GIA

&

THE BLAST FROM THE PAST

The Gustafson Girls #4

BECKY DOUGHTY

BraveHearts
Press

Gia & the Blast from the Past
The Gustafson Girls Book 4
Copyright © 2017 by Becky Doughty

All Scripture quotations, unless otherwise indicated, are taken from the New American Standard Bible, Copyright 1960, 1962, 1963, 1968, 1971, 1972, 1973, 1975, 1977, 1995 by The Lockman Foundation. Used by permission.

Scripture taken from *The Message.* Copyright 1993, 1994, 1995, 1996, 2000, 2001, 2002. Used by permission of NavPress Publishing Group.

Cover Design: Elizabeth Mackey Graphics

Author Info: BeckyDoughty.com

ISBN: 978-1953347121

10 9 8 7 6 5 4 3 2

ONE

GIA STOOD IN THE hushed foyer, dressed in apple green and carrying a button bouquet of peach roses and paper-petaled Bells of Ireland. Beside her, Ricky stood tall and nervous in his dark suit with the slim fit pants that made him look rather debonair. But when he grinned down at her—to her surprise, even in her strappy heels, he still had a good couple of inches on her—she released the breath she'd been holding and slipped her hand into the crook of his proffered arm.

Just in front of them, Renata and Tim waited in silence for their cue, but Tim's large hand curled affectionately around his wife's where it rested on his forearm. The dreamy smile on Ren's face as she glanced up at her man gave away her thoughts; Gia was certain her older sister was remembering her own wedding only six months earlier.

Behind Gia and Ricky, Phoebe and Trevor whispered words too soft to catch, but Gia knew the things they said to each other were tender, and knowing Phebes, probably a little steamy, too, and full of promises of their own.

At the back of the entourage, the matron of honor and Juliette's best friend forever, Sharon Scoville, tended to the bride's every need. She straightened her train for the umpteenth time, checked that her shiny black curls cascaded exquisitely down her back beneath the sheer sweep of her veil, and that her bouquet of French Lavender, Lily of the Valley, Bells of Ireland, and the same peach-hued Sweet Juliet roses were clutched low at her waist so the intricately beaded neckline of her bodice wouldn't be obscured. And of course, Gramps, eyes glistening with tears that would soon spill over as he made his way up the aisle with his eldest granddaughter on his arm, stood in for Papa. His back was still strong, and his shoulders were still broad enough to bear the burdens and joys of each one of his Gustafson girls.

The gentle strains of *Canon in D* wafted from inside the sanctuary, making Gia smile. Her oldest sister and soon-to-be brother-in-law were two peas in a pod with their old-fashioned church wedding, complete with classic wedding songs and traditional vows. Even Trevor's special number he'd written to sing during the lighting of their oh-so-traditional Unity Candle, although heart wrenching and poignant, resonated with ageless beauty, as though surely, it had been part of a hundred million weddings before today.

Juliette and Vic. For a thousand years and a thousand more. Until the end of time. Gia knew it as certainly as she knew the sun would rise in the east and set in the west tomorrow and the next day and the day after that. They were each other's forever.

She darted a glance up at Ricky. Was he her forever? Would the two of them one day stand at opposite ends of a church aisle, waiting to be joined together before family and friends and God? Oh, how she loved him, she readily acknowledged. Every cell in her body thrummed with joyful contentment when Ricky was nearby. Her laughter came quickly, her smiles easy, her sorrows and frustrations handed into his care without hesitation, and she knew he felt the same about her. She couldn't remember her past before he was a part of it; she couldn't imagine a future without him in it.

And yet....

A wave of unexpected melancholy swept through her, and she hugged his arm to her side and leaned her head against his shoulder. She turned her face toward his chest so she could breathe in the heady scent of dark chocolate and cedar notes. It was a cologne she'd given him for his sixteenth birthday, one she knew he wore because she loved it so much.

"Are you sniffing me?" Ricky murmured into her hair. He rested his cheek against the top of her head.

"Why, yes. Yes, I am," she giggled, straightening slowly lest she leave a smudge of face powder on his charcoal lapel. "And I must say, you smell delicious. Good enough to take a bite of." She made a low throaty "meow" at him and then snorted at how ridiculous it sounded. She couldn't pull off sexy, even if she wanted to.

But Ricky gave her a slow smile, and he dipped his head toward her, dropping his voice so the others in the room couldn't hear him. "You know what? I think you'd like that. I think I might like that, too."

Gia's heart skidded to a standstill at the way he looked at her. He was teasing her, she knew, but she'd seen the shift in his eyes more and more in the last year, a growing awareness of her on a whole new level. She'd catch him staring at her from across the room, studying her mouth as she spoke, as she ate, making her just the slightest bit self-conscious, a brand-new sensation where Ricky was concerned. And it seemed the more flustered she got, the more confident he became.

Not that she minded. She kind of liked the way her skin flushed under his heated gaze. She kind of liked imagining what he was thinking when his eyes darkened and his lips parted just the slightest bit. She liked the way he couldn't seem to stop touching her—toying with the copper curls that framed her face, stroking the back of her hand when it rested close to his, pressing the length of his thigh against hers whenever they sat side by side. She liked how his fingers drifted down her spine to rest possessively on her back as he walked beside her, so different from the days when he'd unceremoniously throw an arm around her shoulders and haul her up against him.

When he hugged her these days? No longer did he hoist her off the ground in a rough, brotherly bear hug that squeezed the breath out of her. No, now he stepped into her, hips forward, and slid his hands down her arms to her waist. With his fingers spread wide, he swept his palms across her back, folding her into him, one hand cupping the base of her skull beneath the heavy fall of her hair, and tucking her face into his neck. Full body, nose to toes embraces. That's what they were these days, the kind of hug that sucked all the oxygen out of her in a completely different way. The kind that made her heart race.

Like it was now.

"Take a breath," Ricky whispered, his grin still taunting her. "We're up."

Gia made a small noise, one that almost went unnoticed... but not quite. Renata turned and peered over her shoulder at her, one perfectly arched eyebrow lifted. "Nervous?" she mouthed.

Gia nodded, pressing her lips together in a tight grin that probably looked more like a grimace. She hadn't been a minute ago, but suddenly, her palms felt damp, and her ankles and knees grew wobbly. Beethoven's triumphant *Ode to Joy* suddenly burst from the speakers, and Gia closed her eyes, praying the red splotches of embarrassment crawling up her neck and spreading over her cheeks would be attributed to the emotions of the day, and not the direction her thoughts had wandered.

"You're beautiful," Renata whispered with a reassuring smile, reaching behind her to squeeze Gia's fingers in a quick grab. "Breathtaking." She turned back around, and with one last adoring glance up at her husband, she and Tim led the Gustafson girls and their escorts down the decorated aisle to the front of the church where the handsome groom, Victor Jarrett, stood at attention, awaiting his sweet Juliette.

Gia remembered little of the ceremony except for the way Vic's eyes never strayed from Juliette's face, his expression filled with something so intense, and at the same time so vulnerable, that it almost hurt to look at him. But she couldn't look away. When she did, her eyes met Ricky's from where he stood behind his cousin, Trevor. And what she saw there scared her and thrilled her in equal measures.

But when the pastor said, "You may kiss your bride," and Vic just stood there lost in Juliette's starry eyes, Gia thought it was quite possible that the groom, himself, might not remember everything about the day either, except for the way his bride gazed back at him.

So Trevor, doing best what the Best Man does, stepped close and put a hand on Vic's shoulder. "Kiss her, you fool. Before she changes her mind."

And Vic did just that. He pulled his wife up against him and kissed her, surely and deeply, not once, not twice, but three times, claiming her publicly for all to see, accompanied by the hoots and cheers of the friends and family gathered.

When the pastor cleared his throat, causing Vic and Jules to come up for air, the guests quieted just long enough to hear the other set of greatly anticipated words: "And now I have the honor of presenting to you Mr. and Mrs. Victor and Juliette Jarrett!"

To everyone's surprise, instead of the traditional wedding recessional, the charming song, *Come to Me*, by the Goo Goo Dolls played through the speakers as Vic and Jules practically floated down the aisle. The congregation clapped and sang along as the chorus echoed the request of every star-crossed lover.

Come to me....

TWO

Monday morning came too soon, even for Gia, who was typically wide awake by the end of the opening horn and timpani fanfare of the *William Tell Overture Finale* blaring from her phone alarm. She called it her marching orders wake up call. She loved the celebratory reprise, and usually, it energized her and motivated her to move. But today, Gia listened through the fanfare and into the galloping first movement without opening her eyes. She did, however, roll onto her back and lift her hands to direct the music along with the wild-haired conductor—he always had an Albert Einstein mop-top in her imagination—as the victorious troops marched home in all their due pomp and circumstance.

"Gia, sweetie?" Granny G knocked firmly before poking her head in the door.

Gia never closed it all the way; she didn't like sleeping in the pitch black, and the night light in the hallway cast a comforting warm glow through the three-inch opening. Besides, with the door ajar, she could hear if her grandparents needed her for anything.

Not that they had needed her in the middle of the night at any time in her memory. But they were ridiculously old and cute, and Gia was sure there would come a time when she'd hear one of them beckon her from down the hall. So her door stayed open at night.

"Hey, Gran." Gia, both arms still raised toward the ceiling, cracked one eye and focused on her grandmother. "What's up?"

"Are you alright? Your alarm...." Her words faded into a smile as she realized what Gia had been doing. "You're such a goofball."

Gia rolled onto her side and propped an elbow up under her. "Aren't you feeling a little deflated today, Gran? I mean, it was such an amazing and beautiful weekend and Jules and Vic are so perfect together and everyone was so happy. But today, I just feel kinda… I don't know. Flattened, like a sad balloon that's lost most of its helium, like it happened without me even realizing it, and now I'm a useless, droopy, joyless thing." She flopped back on the bed, her red hair fluffing around her head, a few curls tickling her cheeks. "How am I supposed to get up and go to work when I know I'm just going to be dragging around all day, bumping into things, and sighing dramatically?"

Granny G chuckled as she sat on the edge of the bed and patted Gia's cheek fondly. "Oh, sweetie-pie. It's normal to feel a little let down after such a joyful celebration. It's been months of nonstop hard work for everyone, and now we finally get to relax and just live life again. It's okay to be a little deflated. Can you imagine how exhausted we'd all be if we had to strive for mountain top experiences every single day?"

"I don't know," Gia shrugged against her lumpy pillow. "It seems like it'd be better than this."

"Ah, the voice of youth," Granny G said, nodding sagely. "It's being young that makes us old, sweetie," she said, pulling out one of her myriads of ancient wisdom tidbits. She tapped Gia on the nose with a soft-tipped finger. "But I can promise you this. So long as you don't waste your youth, you won't regret getting old."

Gia didn't take what her grandmother said lightly. Granny G and Gramps had given up some of their best years to be parents to Gia and her sisters, but the older couple had never even joked about the four girls being a burden to them. To the contrary, when people made insensitive comments, even in jest, about the grandparents having to do parenting all over again, they adamantly denied that it had been anything but a joy and claimed to feel all the younger for it. Granny G spoke from experience when she challenged Gia to live without regrets, so she wouldn't have reason to look back and wish she could do it all over again.

Gia did as she was told—usually—and lived as fully as she could. She practiced intentional gratefulness every day; she thanked God for her family, her friends, the loving home she'd be raised in. She was kind and generous. She smiled often, laughed loudly. She'd made it a habit to view the world through sunshine-colored glasses. She didn't mind being sad, but she didn't allow herself to stay there for too long. She wasn't a drama queen, but she didn't care if everyone else around her was. The diversity of people fascinated her, which was one of the reasons she was so good at her coffee shop job.

And if she didn't get up and get going, she'd be late for said coffee shop job.

Granny G patted her cheek again, and Gia was surprised to see how old her grandmother's hands looked. She almost pulled away, not in revulsion, but in concern. Was it because Gia was now an adult that she suddenly noticed things like age and her own aimlessness? Everything seemed to be changing around her... except for her.

She felt stuck... but safe.

Sheltered... but safe.

Safe... but stuck.

She'd graduated high school almost a year ago, and Ricky was turning into a—a *man*—right before her eyes. Her sisters were getting married off one by one and starting—or adding to, in Ren's case—families of their own, and Granny G and Gramps were suddenly stoop-shouldered and scratchy-voiced. Speaking of changing voices, both Ren's oldest boys now squawked when they talked, and Reuben claimed he had man-hair in places Gia hoped never to see.

Even at Ricardo's, where she was now a manager, she sensed a shift in the atmosphere, a subtle, but still tangible upheaval as part-time employees came and went—high school students leaving the cafe behind to go to college, and university students graduating into the real world. Then there were the sidelong glances she received when she was asked what her plans for the future were, and she had nothing concrete to offer.

"I think I could handle living on the mountain top every day," Gia said with an uncharacteristically dramatic sigh. Right now, she felt like the motionless focal point in one of those slow shutter camera shots, lights and action swirling dizzyingly around her, passing her by.

"Well, that's one of the things that makes you who you are, Gia. You're the kind of person who always finds something to celebrate, no matter where you are or who you're with. My little joy bubble."

"Always and never are two words you should always remember never to use," Gia quipped, repeating one of her grandfather's favorite Wendell Johnson quotes. She tried to keep her voice light, but even she heard the undertone of negativity. "Maybe one day I'll stop looking for the mountaintop experience and just be normal, like everyone else."

"Not possible," Granny G said, rising to her feet. Gia heard the disquieting grind of her old knees as she straightened, but Granny G didn't seem to notice. "You can't help yourself. It's who you are." She made her way to the window, where she cranked open the blinds to let some sunlight in. "It's a lovely spring morning. Come on. I'm making Grandpa an egg and sausage burrito. I'll make you one, too."

"I don't know. It's kinda late..." Gia began, tugging the covers from her body and sliding her legs out of bed. "I'll just find something to munch on once I get there." She knew all too well that breakfast was Grandpa's favorite meal, and a plate of eggs and sausage came with a side of conversation, something she didn't have time for today.

"I'll make yours to go," Granny said, not taking 'no' for an answer. "You shouldn't start your day on that processed food, sweetie." She slipped from the room, leaving Gia feeling more like a kid than ever.

She wanted to be crabby today, but according to her grandmother, who knew her better than her own mother did—mainly because her mother had died when Gia was four and she'd been raised by her grandparents—it wasn't possible for Gia to be a glass-half-empty kind of girl. She shoved to her feet, stretched her long arms high over her head, and shook out her hair so it fluffed out like a wild woman's. She really should consider cutting it, or thinning it, or *something*. But every time she said so, her sisters, her friends, especially Ricky, freaked out.

Forty-five minutes later, she pushed through the front door of Ricardo's Cafe, her hair confined in a heavy French braid, and a wide smile she hoped looked real pasted on her face. She wore fighting clothes today, her short black military kilt with wide pleats that slapped against her thighs as she walked, and an olive-green button-up shirt with a black lace camisole underneath. The kilt and shirt she'd found marked down to almost nothing on clearance in the men's department at Nordstrom Rack; she'd hemmed the kilt to show a little leg. On her feet were her favorite buckle-adorned combat boots that could have stepped right out of a Tim Burton movie, and to soften the look, she'd donned a pair of vintage-rose patterned leggings. Granted, the bib apron required for work would completely ruin the warrior princess aesthetic, but she'd be behind the counter most of the time anyway, so it was all about the entrance, right?

At 7 AM, the cafe was already hopping, both with first-timers scouring the chalkboard menu behind the counter, and the regulars who came for Ricardo's excellent coffee and satisfying, if not original, breakfast fare. Salesmen and soccer moms shared tables and counter space. College kids getting their morning sugar and caffeine fixes to help them pry their eyes and minds open for morning classes stood in line with office assistants who picked up to-go orders on their way to their corporate jobs. So yeah, a grand entrance made for a satisfying start to her workday.

Sure enough, a momentary hush—she might have missed it if she wasn't listening for it—fell over the room, and then the rumble of conversation resumed again almost immediately, but she saw the turned heads and double takes.

She knew what she looked like. Tall and straight, no longer gangly and loose-limbed, thanks to the surge of hormones that had been released into her system at the end of her eleventh grade. Over the summer before her senior year, she'd *finally* grown breasts, lost her knobby knees, and discovered the power of good posture and a lifted chin. Although she wasn't exactly Amazonian, she pretty much towered over her three older and rather petite sisters. She had for most of her teenage years. It had been difficult to hold her head high when they were so utterly feminine and curvy and exotic, with their pale skin and dark hair, while she lurched around in their shadows like a lanky kid brother. Although she still had a good three or four inches on her siblings, she definitely filled out her clothing more like they did these days.

Gia paused briefly to greet the Monday morning regulars as she made her way through the shop and behind the counter. After paying her dues on the two part-time shifts—early morning and closing—she was now a manager and worked the perfect 7:30 AM to 4 PM day shift Monday through Friday. She wouldn't be on the clock for another half an hour, but she liked getting there a little early. It gave her time to make nice with her favorite customers, and then sit for a few minutes with Ricardo and a cup of coffee, a beverage she was finally learning to appreciate after working at the coffee shop for more than a year. Ricardo sometimes had a list of work-related things to discuss with her, but more often than not, they were just two people chatting over a hot drink and a box of day-old pastries that had been culled from the shelves at closing the night before.

This morning, however, when Gia shouldered her way into the break room, it wasn't only Ricardo sitting at the small table.

"Ah, Gia! You're here," Ricardo announced unnecessarily, pushing to his feet and offering her his stool. There were only two stools, one on either side of the table, and neither of them very comfortable. Ricardo didn't believe in encouraging long breaks. "Please sit."

The guy opposite her rose to his feet, too, as Ricardo continued. "This is Jupiter Valentine. He's my cousin's boy, visiting for a couple of months. He will be working with you in the mornings."

Jupiter thrust a hand toward her in greeting. She just stared at him. *Dashing.* That was the word that came to mind, but unfortunately, nothing came out of her mouth. Latte-hued complexion and hair that curled playfully over one long-lashed amber eye, a slight overbite that only added to his boyish appeal. He blinked, twice, slowly. Hypnotically. *Snap out of it, girlie!*

"Wait. Wha—huh?" So much for epic warrior woman grand entrances. Gia cringed at the sound of her stuttered response. She looked back and forth between the two men several times until she noticed one side of Jupiter's—Jupiter! Was that even a real name?—mouth hitch up in amusement. *Dang it.* There went one of his eyebrows, too.

And then she realized that her own mouth was hanging slightly open. In shock, of course. Absolutely not in awestruck wonder, even though he was, like his name alluded to—if that really *was* his name—a bit of a brooding Adonis with his broad forehead over deep-set eyes, and his regal Roman nose. He looked like Phoebe's favorite French actor, Louis Garrel, except Jupiter's lips were fuller, shapelier. And was that—no, it couldn't be. Yep. A cleft in his chin. Seriously?

Okay. So maybe she was gaping at him a little. She clamped her jaws shut. She didn't know what question to ask first. Jupiter Valentine? Seriously?

And why hadn't Ricardo said anything last week? And why was it her job to babysit the guy during the busiest hours of the day? Why couldn't he start evenings like every other new employee? And hold up. If he was family, did she have to give him special treatment? And seriously, what kind of name was Jupiter Valentine, anyway?

And seriously, how many times was she going to say the word 'seriously' in her head?

Her teeth clenched, she reached across the table and shook his still outstretched hand once, firmly, then crossed her arms over her chest. She glared at Ricardo, vowing not to look at Jupiter or at his stupid smirk again. "Did I know about this?" She clutched the side seams of her shirt, resisting the urge to wave a hand at the guy who still stood, apparently waiting for her to sit first. She wracked her mind, trying to remember any mention of it. With all the buildup to the wedding, maybe she'd just forgotten, or misheard, or—

No. She was sure she'd have remembered something like this.

Ricardo confirmed it by shaking his head and wrapping a wiry arm around her shoulders. "Jupiter is taking a few local classes. He has insisted on helping out while staying with me." He chuckled and shrugged. "You know me, Gia. I'm not going to refuse an offer of free labor, right?"

Gia shot him a scathing look, not bothering to respond. Ricardo wouldn't be the one babysitting. She would.

"And I knew I could count on you to make my nephew feel at home. You're a good girl, Gia." Ricardo beamed benevolently at both Gia and Jupiter, and then squeezed her shoulders before releasing her to clap his hands together. It was a gesture he made often; he clapped to signify a job well done, a task completed, a done deal.

Oh no, buddy boy. We are not done, not by a long shot. On any other day, she might have nodded her head like the 'good girl' everyone claimed she was and gone about making Jupiter—okay, the name was kinda growing on her—feel at home. But today? She glanced down at her black leather boots and then turned to face Ricardo's nephew. "Have you ever worked in food service before? Do you know how to make a good cup of coffee? Operate a commercial espresso machine?"

Ricardo made an odd noise that sounded a bit like surprise, but Jupiter gave him a look that quieted him. Gia wondered if the guy would teach her the look that would silence Ricardo so effectively; the man often talked a blue streak, especially after his second cup of the high-octane stuff he brewed in the back for his staff... but that request would have to wait until she wasn't ticked about the current situation.

Jupiter gestured at the stool Ricardo had vacated, and his eyelids lowered a little, giving her a look she could only assume was his version of bedroom eyes. Gia had to admit it was effective, even though she wasn't about to give him the satisfaction of letting him know. "Please, sit," he said when she just continued to glare at him. "Allow me to tell you all about my skills."

"Seriously?" This time, she said it out loud, and then felt the heat creeping up her chest and neck.

The guy had an accent. A lovely, lilting, exotic, hypnotic—there was that word again—accent. Mediterranean? Italian? Greek? Or was it South American? Brazil, maybe? She was terrible with accents, but Ricardo, who boasted of being a born-and-raised American citizen, had made mention now and then of distant relatives living in other parts of the world. At the moment, however, she just couldn't remember what those other parts were.

She turned away from Jupiter and grabbed the stool, pulling it close to the table. She sat so she'd have something to do and took her time getting comfortable, straightening the hem of her skirt over her legs as she listened to him settle back onto his own stool. She grimaced in mild distaste; the seat cushion was still warm from Ricardo's occupation of it. Then she rested her forearms on the table, took a calming breath, and lifted her gaze to meet Jupiter's.

"Seriously," the guy said, the grin now encompassing his whole mouth. He had perfectly straight white teeth, too. Of course. "I am sorry about the surprise I am to you. You did not expect to see me today, so I understand. But you are a surprise to me, too."

Gia cocked her head, her long braid slipping forward over one shoulder, drawing Jupiter's eyes away from her face to follow its snake-like swish. "What does that mean?"

"Uncle Ricardo, he tells me you are the best manager he has. He tells me you are a woman of honor and grace with his customers." He darted a glance at his uncle, who nodded in agreement.

"I'll leave the two of you to it. I have to make a few phone calls," Ricardo said, reaching across the table to lay a hand momentarily on top of Jupiter's head. "This woman is your boss when I am not available. You do as she says, you hear?"

Jupiter nodded and shot him a conciliatory grin. "I hear with both ears and my heart, Uncle."

Gia watched as Ricardo disappeared into his little office and then turned back to Jupiter, still not saying a word. By his own admission, he knew a lot more about her than she did about him, and that fact alone made his claim to be surprised debatable.

When the door to Ricardo's office closed with a taunting click, Jupiter leaned forward, bracing his own forearms on the table like she did. "But he did not tell me that you were so beautiful, or that you have eyes the color of the sea water on a summer day. He did not tell—"

Her eyes grew wider with every word until she cut him off. "Stop, please, Mr. Sappy Valentine Card." She paused and cocked her head, considering. "Oh, that's good," she remarked, congratulating herself on her quick wit. "Mr. Valentine Card. Or should I call you Mr. Hallmark?"

At his confused, but still pleasant expression, she shook her head. "Never mind. Listen, your flattery is... acknowledged, but not necessary. It won't change my opinion of the circumstances, nor will it change my opinion of you, since I don't know you well enough to have formed one yet."

Jupiter's eyebrow rose again, this time, in obvious disbelief. Well, she *had* just called him sappy and threatened to call him Mr. Hallmark.

"Keep that up, and I'll form an opinion real quick," she said. They shared an impromptu stare down, and then he relented with a shrug of his shoulders and took a sip of his coffee.

Coffee. She needed coffee. Surely, that would help.

Then she narrowed her eyes at the mug in Jupiter's hand. Her mug. The one that said 'Mrs. Cullen' on it in dripping blood letters. The one Phoebe had designed for her years ago to commemorate the first of many *Twilight* movie marathons. It had been a long time since the girls had gotten together to swoon over Robert Pattinson's brooding, bloodthirsty predator stares. Months ago, she'd found the mug at the back of Phoebe's cupboard and brought it to work with her because it made her happy thinking about her sisters. And every employee at Ricardo's Cafe knew, without exception, that no one—*no one*—used her mug without permission. Which she would never give anyway, so no one even bothered asking. Now into her territory waltzed this guy with the ridiculous name, all suave and entitled, attempting to sweet talk her into putting up with him, and using *her* mug!

"Too late, Mrs. Cullen," she quipped. "Opinion formed, after all." She pushed to her feet, palms pressed to the tabletop, and leaned forward to look him boldly in the eyes. "I'm not on the clock until 7:30. I'll meet you at the front counter in twenty minutes and you can show me your *barista* skills then." She emphasized the word to make sure he understood she wasn't interested in any other skills he might possess. Then she tapped the side of the mug he held. "Let's hope your dish washing skills are up to snuff. I want to see my coffee cup *sparkle* like a naked vampire in the sun—no, like sea water on a summer day!—when you're done with it." *Oh, yeah!* She was back on her game. She might have chortled to herself had she not been so fired up. She spun on her heel and strode out of the break room, her spine straight, shoulders back, her stride long and sure.

At least she made an epic warrior woman grand exit. Seriously.

THREE

Gia couldn't really say why she was so upset about Jupiter being added to her morning shift duties. In fact, the more she thought about it, the more she realized it wasn't really about the guy, himself, but about Ricardo's assumption that she'd be cool with everything. That she wouldn't take issue with him just foisting a complete stranger on her, even though he knew her job was fast-paced and busy all day long, but especially in the mornings. Granted, it was her ability to keep a cool head and a warm smile on her face that made her good at her job, but that didn't mean it was easy. And today, with all the thoughts of change, of the murky future, of new beginnings and time passing, Gia didn't *feel* like the steady creature everyone insisted she was.

None of that, however, was Jupiter's fault. She supposed he hadn't intentionally offended her by using her sacred mug, either. How was he supposed to know he was breaking a cardinal break room rule? Sure, Ricardo knew well enough, but maybe he hadn't said anything because he was trying to help his nephew—was that the right thing to call him? Cousin once removed? Second cousin?—feel at ease. She could have been a little kinder to him, too, she admitted. At least a little more hospitable than she'd been.

It was still early enough in April that the mornings were chilly, so even with a large cup of hot coffee, she was too cold to be comfortable as she mulled over things in the front seat of her car. She wasn't looking forward to facing Jupiter now that her emotions had settled, but she didn't know what to say to him. Sorry I got upset that you showed up to help me today? Sorry I freaked out that some guy with a Roman god name and a Greek god physique and the kind of face that might be immortalized by the likes of

Michelangelo and Donatello showed up to hang out with me all morning long, especially since I look pretty amazing myself today?

At least if she waited until the last minute to head back inside, they could go right to work, and they wouldn't have to endure any awkward conversation—or silence—about her bad behavior.

She cranked up the radio, wrapped her hands around the hot cup, and let her shoulders sag as she leaned her head back and closed her eyes. A throaty voice emanating from the car speakers swirled around her as the heavy base and rhythm section of the band drove the song through her. She didn't recognize the group, but the brooding music resonated with her.

What a craptastic way to start a Monday.

The sharp rap on the window sounded like a gunshot over the music, and Gia jolted upright, sloshing coffee over her hands from the tiny opening in the cup lid. She yelped and then held the cup away from her over the passenger side floor to get her skirt and leggings out of the line of fire. She looked down and groaned. Too late.

A moment later, she felt the burn of the hot liquid on her thigh as it soaked through both layers, and with her free hand, she began flapping the hem of her skirt up and down to cool the spot. And of course, there were no loose napkins lying around her car today—she'd cleaned it out after all the wedding festivities were over.

Gia turned to see who had scared her and didn't even bat an eyelash when she saw him.

Jupiter. Of course.

She stopped the music and rolled down her window, attempting to act nonchalant, even though she knew full well that he'd witnessed the whole thing. There were no tinted windows on her car.

"Did you need something?" she asked.

He didn't speak right away, but instead, fumbled in his back pocket for something. A moment later, he handed her a folded cloth. "Please accept this, along with my apology. I did not mean to startle you." It was a handkerchief. A real, live, old-fashioned snot collector, as Grandpa called them.

"What do you want me to do with this?" She took it, but she didn't bother unfolding it. "I'm not sitting in here crying or anything."

"For your spilled coffee," he said, his tone apologetic. "I insist." He gestured toward the growing wet spot on Gia's skirt and then grinned. "I have not used it, I promise."

She should just go inside and rinse the skirt out now. At least the fabric was dark, but it would still be ugly all day and would totally undermine her epicness. Which had already taken a volley of hits as it was. "Thank you," she said, dabbing at the back of her hand and then at the wet spot. "I'll wash this and bring it back in the morning."

Jupiter just stood there watching her, his hands shoved casually in the front pockets of his pants, but his forearms, exposed by his rolled-up shirtsleeves, goose-fleshed noticeably. Gia sighed and hit the unlock button. "If you're just going to stand there ogling me, you might as well get in. It's cold."

He paused for a moment, almost as though trying to decide whether or not he really wanted to be alone in a car with a crazy woman, and then sauntered around the hood, holding her gaze through the windshield until she dropped her eyes to her lap and continued pressing the handkerchief against her skirt.

"Why, Gia?" she muttered under her breath. "You'll just encourage him."

He opened the passenger door and slid into the seat before she could answer herself. "*Ciao,*" he said, pressing his palms against his knees so the muscles in his forearms rippled effectively. Yeah, she noticed.

"Chow," she replied.

When he said it, even through teeth that were clenched with cold, the greeting sounded exotic, fascinating. Coming out of her mouth it sounded like cheap dog food. And it tasted like humble pie. She took a deep breath and released it dramatically before turning to face him.

"So. I'm sorry I snapped at you in there. Nice welcoming committee, aren't I?" She snorted and added with a slight note of derision, "I'm supposed to be a nice girl."

Jupiter narrowed his eyes and gazed out the window at the cafe's employee entrance. "It's okay," he replied. "I understand your surprise, and I also understand your concern. It is always a bit difficult to start a new employee, yes?"

She nodded, and then shook her head, not wanting to seem too quick to agree. "That doesn't change the fact that I wasn't nice."

"Ah," Jupiter said, turning those lidded eyes to her again. "But perhaps I like you better because you are not so nice."

"Okay, okay. Stop." She held up a hand and smiled politely, even though she could feel her cheeks warm. "I don't know where you're from, but here in America, especially here in Southern California, people get really jumpy about this kind of stuff in the workplace."

"This kind of stuff? What kind of stuff do you mean?" He seemed genuinely curious.

"The whole flirting and flattery stuff," she said. Now she was embarrassed, realizing how presumptuous she sounded. "Not that you were flirting with me, or that I'm upset by it, per se, but as your manager, it's my responsibility to let you know that you could get in trouble for saying those things on the job, especially if you make the other person uncomfortable." Ugh. Now she just sounded like a pompous know-it-all.

"I am making you uncomfortable?"

"No." She quickly assured him, but then faltered. "Well, yes, maybe a little. I'm not used to the whole flowery speech thing from a complete stranger." She waved her hand around in the air between them.

"But how are we to become friends if we do not speak with honesty? It is true. I do think you are a beautiful girl. You make me think of *fragole con panna*—eh, strawberry with cream. Your hair and complexion. But your eyes. Perhaps it is fire and ice, no?"

Good Godiva, he was so cliché with his compliments. She had to narrow her eyes to keep from rolling them.

He continued, oblivious to her reaction. "And it would please me to know if you are impressed by me in some way. Do you like my eyes? Or perhaps my... eh... *fossetta*?" He pressed a fingertip to the dip in his chin, frowned a moment, then said, "What is the word in English?"

"Cleft?" Yeah, she did kinda like it, but she wasn't about to say so.

"No, that is not the word I am thinking of." He pursed his lips in thought, and with his finger resting on his chin, pointing at his mouth, she couldn't help but look a little too long.

"Dimple?" she suggested, her voice sounding... *ummm, stupid? Get it together, girlie!*

"Yes! Dimple. That is the word, yes?" He turned in the seat so that he was facing her more fully, in spite of the fact that there wasn't a whole lot of room for his legs to maneuver in the compact car.

"Sorta." Technically, wasn't a cleft chin really just a dimpled chin, too? "We usually call these dimples." She pointed to the divot in her cheek that appeared when she smiled widely to demonstrate. "It's caused by muscle connected to the skin, so when you tighten the muscle, it pulls in the skin, see? But that—" She reached out and touched his chin without thinking,"—is officially called a cleft, because it's a structural thing in the bones. It happens when the two sides of your jaw don't completely fuse together, leaving an opening or a cleft in the actual bone. You can feel the shape of it underneath the tissue." She pressed a little harder, moving her fingertip back and forth a bit. Sure enough, she could feel the pronounced indentation at the center of his chin. "And yes, in fact. I do like it. My Grandpa has a really prominent one, and I think it's cool."

Jupiter didn't pull away, but reached up and covered her hand, raising it up just the slightest bit to press her fingertip to his lips instead.

Gia jerked her hand back, pulling free of his grasp. "Whoa, there, big boy." Her whole arm tingled, a sensation that quickly spread until she could feel it down to her toes in her boots, like aftershocks. She scooped up her phone from the console and checked the time. "Um, yeah. So we should go in now."

Jupiter frowned, studying her, a look of uncertainty on his face. "So help me to understand. You touch me willingly and it is okay, but I cannot touch you willingly?"

Despite the slightly incongruous words, Gia knew exactly what he was saying. "I'm sorry I'm sending mixed messages." She closed her eyes and gripped her steering wheel for a moment before turning back to look at him again. "Okay. Let me start over. Yes, I think you're very handsome. I think you're probably too handsome for your own good, and I think you probably know that, too. Regardless, you look like some golden Greek god—"

"Roman. Jupiter is a Roman god. So am I." Then he blushed.

Her eyes widened as she watched the color suffuse his neck and cheeks, and she grinned, happy to see the tables turned for once.

"I am not saying I am a god," he hurried to amend. "I am saying I am from Rome. Italy. Not Greece." He waved a hand at her and shook his head. "Please continue before I become a bigger fool."

Gia snorted. "Ha. You might be a Roman god, but I'll have you know that I'm an Amazonian warrior princess. Don't we make a pair." The snort expanded into a chortle as Jupiter eyed her quizzically. He must think her at least the tiniest bit crazy.

But when he asked, "Are you perhaps related to Wonder Woman?" she released a loud guffaw of appreciation and brought her hand up to cover her mouth self-consciously.

Jupiter, too, was chuckling now, and he reached over and pulled her hand away from her face. "I like to hear you laugh. It is a good sound for a Monday morning."

Gia leaned back against the headrest until she could catch her breath, then turned just her head so she could look at him. "Jupiter Valentine, I'm a little afraid of you."

He cocked his head at her. "You have nothing to fear with me, Gia—ah! I do not know your full name."

"Gia Gustafson. Well, my full name is Georgia Amity Gustafson. What about you? Do you have a middle name?"

"Do I have a middle name? A second name?" When she nodded, he said, "My name, Georgia Amity Gustafson, is Jupiter Alonso Damiano Pascal Valentine." He held out the 'n' and then his voice lifted at the end of Valentine, giving sound to the 'e' with a dramatic flair. He lifted one eyebrow again, this time with a look of such pride that she resorted to giggles once more. "What? You do not like my name? You think it is funny?"

"No, no. I love it!" she declared. "Would that we could all be dubbed such a litany of names. It's really quite remarkable."

Jupiter held up two fingers. "That is two things you like about me, then. My *fossetta*—my cleft chin—and my name. It is a good start, yes?"

"Maybe," she grinned, then started scooping up her belongings. "Doesn't mean I'm not still a little afraid of you. But come on. We're going to be late if we're not in there in thirty seconds." The words were barely out of her mouth before Jupiter had pushed open his door. She looked up to watch him circling the car to her side again, where he opened her door for her and offered her his hand. She paused for just a moment before accepting it, even though, to be honest, holding his hand actually made it harder for her to get her too long legs out of the little car. But she soldiered on, letting him be chivalrous. She had to give him 'A' for effort, that was for sure.

"There is something more that you will like about me," he said as they hurried toward the employee entrance.

"Oh yeah?" She was almost afraid to ask, but her curiosity—and the fact that he was so disgustingly charming—got the best of her. "What might that be?"

"My family owns a *caffetteria, a cafe*—a coffee bar in Rome, and I am a certified SCAE barista." He used the English pronunciation of the letters, saying them slowly. "So yes, I do know how to operate an espresso machine very well."

Gia waited while he held the door open for her, then passed through in front of him. "Call me naïve, but what is SCAE?" They were in a short hall that passed by the break room and the combination employee bathroom and laundry room where they washed towels, dishcloths, and aprons.

"Ah. Maybe it is not so important here. Specialty Coffee Association of Europe?"

When she stopped suddenly, he was walking so close behind her that he had to pull up short not to run into her. Even so, he brought both hands up to her shoulders, so when she turned around, they were practically face to face. "Wait. You went to official barista training? Like at a barista school?"

Jupiter didn't release her shoulders, so she stepped back. His hands skimmed down her arms before he let go, sending a shiver whispering up her spine. "I attended my barista courses at the Florence Culinary School of Art."

"Seriously?" Gia muttered, suddenly a whole lot more afraid of him than she'd been only moments before. She didn't wait for his response, but spun back around and led the way toward the front of the shop. Why was Jupiter Valentine, the Italian fancy pants with his bronzed hair, whiskey eyes, and his highfalutin culinary school of art barista certificate *really* here in Ricardo's Cafe?

Was her job in jeopardy?

Why, oh why, hadn't Ricardo warned her about this guy?

FOUR

At first, Gia could find absolutely nothing about Jupiter Valentine to complain over. The guy needed no training whatsoever on operating and cleaning the machinery. He didn't take issue with washing dishes, sweeping floors, or stocking shelves. And he was far more skilled than she or Ricardo or any of the other staff was when making the specialty drinks. Her eyes widened in awe when he made his first latte of the day in one of their signature wide-mouthed mugs used for dine-in customers. With a few practiced moves, he swirled the steamed milk into the espresso base of the drink, sweeping the pitcher back and forth over the tilted lip of the mug in his hand. Using a stir stick, he added a few extra dots of foam to the design, forming a delicate vine and rose pattern.

"Where did you learn to do that?" Gia asked, embarrassed of the simplicity of her signature double-heart pattern she always made for customers.

It really wasn't such a surprise when Jupiter casually mentioned that he'd placed in several latte art competitions over the past few years. Gia knew they took place around the globe, but before today, she'd never minded that her hearts were super basic.

They sold a record number of foam-topped drinks once word got out that Jupiter was skilled in latte art, especially when he refused to do them in to-go cups. He handled customers like he was personally interested in the minutiae of their days, and there wasn't an order he didn't serve with a smile and his catchphrase, "From my heart to yours."

During the noon hour, the place was packed. Actually, the sandwich line didn't seem significantly busier than usual, but the number of people waiting in line to order coffee was out the door... and predominantly women. Giggling, primping, chattering women of a surprisingly wide range of ages.

"Seriously?" she muttered when she finally made the connection after watching one starry-eyed female patron after another coo her drink of choice at Jupiter.

As they took their turns at the coffee counter, many of the regulars who ordered the same thing every day were suddenly asking for suggestions and trying fancy new drinks. When Darby Hardgrave ordered a "ginormous caramel macchiato with two pumps of coconut creme and one pump of vanilla," and asked if Jupiter could sketch his own face in the foam—he made a peacock instead, which Gia thought apropos—Gia had to step outside to get a breath of fresh, perfume-free air. Clearly, he could handle his fan girls without her help.

She hadn't been outside more than sixty seconds before the door opened and one of the other employees, Belinda, poked her head through. "Hey, Gia. Jupiter wants to know if you can trade out his tip jar again. It's spilling over." And, of course, Belinda's eyes had that same dreamy look in them, too. Her next words confirmed it as she simpered, "He's amazing, isn't he?"

Gia drew in a deep breath and pushed past Belinda back into the melee. She plastered the wide smile on her face and stepped up beside Jupiter at the espresso machine where he had four drinks in different stages of production. "How you doing, Mr. Valentine?" She'd wanted to call him Mr. Hallmark, but she refrained, keeping her voice light.

"*Fantastico*!" he exclaimed, swirling the foam on yet another drink before sliding it across the pick-up bar to the woman waiting with her hand over her heart. She then made a show of handing him a five-dollar bill.

"Because your tip jar is too full," she murmured, looking like she'd rather tuck the fiver into the waistband of his pants. Gia eyed her sardonically. The woman was old enough to have birthed Jupiter's mother.

The tables were filled inside and out, but folks were still ordering dine-in drinks even though it was standing room only. Carter manned the register, taking the drink orders for Jupiter, and after replacing the tip jar on the pick-up counter, Gia glanced over at the one in front of Carter's register. It wasn't bursting at the seams, but it needed to be traded out, too. She didn't remember the last time Carter had garnered that many tips in so short a time. "How's your drawer?" she asked as she leaned around him to scoop up a couple of quarters that hadn't made it into the jar.

"Pretty full. It's been a crazy lunch break, that's for sure. Thanks to the new guy." She couldn't quite tell if he was actually grateful or if he was being sarcastic.

"Need a break?" she asked, hoping he was paying attention to his receipts and change.

"No way, Gia," he whispered from the corner of his mouth. There was a momentary pause as the next person in line fumbled in her purse, not realizing she was up. "You seeing those tips?"

Someone cleared her throat and the purse lady lurched forward. "Oh! Hi," she said to Carter and Gia, but her eyes kept darting over to Jupiter who shot her the same half-smile and bedroom eyes he'd aimed at Gia in the break room when Ricardo introduced them.

Gia pressed her lips together to hold in her disgust—one of Phoebe's favorite French exclamations danced on the tip of her tongue—and finally said, "Let me know when you're ready for me to change it out."

Carter nodded. "Yeah, probably soon. I'll holler."

With the two tip jars in hand and relief in her heart because she had an excuse to flee the scene, she headed back to Ricardo's office where she would add the cash tips to the till to divvy up among the crew at the end of each shift. It was how they did it at Ricardo's. When one crew member did well, they all did well.

She returned to the front and kept busy wiping down counters, washing out pitchers and carafes, stocking supplies, and replenishing the pastries and sandwich display, letting the rest of the team interact with the customers. But when the lunch rush had wound down considerably, Gia headed back to Ricardo's office to balance the register drawers with her boss.

They were comparing the last of their figures when Jupiter poked his head into the office. "I must leave soon," he announced, his eyes moving from his uncle to rest on Gia. "My class begins at 3 o'clock."

"Yes!" Ricardo said, waving his nephew inside the cramped room. "Of course. How was your first morning?"

"It went very well, Uncle," Jupiter said, remaining in the doorway, one shoulder against the frame. He no longer wore his apron; it was draped over his shoulder, hooked on the finger of one hand. "Your patrons are easy to make happy."

Gia snorted, the sound slipping out before she could stop it. When both men looked quizzically at her, she shrugged and quipped, "I noticed."

Jupiter grinned, slowly, knowingly. "You have many ladies who drink coffee in this city, yes?"

"Apparently, we do now," Gia replied, then turned back to Ricardo. "Are we finished here?" she asked.

"Yes, yes. Why don't you show Jupiter where to throw his dirty apron while I do a few last-minute things before I head out for the afternoon, okay?" He darted a look past her to Jupiter. "I will meet you out back."

Gia pursed her lips and pushed to her feet. "Follow me," she clipped out as she brushed past Jupiter and out into the little hallway. They walked the short distance to the bathroom that doubled as a laundry room, and she stood back to let him in ahead of her. She caught a whiff of whatever cologne he wore as he slipped past her, a crisp citrus and pine scent that made her nose twitch in response. She wasn't sure if she liked it or not—it certainly didn't make her close her eyes and breathe in the way Ricky's did—but she realized she already recognized it as his, having smelled it hovering in the air of the break room first thing in the morning, then again in her car when he'd climbed in next to her, and over the past several hours of working together.

She stayed in the doorway and pointed out the hamper for soiled aprons and towels, but didn't bother giving him lessons on how to operate the machines. "The night crew runs the washer and then puts them in the dryer. The early morning crew empties the dryer and puts things away. Since you're only working the day shift, you're off the hook."

"But if I substitute for someone during one of those shifts, then it might be good if I learn how to use the machines?" He grinned impishly at her. "Or perhaps I might spill coffee on my colleague's skirt, and she needs me to wash it for her?"

Gia warred with herself momentarily, still not sure how she felt about this guy, but he really was quite charming. She shot him a teasing look and said, "Ha. Don't even think, for one moment, that you can get me out of my clothes that easily."

Goodness. Where had *that* come from? She sounded like she was channeling Phoebe.

Jupiter shrugged. "Ah well. It was worth trying, yes?"

She shook her head and rolled her eyes, but she felt the smile still tugging the corners of her mouth up.

"Tell me one thing, at least, Boss Lady," Jupiter said as he followed her across the hall to the break room.

Gia quirked a brow at him. "Boss Lady? You know, I kinda like the sound of that." Okay. She was officially flirting now. Ricky's endearing face flashed across her thoughts, but it wasn't that kind of flirting. Jupiter was just a really yummy guy who clearly knew his way around the ladies, and hey, she was a lady, after all. And just because Jupiter was confident and sure of himself, that didn't make him a threat. Besides, it wasn't like Ricky had made any moves.

Jupiter had his back to her as he gathered up his things from one of the staff lockers. She watched him move, taking in details quickly before he turned around. His shoulders weren't broad like Ricky's, but he definitely had the whole V-shape thing going on under his pale gray oxford that still looked crisp and fresh after his busy morning. His slim-cut black pants skimmed over his narrow hips and perfectly proportioned legs. They weren't obscenely tight, but he certainly wasn't trying to hide his physique, either. He wore soft-soled black ankle boots she assumed were Italian, and not just because Jupiter was Italian. No, the shoes had that hand-tooled, soft leather look with the slightly elongated toe that combined style and comfort so effortlessly. She didn't quite bite back a tiny sigh as he bent over to pick up a small, leather-bound notebook he'd dropped; the guy even dressed perfectly.

He turned and caught her looking at his backside, but she raised her chin defiantly. He grinned, a knowing glint in his eyes. "How did I do on my first day?" he asked, as he slid his arms into his fitted corduroy blazer the color of roasted red peppers. "Boss Lady," he added.

Two could play this game. She refused to be intimidated by Jupiter's smooth charm. She squared her shoulders a little and straightened her spine so she stood almost as tall as he did and could look him directly in the eye. "Well, other than the fact that you pretty much put the rest of us to shame with your mad skills, I suppose you did all right." She paused dramatically, a look of deep consideration on her face. "Fine. I guess you can come back tomorrow."

Jupiter crossed the tiny room and took her hand, placing a gallant kiss on the back of it. "You will not regret it; I will see to that." Then he lifted that ridiculous—but entirely too effective—heavy-lidded gaze to her face. "And when you arrive here in the morning, I will be waiting for you with the finest cup of coffee you have ever experienced. In your own mug, Mrs. Cullen."

"Ah. Charming *and* clever," she said, but pulled her hand free of his, hoping he couldn't read the conflict behind her smile.

She was not this person, this saucy, flirting girl. Sure, she'd seen Phoebe work a room enough times to know the drill, but Gia was the sweet Gustafson girl, the innocent one. The sister who smiled and made life easier and more comfortable for everyone else.

"I know how important it is to take care of the Boss Lady," he said, lifting a shoulder in a casual gesture. "Please. Walk with me outside." He lifted a hand to indicate she go ahead of him down the short hallway to the rear exit. "Ricardo will pick me up in the back parking lot."

The hallway seemed too narrow for both of them, and their shoulders bumped, sending pleasant waves of sensation through her. It was unsettling how much she found herself responding to even the most casual contact between them.

Jupiter placed a hand on her back, pushed open the employee door ahead of them, and ushered her through, then stood beside her on the small stoop while they waited for his ride. His hand—thankfully—fell away after a few moments, and she closed her eyes and lifted her face to the warmth of the midday California sunshine, partly because it was quite lovely, but also because she needed to get a grip. She could feel him beside her, his shoulder just barely brushing hers as she swayed the tiniest bit.

"Gia, I truly am sorry to have disrupted your day." His voice had lost its teasing quality, and she turned to look at him. He still smiled, but she could see that he was serious, and when he reached up and tucked a wild copper curl behind her ear, his fingertips skimming her cheekbone, the curve of her ear, she didn't pull away. "I only wish to help my uncle for allowing me to stay with him while I attend my courses. He is very generous and offers me his home without accepting payment, but I insisted on working for him in exchange. I learned from my father that a man loses his dignity when he does not have to work for the good things in his life." Jupiter turned to watch as his uncle, who had apparently gone out the front door of the shop, hurried across the overflow parking lot to his car. "My uncle is the same. He understands the value of hard work."

"He's a good boss, your uncle," Gia agreed, turning to glance at the man before cocking her head at Jupiter again. "How old are you, if you don't mind telling me," Gia asked, her arms now crossed over her chest. She marveled at how confident Jupiter sounded, how sure of himself he was, how sure of what he wanted. Something inside her ached a little, and she found herself longing for the same sense of purpose he had. Maybe he was older than she'd first thought and had struggled early on, too. She shifted a little, swiping at the back of her knee. Something—a bug, maybe?—kept flitting against her legs.

"I do not mind, Boss Lady." He watched her swat at whatever was bothering her again. Without warning, he reached up and took her by the shoulders, turning her around so her back was to him. "Your tie is in a knot so one string is hanging long. Let me help you." Jupiter's hands moved confidently against her back—the guy did everything with confidence, it seemed. "I am twenty-two years old. I am almost finished with my culinary program in *Firenze*—eh, Florence," he amended.

Twenty-two. No wonder he was so sure of himself. He had a few years on her and he knew exactly what he was doing with his life. "I am here to take a class in American cuisine."

It took some effort and a little elbow grease, but Gia's apron finally loosened and then tightened snug around her waist again. She felt every bump of his knuckles against her spine as Jupiter looped the apron strings into a new bow.

"There's such a thing as American cuisine?" Gia teased in an attempt to dispel her hypersensitive awareness of him. "I figured people from other countries just brought their own recipes with them when they moved here." Jupiter's hands settled at her waist, his palms cupped around the tops of her hipbones, and for a moment, her breath caught, wondering what he was doing. "Or are you here to learn to make hamburgers and fries and apple pies?" she asked, playing nonchalant. She darted a glance over her shoulder at him, but looked forward again quickly, the expression on his face unreadable. "You done back there?"

Jupiter made some kind of adjustment to the way the apron sat, tugging the fabric gently so that she swayed side-to-side enough to make the hem of her skirt swish against her legs. Then he stepped back, his fingertips brushing over the curve of her hips as he did so. She put another step between them and turned around again.

"It is true, to some degree. American cuisine is a, em, melting pot of many different people and cultures." He spoke casually, evidently completely unruffled by the moment that had just passed between them. "But you have your own way of preparing dishes, and there is much diversity from one state to another, just like in any country. Where I come from, there are many ways to cook the same dish, depending on what region of Italy. Sometimes it is as little as one ingredient changed, but a knowledgeable diner will be able to tell the difference. I think it is the same here in America, is it not?"

She gave thought to his words and nodded slowly. Between the Gustafson family's heavy Swedish influences, the French meals Phoebe sometimes prepared in honor of their mother, Juliette's obsession with Mr. Yu's Green Dragon Chinese food, and the myriad of meals Renata cooked for her burgeoning household, Gia had definitely experienced the "Americanization" of international foods. She thought of Ricky and his pot roast, potatoes, and apple pie upbringing; he hadn't even heard of salmon and potato casserole before eating Granny G's homemade Swedish staple, something they ate in the Gustafson home on a regular basis.

Before she could respond to Jupiter, a movement in the lot behind him caught her eye, and she watched as Ricky emerged from his car and started toward them.

She lifted a hand in a surprised greeting, but a prickling sensation of wariness skittered up her spine as she took in the grim expression on his face.

FIVE

GIA STEPPED OFF THE curb to greet him, looping her arms around him in their usual sloppy hug, but Ricky pulled her right up close in a full body embrace. "Hey there, Georgy Girl," he murmured near her ear, his breath ruffling the small curls at her nape.

"Well, hey there to you, Rickaroni," she quipped. "Miss me much?" She wedged her hands between them and pushed against his chest so that he was forced to loosen his grip. "We'd better get out of the way. Here comes Ricardo and you've seen how that man drives." The cafe owner approached in his older Lexus SUV, but Gia noticed Ricky was eyeing Jupiter over her shoulder, not the man driving toward them. He kept one arm around her waist and moved toward the curb with her.

"Who's your friend?" Ricky asked, a note in his voice making her pause. He stopped when she did and met her curious look with one she didn't remember seeing on his face before. She narrowed her eyes at him in warning, not liking the way he was acting, and in turn, not liking the way he made her feel.

"Let me introduce you," she said, injecting an edge into her own voice. She stepped away from him, but she kept a hold of his hand to reassure him.

To reassure herself.

Because she'd just noticed the look on Jupiter's face, too.

Gia had never been the reason for a standoff before, at least not between guys. Sure, when she was a baby, her sisters had practically wrestled her out of each other's arms, and when she was a bothersome toddler, they'd argued about whose turn it was to be stuck with her. But this was different. And in spite of the fact that it was a new experience, between the lifted chins, the narrowed eyes, and the mocking grins being exchanged by the two young bucks, Gia instinctively recognized it for what it was.

Well, she wasn't up for the drama today, and she clenched her jaw and dragged Ricky forward. She could hear her boss's car pulling up—it was probably a good thing that this was going to have to be quick.

On the sidewalk, she let go of Ricky's hand and gestured at Jupiter. "Ricky, this is Jupiter, Ricardo's nephew visiting from Rome. He's here in the US attending a culinary program."

She turned to Jupiter and said, "Jupiter, this is Ricky." She purposely, and perhaps spitefully, didn't give any indication of their relationship, mainly because she wasn't feeling very friendly toward Ricky at the moment and wasn't sure she actually wanted to claim him.

The red that rose up his neck and the way his eyes bore into her told her he felt the cut of her omission deeply. So when Jupiter offered his hand in greeting to Ricky, Gia stepped back, just in case there was a little more than shaking going on between them.

After the briefest hesitation, they grasped hands in a visibly bone-crushing squeeze, and Gia rolled her eyes. Her response went unnoticed because they were too caught up in their stupid little *mano-a-mano* dance, eyes locked, and half-cocked smiles that looked more like sneers.... Of course, neither of them even winced at the white-knuckled grip they shared.

"Aaannnd..." Gia drew the word out, her voice thick with annoyance. "Here comes Ricardo. Just in the nick of time." The deadlock broken, she snatched Ricky's arm and pulled him toward her out of Jupiter's path. From the broad stance Ricky had taken, she was half afraid he'd try to block the guy from leaving just so they could stare daggers at each other a little longer.

Gia grimaced as Jupiter dusted his palms together in an obvious gesture of dismissal or possibly even contempt, and when Ricky's grip on her hand tightened in response, she stepped forward, not so subtly putting herself between the two. "Okay," she said in a falsely bright but firm voice. "It was nice working with you today, Jupiter. I'll see you tomorrow morning. Have fun in class." And with that, she stepped past him and whipped open the employee door, all but hauling Ricky in behind her. She wasn't supposed to bring anyone but employees through that way, but at this point, she didn't care. Besides, she'd done it in front of Ricardo, who had pulled up at the curb right behind her, so at least he couldn't accuse her of trying to sneak Ricky in.

"Hold up, Gia!" Ricky demanded, coming to an abrupt stop just inside the door. "Stop dragging me around like I'm a—a *dog* or something."

Gia released his hand and lifted both of hers in frustration and surrender. "Then stop acting like an animal. What the heck was all that about?" When he didn't respond immediately, she dropped her hands to her sides and spun on her heel. "Never mind. I have to go back to work. You can let yourself out."

"Wait. You're mad at me?" Ricky grabbed at her arm, forcing her to stop. "I saw the way he had his hands all over you. I saw your face, Gia. He made you uncomfortable. I could see it all the way across the parking lot." He was getting loud, and she narrowed her eyes at him in an unspoken warning. "I was... I was defending your honor," he finished valiantly.

"My *honor?*" If the situation hadn't felt so bizarre and out of character for them both, she might have laughed. But that was exactly the problem. Ricky was behaving like some crazy nut job jealous boyfriend type, and she was—well, she wasn't really herself today either, in part, thanks to Jupiter Alonso—whatever all his other middle names were that she couldn't recall—Valentine. Or Valenteeeen-eh, according to him. She took a deep breath and released it slowly, her cheeks puffing out in exasperation.

Finally, she turned back around to face her friend. "What are you doing here, Ricky? Aren't you supposed to be in school?" Ricky attended classes three days a week at the local junior college, so when he did stop by her work, it wasn't usually in the middle of the afternoon on a Monday. She glanced past him at the closed door, as though seeing through it to the parking lot outside. "And how long had you been sitting there? I didn't see you pull in."

A flash of something unattractive passed through Ricky's eyes and he bit out, "Yeah, that was pretty obvious."

"Seriously?" Man, she had to stop using that word. How many times was that today? "Because it's not weird at all that you were just sitting out in the parking lot spying on me."

"I wasn't spying," he objected.

"Oh. So you just sat in the car and watched us talking for ten minutes, but you weren't spying."

"I wasn't. Or at least I didn't mean to. It's not like I came here to spy on you. I just... was surprised when I saw you... two." His voice ground to a halt, tight with unasked questions.

"So you sat and spied on us."

Ricky clenched his jaw, clearly frustrated. Finally, he spoke, but he didn't answer her question. "How come you haven't told me about this Jupiter guy? And is that really his name? Jupiter? As in the ruler of the gods, Jupiter?"

"Yes, it is his real name." She didn't dare tell him the guy's last name, at least not today. "And I didn't know about him myself until this morning when I showed up for work."

"Wow. You two sure got friendly quick." As soon as the words were out, his face flashed with regret. She saw it in the way his chin dropped, his mouth tightened on one side, and his gaze lowered for a few moments.

She crossed her arms and glared at him.

"Sorry," he muttered. "Uncalled for."

"Yep," she snipped, and started to walk away again.

"Wait. Please." He didn't reach for her, he didn't really beg, either. He just asked nicely.

Dang it. She stopped but didn't turn around. "I really have to go, Ricky. I have a shift change in a few minutes."

"Listen. I'd pulled in right before you came out and was just waiting for your break. I knew you wouldn't get one until Ben showed up at two, but I was getting ready to call and see if you wanted to take yours with me. Can you give me a few minutes? I—I wanted to ask you something. I kinda ditched class today to come see you."

Gia hesitated, her emotions in a turmoil. "I don't know. It's been a crazy morning with Jupiter starting today, and we've been busier than usual, too, so I wasn't really planning on taking one." She shot a meaningful glance down the hall toward the front of the cafe.

"Five minutes. That's all I need."

She bit her lip before continuing, but then lifted her eyes to meet his. "You know, I'm a little ticked off at you right now, so I don't really feel like playing nice, to be honest. Can this wait until I get off work? I can stop by your place on my way home." She wasn't being bitter, she told herself. But he had made her angry, and she needed some time to cool off. She was telling the truth, too; she really hadn't planned to take an official break. As skilled as Jupiter was, the morning had gone by at a near-frantic pace, and she needed to take stock of things before she left for the day, especially if today was any indication of how the rest of the week was going to go now that the word was out on Jupiter's presence.

Ricky opened his mouth like he was going to say something, then closed it again. Finally, he nodded. "Okay. I'll see you after work. My place." And with that, he turned and pushed out the door, not even bothering to say goodbye.

Gia sighed dramatically, smoothed some wispy curls away from her face, and made her way back down the short hall to the front. She dragged her feet the whole way; her boots felt like they weighed a dozen pounds apiece.

Around four o'clock, she received a text message from Renata reminding her that she'd agreed to watch her nephews and niece for the evening for Ren and Tim's date night. She usually loved hanging out with Ren's kids, so the fact that she'd totally forgotten about it unsettled her.

To make matters worse, Ricky never responded to any of her texts letting him know she had to go straight from work to her sister's house. She even offered to come by after Ren and Tim got home—it wouldn't be very late with Charise being only six months old—but when her screen showed evidence that he'd read her texts and wasn't replying, she shoved her phone in her purse inside her tiny staff locker and left it there for the duration of her shift.

"Fine. Be that way," she muttered. So much for cooling off.

SIX

RICKY HELD HIS PHONE down low in his lap so he wouldn't get caught with it in class, and his eyes narrowed at the words on the screen. He kept his pen poised over the half-filled page of his notebook just in case his professor glanced his way, and he started to key in the words *Okay. See you after date nite.* But the picture of Gia and Jupiter standing on the sidewalk behind Ricardo's Cafe today gnawed at him.

Jupiter. Stupid name. The guy had his hands all over Gia, and even from where Ricky sat in the parking lot, he could see the guy's eyes travel all over her, too. "Let me tie *your* apron for you, Barista Boy," Ricky snarled under his breath. "Around your neck."

The room around him stilled, and he glanced up to see Professor Lenarde making his way down the center aisle of the classroom toward the table where Ricky sat with three other students. He said nothing to Ricky, just held out his hand for the phone, and then picked up his lecture where he'd left off as he made his way back to the front of the classroom. He set the phone on his desk beside one other he'd already collected at the beginning of the hour.

Everyone knew Lenarde's strict cell phone rules, so Ricky shouldn't have been angry, but he was. Not at Professor Lenarde, but at Gia.

She was canceling on him. Sure, she said she'd come over after babysitting, but he wouldn't be surprised if she came up with some other excuse to avoid coming over then, too.

Gia had been so distracted by her Roman god that she hadn't noticed Ricky sitting in his truck, even though he'd waved out the window when she'd first walked out the back door... followed way too closely by Barista Boy. With his hand on her back. Then on her waist. And hips. And—

Every muscle in his body clenched as he remembered how slowly Barista Boy had untangled Gia's apron strings, how his gaze had traveled up and down the length of her as his fingers toyed with the knot at her waist. How he'd smiled—maybe at something she'd said, but maybe just at the thoughts that surely were running through his head as he untangled the strings of her apron as though he was undressing her—and how he'd taken his sweet time re-tying it, his hands resting at her waist so intimately. How his fingers lingered on the curve of her hips before she finally stepped away from him.

Ricky was going to go crazy if he kept thinking about it, about them, but he didn't know how to stop the images from playing on auto-repeat in his head. He didn't even have to close his eyes to see it; Gia and Jupiter might as well be standing in front of the classroom acting out the scene again and again for the whole world to see.

He couldn't sit here for another—he patted his pocket for his phone to check how much longer class was before he remembered it had just been confiscated. It occurred to him that if he wanted his phone back, he was stuck there for however much longer the class lasted. He let out a groan.

"Mr. Zander. Do you have a problem with my lecture? My teaching style? Perhaps I'm not entertaining enough to hold your interest?" The professor's words intruded on his misery, and Ricky straightened quickly, bumping his notebook with his elbow and sending it scooting off the end of the table. He lunged for it, knocking his chair backward into the table behind him, making the girl sitting there shriek in surprise. He caught the notebook by a page, but it tore free and fell to the floor anyway, the torn sheet still clutched in his hand.

Ricky straightened slowly, and instead of answering the teacher's sarcastic questions, he simply gathered up his textbook and pen, shoved them into his shoulder bag, then turned and apologized to Amanda, the girl he'd startled. He snatched up his notebook off the floor and then headed to the front of the classroom.

"I apologize for disrupting your class, Professor Lenarde," he said in a low voice as he approached the teacher. "I need to excuse myself for the rest of the day." And without waiting for a response, he veered toward the teacher's desk, snatched up his phone, and left the room.

Fifteen minutes later, Ricky sat slouched behind the wheel of his truck at the back of the employee lot where he could see Gia's blue Prius. Why he was there, he didn't want to admit even to himself, but he'd convinced himself that she might have actually blown him off so she could spend the evening with Barista Boy. *She wouldn't do that to me,* he kept trying to assure himself. *She's not like that.* And yet, only an hour ago, he'd sat in this same parking lot and watched her behave in a way he'd never seen her act with a guy. To add insult to injury, it wasn't just another guy, either. This guy was an Italian god—apparently—whom she'd supposedly just met that morning.

But another thought kept pushing through his head. *Do what to you, Rick? Cheat on you?*

And therein lay the crux of the matter. As her best friend, he may have the right to give his opinion about a guy she was interested in, but he had no claim on her love life. Or at least, he'd never asserted any such claim, even though his heart insisted he had.

He'd pretty much fallen for Gia—literally—the moment he laid eyes on her a week after his family had moved to Midtown when he was twelve. School had just let out, and because he was a new kid in sixth grade in a small town, he was still trying to figure out how to make friends since most of the other kids had been in the same class together all through elementary school. Gia, tall and stick-thin, her pale skin freckled, her long red hair in a wild ponytail on top of her head, had sauntered by with a group of girls just as he'd mounted his bike. Like a scene out of the movies, she'd turned to look at him, and everything in his world had gone slow-motion. Her curls fluttering across her face, her hand reaching up to push them away, those mermaid eyes, big and blue-green and wide and friendly and aware and curious and interested—*interested*—in him... and his foot slipped off the pedal, his backpack flopped to one side, throwing him even more off balance, and he went down, bringing his bike over on top of him.

Only his pride had been really hurt. He'd sustained an ugly elbow abrasion, but that kind of surface injury was nothing new to him. He'd taken his share of tumbles from his bike and skateboard over the years, had shredded a few shins and knuckles, broken some bones, even given himself a concussion after a particularly nasty ramp trick gone wrong. But as the volley of giggles erupted around him, never before had he so desperately wanted the earth to open up and swallow him whole.

And then she was there, leaning over and lifting his bike off him. A moment later, she crouched beside him, and he didn't know where to look. She wore a short, ruffled skirt—didn't girls know you couldn't squat in a skirt in front of a guy?

"You okay?" she asked, and her voice, although light and laced with a hint of humor, wasn't mocking in any way. He nodded, too embarrassed to meet her gaze, and instead, tried in vain to keep his eyes glued to her red Chuck Taylor All-Stars. But he was a twelve-year-old boy, after all, and try as he might, he couldn't help himself. His eyes drifted up her black and white striped long socks, over her knobby knees—one bearing a mottled bruise that looked a few days old—to the pale skin of her inner thighs... and right up her skirt.

He let out his breath in exquisite relief—okay, only slightly tinged with disappointment—at the sight of the black bicycle shorts she wore beneath the purple ruffles. He was already blushing furiously from his fall, so at least he didn't get any redder when she said, "Well, you're obviously not too badly hurt since you just looked up my skirt." She'd thrust out a hand, pulled him none too gently to his feet, and then said, "I'm Gia. You're new, right? Wanna walk with us since riding a bike isn't working out for you?"

Within moments, he'd been absorbed into Gia's group of friends—mostly girls, to his wounded ego's delight—and they'd been inseparable since. They lived only a few blocks apart from each other, rode bikes and skateboarded together, watched movies and did homework together. Pretty much anything they could do together, they did.

Except dating. They'd never done that together. In fact, as far as he knew, Gia hadn't really dated anyone throughout junior high or high school. Oh, she'd giggled with her friends about their hot classmates, about the trending movie stars, musicians, and athletes whose posters they'd taped to their walls, but she was driven to do well in school, and she'd seemed content to just hang with her circle of friends and their boyfriends as they came and went.

To hang with him.

They were a team. Ricky and Gia. Rickaroni and Georgy Girl. They shared the same loathing of their real names—Fredrick and Georgia—but once their friends discovered the miraculous coincidence, they also became Fred and George in honor of the beloved and inseparable twins from the Harry Potter empire, throughout the rest of middle school. In high school, once they commandeered their licenses, they were the TDD—Team Designated Drivers—at extracurricular events. They even had business cards made up and distributed throughout the school. They were the co-hosts of many a high school party themselves, and they often co-officiated school activities because they were popular and unassuming, and people just liked them. They even went to their senior prom together, although Shelby Evans had actually invited him *after* she bought tickets. Shelby had settled for going with one of Ricky's friends who'd been ever so grateful to go on the arm of one of the hottest girls in school. Ricky had also heard rumors that Gia had received at least two invitations, but she'd said yes to him, explaining that he was her best friend, and she couldn't think of anyone else she'd want to share the memories of her senior prom with more than him. At Gia's insistence, they'd wrestled their way through a series of dance tutorials so that they'd look good on the dance floor, because she refused to do the default high school shuffle. Although they'd laughed through much of the process, by the time prom rolled around, they'd found a rhythm they could work with and made quite an impression on their peers.

He'd wanted to kiss her that night. Not that he hadn't wanted to kiss her a thousand times before that night. But dancing with her in his arms beneath the glittering twinkle lights overhead, he'd felt like a prince with his princess. She was make-his-knees-weak gorgeous in an ice-blue dress that draped her body like it had been tailor-made for her, her long hair swept up and away from her face in a cascade of curls that fell from a fancy set of clips at the back of her head. He'd been almost afraid to touch her, not because she looked fragile or out of reach, but because he was so sure that when he did, the floodgates would open and spill out all that he felt for her... and everything would change between them.

Eventually, he knew he'd have to tell her. Eventually, his heart wouldn't be able to go on without her knowing his feelings, without him knowing if she felt anything in return. But he'd been afraid. Afraid of the possibility that his confession would ruin their last year of high school. Afraid she'd withdraw from him, afraid to see the pity in her eyes.

So he chickened out. He told her she was beautiful and then traded dance partners with his friend so that he could regroup, even though he regretted it the instant he saw the flash of hope in Shelby's eyes. Instead, he decided, beyond relieved when he held the laughing Gia in his arms again, he'd tell her right after graduation, maybe on a special summer night. The 4th of July right before the fireworks?

But that summer, Gia had focused a lot of her time and energy on her family and her job at Ricardo's, and the time never seemed right. Before he'd come up with a new plan, a new year had begun. When John Dixon had his fatal fall, once again, everything was put on hold as the Gustafson family rallied around Renata and her kids. In the wake of her first husband's death, she'd needed all the support she could get from her sisters, especially when circumstances led to a wedding for Ren and Tim Larsen that same fall.

Every time he made plans to talk to Gia, it seemed that something came up to deter him. At Christmas, he bought her a special necklace to commemorate his declaration of love... but because it had been the first Christmas without John, coupled with bringing Tim and baby Charise into the mix, and of course, along with the addition of Vic and Trevor all joining in the festivities, well, things had been so different. Ricky knew Gia so well, and he could see how affected she was by the many changes going on around her. He watched her studying her sisters, learning by observation how to cope with life and all its ups and downs.

And now that Phoebe and Trevor were together? Well, even though Gia and Ricky were both thrilled to see people they loved so much find each other, it did put a different spin on things between them. If—no, when—Trevor married Phoebe, Gia would be family by marriage. He knew it shouldn't matter, but it still sounded and felt a little weird, the idea of dating someone who would kinda be his cousin.

But last weekend, during Juliette and Vic's wedding, he'd been so sure he'd seen something in Gia's eyes that told him the time was right—she'd *sniffed* him and sighed like a girl in love, he was sure of it—and he'd made up his mind to surprise her at work with flowers and an invitation to dinner. His folks were out of town on one of their week-long retreats, so it would be the perfect opportunity to have some one-on-one time with Gia. He'd cook Gia's favorite meal of spaghetti with huge meatballs, serve soft garlic bread sticks from Mona's Bakery along with an assortment of Mona's pastries, too, of course. Then they'd top the evening off with a movie of her choice, even if it meant he had to watch *Across the Universe* or *Moulin Rouge* for the thousandth time. Even he had to admit, Ewan McGregor had the best man-cry performance he'd ever seen in a movie.

But now? For all he knew, Gia was having spaghetti and meatballs made by a legit Italian guy who probably made his own garlic bread sticks and pastries from scratch, and loved musicals, too. And how old was he? Thirty? He had the look of a guy who'd been around the block a few times, and Ricky was not thrilled at the idea of Barista Boy offering to take *his* Georgy Girl for a spin....

Except that she wasn't really *his* girl, was she? Because, like a coward, he'd waited. And waited. For the perfect time, the perfect place, the perfect circumstances. Any fool could tell you there was no such thing as a perfect moment showing up on its own. Moments became perfect because of what a person did with the ones he got. At least that's what Gia's Granny G always said. And he, Fredrick Thomas Zander, had wasted almost a decade of potentially perfect moments with Georgia Amity Gustafson by not telling her how he felt about her.

So here he sat, waiting for her outside her work again, hoping against hope that she wasn't just blowing him off—even though he probably deserved it after his little chest-pounding incident—and would give him just a few minutes of her time. He glanced over his shoulder into the back seat where the bouquet of flowers lay wilting and wasted because he'd acted like an idiot. Why hadn't he just taken the flowers with him instead of launching himself out of the car in a state of jealous panic?

Well, he'd go to her empty-handed today and make up for it on Friday night when she came for dinner.

Because surely, she'd say yes to him. Wouldn't she?

SEVEN

Gia threaded her way through the cars in the lot to where she'd parked her Prius that morning. She was running late; Ben had sliced open his thumb with a utility knife while stocking the supplies in the back, and Ricardo had driven him to Urgent Care. Gia had waited for Ricardo to return, anxiously watching the clock, knowing Tim and Ren had dinner reservations at six. Her sister had been understanding, but Gia knew how precious her date nights with her husband were—they only got out together once or twice a month—and she hated making them wait for her.

She had just reached for her door handle when someone said her name behind her. Startled, she spun around to find Ricky standing a few feet away. What on earth was he doing here?

"Seriously?" she asked, and then smacked her forehead with an open palm. *Stop using that word, Gia!*

"I just want to talk to you for a minute." He took a few steps closer, but when she turned and glared at him, he stopped.

"You got my texts, right?" she said, cocking her head, her eyes narrowed. It wasn't really a question, so she didn't wait for him to answer. "I can't talk right now. I'm late as it is."

"I know. I did get them." He grinned sheepishly. "I got my phone snagged in Lenarde's class."

Gia crossed her arms and raised a disbelieving eyebrow at him. "I thought you ditched class today. So Lenarde has your phone now?"

"I ended up going to class, but then bailed halfway through. I got it back when I left. Instead of calling or texting, I just came by here to wait for you so we could—"

"Because waiting for me in this parking lot worked so well for you earlier today? What if I'd come out here with Jupiter again? What if Ben walked me out? Or a customer, some guy you didn't recognize? Would you have jumped out of your car to defend my honor again?" Her voice was hitching up in exasperation. "Why didn't you just text me? I offered to come over after Ren's date night, you know."

"I didn't know—"

She cut him off, not wanting to hear it. "You did know. My phone shows that you read my message. You *did* know."

"That's not what I was going to say." But when he opened his mouth again, she held up her hand to stop him.

"I have to go." She said each word emphatically, like he was a slow-witted imbecile. Then she got into her car, slamming the door behind her.

What was *wrong* with him? Why was he acting like this, lurking around the parking lot waiting for her, spying on her, and assuming things he had no right to assume about her?

She had backed into her parking space, so she started her car and pulled out, glancing only once in her rear-view mirror to see Ricky standing in the spot she'd vacated, arms crossed and shoulders drooping. A wave of guilt pressed against her sternum, but she kept going.

What was wrong with *her*? Two days ago, she'd been hanging on Ricky's arm, breathing in the smell of him and thinking about their forever future together. Right now, she didn't want to entertain even a single moment with him. She cranked up the radio and sang along, doing her best to drown out the nagging thoughts.

Dinner at Ren's was Gia's specialty, macaroni and cheese and piggies in a blanket with the good hot dogs. Of course, the kids had to eat the token pile of greens, too… three peas and at least one giant bowl of green Jell-O with whipped cream (turned green with a few drops of food color) on top. She felt no shame—she knew they got plenty of healthy food the rest of the week from Renata.

While Reuben and Simon did their homework on the coffee table, Gia played a board game with Levi and Judah. Baby Charise, who'd nursed right before Ren and Tim left, had been sweet and smiley throughout dinner, eating hearty spoonfuls of Greek yogurt and Ren's homemade baby cereal. She now slept limply in a carrier on Gia's chest, her tiny pink lips occasionally making an adorable sucking motion.

"Gia, your phone is buzzing," Reuben told her, eying her purse on the floor by the front door. "This is like the fourth time."

"I know. But I'm here with you guys right now. It can wait," she assured him. She knew who it was, and she didn't want to talk to him. She certainly had no intention of going by Ricky's tonight.

But as much as she just wanted this day to be over, she had no real desire to show up at work in the morning to face Jupiter again. She would not apologize for Ricky's behavior—it wasn't her fault he was acting like a child—but that didn't stop her from being embarrassed by it. The fact that Jupiter had accepted the gauntlet all but thrown down by Ricky just meant the guy wouldn't be cowed, and even though she wished it hadn't happened at all, she was glad Jupiter had stood his ground. She didn't like being objectified and that's how Ricky's behavior made her feel, like he had some kind of claim on her.

"Maybe you should turn it off so it doesn't bother us while we're trying to do our homework," Simon said, his voice low and serious. He wasn't intentionally rude, but he often sounded that way. He was just one of those kids who hadn't figured out how to temper his thoughts with social niceties.

"Good idea, dude," Gia said. She got up and went to her purse, grimacing when her phone started buzzing again. This time, it was the rhythmic buzz of a call and not just a text notification. With a hand on Charise's head to keep it from bobbling, she rooted around in her purse until she found her phone, and glanced at the name on her screen.

"Oh!" Her eyes widened in surprise. Ren. "Hey, sis," she said, pressing the phone to her ear.

"Hey, you. How are things?" Renata sounded relaxed and Gia smiled, glad her sister seemed to be enjoying her night out with her husband.

"Great. Homework, board games, booze and cigarettes. You know, the usual. Charise has already passed out from all the wild times. Judah might be next, the little party animal."

"I dint do nothin' wrong," Judah hollered when he heard Gia say his name to his mother. The poor kid was way too used to being told on.

Ren chuckled into the phone. "Well, I hate to cut your shenanigans short, but we sat next to a fussy baby all during dinner who triggered my milk flow. I've soaked through my nursing pads and now I'm walking around with two wet spots on my pretty orange sweater. Poor Tim keeps giving the stink eye to anyone he catches looking."

"Oh no," Gia said, glad that her sister seemed to be taking it all in stride. "So you're coming home now?"

"Yes. At this point, we're just trying too hard to have a good time." Tim said something in the background that made Ren laugh. "That does it. Tim just challenged some poor guy to a duel at sunrise. See you soon."

Gia guffawed, but then asked, "Did you at least have a good time part of the time?"

"We've had a great time," Ren cooed. Her response was slightly muffled, as though she might be talking more to Tim rather than into the phone.

Gia made a face, not missing the lovesick tone of her sister's voice. "Ew. Say no more. I'll see you when you get here."

Less than fifteen minutes later, Renata was taking the now awake Charise from Gia with the desperation of a nursing mother too long separated from her baby. Tim was picking out bedtime stories with the help of the two younger boys. Reuben had finished his homework and sat reading a comic book Gia recognized as one that Ricky had loaned him, and Simon still hunkered over his paper, intense concentration furrowing his young brow. He'd barely acknowledged the arrival of his parents.

It was only 8:30 when Gia climbed into her car. For a few minutes, she simply sat, the stillness of the night settling around her. The stars were bright in the sky overhead, reminding her of their senior prom and the canopy of twinkle lights crisscrossing the ceiling while she and Ricky danced the night away. Not quite a year ago, but it seemed like a lifetime had passed since then. She knew her grandparents were starting to wonder what her plans for the future were. Even though they didn't say anything, she sensed it in the way they watched her, the way they seemed to be marking time.

A thought niggled at the back of her mind, one that scared her when she focused on it for more than a heartbeat. Was the time they were marking hers or theirs, she wondered.

She decided to take advantage of the early hour and head home to watch television with Gramps. He liked his History Channel shows, often commenting on the things they got right or wrong based on his own personal experience. He thought it a hoot that folks considered a good chunk of his lifetime as 'historical' already, but Gramps had lived almost eighty years.

Gia stopped by the market on the way home and grabbed a box of Little Debbie's Nutty Buddy Snack Bars, a favorite indulgence among the Gustafsons.

Sure enough, Gramps was ensconced in his recliner, remote on the wide armrest, bare feet elevated on the footrest. "You're home early, sweetie," he said when she walked in and handed him the open box of treats. "Pull up a chair. Watching an Abe Lincoln documentary. Fascinating man." Gramps was of the mindset that one didn't need a lot of words to say things, but his short sentences never failed to communicate his thoughts.

Gia plopped down on the old sofa beside him. "Sounds good. Where's Gran?"

"She's showering. Should be out soon." He handed the box of treats back to Gia. "Better if you're holding this when she does."

Gia grinned. Granny G appreciated the cheap snack bars as much as anyone, but she always made the obligatory show of disapproval when one of them came home with a box. Then she'd indulge right along with them.

"I'm going to make a cup of Chai tea. Want some?" she asked, but she already knew the answer.

Gramps didn't drink much of anything after dinner. He'd begun having some bladder control issues over the past couple of years and had found that not having liquid past a certain hour made for a much more peaceful night's rest for everyone, especially since he refused to sleep in 'old man diapers' as his doctor had suggested.

But she always offered anyway, knowing that if she didn't, she'd not only be acknowledging his weakness, but also accommodating it, too. So even though they all knew his reasons for refusing, she kept asking, allowing him the dignity of turning her down of his own free will.

Granny G, however, loved the flavorful Chai blend Gia kept stocked, so she made enough for both of them, and by the time her grandmother emerged from the back hall in her flannel pajamas, Gia had a steaming cup of tea and two Nutty Buddy bars on a napkin waiting for her on the coffee table. It was a peaceful night in the Gustafson home, and Gia settled into the corner of the sofa and tucked her feet up under her the way she'd done for as long as she could remember.

Because she didn't remember any other home before Gramps and Granny G's.

Snippets and snapshots of her parents flickered across the screen of her memory like old movies without sound, but truth be told, she wasn't sure if they were even her memories, or if they were pieced together from family pictures and everyone else's stories.

Gia had just turned four when her parents had been killed by a drunk driver, a girl named Angela Clinton who'd been in Juliette's graduating class. In fact, it had been on the way to her own graduation ceremony that Angela had run a red light and plowed into Paul and Simone Gustafson who were also heading to the event, killing Simone almost instantly when her head slammed against the passenger door window. Paul had lasted long enough to say goodbye to Gramps before he had joined his beloved wife, making the four Gustafson girls orphans. The sisters had moved into their grandparents' guest bedroom before the night was over, the three older girls commandeering the guest room suite, while Gia slept on a mattress on the floor of her grandparents' room for the first couple of months. She eventually moved into a tiny room that had once been her grandfather's TV den, but when she turned thirteen, the whole gang got together and redecorated the 'big girls' room' for her birthday gift. It had been—and still was—a teenager's dream room, complete with a four-poster bed, furry throw rugs, beaded window and door curtains, and a bejeweled chandelier that rotated like a disco ball with the click of a remote. No, the only home she knew was the one provided by the grandparents who raised her like their own since the day Angela Clinton had taken Paul and Simone's lives.

Angela Clinton. Now *that* was a cauldron on the brink of bubbling over.

EIGHT

Angela Clinton was scheduled to be released from prison on parole in less than a month, and the pending event loomed over them all like a storm cloud on the horizon. Each of her sisters seemed to be handling the situation in their own way. To help her process through her own myriad of emotions, Juliette had initiated contact with Angela via letters, and the two had been writing back and forth for over a year.

Last summer, Angela had informed Juliette of her pending release, and had asked if the sisters might be willing to get together with her once she had settled back in Midtown.

Renata had been hesitant at first, but she had eventually agreed that getting together with Angela would bring a sense of closure, if nothing else. She hadn't known Angela the way Juliette had, so she didn't feel the same obligation Juliette did to repair a broken relationship.

Phoebe, on the other hand, had encouraged Juliette, and subsequently Renata, to do whatever they needed to do to heal, but had remained uncharacteristically resolute about not wanting to connect with Angela. Ever.

Then, a little over a month ago, through a series of remarkable circumstances, Phoebe was introduced to Alice Masters, Angela's mother. She'd discovered a woman who had also endured devastating loss and grief because of the tragic accident.

Alice and Phoebe had forged a fragile connection, and now, between Juliette's pen pal friendship with Angela, and Phoebe's developing relationship with Alice, it seemed inevitable that the two families—what was left of them, anyway—would converge at some point in the near future. Gia knew all three of her sisters, each in their own way, were looking forward to meeting Angela Clinton.

However, Gia felt completely detached from the situation, although she couldn't bring herself to admit as much to the rest of her family. Her sisters assured her that she, too, had been a mess, had cried at night, had begged to go home to her own house. They told her how she'd started wetting the bed again, and how she'd refused to eat anything unless it was served in the Little Mermaid dishes her parents had given her for a birthday present a few months before they'd died. How she'd religiously worn her daddy's tie and incessantly rubbed the end of it until it was just a frayed tassel that kept getting shorter and shorter as time went by. How she'd cried when it wasn't long enough to knot around her neck anymore.

But Gia couldn't remember any of that. Even though she'd been well old enough to have memories of those months before and following her parents' deaths, she simply couldn't dredge them up.

And so, in light of having no real concept of the loss, and the grief that accompanied the loss, she also believed she harbored no bitterness or lack of forgiveness toward Angela. She simply felt no compulsion to connect with the girl, not even for the sake of resolution.

As far as Gia could determine, she had no unresolved issues with Angela. Her unresolved issues were much closer to home.

In fact, it was only a sense of familial obligation that drove her decision to agree to meet with Angela upon her release. If not for Juliette's desire to do so, Renata's need for closure, and Phoebe's curiosity about Angela's part in the connection she and Alice Masters shared, Gia could have gone her whole life without ever knowing what became of the Angela Clinton Gia didn't know who took the lives of the parents Gia didn't remember.

However, that sense of detachment seemed to permeate everything in her life these days. She didn't know what she wanted to do with her life, but she felt no motivation to figure it out. She wanted to love and be loved by someone—Ricky? Jupiter? Someone she had yet to meet, some future man of her dreams? Or someone from her past? What about Jackson, who had begged her to go out with him throughout their whole senior year, who kept in touch even now, claiming he loved her and wanted to take care of her? Of all people, Jackson Plains could do just that. He came from money, and even though he was off at college getting his business degree so he could one day step into his dad's big shiny shoes, she knew she had but to say the word, and he'd rearrange his world to make a place in it for her. Why couldn't she let herself love someone like Jackson?

And what *about* Ricky? He was her best friend. He was the brother she had never had. He was her comforter, her companion, her trouble-maker twin, her conscience. They were already practically one person in so many ways, and she loved him to the point of obsession. But did she love him *only* like a brother? A friend? Or did she love him the way she would a husband? A lover?

Well, yes. Yes, to all the above. And that's what made it so confusing and frightening. How could she love someone like a brother and want him to also be her boyfriend? Where was the line between platonic and romantic, or even carnal love? It freaked her out to think about kissing Ricky, about his lips on hers, his tongue in her mouth, his hands caressing her, his body hard against hers... and yet she longed for it, too. And that made her feel guilty, partly because he was her buddy, her pal, Rickaroni Baloney Thomas Zander she was thinking of in such a way.

And yet, *still*, she ached for it.

Listening to her friends carry on about the guys they dated, about making out, about sex. Gia wasn't only the last virgin she knew; she was also the only girl she knew who hadn't even had a real open-mouth kiss before. She was a full-grown legal adult, for Pete's sake, and she hadn't even been to first base with a guy. Didn't that make her some kind of a freak?

What she really longed for was a mother to talk to. For Simone specifically, she supposed, to sit beside her on her bed and help her sort through these feelings.

She couldn't ask Granny G to help her. As much as Gia loved and respected her, the woman was almost four times her age and when she and Gramps had met, things had been different. They'd known each other six months before they married. Six months! They hadn't witnessed each other's ups and downs of adolescence and puberty. They'd never had to sort out their conflicting feelings about each other. They'd met, fallen in love, and agreed they couldn't live without each other.

She couldn't talk to Phoebe, either; there wasn't a maternal bone in Phoebe's body. Well, at least there hadn't been until recently. And although the heartbreaking story of Phoebe's daughter had been exposed and her sister had begun the process of freeing herself from the pain of that person she'd been, it was still too early to lean on Phoebe as a mother figure.

Juliette, as soft and gentle and loving as she was, wouldn't be any good to talk to either. She'd never understood why Gia and Ricky had stayed 'just friends' all this time. "He's perfect for you in every way, Gia, and I can see how much you both love each other. I don't get it. Why is nothing happening between you?" But since Gia couldn't explain it to herself, it would do no good to confide in Juliette, who seemed to have the same questions she did.

And Ren? No. Just no. Not because she didn't trust her, but because Ren would over-analyze the whole thing, come up with some insane intervention plan, and the whole thing would backfire, and without a doubt, someone would lose an eye. At the very least, someone's heart would end up broken.

Her friends from high school? As much as she'd believed they'd be forever friends and closer than sisters, in the time since graduation, she felt the separation that came from everyone taking different paths. There wasn't one of them who could relate to what she was dealing with—they knew Ricky in the same context she did, and she really needed a fresh perspective.

So what about Jupiter? Maybe she should see where things went with him. Not that she really believed he was interested in her. Sure, he flirted and teased and touched her in ways that made it seem like he was attracted to her, but everything about him felt polished, like he'd had a lot of practice at playing the Casanova.

Gia toyed with a long curl, winding and unwinding it around her finger as she thought about the disruption Jupiter had brought to her life in the course of one day. She marveled at how self-assured he was, how he seemed to know exactly what he wanted and went after it. Perhaps he wasn't exactly serious about her, but his behavior did indicate that he wanted her on some level, even if it was just a physical attraction. How could it be anything else in less than seven hours spent together?

And yet, maybe the fact that he wasn't serious about her—and indeed, couldn't afford to be since he was only here temporarily—was just the thing she needed to help her breakthrough whatever barrier kept her from letting anyone love her.

The idea thrilled her and terrified her at the same time, and she found herself growing more and more antsy, fidgeting in her seat. She certainly wasn't paying a bit of attention to the television show. She glanced over at her grandparents. Gramps' eyelids sat at half mast, heavy with sleep, but she found her grandmother studying her, a look of concern on her face.

Before the older woman could ask her any questions, Gia sat forward and said, "I'm going to call it a night. I'm having a hard time concentrating on the show, and I think I'm just super tired. Do you want me to take your cup, Granny G?" She stood and held out a hand toward her grandmother.

"No, sweetie, I'm not finished with it yet, but thank you." Granny G took a sip as though to validate her statement. "Are you sure everything is all right?"

"Absolutely," Gia assured her. "It was just a long day, and I think I'm still coming down off the wedding high from the weekend, that's all."

"A good night's sleep often cures what ails ya," Gramps interjected, his voice groggy with fatigue. He muted the volume on the television and reached a hand toward each woman. "Come. Let's do our prayer here, then." Together, they bowed their heads and lifted up their nightly prayer of thanksgiving for family and friends, for provision, and salvation.

It took Gia a few moments to quiet her spirit enough to feel the gratitude Gramps claimed for them, but she was grateful. For her grandparents, who'd taken them in without hesitation, for her sisters and how close they'd remained over the years, despite their differences. For Ricky... yes, for Ricky, her best friend in all the world. For her job, her cute little car, her grandparents' health, for the way God had provided for the whole family in the aftermath of the tragic accident.

Angela Clinton. Could Gia be thankful for her? With her head bowed, she tried to imagine the petite girl with corn silk hair and the voice of an angel her sisters had told her about. A girl beloved by all who knew her, a girl from an upstanding, church-going family that was prominent in the community... getting drunk all alone on what should've been one of the best days of her young life.

A girl who'd spent the last sixteen years in the women's prison forty-five minutes away from her hometown where her mother, Alice Masters, waited with the support of her new husband for her daughter's safe return.

Could she be grateful for the girl who had turned the lives of so many people upside down with her irreversible actions that day?

Something in Gia longed to say yes, but the longer she thought about it, the longer she considered how desperately she needed her mother these days, the more difficult she found it to even be content with the way things were, no less grateful. She loved her grandparents, her sisters, and she loved what they'd made of the life that had been forced on them, but would any of them have chosen this for themselves?

No. A thousand times no. Of that, she was certain.

Gramps squeezed her hand as he ended with a reverent "Amen," but Gia didn't echo him the way she usually did. A dark cloud of disquiet hovered over her as she leaned down to plant a kiss first on Gramps's cheek, then on Granny G's.

And although neither of them said anything, she could feel the weight of their concerned gazes on her as she headed down the hall.

NINE

Just as he'd promised, Jupiter Valentine was waiting for her the next morning. Not in the break room with Ricardo, but at a table near the back hallway, where he'd be certain to see her the moment she came in the back door.

And boy, did he certainly see her. The appreciation in his eyes almost made her second-guess her bold look, although it was nothing new to her co-workers and regular customers. She often changed up her style from one day to the next, but she'd taken extra care with her appearance today, and she knew it worked well with her height.

Jupiter rose, closed the notebook he'd been writing in, and stepped into her path. She pulled up short and looked him in the eye.

"Good morning, Jupiter." She was pleased to hear her voice sounded chill. Just the opposite of how she felt. That said, if he didn't move, or say something, or at least stop looking at her like she was... well, *edible*, she'd get nervous and one of her eyes would surely start twitching, or something else equally embarrassing.

Without warning, he took her by the shoulders and leaned in. First, he kissed one cheek, then the other, and then, without releasing her shoulders, he looked her in the eyes again and murmured in that silky voice, "Come. I will brew you a cup of coffee that will make you fall passionately in love with me at the very first taste."

Either that first taste or the way you say 'passionately in love with me' in that yummy accent, she thought. She knew her cheeks flamed at his flirting, but she'd come prepared for his assault on her senses. Yesterday she'd dressed as a warrior woman ready to take on the world. Today, she was an All American Beauty going toe to toe with an Italian Stallion named Jupiter Valentine.

She wore black and teal plaid twill cigarette pants, a 3/4-sleeve black ballerina top cinched at the waist with a wide red belt, black Mary Jane shoes with red bows on the toes, and a teal bandanna sweeping the big victory curls she'd tamed her hair into up and away from her face. When she wore her hair piled on top of her head that way, she gained several inches. Jupiter wasn't as tall as Ricky—he might only have a couple of inches on Gia at best, since they were looking at each other pretty much eye-to-eye. But he was bigger than life in other ways, so she'd grab whatever advantage she could get.

"Bring it, baby," she said, putting one hand in the middle of his chest and pushing him gently. He didn't resist, but he stepped aside to let her pass. He scooped up the espresso cup and saucer he'd had at the table with him, along with his notebook and pen, and followed her to the break room where Ricardo leaned against the counter, talking on the phone. The older man acknowledged them with a nod, but he didn't pause in his conversation. Gia smiled in greeting and stashed her bag in her locker as quietly as she could.

"I'll be back with your coffee," Jupiter said quietly, a little too close behind her. "Please sit." He gestured to the table and one of the stools.

But Gia didn't feel like sitting and waiting to be served, especially with Ricardo talking a mile a minute on the phone. The guy rarely used his office for anything but paperwork, and Gia didn't blame him. It was practically a windowless closet. She also figured he used the break room as often as he did as part of his ploy to keep his employees from spending too much time back there. Well, she wasn't on the clock yet, and she was too antsy to sit, so she headed out to the front of the shop to greet some of the regulars.

A few minutes later, she noticed that Jupiter had stepped behind the coffee bar and was helping Belinda and Lacy fill coffee orders as Carter manned the register, apparently taking her unwillingness to sit and wait for him in stride. She could feel his eyes on her as she made her rounds, and at one point, she glanced over to find him smiling at her with a knowing look in his eyes that irked her.

She wasn't avoiding him, even though it was obvious he thought she was.

Among the regulars who had snagged tables and stools along the high counter that ran the length of one wall of windows, there were several customers she recognized, even if she didn't know them all by name, but she greeted everyone warmly all the same. There were many new faces, too, primarily of the college age, female persuasion, and Gia couldn't help noticing how many of them followed Jupiter's movements the way he was following hers. News traveled fast in their small university town, and Jupiter Valentine was an attention magnet, with his swarthy good looks and his classy style, those heavy-lidded eyes and artfully messy hair.

Of course, there were those who had simply come for coffee and pastries, and Gia was glad to see that the whole world hadn't gone goo-goo eyed over the guy behind the counter.

She noticed in particular a couple of women at a table that was tucked back a little from the fray. When she realized their heads were bowed in prayer over their breakfasts, she didn't approach them, but watched them nonetheless, curious. It wasn't often that people said any kind of a blessing over their food at Ricardo's, so although the ladies didn't make a show of it, Gia did notice.

Sisters, she decided. They shared similar features—blue eyes, blond hair faded with age and both showing a little gray at the temples, slender shoulders, long, elegant hands—and when they spoke, Gia could hardly tell the difference between their voices. The older one seemed almost fragile, and the younger one made reassuring gestures, like a quick hand squeeze, or brushing her fingers along her sister's forearm. Maybe they hadn't seen each other in a while, or perhaps they'd had a falling out and were on their way to making amends.

Gia often found herself creating stories around folks who crossed her path. She loved to people watch, and she was especially fascinated by female relationships of all kinds: friends, sisters, mothers and daughters. Especially mothers and daughters, because she couldn't remember much about her own mother, and certainly not enough to be able to compare what they'd had to what she saw in others.

Not that her relationship with her sisters would be considered normal, either. Juliette, Renata, and Phoebe were stair-step siblings with less than two years between each of them. Gia, however, had come along eleven years later. Jules, Ren, and Phoebe *looked* like sisters with their similar builds, dark hair, gray eyes, and porcelain skin that blushed prettily in the sun.

Granted, Gia had pale skin, too, but hers had the propensity to go blotchy and freckle. Gia had a good three inches on Juliette, who was the tallest of the older three, and even though Gramps was on the tall side of average for a man—he stood right at about six feet—the top of Granny G's head barely reached Gia's chin.

The hair was the worst. Although Gia had learned to turn her crazy red frizz into an asset, there were many mornings she longed for the black velvet locks of her sisters and mother. Just once, to be able to crawl out of bed and run a quick brush through her hair; oh, what a fine thing that would be.

But more than the differences in their ages and appearances, Gia felt the lack of mutual experiences between her older sisters and her. Jules, Ren, and Phoebe shared memories of family vacations and road trips. They recalled fondly their parents' arguments and kitchen kisses. Daddy's stories, Mom's strong accent, and her refusal to give up her French exclamations no matter how long she lived in America. How Daddy smelled like old books after a long day at work.

Paul Gustafson had been an antique book dealer specializing in European literature. It was how he and Simone had met, in fact. She'd inherited a collection of Benedictine liturgical texts from a doting uncle, but having no interest in the collection herself, she'd contacted Paul to find her a buyer who would appreciate the value of them. Paul, fascinated by the collection—and by the French woman who insisted on delivering the collection to him in person—took far longer than usual to find a buyer just so he could extend the amount of time spent with Simone.

Granny G liked to tell the story of Simone finally calling Paul's bluff. "Your mother, with one hand on her hip and the other waving dramatically in the air between them, bent over our son's desk and said, 'Will you please just find me a buyer soon so I can afford my wedding dress? I will not marry you without the dress of my dreams." Paul, in his usual stoic manner so much like Gramps', had simply nodded, picked up the phone to dial one of the buyers he already had lined up and waiting, and completed the transaction on the spot right in front of Simone. They were married in six weeks.

The three older sisters also shared the experience of their mother's pregnancy with Gia, the excitement of her birth, and the struggle with postpartum depression Simone had, something to which Gia often attributed her own sense of detachment. Wasn't it true that postpartum bonding was essential for babies to thrive? That babies whose mothers couldn't bear to be around them during those first few weeks and months often struggled to connect to others throughout the rest of their lives? But the few times she'd suggested as much to her sisters, they'd assured her their mother's depression had only given them the opportunities to step in and help more. "You had four mothers, Georgia Gustafson," Ren would say. "When one of us wasn't available, there was always another mother who was. You were loved and cuddled and kissed and played with more than any baby I've ever known."

Juliette, too, had insisted the depression was short-lived, that by the time Gia was a month old, Simone had gotten through it and was, as usual, the best mother any little girl could ever want. "We just remember it so vividly because it was completely out of character for her. But Gia, you have to realize that having a baby older in life affects people differently than when they're young and fearless." Gia didn't ask, but she wondered if that thinking would now affect Juliette and Vic's decision whether or not to have children since Jules was in her mid-thirties, only a couple of years younger than Simone had been when she'd given birth to Gia.

Even so, when Paul and Simone Gustafson had been killed that horrible night, as much as she'd been loved by her older sisters, by her Granny G and Gramps, and by the smattering of international relatives in France—Simone had been the only child of an only child—Gia had sort of fallen into the in-between places. She didn't really belong in the tightly knit three-corded sister thing the older Gustafson girls shared, even though they eventually allowed her to join their sister group—and subsequently changed their name from G-Force3 to G-FOURce.

Granny G was quite a bit older than any other mother she knew, and she simply never thought of her as a mother figure. Granny G was the quintessential grandmother. Cute, gray, sweet, gentle, and old. And more often than not these days, Gia felt the roles reversing, that she in fact, was becoming more and more responsible for taking care of Granny G and Gramps, not the other way around.

And Gia's best friend was not another little girl, but a rough and tumble boy who lived a couple of blocks away. Sure, Gia had lots of female friends. She'd always hung out with a group of girls until Ricky joined them, and then it was Ricky and the girls. But the reality was, she didn't just *hang out* with them. She *led* them. And it wasn't until after high school that she realized how the role of leader allowed her to remain detached. Isolated. For whatever reason, only Ricky got through her invisible force field of self-preservation, and she'd been fine with that.

Until Ricky started looking at her in a way that buddies didn't look at each other.

Not yet, she wanted to wail at him every time she saw his eyes darken with something she didn't want to define. *Give me more time. I'm not ready. Not yet.*

TEN

RICKY DIDN'T BOTHER GOING inside. He could see her through the long row of windows chatting with customers and being her usual friendly, warm self. She looked amazing today in her Rosie the Riveter outfit. He knew a guy in love was supposed to prefer his girl *au natural*, but he got some kind of buzz out of Gia's different looks. It was like cosplay on a more normal level; instead of dressing like a favorite movie or comic book character, she dressed up like her mood. It definitely made her easier to read; Gia wasn't a game player by nature, but she was still a woman.

Honestly, it didn't matter what she wore. His Georgy Girl was beautiful in ratty shorts and tees while gardening with her grandparents, in flowery dresses that showed off her long pale legs, or sleeveless tops that made him want to touch the soft skin on the inside of her arm just above her elbow. Her blue jeans and hoodie at the movies, her flannel pajamas on lazy Saturday mornings. Rockabilly Babe, Hollywood Glamour Girl, Steampunk Rebel, Boho Chick.

Biker boots and military kilts like she wore yesterday.... He should have known that she wasn't in the mood to be challenged yesterday.

His eyes narrowed when he spotted Barista Boy behind the coffee bar. Staring at Gia. Even with the morning sun reflecting off the plate-glass windows, he could see the hungry look in the guy's eyes. His fingers tightened around the steering wheel. He should go inside and stake his claim. She wasn't on the clock yet. She could have a quick cup of coffee with him before work.

No, that would only tick her off more.

But he couldn't just sit here watching. Spying.

Why was he here? What had he hoped to accomplish this morning?

If only he'd gotten here earlier, maybe he could have caught her in the parking lot before she went in.

As he watched, Gia headed around the end of the coffee bar and struck up a conversation with Barista Boy. A moment later, she headed to the back. His relief was short-lived when Jupiter followed her not more than three minutes later, a cup of coffee—Gia's Mrs. Cullen cup—in hand.

Barista Boy was taking her coffee in the back room.

Ricky's face went so hot he thought the blood in his veins might burst through the skin. His pulse roared between his ears and his chest tightened, squeezing all the air out of him. He had to get out of there before he did something stupid again.

Resting his forehead against his knuckles, he forced his emotions under control, his lungs to expand and contract. When he no longer saw bright sparks at the periphery of his vision, he started his truck and eased out of the parking spot beside Gia's car.

"Idiot," he snarled through the tightness in his throat. For coming here yesterday, for being here this morning, for waiting, and waiting, and waiting.

Oh, he wasn't giving her up without a fight, but he needed a plan. Work was going to suck today. Big time. For once he was glad that he was on tire duty at the shop today. Nothing like loud tools and heavy lifting to cool him down a little. Hopefully, he'd be working alone so he wouldn't have to play nice with anyone. He needed to think.

ELEVEN

When she could put it off no longer, Gia headed back behind the counter to where Jupiter was busy cranking out the coffee drinks. Without looking at her, he said, "It seems that there is no one who does not love you, Georgia."

"Gia," she corrected, crossing her arms and propping a hip against the counter. "I prefer Gia."

"Then Gia it is. Are you ready for coffee now?" He gestured at her Mrs. Cullen mug on the counter nearby. It sat at the ready with an empty single serving pour-over cone perched atop it. "I will bring it to you in the lounge."

"The lounge?" Gia's eyebrows rose at the absurdity of the tiny messy break room being called a lounge.

"Please," he said, pushing a cup topped with foam toward Belinda. He stepped back away from the machine and turned to face Gia fully. He did look at her then. "I promised you a cup of coffee to start your day. Allow me to serve you."

"Fine," she said, sending him a conciliatory smile. Good grief, the guy was relentless. He was definitely flirting with her, and although it didn't bother her—in fact, it was really quite flattering—it might make someone else uncomfortable. As a manager, she supposed it was her job to talk to him about it, to explain that things might be a little different in California than in Rome where sexual harassment on the job was concerned, and that he had to be more reserved while at work.

How on earth was she going to start *that* conversation? *Hey, so, Jupiter. You know how you smile at me with those sexy eyes and tell me you want to make me a cup of coffee to die for? That will make me fall passionately in love with you? Yeah, well, someone might think you're flirting with me and get upset because you're making them uncomfortable. So think you can tone it down a little and maybe be a little less...less beautiful in every way? Who, me? No, I'm not uncomfortable with it. I kind of like it. But someone else who sees you flirting with me might be offended by it. Why? I don't know. Maybe because they think you should be making their coffee and not mine? Jealous? No, that's not what I mean. Okay, yes. Ricky was acting jealous, but that's not what I'm talking about. I'm talking about a customer who might feel like it's inappropriate for you to flirt with me when they're paying you to make them a cup of coffee. I know they're not paying you since you're working for free... oh, never mind. Just don't look at anyone, don't talk to anyone, don't touch anyone, and you might be okay.*

"I hate being a manager in today's workplace," Gia muttered under her breath. Just as she was about to head to the back, a movement out the window caught her eye and she looked up to see Ricky's truck pulling out of the driveway. What on earth had he been doing? She hadn't seen his truck when she parked, so he couldn't have been here that long. Why hadn't he come inside?

Or was he out there spying on her? "You have got to be kidding me." She rolled her eyes and pushed through the break room door. But hey, she hadn't said 'Seriously?' again.

A few minutes later, Jupiter entered with her mug held in both hands. He paused just inside the room, grinned cockily, and said, "Are you ready for this?"

Gia snorted and patted the table in front of her with both hands. "Bring it, baby." Ugh. Why was she saying all these stupid things around this guy? Bring it? Who even said that anymore? And she'd said it earlier, too, along with 'Seriously' a million and one times. And how on earth was she supposed to call him on the carpet for flirting when she'd called him 'baby' just now?

Jupiter set the cup down in front of her, and she smirked at the image in the golden foam on top; the Wonder Woman logo was unmistakable. "I love it," she declared, grinning down into the drink. Her thumb traced the slightly raised lettering on the side of the mug, drawing his eyes to the movement.

"You have not even tasted it, Mrs. Cullen."

She looked up at him, her eyes as wide as her grin. "I don't want to mess it up. It's remarkable. So what is it? I'm pretty picky about my coffee, just so you know."

Jupiter lowered himself to the stool opposite her, braced his forearms on the table, and leaned forward. "Taste it. It is authentic. Very elegant. Like you, I think." He tipped his head just a little, waiting, watching, making her think of the Mr. Cullen. She took a deep breath and lifted the drink to her lips.

And closed her eyes as the full-bodied smoky flavor of the dark roast mellowed by steamed heavy cream washed over her tongue, making it curl with pleasure. She swallowed, the liquid sliding down her throat, warming her chest and leaving behind traces of oak and caramel, even though she was fairly certain he hadn't added any flavored syrups. Not honey, either. Brown sugar, perhaps? She didn't say anything, didn't open her eyes, just took another sip, letting the brew linger in her mouth a little longer.

"Does it satisfy you?" he murmured, his voice hushed in the quiet room, almost as though he didn't want to interrupt her nirvana moment. But she could hear the smile in the way the words were formed. Clearly, *he* was satisfied.

"Jupiter Valentine, you are a magic man. This is amazing. What did you do to this coffee?" She finally set the cup down and looked up at him.

He straightened and pressed a palm to his chest. "Your words are ambrosia," he purred.

"Stop, please." She waved a hand at him, brushing off his melodrama. "Seriously. What is it? I think we should add this to our menu and name it after you. We could call it, um..." She furrowed her brows in thought. She took another sip. "Mmm. This is like the perfect get up and go morning cuppa Joe."

"Ah, but maybe it is my secret recipe and—."

"I got it!" She cut him off and reached a hand across the table to grab his. "Jupiter Rising. You know, like Venus Rising? Since it's a get up and go cup of coffee, right? Or, hey. Cuppa Jupiter! What do you think?" Okay. Two sips of the strong brew weren't enough to send her buzzing already, but she was definitely feeling a little stirred up by the way the guy across the table was looking at her.

"And if I told you," he continued, as though she hadn't interrupted, turning his hand over and clasping hers, "I would have to kidnap you and take you back to Rome with me when I go home."

"I'll fire you if you don't tell me," she said, both of them knowing she would do no such thing, especially since his hours were volunteered as appreciation for his uncle's hospitality. "I have no scruples." She tugged her hand free and took another sip, hoping the cup hid the blush she was sure had pinkened her cheeks.

Jupiter laughed out loud. "You blackmail me. Fine. I will tell you how I make it. I know you Americans like your coffee in a large size. I think you believe a demitasse cup is not such a good value?" He waved away her response before she could get one out, but she didn't mind. She was too busy sipping on the best cup of coffee she'd ever had in her life. "If I filled your cup with only espresso and cream, you would be like a Grand Prix race car driver." He lifted both hands like he was steering a car and made speedway sounds that had Gia giggling. "So I made a pour-over with Ricardo's favorite bold roast coffee, then I add a shot of espresso alternately with steamed heavy cream and sweetened it with, eh, *melassa*. In English, it is nearly the same word: molasses, yes? Of course, you might prefer caramel syrup or a different flavor?"

Gia shook her head. "No, I think a flavored syrup would take away from the balance. I like the molasses, which is a surprise, honestly, but I guess I can see using caramel, too."

Jupiter nodded. "Yes. I agree, it is good this way. Like I said, genuine and elegant, yes?"

"Genuine and elegant. Excellent way to describe it." Gia pointed at him. "Now, you know you're going to have to make me one of these every morning. Unless you teach me how to do it." She knew enough about coffee to understand that there was so much more to making a perfect drink than just using a specific formula. A good barista had an intuitive sense about balance and blend, about the texture of the grounds, the temperature of the water and cream, the consistency of the *crema* cap on the espresso and the milk foam, the method of layering ingredients, cup size and shape, and presentation. Every detail mattered.

Jupiter rubbed his jaw as though weighing out the options, but after only a moment's pause, he said, "I think perhaps I will continue making it for you." He reached up and cupped the back of his neck, his biceps flexing visibly beneath the sleeve of his fitted oxford shirt. She dropped her gaze, hoping he hadn't noticed that she'd noticed. "But maybe we will call it Venus Rising, I think. You are the beautiful Venus with your white skin and fire in your hair. And my coffee will wake you up each morning."

Gia tried not to think about the fact that he was comparing her to the naked goddess emerging from the sea on a half shell. She smiled kindly, knowing now was the time to say something. "Jupiter, listen. I appreciate your compliments. I really do. You make me feel great. Self-conscious, but great," she chuckled, a little embarrassed. She hurried on. "But while we're at work, I really need you to be...." Man, how on earth did she say this? "Maybe don't flirt so much, okay? Sometimes people can misunderstand and get the wrong idea about you. I just don't want anyone to cause trouble for you, so...."

But Jupiter was shaking his head before she even finished. "I know this already, Gia. My uncle told me." He reached across the table and brushed her arm with his fingertips, then pulled away as though thinking twice about touching her. "It is different in Italy. Flirting is good business."

"I understand," Gia assured him. She didn't know what else to say. She fought the compulsion to apologize for the expectations in the workplace, but she also understood how awful it could be when uncomfortable behavior went unchecked.

He shrugged good-naturedly. "I will try very hard to behave like a gentleman."

She wrinkled her nose at him and said in a light voice, trying to smooth things over the best she could, "You're free to flirt as much as you want when you're not on the clock."

Jupiter grinned. "So, I may flirt with you in the parking lot?"

Gia snorted and pushed to her feet, not bothering to answer him. "Thank you for the coffee, Jupiter. You were right. That truly was the best cup of coffee I've ever had."

"And now you are passionately in love with me, yes?"

This time Gia laughed out loud. Clearly, the message hadn't quite sunk in all the way. "Oh, Jupiter. What am I going to do with you?"

"I have many suggestions," he replied, hardly missing a beat. Then he held up his hands in surrender and chuckled. "Do not worry. I will wait to share them with you until we are in the parking lot."

It was going to be a long week, but Gia was suddenly looking forward to the challenge of keeping Jupiter in line.

TWELVE

Friday morning showed up garbed in gray clouds dripping with pearls made of rain. Gia sat on the edge of her bed, brush in hand, staring out the window at the heavy sky. April was as unpredictable in Southern California as her moods these days, switching from sunshine and blue skies to heavy shrouds overnight, sometimes without warning. Gia loved the gloomy days of spring, not because they made her feel good. On the contrary, when the weather was like this, she felt like she had permission to feel a little down in the dumps, too. And since it had been such a bizarre week, she didn't think she had it in her to feel any other way today. So the rain clouds brought relief, knowing she didn't have to fake a bright smile today.

Jupiter Valentine had been on his best behavior all week. He was always at Ricardo's before she got there, and within minutes of her arrival, she had her mug of Venus Rising in hand, complete with a new bit of foam art every day. But other than those few moments of him paying special attention to her before she clocked in, during actual work hours, his behavior was above reproach. Sure, he had a bit of trouble with personal space. He tended to stand too close and look into her eyes too attentively when she spoke to him, but she realized he was that way with everyone. As though whomever he conversed with might be the only other person in the world. She couldn't complain. His undivided attention wasn't just flattering; he actually did listen to everything she said, everything anyone said to him. He had yet to get a drink order wrong, he was already calling the regulars by name, and even during the busiest hours of the morning, he seemed to find time to interact with everyone.

At his request, she made it a practice to walk him out the back door and wait with him each afternoon just before two o'clock when he left for his classes, and she found herself looking forward to those few minutes alone.

There was never enough time to get into any deep conversation, but Gia was all right with that. She actually liked getting to know him in little snippets. He spoke about his older brother, Adamo, often. The two were close and had plans to open a restaurant one day. Adamo had already completed his culinary education and was currently a *sous chef* at a restaurant in Sorrento where he intended to remain until Jupiter was ready to join him in their own endeavor.

Gia listened to his well-planned life with sincere fascination, but she couldn't relate at all. Not because of the chef thing—clearly, Jupiter had a gift for working in the culinary world—but simply because he had a plan and was working methodically through it. She, on the other hand, had no clue what she even wanted to do beyond getting up and going to work at Ricardo's.

The wide-toothed brush she used caught in a snarl, pulling her hair and making her wince. Bending to the task of untangling the curls, she sighed deeply. It was Friday. She should be excited. The weekend was almost upon her, and she had nothing planned. It was such a relief after the frenzy of the last several months of wedding activity.

Even when she had nothing on her schedule, though, in the past, she'd usually done that 'nothing' with Ricky. And Ricky hadn't called since late Monday night when she'd ignored his messages and texts.

As if on cue, her cell buzzed on the nightstand where it was still plugged in. The image of Fred Weasley showed on the screen, and she hesitated only a moment before swiping the text message open.

Can you stop by my place just for a minute on your way to work?

No apology, no chitchat. But she knew better than to try to read between the lines with Ricky. Lately, he'd been as all over the place as a teenage boy's voice—she saluted in the general direction of Renata's house full of boys—and she didn't trust herself to be able to read him correctly with only a text.

Can you come by here instead? I'm already running a little behind and you know what cloudy days turn me into. Did that sound too carefree? Like she was pretending nothing was wrong? But she wasn't. She was being completely straightforward. She still had to shower and figure out what to wear while her hair dried, and she had to do it all while feeling like a sludge monster.

I'll be there in half an hour, Sludgy.

Gia smiled. He knew her well.

By the time she'd showered and all but emptied her closet, only to wind up wearing the first pair of jeans she'd pulled out and a cobalt blue ribbed sweater that hugged her curves, she could hear Ricky's voice coming from the kitchen where he'd most likely joined Gramps for a cup of coffee at the breakfast table. She glanced at the clock. If she opted not to go in early this morning, she had some time to give him. She slipped on a pair of ankle socks and then shoved her feet into her favorite Chelsea boots. With her damp hair loose down her back—she'd give it a little more time to dry first and then pull it up into a topknot when she got to work—she strode down the hall to face the day.

The look on Ricky's face when she swept into the room got her a little choked up. He was so transparent sometimes, and she couldn't help comparing his open and honest features to Jupiter's bottomless hooded gazes. Ricky's eyes moved over her quickly from head to toe and back again, bright with genuine appreciation, and then he stood to greet her. He didn't rush, but took his time, politely sliding his chair in before making his way around the table to get to her.

Under her grandparents' speculative regard, Gia looped her arms around his shoulders before he could say anything and hugged him. He pulled her up close and tight, and dipped his head to whisper, "Hey there, Georgy Girl."

"Hey there, yourself, Rickaroni." And all was right with the world, gray clouds and pearl raindrops included.

"Would you kids like something to eat?" Granny G asked when they'd stepped apart, a tinge of lingering awkwardness in the air between them. She didn't even bother to get up from the table. Needless to say, she wasn't surprised when they turned her offer down. "Well, there are Pop Tarts in the pantry. Won't fill you up and you'll have nothing but sugar and chemicals to fuel you for the morning. But knock yourselves out."

She said it all good-naturedly, and Gia bounced over, kissed her grandmother's soft cheek, and ruffled Gramps' bed head hair. He'd been a little run down, especially since the wedding, so hopefully, the fact that he hadn't gotten all spruced up for the day before breakfast, as was his usual regimen, meant he was getting extra sleep.

He'd had a couple of nasty colds over the winter, and the girls had practically hogtied him to get him in to see his doctor after a cold had run its course, but the cough remained. Sure enough, Dr. Adler had diagnosed him with what he called walking pneumonia and had given Gramps a stern lecture on taking better care of himself. He'd gone home with a course of antibiotics and strict orders to do nothing too invigorating—which was practically against his religion—sleep lots, eat healthy, and get plenty of fluids. It had taken more than a month for Dr. Adler to give her grandfather a clean bill of health, but between Granny G and the four sisters, Gramps had come through like a trooper.

Now, seeing him dragging again concerned Gia, but at least they knew what to watch for. Granny G didn't seem too worried, as far as Gia could tell, and at least he didn't have that hacking cough that had sounded so awful back in December.

Gia grabbed Ricky's hand and dragged him over to the pantry with her. She opened the door and started tugging him inside the small walk-in space with her. Suddenly, she remembered his words from the coffee shop and let go of him as if he'd shocked her. "Sorry. Didn't mean to drag you after me like that." She flashed him an embarrassed smile.

Ricky stood framed in the narrow doorway, his broad shoulders filling the space. "Hey," he said, then he reached out and took her hand back, lacing his fingers through hers. He stepped into the pantry, pulling the door half-closed behind him. "I'm sorry I said that. I'm sorry about that whole thing. It was a crap thing to pull, and I was a jerk. Forgive me, please."

Gia looked up at him—grateful she'd worn her flat-soled boots so she actually could—and smiled, not caring that she was blushing. "Well, you were being a big, stinking pile of—eep!" She squealed as he tugged on her hand, hard, jerking her toward him. The tiny space was barely big enough for them to stand upright face to face, so closing the distance between them didn't really take much effort. His arms came around her again, this time in that slow, thoughtful way he did these days, drawing her tightly against him.

He was going to kiss her. Right there in Granny G's pantry, he was going to *kiss* her. She could see his intention written all over his face, she could feel it in the tautness of his body, in the tenderness of his embrace. She saw it shining in his eyes as he dropped his gaze to her mouth and then dragged it back to her eyes.

Not yet, a voice screamed inside her head. *Not here. It's changing too fast.*

Gia tensed, but didn't pull away. Instead, she rested her head against his shoulder, turning her face into his neck. He smelled like body wash and shaving cream and the cologne she'd picked out just for him. Her cheek brushed against the underside of his jaw and she noticed how smooth it was; he must have shaved just this morning. She closed her eyes and breathed him in.

A moment later, Ricky rested his cheek against the top of her head.

This. "Let's just hide out in here all day," she whispered, the words slipping out on a breath.

"We won't starve," Ricky said with a chuckle, the sound rumbling against her ear. When had his voice gotten so low? And so soothing? She suddenly recognized how wound up she'd been all week, the thrill of working with Jupiter, of being acutely aware of him at all times, knowing she'd turn, and he'd be watching her, smiling, teasing. Wondering what he was thinking, what he wanted from her, why he wanted anything from her at all. On, on, *on* all morning long until finally, *finally,* he'd leave for class and she'd be able to breathe normally again. It was exhilarating and exhausting, stimulating and stressful.

But this, tucked into her grandmother's pantry with Ricky? This was sanctuary. Peace. Comfort.

This was shelter.

This was... safe.

A trickle of resistance skittered down her spine, and she straightened, pulling slowly away from him. She didn't look at him as she stepped back, putting space between them again. His hands slipped to her waist until she turned away from him and made a show of perusing the shelves for the breakfast treats, even though she knew exactly where they were. "Come on," she said, snatching the whole box from its spot next to the cereal and backing out of the pantry and out of reach of his touch. "Time to be grown-ups. You have class in an hour, and I don't want to be late to work." She tried to make her voice light and breezy; she didn't want him to know how unsettled she felt.

"Wait," Ricky said, grabbing her hand and pulling her back into the tiny room. "I have to ask you something. Two things."

She shuffled forward a few steps, but stayed in the open doorway and leaned against the frame. She grinned up at him, finally braving a look at his face. "You mean, you didn't just come over to apologize for being a turd butt the other day?"

Ricky snorted. "I supposed I've been called worse—"

"Oh, yeah. I've definitely called you worse," she agreed, pulling her hand free of his and tucking it behind her back.

"And yes, I came to apologize."

"Which you did quite nicely, thank you very much." She nudged his foot with her toe.

"You're welcome. I also came to ask you if you'd let me try to make it up to you by cooking dinner for you tonight. My folks are gone again, so we'll have the place to ourselves." He stepped closer and put his hands on her waist. She clutched the box of Pop Tarts to her chest. "Your favorite. My spaghetti and giant meatballs." He rocked her hips a little, almost like he was trying to shimmy loose the answer he wanted from her. "I'll get bread sticks and chocolate éclairs from Mona's, too."

"Oh wow. You really drive a hard bargain." She wrinkled her nose at him. "I don't know if I can cancel my wild and crazy Friday night plans at such short notice," she teased.

She felt him stiffen just for a moment and she wished she could take the words back. She didn't want him thinking about Jupiter right now. She hurried to add, "Granny G will be so disappointed that I won't be able to watch 'Murder She Wrote' reruns with her."

"Then I have one more card to pull out of my sleeve," he said, relaxing his shoulders noticeably. "I'll even let you pick the movie we watch."

"Sold!" she said, almost cutting him off. She pushed out of the pantry and walked backward as she continued. "No backsies, Fredrick Thomas Zander, you hear me? Spaghetti, giant meatballs, garlic bread sticks, chocolate éclairs, and *Twilight*. All of them."

"Oh, please, no," he moaned. "Anything but the Cullens."

"Actually, no, not *Twilight*." She didn't need any reminders of Jupiter if she was spending the evening with Ricky. "How about *Dirty Dancing*?"

"No." He shook his head, but he was grinning. "You'll make me dance with you, and I didn't say anything about dancing." He followed her as she continued to move backwards through the living room. "How about *Mad Max: Fury Road*?" he suggested. "You like Tom Hardy. And that Nicholas guy."

"Ha!" she retorted, rolling her eyes, knowing just how much Ricky liked the brutal Charlize Theron and her rescued bevy of beauties. "Not a chance. *The Notebook*?"

"No."

"You said I could pick the movie," Gia pouted, coming to a stop in the front entry. "Bye Gramps, bye Gran!" she called out, getting return salutations from the other room. She gathered her purse and coat from the coat closet and let Ricky help her into it.

"You can. You just can't pick any of those movies." Before she could come up with a rebuttal, he continued. "And the other thing I was going to ask you was if you'd like me to take you to work. That way I can pick you up at the end of the day on my way home from school and we can go home together. Save you the gas."

"But your classes don't start until nine this morning." She didn't want him sitting at Ricardo's while he waited for school to start.

"I have to do some research at the library before my first period, so I'd planned on getting there early today, anyway."

Gia considered a moment longer, and then nodded. "Okay. Sure. I should let my grandparents know so they don't wonder about my car in the driveway all day."

"I already did. I told them about tonight, too."

"But they don't know I accepted your invitation," Gia reasoned.

Ricky had the grace to look sheepish as he admitted, "I kinda just told them you were doing stuff with me tonight. I figured since you were willing to let me come over this morning that it was a safe bet you'd agree to dinner, too. Sorry."

There went that frisson of resistance again, and she twitched just the tiniest bit before responding, "Safe bet. That's me." But she flashed him a smile to soften the sarcasm and turned to head out the door in front of him.

On the front porch was a large black and white umbrella, already wet from use. Ricky scooped it up and held it above their heads. "I came prepared," he said. "Stick with me, Georgy Girl, and I'll keep you safe and sound." He wrapped an arm around her shoulders, and together, they made their way through the drizzle to his truck.

A hollow disquiet settled in her stomach at his words. Safe. Is that what she really wanted?

THIRTEEN

"So tell me, Gia." Jupiter leaned on his forearms across the break table toward her. There was a lull in the morning rush, and because she'd come in so close to when she was supposed to start, she'd asked for a rain check on Jupiter's Venus Rising and settled for a double shot of espresso to get her going instead. It had been bitter and intense and left a harsh taste in her mouth, but the jolt had come after only a few minutes as the caffeine hit her system. Now, three hours later, she was ready for a refueling, and Jupiter had obliged her with a cup of his special brew.

"Tell you what, Mr. Coffee?" She sighed blissfully as she took another sip from her cup. "How you make this perfect every single day is like magic."

Jupiter grinned with satisfaction and watched her mouth as she licked the foam from her lips. She felt her cheeks grow warm and dropped her gaze to what was left of the cute little bunny face he'd made in the foam. "Tell me, what should a man like me do on his first weekend in America? And please tell me you will do whatever you suggest with me. I have only one class this afternoon; would you like to have dinner with me?"

Gia bit her lip, hating to disappoint him. But part of her was relieved to be able to tell him no. She was actually looking forward to the break from him and the way he made her feel. She couldn't imagine being alone with him on a... well, a date, for lack of a better word, without the parameters of work to hide behind. She had no clue what he'd expect from her if they went out together, even if it felt like a harmless flirtation to her. What if he thought she was more experienced than she was and expected a goodnight make-out session—or *more*, God forbid—at the end of the night? Or in the middle of the date, for that matter?

"Oh, Jupiter. This town is tiny. Just because we have Mid-U here doesn't mean we have a happening night life. I think most of the college kids head out toward Los Angeles or Pasadena, where there are all kinds of hot spots with live music and entertainment. You won't find much of that here in town."

"I don't need a hot spot. I was thinking more like a quiet dinner where we didn't have to worry about customers needing our services, where we could talk. I would like to get to know you better." He dipped his head toward her drink. "Now that I have figured out one of the most important things—how you like your coffee—perhaps I can figure out how you like other things in your life, too."

"Right. Um," Gia set the cup down on the table and wrapped both hands around it. The rain had stopped outside, but the day was still overcast and chilly, the kind of damp cold that seeped into your bones and didn't let up. The heat from the cup felt wonderful against her cold palms. "Well, I have plans for tonight. I'm sorry." Ugh. Why did she apologize? Having plans was nothing to be sorry about. He could have asked her before the last minute if he really wanted to do something with her.

"Of course, of course. I assume too much. Maybe another time, then." He straightened a little, bracing his hands on the surface of the table like he was going to rise and leave. "I will ask Ricardo if he is free to escort me. Perhaps he is a fun guy?"

Gia laughed out loud at the idea, not because she couldn't imagine Ricardo being a fun guy, but because she couldn't imagine him leaving the cafe for a night to have said fun. "Good luck with that," she said, not unkindly. "Listen, I'll see what tomorrow night looks like. Maybe we can do something, then?" Now why on earth did she put that thought into words? Especially where he could hear them? *Think before you speak, remember?*

Jupiter nodded slowly, his eyes crinkling at the corners as he smiled broadly. He pulled out a phone from his back pocket. "What is your phone number? I will call you tomorrow morning, okay? At ten o'clock?"

Argh. Now she'd gone and done it. But after only a moment's hesitation, she gave it to him. She wasn't worried about him stalking her or anything sinister like that, and she really did enjoy spending time with him, even though it was a bit like walking too close to an electric fence most of the time. She could feel the tingle of current between them and had a sneaking suspicion that if she were to ever initiate anything, she'd get a jolt that would knock her off her feet. "I'm not promising anything, okay?"

He grinned at her, clearly reading between the lines, but didn't say anything. Feeling an overwhelming need to explain her disclaimer, she added, "I need to check with my grandparents first. They may have plans for us for this weekend. My oldest sister just got married, so it's been super busy around our place. They may need me to help out with some of the stuff we put off because of the wedding. Like gardening. Gramps always puts in a big garden each spring..." The longer she talked, the higher his brows rose. "...and I know he's behind, so he may need my help," she finished, her voice fading with embarrassment. Gia closed her eyes briefly; she sounded like Jules when she got nervous.

"I like to garden," Jupiter said with a shrug of his shoulders. "My family has always grown a garden. If your grandfather needs assistance, just tell me and I will come and help."

She was fairly certain he was just trying to put her at ease. She glanced at his elegant hands, his long fingers, with square nails that looked manicured. Nope. The guy didn't garden much, at least not in recent days. "Um, sure. I'll tell you if he needs help." She took another long sip of her coffee, draining the cup, and then moved to the sink to rinse it out. "I suppose we should get back out front and help. Thanks for the coffee, Jupiter. As always, it was absolutely amazing."

"It is my desire to pleasure you," he replied, still sitting with his phone in his hands, watching her every move. Gia stilled at his provocative statement, but when she braved a look at him, he just smiled and added, "And thank you for your phone number. I texted you just now so you will know it is me when I call in the morning."

Clearly, it had been a translation issue, not an outright innuendo, right? "Sounds good," Gia responded, hoping he didn't hear the slightly breathy quality of her voice. But the images that had just flashed through her mind at his statement about what he desired had her thinking that perhaps she'd just stepped a little too close to the electric fence.

FOURTEEN

Gia stood on the curb with her jacket clutched in one hand at her side. A beam of sunshine had broken through the clouds and she lifted her face to it, her closed eyes and upturned mouth evidence that she was relishing in the spill of warmth on her cheeks.

Ricky swallowed hard around the lump in his throat. Man, she was beautiful. That hair, those long legs, the way her blue sweater hugged her body. It all wreaked havoc with his thoughts. She really shouldn't be allowed out of the house in anything but a potato sack. Then again, a potato sack would be a lot easier to remove than all the layers she usually wore.

Scratch that.

"Dude," he reprimanded himself as he pulled his truck up next to where she stood and hit the unlock button on his door panel. "Get a grip." She just stood there, face still tilted up, so he rolled down the passenger window. "Hey there, pretty lady. Want some candy?"

Her lips twitched, but she didn't look at him. "No, thank you. I don't have a sweet tooth."

They both knew that was a lie. "I have a collection of cute puppy pictures you might want to see."

"Nope. I'm a cat girl." They both knew that was a lie, too. Phoebe was the only Gustafson girl who actually liked cats, but she was allergic to them, so she pined for them from afar.

"I see. Well, I also happen to have a stash of cat memes on my phone. Wanna see them?" He held his phone between thumb and forefinger and swung it back and forth in the window.

Gia finally looked at him—*finally*—and Ricky could have sworn he felt the heat of the sun radiating off her skin when she did. "You are a determined and desperate man, sir." She stepped to the edge of the curb and leaned down to peer in the window at him. "Do you cook?"

"My prison tattoo says 'Chef' so I'd say that's a yes." He was grinning like a lovesick baboon, but he didn't care. "I make a killer pot of spaghetti and meatballs," he added.

"Ah. The reason you went to prison, I presume? Your killer spaghetti?"

"Or my to-die-for quesadillas."

"Or maybe you just got caught luring helpless women into your truck with your offer of candy and baby animal porn."

Ricky laughed and shook his head. "Nope. Not possible. It hasn't worked even once."

Gia narrowed her gaze at him as though considering his offer. "Spaghetti *and* meatballs?"

"And bread sticks and éclairs." When she still didn't look sold, he added his *coup de grâce.* "I will not be serving salad or anything else in the vegetable family tonight."

Gia yanked open the door and slid into the seat. "You just got yourself a dinner date, mister." She slammed the door behind her and turned to face him.

They sat in silence for a few moments, her breathing quick and shallow, his held tightly in his chest, and then she burst out laughing. "You are such a perv, Rickaroni."

He shrugged. "Yeah, well, it worked, didn't it?" He hit the lock button and rolled up her window from his door panel, then wiggled his eyebrows at her suggestively. "Now I'm going to kidnap you and take you back to my dark lair—"

Gia reached over and shoved him in the shoulder. "Stop it. You're just creeping me out now. Besides, I get enough of that stuff at work already."

Ricky swayed with the push and he chuckled, but he hadn't missed the odd look that crossed her features. Her words sunk in and he stilled, but he didn't look at her. Instead, he leaned forward and turned the key in the ignition. As he pulled away from the curb, he asked, "What do you mean, you get that stuff at work? Is there a customer bugging you?" *Please tell me it's not Barista Boy, please tell me—no, wait. Please tell me it IS Barista Boy so that I have an excuse to mess up his pretty face...* Good grief.

But one glance over at her gave him all the answer that he needed. "It's Barista Boy, isn't it?"

Gia's head snapped around and she let out a sound that was halfway between a giggle and a snort. "Barista Boy?"

"Yeah, your Italian coffee god." He didn't mean for it to come out so sarcastically.

Gia sat slumped in her seat, her jacket in a heap on her lap, but he knew her too well not to notice the tension tightening her neck and shoulders. And the fact that she stared straight out the front windshield now only made him more wary of her response.

"First of all, he's not *mine* at all, Italian coffee god, barista boy, or whatever else you want to call him. He is, though, the new kid in town—remember what that feels like?" She shot him a hard glare, but as soon as he caught her eye, she lifted her chin and looked straight ahead again. "He is also my friend, and he is my co-worker."

"Sorry," Ricky interjected, even though he wasn't. Her adamant reaction alone told him he had good cause to be worried, but the fact that she was claiming him as a friend after knowing him less than a week bugged him to no end. "I just wanted to know if you were being bothered by someone, okay? You're the one who said you were getting hassled at work."

"No," she dipped her head dramatically. "I did not say I was getting hassled at work. I said I was getting... *stuff*... at work."

Ricky knew he should just drop it, that asking for clarification was tantamount to jumping into the middle of a cactus patch, but he couldn't bite the words back fast enough. "What kind of stuff?" He emphasized the word the same way she had. "Perv stuff? Teasing? Flirting? I know the guy makes you coffee—" *Dang it. Shut up, man.*

For the most part, he kept his eyes on the road, but a few sideways glances told him she was shutting him out. Arms now crossed, jaws clenched, chin up.

"Fine. Never mind," he finally said when she didn't offer an explanation. "But if I catch that guy harassing you, he's going to have to answer to me."

"Seriously?" Gia asked, swiveling around in her seat to glare at him. She said that word a lot these days, he'd noticed, like she couldn't quite believe what other people around her were thinking and saying. It bugged him.

"Yeah, seriously," he grouched.

"Okay. How about this," she began, her tone laced with venom and false cheer, and Ricky knew his plans for the evening were on the verge of imploding right before his eyes.

He spoke first. "Gia, please. I don't want to fight with you. This is about us making up, okay? Forget I said anything. We were having a good time a minute ago."

"Yeah, until you ruined it by pulling the jealous boyfriend card. Again. Dude. I'm not your girlfriend." She accentuated each word as though he were thick in the head. But then she faltered a little, and Ricky's heart twitched with hope, hope that she didn't like the sound of that any more than he did. "It would never work, not in a million years," she continued, her words falling from her lips like anvils.

Nope. No hope there.

Gia pressed back into the corner of her seat and up against the door, like she was trying to get as far away from him as possible. "We're not even friends with benefits."

Ricky blinked long and slow as he processed what she was saying. And then, because he wanted to take a jab at her the way she was at him, he let the words fly. "Whoa. You mean that was an option? You've been holding out on me, woman."

The air between them went deathly still, like they'd both been struck and were holding their breath to determine how much pain had actually been inflicted.

"Stop the truck."

"No."

"Stop the truck!" she cried out, the words tearing from her throat in a voice Ricky had never heard before. When she began fumbling for the handle, he realized she was dead serious. Terrified she might actually launch herself out into the street, he pulled over to the curb.

Before she could untangle herself from her seat belt, he grabbed her arm. "I'm sorry. I'm sorry, okay? That was totally out of line." He tugged a little in a futile attempt to pull her toward him. This was not happening. *Not* happening.

"You think?" She wouldn't look at him. Instead, she stared at his fingers wrapped around her wrist. "Let go of me. Now."

"Gia, please. Please." He was begging now, but he didn't care. "Don't go like this. I have dinner. We can—"

"Let go of me or I will scream." She lifted her eyes to his, and he released her arm as though he'd been burned, even though what he saw in her face turned his blood to ice.

Over. It was over. The fight. The night. Maybe even the friendship. Definitely his lovesick dreams for a happily ever after between them.

She pushed open her door and swiveled in her seat to get out.

"Let me at least drive you home," he murmured. It was almost five miles across town to her place. "Please." He was still begging.

"I'll find my own ride. And I'm not going home." With that, she stepped out onto the sidewalk, slammed the truck door much harder than necessary, and turned on her heels to go back the way they'd come.

Ricky knew where she was going. And he was pretty sure he also knew who would be giving her that ride. Juliette and Vic were on their honeymoon, Phoebe and Trevor were always busy on Friday nights, and Gia would only call Renata if she was desperate.

Ricky couldn't ever remember Gia being that desperate.

He stared at her retreating back in his rear-view mirror, her long strides eating up the sidewalk under her. Sure enough, she pulled out her cell phone, dialed, and held it to her ear. A moment later, she glanced back over her shoulder at him, and even though he didn't think she could see him watching her, he hated that she witnessed him just sitting there.

But he couldn't move. He wouldn't just leave her alone on the sidewalk. Even if he was angry and jealous and gutted, he had to make sure she was going to be okay, no matter where she was heading. Before he could talk himself out of it, he put the truck in gear, made an illegal U-turn across the double yellow lines and drove after her. By the time he was parallel to her, she'd put her phone away. "Can I give you a ride to Ricardo's?" he asked, even though the words felt like broken glass on the way out.

"No thanks. I've got a ride, and I'm not going to Ricardo's."

Ricky bit the inside of his cheek so hard he tasted blood. "I'm not going to leave you out here by yourself, Gia. Please get in. I'll take you wherever you want to go."

She stopped, braced both feet wide on the pavement, and said, "Go home, Ricky."

He sat stone still, not even feeling the vibration of the idling truck under him. He might not have the will or strength to say anything else, but he wouldn't drive away until he knew she was safe. It wasn't a bad part of town, *per se*, but it wasn't a very busy street, either. If anything were to happen to her out here, there would be no one around to help.

A few moments passed, and then she turned and started back down the sidewalk. He waited until she was several yards ahead of him and then let his foot off the brake just enough to creep along behind her, close enough that he could jump out and intercede if he needed to, but far enough away that she wouldn't think he wanted to talk.

At the end of the block, she waited for the light to change, and then crossed the street and went inside the little taco shop on the corner.

Ricky pulled into the parking lot and backed into a spot so he could keep an eye on her through the plate-glass windows. He knew she'd accuse him of spying on her or stalking her, or of 'pulling the jealous boyfriend card' but he hoped after she calmed down a little that she might see he was really pulling the 'true friend' card now. He would leave as soon as he knew she wasn't going to be walking the five or six blocks back to Ricardo's alone.

No matter who showed up to give her a ride.

FIFTEEN

GIA'S HANDS WERE SHAKING so badly she could hardly get the zipper open on her coin purse where she kept her spare change. Her mouth was so dry; she just needed something to drink. Stepping up to the counter, she ordered a large cup and took it to the soda fountain near the front window. First, she filled it half-full of water, gulped down several swallows, and then started to fill the cup again with Sprite. From the corner of her eye, she recognized Ricky's truck pull into the parking lot.

"Why won't you leave me alone?" she growled under her breath. A man who had stepped up behind her looked at her curiously, and then followed her gaze out to the parking lot where Ricky was now backing into a spot.

"You alright?" he asked. "Someone bothering you, young lady?"

Caught off guard, she turned around to face the man, sloshing her soda over her hand as she did. Probably mid-forties, the guy reached around her to steady her cup, and with his other hand, tugged a clump of napkins from the dispenser on the counter nearby. "Oh, gosh. I'm sorry. Did I get you?" Gia asked, her nerves zinging like an electrical surge through high wires.

"Not a drop on me," he assured her. He dabbed at her hand with the wad of napkins. "And I don't mean to be nosy, but I overheard what you said. I have a daughter about your age, and I just wanted to make sure you're not in any trouble." He glanced toward the window again.

Gia peered around his shoulders to see Ricky launching himself out of his truck and dashing like a madman toward the nearest entrance, nearly getting taken out by a car just leaving the drive-through. She let out a short gasp when he leapt onto the curb to safety, but it dissipated almost immediately when he dragged open the glass door.

"Hey!" he called out, eyes on the man who was still dabbing at the spilled soda on Gia's arm. "Get your hands off my girlfriend."

Gia's eyes widened in stunned surprise as Ricky strode toward them, fists clenched at his sides.

"You mess with her, you're gonna have to deal with me," he snarled.

The man straightened his shoulders and stood a little taller. He did let go of Gia's hand, but stayed right beside her in what she could only call protection mode. "Is this guy bothering you?"

Ricky pulled up short and practically sputtered, "Am I bothering her? I just watched you through the window, old man. You're the one manhandling her." He started forward again, but Gia stepped in front of her would-be savior. The older one.

"Ricky, stop. Stop!" She put a hand up, ready to strike him if he came any closer. "What are you doing? Are you out of your freakin' mind?"

"I *saw* him, Gia. I saw him grab you." Ricky stared at her like she was the one out of her mind.

"He didn't grab me, you idiot. He grabbed my cup to keep it from spilling because I almost knocked it over."

"But—but I saw him grab your arm." The look of disbelief coupled with relief on Ricky's face stirred up conflicting emotions in Gia, making her want to cry and laugh at the same time.

"I think you'd better leave, kid," the older man said. He'd stayed behind Gia, but when she looked back at him, she could see it wasn't because he was afraid. He'd wrapped a hand around one of the heavy metal pump canisters that held condiments, ready to take action should Ricky make any more threatening moves.

"It's okay, mister. Sorry about all of this." She stepped toward Ricky and put a hand on his chest, pushing him back a few paces. Both mortified and more than a little angry, she added dryly, "He's just a little overprotective, you know?"

The man didn't let go of the canister altogether, but he relaxed his stance slightly. "Seems more aggressive than protective."

"I know. He just doesn't like me wandering around alone." Gia turned so her back was to Ricky and looked the older man square in the face, so he'd believe her. "He's not dangerous—"

"Looked pretty dangerous to me," the man cut in.

"Well, he might be dangerous to someone he thought was going to hurt me."

"Hey. I'm right here," Ricky interjected from behind her.

"Shut up, idiot," she growled, not bothering to look at him. Instead, she addressed the man again. "He'd die before he hurt me or let me be hurt, so you don't have to worry, okay?"

She suddenly noticed how quiet the little shop had gotten, how the few other diners—a couple of guys at one table, and a woman and two children at another—were hushed, wary. Her eyes darted over to the register counter where the employees were paying close attention to what was going on. Three of them had cell phone cameras rolling and Gia closed her eyes in humiliation. "Come on, Ricky. Let's get out of here." She spun on her heels, darted around him, and left out the door he'd come through. He'd shoved it so hard it had stayed open.

She heard Ricky's apology to the man before she pulled the door closed behind her. "Sorry, man. No hard feelings, okay?" He followed her outside a moment later.

She was beyond livid now, pacing back and forth at the back of the truck where the people in the shop couldn't really see her. Ricky approached slowly but didn't come past the wheel well.

"Sorry, Gia. I really thought that guy was working you over."

She stopped and stomped her foot, hard, and pain shot up the front of her shin. "In front of all those people? What? He was just going to grab my soda right out of my hand and make a run for it? Or was he going to throw me on the ground and have his way with me right there on the cold, hard tile? No wait, there was a nice rubber mat on the floor—"

"Stop, Gia." Now Ricky came around the end of the truck, his hands out, his face earnest. "I'm sorry, okay? I just freaked out when I saw him grab you."

"He. Didn't. Grab me!" She threw her nearly empty cup, and it hit him square in the chest, sloshing the clear sticky liquid all down one side of him. "He didn't grab me," she said again. She started around the other side of the truck, but Ricky lunged for her, grabbed her arm right above the elbow, and pulled her to a stop.

"Do not walk away from me, Gia. Please. How many times do I have to say 'please' to you?" He shook her gently when she kept her back to him. "Do you hear me? I'm begging you to stop and talk to me. I'm begging you to forgive me. I'm an idiot, okay? I'm a fool. And yeah, you're right. I'm playing the jealous boyfriend card."

His voice hitched and cracked like he was on the verge of tears himself, and Gia squeezed her eyes shut and covered her ears with her hands like a little girl trying to shut out the ugliness of the world. But she heard his next words loud and clear, even though they came out in barely more than a hoarse whisper.

"It's because I'm in love with you." His grip on her arm loosened, but he didn't let go. The air between them practically sizzled with the tumult of emotions they were both experiencing. "I love you, Gia," Ricky said, his voice throaty and ragged with feeling. "Not just as your buddy. I want to be your boyfriend. I want you to be my girlfriend. For real."

Gia's heart ached with the impact of the words, realizing in that moment how badly she'd longed to hear them from him. Her body trembled with the need to turn around and throw herself into his arms, to tell him that she was sorry for yelling at him, sorry for throwing her soda at him, and that she loved him, too.

But something in her had opened up this week, maybe even before that—a wound, an old scar she'd forgotten she even had—and here in this meaningless random parking lot, spoken in anger and frustration, words that should have been the most precious of all shared between them, were somehow tainted, tarnished by the events of the week that had brought them here.

"Gia?" he murmured, her name a plea.

What was stopping her? What was holding her back? This was Ricky, for Pete's sake! Rickaroni. Fred to her George. The dynamic half of their duo. Why couldn't she make her feet move? The question formed on her lips as she thought it in her head, coming out incomplete and ambiguous. "How long?"

Ricky's hand skimmed down her arm until he curled his fingers around hers. He tugged gently, but she didn't budge.

"How long?" she repeated, louder this time, her jaws clenched, not caring that she didn't clarify. This was Ricky, after all. He should know exactly what she meant.

"I don't know, Gia. For a while, I guess."

She jerked her hand out of his and rounded on him, thrusting the heels of both palms into his chest and sending him stumbling backward a few steps, tripping over the plastic cup she'd thrown at him. He didn't bother picking it up.

"You guess? I don't want you to guess, Fredrick Zander. Tell me. How long have you known you loved me?" she demanded.

But that wasn't really what she wanted to know. Not exactly. The bridge of her nose prickled, and she knew she was going to start crying at any minute. "How long have you been lying to me?"

Ricky's eyes widened, his mouth opened and closed a few times, but when no words came out, he shook his head, clearly not sure what she wanted him to say.

"How long have you known you loved me, Ricky?" she asked again, her voice snagging at the back of her throat so that his name broke halfway through.

Ricky made to move toward her, but she put her hands up to stop him and took a step back. He halted and reached up to rub the back of his neck with one hand, a grimace twisting his features. "I guess—I think—I mean," he nodded, just the slightest up and down movement at first, then more vehemently, like he was crosschecking his facts. "I *know* I've loved you since the first day I saw you. It was the second week of school, on a Tuesday. Sixth grade. Gia, you knocked me off my feet. Do you remember?" He didn't move closer, but he dipped his head toward her, shoving his fingers in the front pockets of his jeans as though to keep from reaching for her. "I fell off my bike when you smiled at me and that was it. I was in love." He chuckled and raised his eyebrows sheepishly. "Or maybe it was when you let me look up your skirt, but I can't be sure of the exact moment."

"So you were a perv back then, too." She might have been half-teasing, but she wasn't smiling. This all felt broken. Wrong. The timing was off or something was misfiring somewhere.

Ricky shrugged, "Nope. Just a twelve-year-old boy going belly up for a twelve-year-old girl. You don't know how glad I was that you were wearing shorts under your skirt that day. I would have spontaneously combusted right there in the parking lot if you'd flashed me an actual real live panty shot."

Ah yes. A purple skirt with lots of ruffles. Ruffles the wind wouldn't leave alone. She'd learned the hard way to always wear something under that skirt. But even though she wanted to laugh at the memory, to tease the man in front of her who'd been that skinny, short, awkward boy on a bicycle that was too big for him, the truth of his revelation was beginning to burn. "So you've been lying to me for more than seven years," she said, her eyes resting on the wet half of his shirt where it stuck to him, clinging to the outline of his chest muscles, the ridge of his collar bone, the rounded curve of his shoulder. "You've been pretending to be my friend all this time."

"No, Gia. No." He took a tentative step toward her, but she held her ground. If he touched her, though, she thought she might release like a coiled spring. "I haven't been pretending at all," he insisted. "You are my best friend, and I have tried to be a best friend to you, too."

"So, then, you've been pretending not to love me." She knew she was goading him. Not because she wanted to, but because if what he said was true, that he'd loved her through junior high, through high school, since graduation, if he'd been in love with her this whole time and she'd only just started to realize it? Then she was either as dumb as a rock, or Ricky was really, really good at faking his feelings. "You played me, Ricky."

"I don't get it, Gia. Why are you doing this?" He turned away from her, spotted her cup on the ground near his feet, and kicked it so that it went skittering out of sight under the car next to his truck. "I wasn't lying to you. I wasn't trying to trick you or play you. I was just waiting. For the right time. For you to be ready." His sentences came out choppy, short, frustration ringing in his tone.

"For me to be ready? Ready for what?" she challenged.

"I don't know. Never mind. Forget I said that about you." He shrugged his shoulders so roughly that she winced. She could see his fists balled inside his pockets and felt his frustration in every word. "Like I said, I was just waiting for the right time."

"And this—" she flung out her arm in the fading twilight, waving her hand at the odd collection of vehicles in the lot around them. "You thought this was the right time?"

"No, no, no. Of course not. But I was kinda under the impression it was now or never, the way you were storming around and throwing crap at me." Now he was waving his arm around, too, gesturing in the direction he'd kicked her cup.

"You're accusing *me* of acting like a freak? Let's see." She held up her hand and started ticking things off with her fingers. "Monday you practically launch yourself across the parking lot to all but accuse Jupiter of getting frisky with me. Tuesday you lurk out in the parking lot, spying on me like a stalker—yeah, I saw you," she added when his eyes rounded in surprise. "Then you don't talk to me all week, but you show up this morning acting like nothing happened. You try to—to—I don't know." She twirled a hand in the air near her head. "To get all up in my personal space in Granny G's pantry. And now this whole ridiculous show of... of whatever this is!"

"Wait. Wait just a minute. Up in your personal space? What does that mean? We're always in each other's personal spaces, and it's never bothered you before. Or has it? Maybe you've been lying to me, too!" Ricky interjected, his hands shoved deep in his pockets again, his shoulders up, like it was all he could do to keep from grabbing her and shaking some sense into her.

"You wanted to kiss me," she blurted out. "It was written all over your face."

Ricky took a step toward her and dipped his head so that his nose was less than a foot away from hers. "Yes, I wanted to kiss you," he practically snarled. She could see that his pupils were huge in the waning twilight, the blue irises like rings around black moons, he was so close. "I really, really wanted to kiss you. I thought I might die if I didn't, but nope. Still standing here, still an idiot, still begging. Because I *want* to kiss you now, too, but I'm afraid I'll lose a limb if I try. I love you, Gia!" He wrenched his hands free of his pockets and cupped her face between them. "I *love* you. Please give me a chance to prove—"

"No!" She ground the word out, trying to pull away, but his fingers curved around the base of her skull, and he didn't let go. The pads of his thumbs brushed against the hair at her temples in tiny, caressing movements that made her skin tingle. She grabbed his wrists, but instead of trying to pry his hands free, she just held on. "No," she said again, this time without quite as much force. "Stop, Ricky. Please."

"Gia…" His voice was a whisper; he was so close she felt his breath against her lips.

And because she suddenly wanted his kiss more than anything else in the world, she turned away, wrenching her face from his grasp. She still clung to his wrists, his empty hands in the air between them, his fingers wide, then closing into fists. Every muscle and tendon in his forearms were rigid under her hands.

"No. Not like this," she said, trying not to cry, wanting something more, but what, she didn't know.

He lowered his arms to his sides, and she released him, lifting her eyes to his. She felt a single tear spill over her bottom lid, and his gaze followed its trail down the curve of her cheekbone. He didn't touch her.

"You know what's so ironic about all of this?" she asked, a dry, humorless chuckle making its way from her throat. "If I were your girlfriend, I'd have broken up with you tonight. But I can't even do that because you never asked me out."

"I'm asking you now," he declared, his voice ardent, hushed. "Be my girl, Gia. Be my girlfriend."

Another tear slipped down her cheek, hung from her jaw for just a moment, then fell to her chest just above the neckline of her sweater. It seemed to burn a hole through her skin, piercing fascia and muscle, through the bars of her rib cage, until it bore a hole into the innermost chamber of her heart where it turned to ice. "No. Not like this. No."

"No?" It was a question asked in the hope of getting a different answer, but the expression on his face told her he knew it was asked in vain. His eyes dulled, his mouth tightened, and she felt him pull back just the tiniest bit.

She simply shook her head. She swiped at another tear before it fell, and then turned away from him. Everything inside of her sagged, not with relief, but with weariness of soul and exhaustion of spirit. "I need to get back to the coffee shop. I was going to walk, but it's going to be completely dark soon, so if you wouldn't mind, I will take the ride."

"You won't come to dinner tonight?"

But she could tell, even without looking at him, that he already knew the answer to that. She didn't bother responding.

"Of course I'll give you a ride. Are you sure you don't want me to take you home instead?"

"No," she murmured, not sure if he could hear her. "I already made arrangements to be picked up from the cafe in about half an hour, and I don't want to call back and cancel. I'd have to give some explanation, and I'd rather not."

From the corner of her eye, she saw him nod slowly. "Alright." He circled her and pulled open the passenger door. "Climb in."

SIXTEEN

Ricky wondered if he might just stop breathing, if his lungs would cease to expand and contract, if his blood would slow to a standstill in his veins. He listened to the throbbing of his own pulse in his head, fully expecting his heart to simply wind down like a kitchen timer. There'd be a loud, obnoxious clanging sound between his ears, followed by dead silence, and then dark oblivion.

In the terrible stillness of the truck cab, he could actually hear her breathing, and without meaning to, he found himself matching his own respiration to hers. As long as she sat beside him, breathing for him, setting the pace, in and out, in and out, he'd keep going.

But when she got out of the vehicle? What then?

Not five minutes later, they pulled into the parking lot at Ricardo's. He headed down one lane to look for an open spot, but she spoke. "Just drop me off at the back door."

He opened his mouth to protest, but one look at her profile told him it would do no good. In fact, it might even make things worse, if such a thing were possible. He turned the truck up the next aisle, pulled along the curb, and turned off the engine.

And he'd thought it had been quiet before.

He propped one arm on the window frame, his elbow hitting the glass a little too hard, making him wince, but he didn't make a sound. His other hand rested on his thigh, his fingers itching to reach across the chasm between them to touch her. Gia sat stiff and upright in the passenger seat, as she had the whole drive back from the taco shop, her hands tucked under her jacket balled up on her lap.

Finally, she spoke. "Thank you for the ride. I'm sorry... I'm sorry for...." Her voice faded away. She seemed as at a loss for words as he was. But she took a deep breath and started over. "You were right to wait. It seems I'm not ready after all."

She fumbled for the door handle and tugged, and Ricky wracked his brain for something to say—anything—that would keep her in his truck a little longer. "I'll wait," he said, pouring as much love as he dared into his promise. "I'll wait forever if you ask me to, if that's what you need."

Gia nodded, but didn't look at him. "I know, Ricky." There was something in her voice that wrenched his insides, something final. Something fatal. She sounded emptied out, hollow. She pushed the door open, but then drew it almost closed again. "Just give me a little time, okay? Everything feels upside down inside my head right now and I—I'm sorry."

"You don't need to apologize," he said, at last giving in to his need to touch her. He reached across the console and brushed her cheek with the backs of his knuckles. "I understand." He hesitated and then let out what he meant to be a chuckle, although it sounded more like a whimper to his ears. "When you're ready, I'll be here." He didn't say the words out loud, but he made a decision, then and there, to give her whatever time she needed, to let her have all the space she needed, and to wait until she came to him.

"Thank you." Gia reached up, grabbed his hand before he could pull it away, and pressed a kiss to his knuckles. And then she slipped out and disappeared inside the back door of Ricardo's Cafe without looking back.

Ricky sat at the curb for several minutes, going over and over in his head what had just happened. Not quite an hour ago, he'd picked her up at this very spot, both of them all smiles and teasing on their way to a romantic dinner for two. Where had things gone wrong? Was it all his fault? Had he really stepped so far over the line that the night should end this way? Yes, his crass response to her remark about friends with benefits was out of line, but wasn't her remark, itself, inappropriate, too? And he'd been beyond frustrated. Gia wasn't usually manipulative, she didn't play the semantics game, and it wasn't like her to be irrational, especially in their relationship. But tonight, she'd been all three.

He used to think he knew her so well, but now he wondered if maybe he'd just been fooling himself into believing that. What was going on in her head that he wasn't getting?

SEVENTEEN

GIA MADE IT INTO the customer bathroom without anyone really noticing her. She'd hide in one of the stalls until she could regain her composure, and then she'd take a few minutes to touch up her makeup before heading back out to wait for Jupiter.

"Oh, God," she whispered into the quiet bathroom. "What a mess I've made of things."

She wasn't about to call Jupiter back and tell him she'd changed her mind, nor did she feel like going to dinner with him and pretending everything was hunky dory. Why, oh *why* had she called him, of all people, in the heat of the moment? Anyone else on her admittedly short list of friends and family would have been understanding of the situation, mainly because everyone in her life besides Jupiter knew and loved Ricky already. Sure, she might have inconvenienced someone else, but they would have forgiven her and moved on.

She also didn't want anyone at Ricardo's to know she was spending time with Jupiter outside of work, so why she'd instructed him to pick her up at the cafe was beyond her; she clearly wasn't in her right mind today. Gia had seen too many employees come and go because of workplace romances gone bad, so she made a point not to mix work with her personal life as much as possible. She was pretty sure that was one of the reasons Ricardo had promoted her... and now here she was, breaking her own rule with Ricardo's nephew. Although she justified it because the guy was only going to be here on a temporary basis—she'd have to remember to ask him how long he was staying—she still felt uncomfortable about it.

She'd have to make the best of it. And maybe, when all was said and done, tonight was the perfect night to go out with him for the very reason that she really didn't want to. She'd fulfill any obligation she had inadvertently agreed to, and she'd be ready to turn in early. She'd get a better feel for the kind of person Jupiter was—in particular, what he wanted from her—and would then be better prepared to interact with him the rest of the time they worked together.

Feeling like she had at least some semblance of a goal for the night, if not a plan, she pulled her hair loose from the messy bun she'd worn all day, releasing a sigh as the whole mass tumbled down her back. Her scalp always ached a little when she wore her hair up and she ran her fingers through her roots, relishing the relief. Curls now fell playfully around her face, and she hoped they'd help mask any residual evidence of her emotional outbreak. She hadn't cried a lot, thank goodness, but enough that anyone who knew her would be able to tell. She dug in her shoulder bag for what little make-up she carried with her—a powder compact, mascara, a Merlot-tinted gloss that made her lips look fuller, if not exactly pouty. Then she stepped back, smoothed her blue sweater over her waist, and squared her shoulders.

"As ready as I'll ever be," she said to her reflection.

She cracked the door to make sure the coast was clear, then darted out into the hallway and made her way toward the side customer exit of the cafe. She kept her head down, not wanting to be noticed, and made it outside without anyone halting her escape. A few minutes later, she'd skirted the building to the back parking lot and stood on the curb outside the employee door, praying that no one would be coming in or out anytime soon. Seriously, it was like *deja vu* on automatic replay. How many times was she going to stand on this stupid sidewalk tonight?

She kept her eyes peeled for Ricardo's Lexus, her phone in hand, checking the time. The longer she stood there, the more she wanted to retract her offer to spend the evening with Jupiter, to call her grandmother to come pick her up, to crawl under her covers and pull her pillow over her head.

She closed her eyes for a few moments and let the thoughts that had been fighting for an audience take center stage. Ricky loved her. Nothing new there, not really. But he didn't just love her. No, he was *in* love with her. And supposedly had been for a lot longer than she'd estimated. The notion made her knees a little wobbly, and she quickly opened her eyes to keep from stumbling.

A car rounded the side of the building and eased up to the curb in front of her, a low, sleek little slate blue Miata, the throaty rumble of the engine punctuated by the bass kicks of the music being blasted inside. "No way," Gia murmured, not sure if she was impressed or put off. Of course. Why wouldn't Jupiter Multiple-Italian-Names Valentine drive not his uncle's car as she'd assumed, but a little sporty roadster on the weekends?

He didn't turn off the car, but the music stopped, and a moment later, he was unfolding from the low bucket seat and making his way around the streamlined hood. Her eyes grew even wider at the sight of him. He wore a pair of tight black dress pants, a deep plum-colored V-neck sweater over a crisp white button-up shirt with a wide collar, and the whole ensemble was topped with a buttery Havana suit jacket and a chevron scarf knotted loosely around his neck. Jupiter radiated casual elegance, and the car only completed the picture. He approached her with all the confidence of a young man who had the world at his fingertips, and without any hesitation at all, took her face in his hands and kissed her, first on one cheek, then the other, and then— Yep, on the lips. His mouth was warm and purposeful against hers, and although he lingered just long enough for her left knee to buckle, she quickly righted herself, blushing hotly when she saw the satisfied grin on his face. She'd barely caught her breath before he'd grabbed her hand and was leading her to the passenger side door.

"I am so happy you changed your mind," he said, his voice cool and bright, apparently completely unaffected by their first kiss—something she'd refused Ricky not more than half an hour earlier, but boldly taken by Jupiter—and pulled open the car door to help her inside. Closing her in, he headed back around the hood of the vehicle and within moments, he was tucked back into his own seat behind the wheel. "So, I will take you home to get ready first, yes? Tell me where to go."

Gia felt her eyebrows rise of their own accord. She bit back the ready retort that begged to let fly—she'd tell him where to go all right—and considered the circumstances through his eyes. All she'd told him was that she'd gotten a ride to work from a friend, but because of a change in her plans, she no longer had a ride home. And because of said changed plans, she was also free to do something with him if he was still up for it. So really, he had every right to assume she'd want to go home and at least change, didn't he? He'd taken the time to spiff up a little, so of course he'd expect the same from her.

But what would she say to her grandparents if she showed up with Jupiter? They'd known about her plans for the evening with Ricky. What would they think of this suave character escorting her home? Of her? How on earth did she get herself into these situations?

Jupiter paused before pulling out onto the street. "Which way? Left or right?" He turned to look at her, a shock of curls falling forward over his forehead, his smile wide, disarming. He tapped the GPS on the dash. "You can enter the address if you like."

"Um, go left," she said as she entered her grandparent's street information. A female voice greeted them before indicating the next upcoming turn. Gia would just have to pray her grandparents wouldn't ask any awkward questions. "I'll try to be quick, okay? What do you feel like eating? I'm not taking you to any Italian food places."

He whipped the car out into traffic like he'd been born behind the wheel. Gia clutched the strap of her purse tightly, surprised, but not alarmed.

"It would not matter where we ate because tonight, it is all about the company." He flashed her another grin, and to Gia's embarrassment, she giggled. Not quite like a schoolgirl. No, it was more the sound of a woman realizing she was in way over her head and not sure whether to be thrilled or terrified.

"You are..." She hesitated, shaking her head as she eyed him in the glow of the streetlights passing overhead. "You are pretty dang sure of yourself, aren't you?"

Still grinning, Jupiter glanced over at her and then back at the road ahead. It suddenly occurred to her that he was awfully comfortable driving in America. How long had he been here already, and where had the car come from? Had he actually bought a new car this week? For the short amount of time he was here? Surely, there was more to his story than she thought.

"Is there a reason not to be confident?" he asked. "I am a good-looking man who has his youth, a decent level of intelligence, a promising future. I am driving a fast car and I have a beautiful woman at my side."

Gia laughed again, the same conflicting feeling flooding through her. Drawn to him, almost against her will, relishing the way he so boldly went after her. No one had ever treated her the way Jupiter was, like she was someone to be sought after, fought for, pursued. Especially not Ricky, at least not until today. In his own words, her friend would wait forever... but who had forever to wait? Just being in Jupiter's presence was stimulating and intoxicating, to the point that she wasn't quite sure where his pursuit ended and her desire to be caught began. And did she want to be caught? By Jupiter Valentine?

Or did she want to be pursued by Ricky Zander the way Jupiter was pursuing her?

The question gave her pause, and she stilled.

"At the next intersection, make a right turn," intoned the automated GPS robot.

Why hadn't Ricky ever pursued her? Sure, this week he was making a real go of it, but only because Jupiter showed up and was suddenly giving him a run for his money. What had held him back all this time, especially if what he said was true, that he'd loved her for so long?

"Are you alright?" Jupiter's quiet question interrupted her pondering. Good. She didn't want to think about Ricky right now.

"I'm fine. It's nothing. Just thinking about how the plans got changed this evening." At least there was truth in that. "You know how I told you I live with my grandparents? They're not really expecting anyone, even me, at least not until late tonight, just so you know." She figured they'd be doing what they normally did on Friday evenings—dinner around six, maybe a Netflix movie instead of a sitcom or a game show, and definitely a heaping bowl of ice cream for each of them. "You don't have to be nervous or anything because they're great people. But they do like to chat, so be warned. You'll think they're sweet old folks, but if you're not careful, they'll have dragged all your deepest, darkest secrets out of you without you even knowing it."

"Ah. No one suspects the elderly, in spite of their wisdom and years of experience." Jupiter laughed. "My own grandfather was the same way. Somehow, he *knew* things. There was no tricking *mio nonno.*"

"Right? I think they should use grandparents in the CIA or FBI. They could get the dirt on anyone. All Granny G would have to do is show up with a plate of cookies and the worst criminal would buckle." She poked him in the shoulder. "So you'd better be careful."

She saw Jupiter's eyebrow arch, even in the dark. "What makes you think I have deep, dark secrets, pretty lady?"

"Ha! Because," she retorted. "No one can be as perfect as you are and *not* be hiding something." Gia thought she heard a tiny pinging sound somewhere between her ears. *Warning! Warning! Danger zone!* "That didn't come out... the way... I..." *Detour! Hazardous curve ahead!*

After an interminable silence, Jupiter spoke, his voice like caramel syrup. "Do you want me to have a deep, dark secret, Gia?"

"What? No!" she exclaimed, her cheeks blazing. Hopefully, it was dark enough he wouldn't be able to see. "Of course not. I don't like secrets. My family has carried a lot of them over the years," she expounded, thinking of Phoebe and the daughter she gave up for adoption almost fifteen years ago, and of course, Ricky and his secret love for her all these years. "I actually am a little tired of secrets, so if you could figure out a way to *not* have any, I'd really, really like that."

"No secrets, Gia. What you see is what you get. Contrary to what you seem to believe, I am not perfect, something you will quite likely discover as you get to know me better." He reached over and brushed her cheek with his knuckles, an echo of the way Ricky had earlier, and she almost flinched. He must have sensed her discomfort, because he returned his hand to the steering wheel. "I already know you are not perfect, so—"

"Excuse me?" She snapped her head around to gawk at him, her mouth open in shock. "What's that supposed to mean?" So much for smooth charm, she thought.

"Well, it is obvious you have some kind of deficiency, since you have suggested I'm perfect. Only someone who is a little bit crazy would think that." He shrugged and shot her a crooked grin. "But I am willing to lower my standards for you."

"Oh, my gosh!" she gasped. She poked him again, but this time, he reached across his body with his left hand and wrapped his fingers around her wrist before she could pull away. He turned her palm up and brought it close to his mouth. But instead of kissing her, he pursed his lips and blew softly into her cupped hand.

She definitely flinched. Or trembled. Or quivered. Or something entirely too inappropriate. She jerked her hand from his grasp and tucked it under her thigh, every inch of her skin tingling as though she'd just stuck her finger in a socket. "You are so smug," she said, her voice snagging on the breath she couldn't quite catch.

"Your destination is on the left."

Jupiter eased the little car into the driveway and parked. He turned in his seat to face her. "I will be on my best behavior with your grandparents. I wish to make a good impression with the people who love you the most." Then he flashed her another grin, making her chuckle self-consciously again. She was finding it really difficult to stay depressed, and although she still planned to get the night over with as soon as possible, it was no longer looking to be such a tiresome ordeal. They just had to get through the next half an hour while she got ready.

EIGHTEEN

GIA STOOD AT HER mirror, hands pressed to her cheeks, as she studied her reflection. Even to her, the eyes that stared back at her were huge, luminous, and maybe a little shell-shocked. And the upward turn of her lips seemed permanently molded there. She couldn't stop smiling.

Granny G met them at the door, having heard the car pull in, and although Gia could tell she'd been surprised to see the young man at Gia's side, she'd masked her reaction quickly and seemed to take it all in stride. She'd even gone ahead into the living room where Gramps was poring over a set of porch swing plans. Juliette had told him how much she'd miss the swing in her backyard once she moved to Vic's place after they were married, and he'd promised to make her a new one.

"Honey, Gia's night is going a little differently than she'd planned." Gia didn't miss the pointed look Granny G shot her husband. "She's brought this young man by to meet us. Jupiter, this is my husband, Henry."

Gramps stood, shook hands with Jupiter, and gave Gia a fatherly hug. "Good to meet you, Jupiter."

"Jupiter is Ricardo's nephew, Gramps," Gia explained quickly. "He's from Rome. He's here—" she broke off. "He can tell you. I'm going to go freshen up." She turned to Jupiter. "I'll hurry, I promise. And remember. Be afraid. Be very, very afraid of them." She pointed a finger back and forth between her grandparents, and then scurried from the room, giggling at the look on Jupiter's face.

She already knew exactly what she wanted to wear, so she dug through her closet for what she needed and darted across the hall to the bathroom where she took possibly the fastest shower she'd ever taken in her entire life. It was exactly what she needed to wash away the last vestiges of the frustration—and guilt, she admitted, although with much reticence—over her falling out with Ricky.

"But what did he expect?" she said to her reflection as she finger-combed Argan oil into her hair to calm some of the flyaway frizz and make it shine. "Did he think I've just been hanging around my whole life waiting for him to bare his true feelings for me? That I'd throw myself into his arms in lovesick gratefulness because he finally had the guts to tell me he lo—loved me?" The word tripped over her tongue, but she forced it out, anyway. "Why does everyone just assume I'll say 'yes' to everything? That I'll just do whatever they want me to whenever they want me to?"

She mulled the thought over as she carefully applied bronze and cocoa eye shadow and a smudged dark brown liner that made her eyes look smoky and maybe even a little dreamy. Her lips weren't full like her sisters', so she often downplayed them as she did now, smoothing on a clear gloss that tasted like peaches and cream. She gave herself one last perusal, fluffed her curls around her face, and cocked her head to one side. "Maybe I have some deep, dark secrets of my own, people. Like maybe I'm not really a 'yes' girl after all, you know? Maybe I might just start saying no. See what you all think about that."

On that note, she tightened her bathrobe around her middle, hurried back to her room, and slipped into the dress she'd laid out on the bed not more than fifteen minutes earlier. It was a wrap-around maxi dress that tied at one side of her waist and flashed a long line of leg when she walked. The neckline crossed modestly above her cleavage, and long bell sleeves fluttered over the backs of her hands at the perfect length. The fabric pattern could have come right off the wall of a Monet art gallery, the plums and turquoise palette giving the impression of florals and blue skies. It was busy and bold, but on Gia's tall frame coupled with her mane of fiery hair left loose around her face and shoulders, she knew she wore it well. She slipped her feet into a pair of ballerina flats—she didn't want to tower over Jupiter—and squared her shoulders.

"Just say no," she told herself, and then stepped out into the hallway.

Sounds of comfortable conversation and clinking silverware and dishes came from the kitchen, and she headed that direction.

She pulled up short at the sight that met her. Jupiter, sans scarf and jacket, with his sleeves rolled halfway up his forearms, was standing over the stove stirring a pot of what could only be pasta. Gramps was setting the small kitchen table with four—*four*—place settings, and Granny G bent over a huge wooden dish of fresh kale, her hands shiny with olive oil as she massaged the dark green leaves to soften them.

"Hey. What's going on in here?" But she needn't have asked. She could see for herself what was going on.

Jupiter turned toward her, his eyes wide with appreciation. "Gia. Wow." He set the spoon he'd been using a little too close to the edge of the counter and had to scramble for it when it started to fall. "You are a beautiful work of art."

Gia almost giggled when Gramps' bushy brows shot up in amusement. But because he maintained his composure, she found the will to hold hers in check, too. "Thank you, Jupiter." She darted a look at her grandmother, who had added a handful of pine nuts to the fresh greens and was now grating fresh Parmesan over the top of it. The salad was a favorite of Gia's. She narrowed her eyes at Granny G. "So?"

"Your young man offered to make us a special meal tonight," Granny G said, smiling impishly at Gia. Oh, the conniving going on behind those bright gray eyes. "Seeing as how he's a real chef and your absolute favorite food is Italian, I wasn't going to turn him down, sweetie."

"Your grandparents had not yet eaten dinner," Jupiter jumped in, confirming her suspicions. "So I am cooking for all of us. The pasta is simple fettuccine, but the sauce?" He turned back to stir the noodles, but he eyed her over his shoulder, grinning. "It is my one deep, dark secret that I will take to the grave with me."

She laughed out loud and kicked off her shoes before pulling out one of the mismatched chairs and dropping into it. Resigning herself to staying in for the night, she directed her next question at her grandfather. "Fine. So what movie are we going to watch, Gramps?"

"Don't look at me, Gia pet. This is your grandmother's doing," he said as he circled the table, filling glasses with ice water.

"You're not staying for a movie," her grandmother spoke up. "Just dinner. Then we're kicking you youngsters out so we can watch something that doesn't have explosions or vampires or magic wands."

Gia looked down at the fork she toyed with. Maybe she wanted to stay in for the night. Had anyone bothered to ask her opinion?

Dinner turned out to be a delight. Jupiter talked openly about his family back in Rome, about his restaurant plans with his older brother, about his home above his parents' coffee shop where he'd grown up. "But I have family in many parts of the world, like Uncle Ricardo," he told them. "And we are not all in the culinary industry. I have an aunt—em, she is my mother's sister-in-law—who owns three car dealerships around Los Angeles and Orange County." He turned to Gia and said in a somewhat chiding tone, "You did not ask me about my automobile."

"I meant to," she insisted, touching his forearm briefly. "It's something else, that's for sure. It seems your aunt took good care of you."

"Yes, well, we might be family, but there were no special deals made, except that she did not require a credit check for the lease. She knows my mother will see to it that I fulfill my end of the contract." He chuckled, his eyes going soft. "My mother is a woman not to be challenged."

"How long are you here in Midtown?" Granny G voiced the question Gia had been dying to ask all night.

"I am taking two classes locally for seven more weeks. Then I will move to my aunt's home in Pasadena to attend a summer program at Le Cordon Bleu Culinary Arts School. I will return to Rome at the end of September."

Five months. But less than two months here in Midtown. A tiny bud of disappointment took root in her heart. Only two months. Not even that, if he left as soon as his classes in town were over.

Her grandparents declined coffee and bustled the two of them out the door. "I've got clean up, young man," Granny G insisted when Jupiter offered to wash dishes. "Go and have yourselves a nice evening. I know the last thing you'd planned on doing was hanging out with a couple of old folks like us."

Jupiter took Gramps out to show him the car, but Granny G put a hand on Gia's arm when she started to follow. "Is everything all right with you and Ricky?"

Gia took a deep breath and let it out slowly, turning to face her grandmother. "Yes. No. I don't know. We've had a rough week."

"I could tell. You've not been yourself ever since the wedding, and then this morning Ricky was practically bouncing off the walls with nervous energy." She straightened the sash around Gia's waist, then added, "But I thought things were better between you when you left with him."

"They were. But then he got a little... I don't know." Gia sighed. She didn't mind talking to her grandmother, especially since Granny G knew Ricky so well, but she didn't want to do it now, not when she was looking forward to spending some time with someone else. "Can we talk tomorrow morning? I could use your advice."

"Of course, sweetie." She reached up to cup Gia's face in her soft hands. "Have fun, dear," she said, and then her brows furrowed just a little. "Just be careful, okay? Your heart is precious to me."

"I love you Gran." Gia leaned down and hugged the old woman fiercely. "You're the best grandma in the whole wide world, and don't you forget it."

An hour later, after a couple of cappuccinos and a shared piece of apple pie at one of Gia's favorite joints in town, the two of them agreed that the Friday night diner crowd was getting too noisy for them to converse. Jupiter didn't ask her where they should go, but instead, pulled up an address on his GPS and headed out of the parking lot. "It's a surprise," he said, his eyes bright with anticipation. A block away from their destination, she realized where he was taking her.

"Salden Park?" she asked, pleasantly surprised.

"We can sit in the moonlight and talk," he said as he pulled into a parking spot and turned off the car. "I even have a blanket in my trunk," he added. "In case we get cold."

"Wowee-wow," she quipped. "You even brought a blanket?" Gia shook her head, laughing at his cocky expression. "You really are smug, aren't you?"

"I prefer to think of it as hopeful," Jupiter said. "So, what is your answer? Will you come sit on my blanket under the starry sky?"

Gia let the events of the evening play through her mind, remembering her commitment to just say no. Clearly, Jupiter thought she'd say yes to him; he'd even brought a blanket. But the coat she wore wasn't thick enough to sit outside for very long, and she wasn't sure that she was ready to snuggle under a blanket with this guy.

"You know what?" she began, dropping her gaze to her hands in her lap. She didn't want to see the disappointment on his face. "I think I'm going to have to pass on the park. It's been a busy couple of weeks for me, and as much as I've enjoyed this evening with you, I don't think I'm going to be very good company for much longer."

Jupiter chuckled softly, making her pulse jump start a little. "Are you Cinderella? Will you turn into a gourd soon?"

Gia snickered. "A pumpkin? Cinderella didn't turn into a pumpkin, silly. Her ride did." She lifted her eyes to meet his. "But in the state that I'm in, who knows? I actually might turn into a pumpkin if I stay out much longer."

Jupiter reached across the console between them and tugged one of her hands free. Lacing his fingers with hers, he said, "I happen to like gourds. And pumpkins. Very much, in fact."

Gia meant to laugh, but instead, it sounded more like a whimper. He lifted her hand to his mouth again, and she tensed, remembering all too well the way his warm breath had felt against her palm. This time, however, he pressed his lips to the sensitive skin on her wrist, as though in search of her pulse. Her breath caught as he began planting soft, tender kisses in a slow trail up the inside of her forearm, and it took all her willpower to speak.

"Jupiter, stop. Please."

He did, immediately. He didn't let go of her, but he lowered their laced hands to the console between them. He studied her in the glow of the streetlamp nearby, but he said nothing.

"Why are you—doing this?" It was little more than a whisper, but she knew he'd heard her.

"Doing what? Kissing your hand?" His thumb now stroked back and forth over the spot on her wrist that still tingled from the pressure of his mouth.

"Why are you flirting with me? Coming on to me? What do you want from me?" Her breathing was shallow, and she felt a little lightheaded. "I mean, you're leaving in a couple of months."

Jupiter still studied her, but she saw something shift in his gaze, a flicker of determination. "I like you, Gia. I like you very much. I know we only met this week, but you are a beautiful woman, and I am very attracted to you."

When it seemed like he wasn't going to say anything more, she frowned and reiterated, "But you're only here for two months."

"What does it matter? Perhaps my mind understands the limitation of time, but my heart, I assure you, does not. My heart believes every single moment with you is forever." He smiled, a little sheepishly, and then said, "My heart tells my mind I am in love with you, Gia Gustafson, and my mind is not arguing tonight."

"Jupiter, stop. Stop, please," she pleaded. This was turning into the ultimate Ground Hog Day. In all her nineteen years, no one had ever declared their love for her before today, and now two guys from opposite ends of the spectrum had come to her claiming just that. "This is crazy," she muttered, more to herself than to him.

He suddenly leaned toward her, bracing his free arm on the dash in front of her, with his other, pressing her hand tightly to his chest over his heart. "Perhaps it is crazy," he began, his voice earnest, intense. "But what if tonight is all we have? What if the world ends tomorrow? What if I die in an automobile crash on my way to work in the morning?"

"Don't say that," Gia interrupted. "That's a terrible way to think."

"No, it isn't," he argued, his face so close she could see the individual hairs in his spiked lashes. "It's the way life works. If we deny our love because we think two months is not enough time, and then somehow, we were to be separated forever before morning, wouldn't we regret that we didn't take advantage of every single moment we had together, no matter how small, how short?"

It was ridiculous. His reasoning was riddled with holes, she was certain... but she couldn't seem to pin down a solid counterpoint to offer him.

"So what if we only have two months together?" he whispered, leaning closer still. "It will be the most beautiful two months in the history of lovers. It would be better to have two months of bliss than a lifetime of knowing we missed our chance to be together."

In a smooth, slow descent, he brought his mouth down on hers, and she didn't pull away. The taste of coffee and cinnamon mingled with the subtle scent of his cologne and something else, a fragrance her mind recognized as uniquely Jupiter. Or was it her heart that recognized it?

She gave in to the kiss, moving with him, letting him explore her mouth with his. He released her hand to thread his fingers through her hair at the back of her head, closing around the heavy curls and tugging slightly so that her face tipped up, giving him access to her jaw, her neck, the tender hollow where her pulse hammered beneath her skin. His voice rasped in her ear, "*Bella mia*. My beauty."

Gia brought one hand up to rest against his face, her fingertips brushing the hair at his temple, his jaw moving against her palm as his mouth continued its ardent assault on hers.

This was her first real kiss, that of a man and woman communicating in a language that knew no barriers, a mingling of souls and hearts and desire unleashed.

He murmured against her lips. "Say yes to me, *belleza*. For this moment is forever."

She cooed softly, a tiny sigh of submission... and then her eyes began to fill, the tears coming as unexpectedly as a rainstorm in the middle of July in the desert.

No! A tiny voice cried out in her head. *Say no, Gia. Not like this. No, not like this.*

Jupiter pulled back a few inches, just enough that he could look at her. "Why are you crying, Gia? Did I hurt you?"

She shook her head, not trusting her voice.

He pressed his forehead to hers and closed his eyes. "Tell me," he whispered. "What is making you cry?"

"I don't know," she whispered back. "But I think—I think I was saving that kiss for—for someone else."

NINETEEN

GIA STAYED IN BED as long as her bladder would allow. When she finally did get up, it was nearly noon, and the house was quiet around her. On the refrigerator was a note from Granny G. *We're having lunch with Ren and the gang at Salden Park. You're welcome to join us!*

Any other day, she would have said yes. She would have squared her shoulders, put on a happy face, and headed off to the park to join her family.

Not today. Today, the answer was no. Gia thought she might be okay if she never went to Salden Park again after last night.

Her stomach felt too hollow for coffee, so instead, she filled the teakettle with water and put it on the stove. While she waited for it to boil, she scrounged in the fridge for some vanilla yogurt. She dolloped a large helping into a bowl and topped it with two handfuls of Granny G's homemade granola and then stood against the counter eating it.

When the whistle sounded on the kettle, she pulled a travel mug from the cupboard and dropped two country peach flavored tea bags into it and filled it with the boiling water. After downing the rest of her yogurt in a few huge bites, she washed the bowl and spoon, set them in the drainer, and headed back to bed with her tea.

She dug her phone out of her purse and groaned when she saw several missed calls and text message notifications. Scrolling through them, she found three text messages and a voice mail from Jupiter, a text from Ren, one from Jules, and one text message from Ricky. She started with the message from Juliette; it was a group text to all the sisters.

Having a great time - we'll be home on Monday. Can we have a G-FOURce on Wednesday night at my condo? At 6? Now that they were married, Juliette would share Vic's house, which meant her little condo next door to Mrs. Cork would be empty. She still hadn't decided what she was going to do with it. The condo was Juliette's first home away from their grandparents' home, and she'd lived there for almost a decade before meeting Vic. But Vic's place was larger, better suited to a family, or at least that was the unspoken hope. Which meant the cute little condo would need to be sold or rented, because they couldn't afford to leave it sitting there empty. But for now, it was the perfect place to have their G-FOURce meetings. Gia replied to the group text saying that she was available. Phoebe had also responded; she and Trevor would be home by then, too, so it was settled.

Renata's text was an invitation to their picnic at the park, so Gia jotted off a quick reply, thanking her, but telling her no anyway. She had plans, she wrote. Ren didn't need to know her plans included having no plans at all.

She stared at her phone a long time before deciding to read the rest of the texts, starting with Jupiter's from late last night, which had come in long after he'd dropped her off.

12:32 AM *Thank you for the beautiful evening. Are you asleep, mia bella Gia? I lie awake thinking of you, imagining your tears, and my heart breaks.*

10:03 AM *Mia bella Gia. I called you at 10 o'clock, just as I promised I would. Do you know what your kisses have done to me? I do not know how I will be able to wait until Monday morning to see you again. Will you listen to my message? It is from my heart.*

She wouldn't listen to the voice message. Not yet.

11:14 AM *Mia bella Gia. I am going to Pasadena to see my aunt. Please call me. I must speak with you. I cannot wait to hear your voice.*

She wouldn't call him, either. Not yet.

She took a deep breath and swiped open Ricky's text from last night.

8:16 PM *You are worth waiting for. Goodnight, Georgy Girl.*

Oh, Rickaroni.

The difference between the two guys screamed at her, even through their texts. Jupiter. Suave, handsome, charming, relentless. Seemingly unruffled by her tearful retreat. He'd teased her about turning into a pumpkin after all, and assured her he really did like pumpkins, even ones who wept in his arms. He'd been kind and gracious... he hadn't even asked her what she meant, or *who* she meant when she said, 'she'd been saving the kiss for someone else'. But now... *now* she thought she understood. Apparently, it didn't really matter to him. Apparently, he was just fine with her admitting she might be pining for someone else while kissing him. Apparently, it didn't matter what she wanted, only what he wanted.

And that line! *My heart believes every single moment with you is forever.* Holy smokes. How many times had he used that on some poor, unsuspecting female? Gia grabbed one of her pillows and pressed it over her face, then released a cry of embarrassed anger into it. How could she have been such a pushover?

He'd worked her over all week long, worn her down with his assault to her senses, and then swept in on his shiny steed—a slate blue Miata Roadster—and rescued her, a damsel in distress. He'd even taken the time to woo her grandparents—he probably knew it would soften her up, and he was right. It had.

She'd been blindsided by his charisma, to the point where until that kiss, until he'd asked her to say 'yes' to him, she hadn't been sure she'd really wanted to say 'no.'

You are worth waiting for.

And she'd said 'no' to the person she really wanted to say 'yes' to... didn't she?

What a mess. What a *mess!*

She yanked a pair of earbuds from her bedside table and shoved one of the little speakers into her ear. Scrolling through her extensive playlist, she pulled up one song after another, but they all reminded her of Ricky. Every single song in her library had been shared at one time or another with him. Some he'd laughed at, some he'd teased her about, some he'd shushed her on so he could listen. Some he'd sung along with; some he'd grabbed her hand and danced to with her. These songs had been the soundtrack to their arguments, their struggles, their triumphs, their joys, their sorrows, their friendship. They'd studied to these songs, they'd lain on their backs and watched for shooting stars to these songs, they'd walked without speaking, the music between them binding them together in time and space.

By the time she gave up on finding something that would distract her from her troubles, tears were streaming down her face. When she heard the front door open and Granny G talking animatedly to Gramps down the hall, Gia burrowed under her pillow again, feigning sleep.

But Granny G was having none of it. She pushed open the door when Gia didn't respond to her knock and crossed the room to sit on the side of the bed. "Sweetie, you've been in bed too long. Tell me what's wrong." She pulled the pillow from Gia's face and brushed her messy curls back. There was no surprise in Granny G's eyes when she saw the tears in Gia's.

No matter how many times she opened her mouth to speak, however, no matter how hard she swallowed and tried to force the words past the lump in her throat, nothing came out. She wasn't even sure she knew what to say. She didn't know how to explain her feelings to herself, let alone to someone else.

Stuck. Safe. Stuck. Secure. Safe. Stuck. Stuck. Stuck.

"I don't know who I'm supposed to be," she finally whispered. "And I don't know how to be anything else than what I am, and I'm afraid what I am isn't really me."

After a lengthy pause, Granny G said, "Well, that's a good place to start." Her fingers stroked the top of Gia's head, the comforting gesture as familiar as the sound of Granny G's voice. "This isn't just about Ricky, is it? Or Jupiter."

"No. But they play a big part in making me crazy and confused."

"I see."

"I love Ricky, Gran. And he loves me. But he's my best friend—or at least he was until he started acting like an idiot."

Granny G chuckled softly. "They do that when they fall in love, you know."

"No, I didn't know," Gia retorted. "Why didn't you warn me?"

Granny G tugged on one of Gia's curls, then wound it around her finger. "You really didn't see this day coming, sweetie? We've all known Ricky has been in love with you, almost since the first day he set eyes on you."

Gia pulled her blanket up over her head and asked again, "If you all knew, why didn't anyone warn me?"

Granny G tugged the blanket back until Gia's eyes were visible. "Warn you about what?" she asked.

"About how weird it feels." Gia's voice was muffled behind her pillow, but the words were clear enough to be understood. "He's like my brother. Isn't that weird? Gross? My brother has the hots for me. He wants to make out with me! And you don't think that's a little sick?" Admittedly, she was trying to shock her grandmother just the slightest bit, but she should have known better.

"And the feeling isn't mutual? You haven't thought about how nice it would be if he actually did kiss you? Checked him out a little too closely the last time he had his shirt off? You haven't imagined him naked?"

"Granny G!" Gia gasped, sitting upright in bed. "Gramps!" she hollered, knowing her voice would carry to him wherever he was in the house. She'd heard his heavy footsteps coming down the hall earlier. "Do you know what your wife just asked me?"

Her grandfather appeared in the doorway and leaned against the frame. He looked tired after the last couple of hours in the sun. She was sure Ren's boys had given him a run for his money at the park. He'd probably been hoping for a nap this afternoon. "Hey Gia pet. What did my wife just ask you?"

Gia blushed, refusing to repeat it to her conservative grandpa. "Never mind," she said. "Suffice it to say, she's got a dirty mind."

Gramps shrugged. "That's one of the reasons I married her."

"Gramps!" His name came out on a half laugh. "Scarred for life, you guys! Seriously?" But in that moment, under the loving gazes of the two people who had been home to her heart for as long as she could remember, she thought she caught a glimpse of who she was supposed to be. Who she wanted to be.

"Did that boy hurt you?" Gramps asked, but she could see on his face that he knew she was all right.

"No. I think I kinda hurt myself."

"Because I oiled my shotgun last night after you left, just in case," Gramps added.

"I figured as much, you crazy old man."

"If you're sure," he said. When she nodded, he did, too. "Then I'll leave you two ladies to your boy talk. Gonna lie down for a bit."

"Sleep tight, Gramps. I love you."

"Love you, too, Gia pet."

Gia waited for his footsteps to fade and then turned to her grandmother again. "I know I'm way behind everyone else when it comes to lovey-dovey stuff."

"You're only behind those who have gone ahead of you," Granny G murmured with a smile.

"Yeah, well, that's pretty much the whole rest of the world." Gia brought her knees up and rested her forearms on them. "I gave Jupiter my first real kiss last night. Or he took it." She frowned, immediately ashamed for making him responsible. "Actually, it was both of us giving and taking. *We* kissed. And I liked it. A lot. Until I realized I'd been saving that kiss for Ricky." The telltale tingle in the bridge of her nose warned her of impending tears, and she lowered her forehead to rest on her crossed arms.

Granny G sighed deeply, once again stroking Gia's hair, smoothing it down her back. She didn't ask for details, didn't question if they'd done more than kiss, and for that, Gia was grateful. "It's a little like swimming in the ocean, I think, Gia pet," she began, her tone thoughtful. "The vastness of the water, the unplumbed depths, the endless horizon, that's how love feels. Standing on shore, watching the waves crashing on the sand and rushing toward you, the water licking at your toes. It calls you, beckons you to jump in, join the others who are out there riding those waves. You finally do, and then the first wave hits." She chuckled, shaking the bed slightly. "If you're lucky, you'll get swept up over the crest of it and your stomach will do that wild flippy thing as you ride the swell. Or you might get tossed on your keister, head over tail, the world spinning out of control. You stagger back up onto the beach, seaweed in your hair, sand in your bathing suit, and wonder what on earth just happened, right?"

Gia nodded slowly, her forehead still resting on her forearms. How many times had she experienced that chaos during all the endless summer days on the beach with friends and family?

"But then you learn to watch the rhythm of the waves so you can get the thrill of riding them again and again, and it's magnificent and exhausting and exhilarating and always just a wee bit dangerous."

"Sure. Yeah, I can see that," Gia concurred, lifting her head to give her grandmother a quizzical look. It did seem a good analogy of love, from what she could surmise. But how did that apply to her own experience? Where was her grandmother going with this?

"To me," Granny G continued. "Falling in love with the right person is a little like choosing the right lagoon to swim in. From a distance, they're all beautiful. But up close and personal, you discover the dangers that lurk amidst the beauty. Jagged coral, poisonous sea creatures, crashing waves, fluctuating tides. However, if you don the right footwear and a good set of snorkeling equipment, maybe learn how to surf, you can find beauty even in those things. Love is treacherous, no two ways about it, but isn't just about anything that's worth doing?"

Gia nodded again, although she kept silent. She had a feeling Granny G still hadn't quite gotten to the point. She was correct.

"But what happens when you choose a beautiful lagoon that's home to a pod of sharks—"

"A gam," Gia corrected without thinking. "A group of sharks is called a gam, or a frenzy, or a school or shiver. Oh! And you can call them a herd of sharks, too."

"Thank you, Google Girl," Granny G said, tugging on a strand of Gia's hair. "I like a shiver of sharks, since that's what I tend to do when I think too much about them."

"Sorry." Gia had the good grace to be embarrassed for interrupting. "Go on. Swimming in shark-infested waters and all that."

"Yes." Granny G paused, probably trying to collect her disrupted train of thought. "Here's my point, Gia. I would venture to say that jumping into things with Jupiter, as lovely a young man as he is, might be compared to swimming in a beautiful lagoon with a *shiver* of sharks. All the basic qualities of lagoon life are still there, right? The waves, the tides, the reef. But the risk of swimming in those waters may not be worth it, even if you're in a full wetsuit and life vest. Jupiter's heart and mind have been infiltrated by things of the world—things that should remain beyond the reef—because his guard has either fallen, or it was never up in the first place. He's let those things take over."

"You think Jupiter is like a shark?" Gia knew that wasn't exactly what her grandmother was saying, but it sure would have made things more cut and dried if he was.

"No, I don't. He's not the shark. Sin, or the things that would cause us to sin, are the sharks. I think Jupiter is just as much a beautiful creation of God as you or me, or Ricky. But because he doesn't understand God's design on his life—that a lagoon, in fact, was never intended as a place for sharks—he doesn't know to keep his boundaries firm, his safety nets in place, his guard up. It's not always bad stuff—there's nothing inherently wrong with fancy cars and extra cash, or even kissing, right? Just like there isn't anything inherently *wrong* with sharks." Her grandmother's slight shudder belied her words, making Gia grin. "I mean, you can't begrudge a shark for killing and eating, right? That's its nature. But that doesn't mean they're not a danger to you, sweetie. You need to learn to steer clear of the waters where sharks are allowed free rein."

"But Jupiter's not a bad guy, Gran." Gia felt the need to defend him. Sure, he was worldly in his thinking, but did that really qualify him as being "shark-infested"?

"No, he's not," Granny G wholeheartedly agreed. "In fact, I think I said he's a lovely young man. But he's still ruled by what he allows into his lagoon, Gia. Unless he gives his life over to be ruled by God, who will flush out those sharks, he's going to be dangerous waters for you. Exciting, yes—and perhaps his sharks seem tamed right now, or too young to be too threatening at this point—but he's still dangerous, nonetheless."

"I suppose," Gia murmured, once more feeling the weight of the mess she'd made of things. "But what do I do about Ricky now? I feel like a total jerk. I want to take back that kiss I gave to Jupiter and give it to Ricky, but it's too late."

Granny G tapped her on the nose. "Think of it this way. You jumped into the wrong blue lagoon with your eyes shut, got a warning nip in the ankles, and skedaddled on out of there before you lost a limb... or your heart. Now it's time to go swimming in the right lagoon with your eyes wide open."

"What if every time I kiss Ricky, I think of Jupiter?" Her question sounded silly, even to her own ears, but she legitimately feared it might be the case.

"You know what I think?" Granny G didn't wait for Gia's response. "I think the only way to get the handsome young Italian boy out of your mind—and he really is quite an eyeful, sweetie—"

"Not helping," Gia snipped.

Granny chuckled and started again. "I think the only way to get Jupiter out of your head is to fill it to overflowing with Ricky. If you love that boy, and I know you do, you'll figure it out. He's worth it, you know."

"That's what he said about me when I wouldn't let him kiss me yesterday."

"And he's right."

"But I kissed Jupiter first." She was bemoaning the issue now, she knew it, but still... She lifted her eyes to her grandmother's. "I mean, I really *kissed* him."

"Good for you. I probably would have kissed him myself after tasting that amazing sauce last night. If not for your grandfather, that is."

"Gran, stop trying to be a cougar. I'm not buying it."

"Well, then stop trying to be a prude. I'm not buying it, either." Her grandmother patted Gia's cheek gently. "So you kissed the wrong guy. If you hadn't liked it, I'd be worried. But now you just have to start kissing the right guy."

Gia reached down and ran her fingers over the lace trim of her pillowcase. "It's still weird to think about Ricky that way."

Granny G snorted. "It won't be once you start kissing him; I can pretty much guarantee you that." She tapped Gia's nose with a finger. "Why don't you give Ricky a call? Maybe you can spend some time with him this evening."

Gia nodded. "Maybe I will." She reached over and hugged her grandma. "Thanks for not thinking I'm a freak."

Granny G hugged her back. "Oh, sweetie. We're all freaks in this house. I'd be worried if you weren't."

However, as Gia was getting dressed and working up the courage to call Ricky, her phone rang. Ricardo had a weekend crew member no show and wondered if she could fill in from four until closing. She wasn't quite brave enough to ask him if Jupiter would be there or not, nor was she brave enough to tell him no, even though that voice in her head practically screamed at her.

As it turned out, neither Ricardo nor Jupiter made appearances at the cafe all night. And when she locked the doors at 10:30 PM, she sat in her car for several minutes debating whether or not she should call Ricky, finally deciding that some things were better dealt with on a good night's rest and the clearer perspective of daylight. She'd go to church with her grandparents, and then call Ricky afterward.

Ren and Tim and the kids came for lunch, though, and Gia spent the afternoon beating her nephews at X-Box games and playing cuddles and patty-cake with Baby Charise. By the time she and her grandparents sat down for dinner, she'd convinced herself that maybe it would be better to give herself a little more time before she talked to Ricky. She still had to face Jupiter in the morning, and she could only handle so much at one time.

TWENTY

Monday morning dawned as bright and cheerful as a day could be in spring. Gia rolled out of bed as though the weight of the world rested on her shoulders. She'd missed Ricky more than she wanted to admit yesterday. She usually went to church with him, sitting in the same pew as Jules and Vic, Phoebe and Trevor, but she hadn't been brave enough to go without talking to him first. She'd thought about having him over for family dinner—his parents weren't religious and most Sundays, Ricky was free of any family obligations—but she'd chickened out.

And now she had to go to work and sort things out with Jupiter. How was he going to act around her? Would he assume they were an item now? Would he act possessive and unprofessional? She couldn't imagine he'd intentionally stir up trouble, but how was she supposed to act around him? Should she tell him right up front that she was sorry, and that she wasn't interested in him that way? He'd said he was in love with her—or at least, his heart was in love with her, whatever that meant—so what if he got all hurt and bitter? What if he told Ricardo? Would she lose her job? Should she just quit?

"Crap, crap, crap," she muttered under her breath as she dug around in her closet for something to wear. She would not be sexy today. Casual. Downplayed. She'd be a wallflower today.

She pulled on a pair of black jeans and a pale peach polo shirt, shoved her feet into black Converse sneakers, and swept her hair back into a tight French braid. She went lighter than usual on the makeup and even agreed to join her grandparents for coffee and a plate of scrambled eggs and toast, waiting until the very last minute before heading out the door for work. She arrived with just enough time to shove her gear into her locker, say a quick hello to the rest of the morning crew, and poke her head into Ricardo's office to let him know she was there.

"Good," he said, barely lifting his eyes from the folder of paperwork in front of him. "It's been a busy morning already. I am glad you are here."

She hadn't missed the fact that Jupiter wasn't around, but she didn't ask. He wasn't officially an employee, so it wasn't really her responsibility to worry about whether he clocked in or not. She slipped her apron over her head, tied it around her waist, and headed to the register to start to her workday.

It was indeed a busy morning. The regulars streamed in and out with their coffees and breakfast sandwiches. The tables were full until well after 10 AM, and Gia noticed the two sisters she'd seen the week before at the table in the back corner again. From the open Bibles and notebooks in front of them, they seemed to be having some kind of a Bible study. She marveled at the notion; as much as she loved her sisters, she couldn't really picture her and any one of them going out somewhere so they could spend an hour studying the Bible and praying together. Even though they were all confessed Christians now, they just didn't talk about their faith much, at least not in public. There'd been a time when it had been a really touchy subject, and she supposed they'd just gotten into the habit of steering clear of all things to do with God. "But it might be nice," she thought to herself.

As had been the case all last week, there were more college-age girls than usual up so early on a Monday morning, playing it cool, but not fooling anyone. Her shift comprised of hours of fielding questions about Jupiter's whereabouts—Midtown was a small college town, but even so, it surprised and amused her how many people asked about him—to which she simply answered, "He isn't here right now." Since she didn't know any more than that, she finally cornered Ricardo in his office. "What's up with Jupiter? Is he coming in today?"

Ricardo looked up at her, a look of consternation in his big brown eyes. "I didn't tell you?"

"No," she said, drawing the word out as she slipped into the tiny room and dropped into her customary chair. She blew over the top of a cappuccino she'd made for herself; she'd missed her custom Venus Rising drink from Jupiter. "What's going on?" Had Jupiter told Ricardo about them? Was he in trouble with Ricardo?

"My head is in the clouds today. I'm sorry. Jupiter's aunt. Did he tell you about her? The one in Pasadena?"

Gia shrugged. "A little. She leased him that slick car, and he's going to stay with her when he goes to Le Cordon Bleu, right?"

"Yes, yes. Louisa. On Saturday morning, her husband was in a terrible accident," Ricardo began, gesturing dramatically with his hands as he often did when he was frazzled or frustrated.

"Oh no. Is he—?" She couldn't bring herself to say the words.

"He's injured pretty badly, but his doctors believe his prognosis is good. I really don't know all the details, but he fractured some of the vertebrae in his back, so he's laid up in the hospital for now, and will eventually need surgery to repair the damage. Jupiter has gone to stay with them early so he can help out."

"Oh. Wow." Great. Now she felt terrible for not calling him this weekend. She just couldn't seem to get things right, no matter what she did. "What about his classes here in Midtown?"

"He'll drive out here for those. It's only two classes back-to-back, from 3 to 7 in the evening, so he'll miss the worst of the traffic both ways. But that way he can be there during the day to help with the kids, and then again after the kids go to bed so Louisa can go back to the hospital. It's actually rather providential that Jupiter is here in the US and available to help out." Ricardo chuckled. "And that Louisa leased him that car. He almost doesn't mind the drive."

"Wow," Gia said again. "I'm sorry. I'll be sure and keep Louisa and her family in my prayers. And Jupiter, too, with him out there driving our crazy freeways." She took a sip of her coffee and made a face at the bitter bite. Either she'd lost her touch, or she'd been spoiled by Jupiter's expertise.

Ricardo chuckled again. "Jupiter knows our freeways well. He's been coming to California every summer for years," Ricardo said, waving a hand as if batting away her concern. "He usually doesn't stay with me; he prefers the big city life where his aunt lives, and the beaches, of course." He narrowed his eyes and studied her a moment before adding. "Watch out for that kid, Gia. He'll break your heart if you let him."

"Right. He's quite the Casanova, isn't he?" she asked, glancing down into her mug.

"Oh, no." Ricardo shook his head and folded his hands over the pile of papers on his desk. Leaning forward a little, he said, "Don't tell me. It's too late, isn't it?"

"No," Gia insisted, embarrassment making her skin prickle. "He's been very nice. A little... um, aggressive, maybe, but not inappropriate. But no, he hasn't broken my heart."

"Good," Ricardo said, pointing a thick finger at her. "Keep it that way. Jupiter *is* a good kid. He loves his family, he's a hard worker, and he's extremely committed to his restaurant plans. But women?" He grimaced, shaking his head. "They don't say no to him. And when a man doesn't have to fight for what he wants, more often than not, he doesn't appreciate its—or her—value." He stood up and planted his hands on his desk, leaning across until he was looking her in the eyes over her coffee cup. Gia sat straighter and tried not to stare at the single white curl that stood straight out from his otherwise black bushy left eyebrow. "I appreciate your value more than that boy ever will. Don't you dare quit on me; you hear? I will disown Jupiter before I let you leave on his account." Then he reached out and patted her on the shoulder.

Gia giggled, embarrassed, but also flattered. "So, about that raise?" she quipped.

Ricardo straightened and laughed heartily. "Ah, see? You are right. You are worth far more than anything I could ever pay you. Don't you forget that." He circled the desk and held out a hand to help her up. "That said, I will think about a raise. Maybe it's time. We will talk next week, okay?"

Gia stood, pleasantly surprised. "Well, okay! That sounds great. Thanks." She'd had no intention of asking for a raise—he'd just given her one right before Christmas—but hey, he thought she was *worth* it.

Three different people in the last three days had used that word to describe her. She was *worth* something.

That night, Ren called and asked if she wouldn't mind sitting with the three younger boys for a couple of hours after dinner. "I know it's short notice," Ren said. "So no pressure, okay? We're scheduled to have a meeting with Reuben's teacher, and I just planned to go on my own and leave Tim home with the kids, but he wants to go, so we thought we'd take Reuben out for dessert afterward." Tim was doing everything he could to get involved in the boys' lives. He had no aspirations to replace their dad, John, who had passed away a little over a year ago, but he wanted to be the best father figure he could be to the kids, and his efforts seemed to be paying off. The kids loved him.

Gia thought about saying no. She needed to call Ricky and she really should call Jupiter, too. But she knew how much a night alone with his parents would mean to Reuben, even though the sarcastic teenager would never admit it in a million years. She agreed.

She ate a quick meal with her grandparents, remembering to fill them in on Jupiter's situation. They prayed for him and his family and then she headed out the door, gearing up for an evening of building forts and telling ghost stories. Of course, the serious Simon would pretend he wasn't interested, and that the creepy tales didn't scare him, but she knew better. He was at that awkward age between little boy and teenager, and he couldn't seem to decide from one day to the next which one he wanted to be. Gia could relate.

When she returned home just after 8:30, she found Granny G alone in the living room with an open book and a cup of hot tea. "Hey, Gran. Where's Gramps?"

"Hi, sweetie. How are the kids?" Granny patted the sofa beside her. "Join me. I was just trying to decide whether I should go to bed with your grandfather or watch something on television. You can help me decide."

"Gramps is in bed? Is he okay?" He rarely went to bed before ten, even if that meant he dozed in his chair for an hour or so before giving up the fight to stay awake, but never before nine.

"Oh, he's fine," Granny G assured her. "He spent several hours tilling up a new patch of garden—we're expanding this year to put in more corn."

"You can never have enough corn on the cob," Gia interjected.

"That's right. Anyway, he overdid it again and is simply worn out. He's going to be sore tomorrow, I'm certain." Granny G sighed. "Poor thing. He actually took a couple of ibuprofens before going to bed."

"Really?" Gramps only took stuff for his aches and pains if he was really uncomfortable. "If he waits until this weekend, Ricky and I can help," she offered.

"So you've patched things up with Ricky, then?" Granny asked.

"No, not yet," she admitted. "It just hasn't been the right time. Every time I get ready to call him, something comes up or someone needs me for something else. I want it to be right, you know?"

Granny G didn't respond right away, but by the furrow that formed between her brows, Gia could tell she was concerned before she finally said, "Isn't that what he said to you?" her grandmother asked, her question probing, but gentle. "That he was waiting for the right time?"

"I know," Gia sighed and flopped back against the couch cushions behind her. " But honestly, I don't quite know what to say to him."

"You could start with 'I'm sorry.'"

"I know." Gia said again, closing her eyes. She wanted to apologize, but for what? *I'm sorry I didn't tell you I love you, too? I'm sorry I kissed Jupiter instead of you on Friday? I'm sorry I'm such a jerk?*

Granny G patted her knee. "You'll figure it out. You always do. Let's watch some *Gilmore Girls*. What do you say?"

After Granny G went to bed, Gia pulled out her phone and scrolled down to Jupiter's voice message, and she finally listened to it.

"Beautiful Gia. My heart misses you. My lips miss you. My hands miss you. I want to see you tonight. Today. Now. Tell me you want to see me, too. Call me back."

That was the message from his heart? He hadn't asked how she was, nor had he mentioned his uncle's accident. Granted, he might not have learned of it until after he left the message, but if he was so desperate to see her, wouldn't it make sense for him to at least call her back and let her know he was heading out of town? She wanted to throw the phone across the room. Geez! He must've thought it was like taking candy from a baby with her. She opened her text messages and keyed in a quick note to him. *So sorry to hear about your uncle - Ricardo told me what happened. We are praying for you and your family. Be safe.*

He didn't text back. Maybe he was at the hospital. Or in bed? Or maybe he was enjoying the big city life like Ricardo said.

She shook her head to clear her thoughts of Jupiter. Then, before she could change her mind, she pulled up Ricky's text and keyed in a message to him. After only the tiniest moment of hesitation, she hit 'send' and there was no turning back.

Can we talk after work tomorrow night?

Laying the phone face up on the bed beside her, she leaned back against the headboard to wait for his response.

What about Wednesday? I have soccer tomorrow night – or you can come to the game. We can talk after. Ricky coached a soccer team for a local AYSO league. He'd played all through junior high and high school, and although at nineteen, he was on the brink of aging out, he'd found a way to keep playing by becoming a coach. He was great at the sport and the kids on his team loved him.

But Gia didn't want to sit through several games in the hopes that she'd get a little time with him at the end of the night. Sometimes the kids played until ten o'clock, depending on how the games went, and Ricky was a rather... *active* coach. By the end of the night, he was as sweaty and pumped up as the kids. She wrinkled her nose at the thought of kissing him like that.

I'd rather not. No offense, but you'll need to take a shower before we talk. And I have a G-FOURce Wednesday night. Could be a long one—we're talking about Angela C. Maybe Thursday night?

A few very long minutes later, her screen lit up again. *I'll need to shower first? Are you sure we're just talking?*

Gia snorted out loud. She felt the earth shift a little beneath her, but in a good way. Evading his question, she texted, *So Thursday night?*

His response came back less than a minute later. *Thursday night. Your place? Mine? My folks are back—can we use Juliette's condo?*

A tiny thrill raced up Gia's spine at the thought of talking with Ricky alone in Juliette's little house. Probably not a good idea, especially if she planned on asking him to kiss her. *How about your treehouse? See you at 5?*

My tree house at 5. I'll bring drinks, chips, and éclairs. You bring sandwiches from Ricardo's.

Deal. She sighed with relief as she scrolled back through the short series of messages, rereading what she'd written and his response. She froze when she saw the three dots flashing at the end. He was writing something else. She waited, biting her lip, her hands shaking slightly.

They disappeared. She waited, but no message came through.

There they were again.

And again, they disappeared.

Finally, a message came through. *Nite, Georgy Girl.*

Nite, Rickaroni.

TWENTY-ONE

Tuesday afternoon, Jupiter made an appearance at Ricardo's. Gia had slipped out the back door for a quiet break—some days the espresso machine seemed so loud, and the noise level of the customers increased accordingly, until Gia's skin seemed to crawl. She often ducked outside when that happened, and it rarely took more than a few minutes to get her nerves under control.

She loved her job, she really did, but more and more she was plagued by thoughts about her future and what she was going to do with her life. She didn't want to be a manager at Ricardo's forever... but she didn't know what it was she *did* want, either.

She sat on the bottom step of the little stoop and stretched her legs out in front of her, relishing in the warmth of the sun penetrating the black knit leggings she wore under a fluttery miniskirt. She closed her eyes and tipped her face up to the sun, too.

The door opened behind her. Someone needed her. Someone always needed her.

"*Ciao, bella* Gia. I wondered where you'd taken yourself." Jupiter lowered himself gracefully to the step beside her. It took a great amount of effort to remain relaxed, not to draw her legs up close and tuck her ankles under her, to make herself somehow smaller, *less* than what she really was.

That thought gave her pause. Why on earth would she want to be less than what she really was? And why did Jupiter spark that reaction in her?

Jupiter made to brush her cheek with the back of his hand, but she tipped her head away from him. She kept her eyes on her crossed ankles, but in her periphery, she saw his smile. "What is it, Gia? Are you angry with me? Do you think I abandoned you?"

Gia grimaced. "No, Jupiter. I didn't think you leaving this weekend was about me at all. I know what you did—what you're *doing*—for your family, and I think it's wonderful. You're a good guy, you know." She finally lifted her face to look at him. "I'm sorry I misled you on Friday night, or all last week, in fact. I'm really sorry, because it wasn't fair to you, especially after you were so open and honest with me. I—I've been a little confused about things lately, and I think I might have taken advantage of you. Not intentionally, but still..." Her voice drifted to silence. She hadn't meant to say any of this to him. She hadn't really thought much about what she might say if she got that chance. But he'd shown up unannounced, and the words just seemed to flow, so she let them. They made sense to her.

"I do not think you are the kind of girl who would ever intentionally take advantage of anyone, Gia." Jupiter's words were soft, kind, just like they'd been Friday night after she'd broken down. But having had the weekend to process things, having spoken to Granny G, and more importantly where Jupiter was concerned, to Ricardo, Gia wasn't quite so easily waylaid by his flattery.

"Actually, you know what? Maybe it wasn't premeditated, but there's no question that I intentionally took advantage of you on Friday night." She picked up a pebble from the step beside her and tossed it out into the parking lot. "I'd just gotten into a fight with my friend. We had plans for the evening, and when he made me mad, I called you." She released a self-deprecating snort. "Apparently, I am that kind of girl, Jupiter. Like I said, it might not have been premeditated, but it was definitely intentional," she reiterated.

"I see," Jupiter said, his smile still in place, but no longer quite so flashy.

"I'm sorry. It was a crappy thing to do to you, calling you to come rescue me that way. But then, to mislead you the way I did only made it worse."

"No." Jupiter reached over and took her hand in his. Turning toward her, he said, "Do not say that. I didn't mind being there for you when you needed me. In fact, if you need to take advantage of me again, I am at your service." Then he lifted her hand to his lips and kissed the back of her knuckles in a rather gallant gesture.

She almost pulled away, remembering the delicious sensations his mouth had stirred in her when he'd kissed her, but at the last moment, she let him do his thing. When he released her hand, she patted his cheek, perhaps a little more brusque than absolutely necessary. "You really are something else, Jupiter. I kinda can't help but like you."

"That is good, because I can't help but like you, too," he replied, his eyes on her in a heavy-lidded stare. "How about this? Let us be friends for now, and if one day you think you might want to take advantage of me again, I am willing to discuss the option of being friends... how do you say it here in America? With benefits. I do come visit Uncle Ricardo every year, you know."

"Wow. Hm." She tipped her head to one side and stroked her chin like she was contemplating something deep. "Let me think on that offer... no. But thank you." She pushed to her feet, then offered him a hand up, which he took. When he stood in front of her, his smile broad and friendly, not offended at all, she stepped forward, put her arms around his neck, and hugged him hard. "Thank you for being a gentleman, Jupiter," she said close to his ear. "Things could have gone a lot differently both Friday night and just now." Then she stepped away from him. She felt him resist, just for a moment, his hands resting on her waist, but then he nodded and stepped back, too.

"I will be staying in Pasadena for the rest of my time in America," he said. "But I am only a little more than an hour away." He didn't try to extract any commitments from her, nor did he make any promises himself, for which she was glad.

"Thank you, Jupiter." She cocked her head and narrowed her eyes at him. "So since you're not going to be here every morning to make me my Venus Rising...." She pressed her hands together as if in prayer. "Please teach me how to make it. I promise I won't tell anyone."

Jupiter laughed out loud and shook his head. "Aha. It will be your punishment for taking advantage of me." Gesturing toward the door, he indicated that she go in first.

"Please, Jupiter," she whined, walking backwards ahead of him. "I need it. I want it. I must have it."

Jupiter chuckled and shook his head. "You only get my coffee when you get me. So if you don't want me, you don't get my coffee."

"That's not fair," she grumbled.

"Let us compromise," he teased, grabbing her shoulders and maneuvering her around a table she almost backed into. "I will make you a Venus Rising whenever I come to visit. It will be our commemorative drink reserved only for when we are together. Okay?"

"Does that mean you'll make me one now?" She stopped in front of him, blocking his way in the narrow hallway. "If you don't, I'll think you're mad at me." She planted a hand on her hip and narrowed her eyes at him.

Jupiter laughed, took her by the shoulders again, and turned her around. "March," he commanded, nudging her forward. "I have fifteen minutes before I must go to class. I will make you a Venus Rising."

After he left, Gia felt such a sense of relief that she almost changed her mind about going to Ricky's soccer games, but she stuck to the plan. She wanted his undivided attention, and she knew his team, the Diesels, would be his number one priority long after the last game ended. He was the kind of coach that didn't let any of his kids go home without feeling valued if they lost and celebrated if they won. Besides, she still hadn't figured out what to say to him.

On the other hand, maybe she shouldn't overthink it. Look how well the impromptu talk with Jupiter had gone, and she'd gone into that with no forethought at all. That said, there wasn't as much at risk with Jupiter. They didn't have a decade-long friendship between them, nor did they have a future ahead of them to figure out together. No, she had to do this right.

She did, however, text him from her driveway as soon as she got home at the end of the day. She knew he'd already be at the park, making sure everything was ready.

Thursday seems a long way off, but you're worth waiting for, Rickaroni. Go Diesels!

His reply came almost immediately.

Thursday can't come soon enough.

TWENTY-TWO

Ricky stared down at the phone in his hands. His heart pounded inside his ribcage as though he'd been running laps with his team for the past hour. He could hear her voice in his head when he read her words. *Thursday seems a long way off.* Did he dare hope? *You're worth waiting for.* How the heck was he going to concentrate on the games tonight?

He shoved his phone back into his gym bag and kicked it under the players' bench where he'd have access to it. More often than not, he left his gear in his truck, but tonight, he'd brought it all onto the field with him, and boy, was he glad he had. It was early and only a few of the kids had shown up. He'd sent them out onto the field to do some goal shots, so he'd been sitting on the bench alone, going over game plans and strategies he'd worked on with his team when he'd heard the text notification.

But Ricky was sticking to the plan. He'd made a promise to himself to give Gia whatever time she needed, and to let her come to him when she was ready, and that's what he was going to do. He wouldn't call her, no matter how badly he wanted to. He wouldn't text her unless she texted him first and needed a response. And he wouldn't, come hell or high water, stop by her work to have lunch with her like he usually did on Wednesdays. No, he'd wait until Thursday night at five o'clock, just like she'd requested.

Even if it killed him.

His composure slipped a little as he thought about Barista Boy and all the time Gia was spending with him. He was the kind of guy to whom she'd never have to say things like "You need to shower first," the kind of guy who dressed for dinner, who wore blazers on his days off. "He probably doesn't wear socks with his shoes, but his feet never stink," he muttered to himself as he stood to greet several more team members arriving on the field. "Enough, man."

Giving his whistle two sharp blows, he rounded his players up and lined them up for warm-up drills. The Diesels were twelve- and thirteen-year-old kids who'd been playing soccer since they were five and six. He loved this age because they were young enough to think he was old enough to be treated like an adult, but they were old enough to really love the game. This was the age when most of the kids in AYSO really began focusing on skill and technique, and not just playing by the rules and hoping to win. They practiced strategy and different plays, capitalizing on each player's strengths and targeting the opposing teams' weaknesses. When they lost, they raged, and he let them, as long as they did so with dignity. And after they raged, they put their heads together to come up with new plans, new strategies, and different ways of getting the ball down the field and into the net. He wanted them to feel the frustration of not getting it right, to find the motivation to do better next time. When they won, they celebrated hard and loud, and he celebrated right alongside them... as long as they did so with dignity. And after they celebrated, they still put their heads together to come up with new plans, new strategies, and new ways of getting the ball down the field and into the goal, because that's what team practice was all about.

One of his most impressive players was a girl named Tiffany. The crazy thing about the girl was that she looked like a Tiffany—she'd developed early and stood a good couple of inches taller than the biggest boy on the team—but she played soccer like she'd been born in cleats and shin guards. He'd seen something in the girl's eyes that reminded him of Gia—someone who would go the distance no matter what they threw her way—and the first time he heard one of the boys say, "Good morning Stiffy—I mean, good morning, Tiffany," to her, followed by a chorus of snickers and guffaws from some of the other boys, he'd taken them to task. The culprit was kicked off the team—Ricky had zero tolerance for that kind of behavior—and the other four boys who'd laughed at the crude greeting had been benched for four games.

Of course, as irony would have it, they were some of the team's best players, and it hurt for them to have to sit on the sidelines and watch their team lose because of their bad behavior...except that they hadn't.

Ricky had hoped Tiffany would come through, and she did. He played her in each of the four positions that were usually played by the boys on the bench, and she'd proved herself a champion in every one. She'd almost single-handedly won the second game for the team when she filled in for the goalie and blocked every goal attempt the other team made. And somehow, throughout the whole ordeal, Tiffany still made her team members feel important, going so far as to ask the boys on the bench for pointers when she filled in for them. By the end of the second game, she'd become a team favorite, and although she wasn't the official team captain this season, Ricky was pretty sure she'd be nominated for the next.

Tiffany's mother, Trina, however, was a different story, and one Ricky was struggling to know what to do about. Because Tiffany never missed a game, a practice, or any of the team's celebratory outings, neither did Trina, but Ricky couldn't tell if Trina came for her daughter... or for him. The woman had a good ten or fifteen years on him, but she flirted with him outrageously, to the point that he was more embarrassed for her than he was for himself. He'd done everything he could think of—without coming right out and saying so—to let her know he wasn't interested in whatever it was she was offering, but he knew the time was coming when he'd have to confront her.

He glanced over to the bleachers. Sure enough, Trina wasn't paying any attention to her daughter's phenomenal dribbling skills, but instead, was watching him, an expression on her face that made him grab at the collar of his shirt just to be sure he was actually wearing one. He looked away quickly. How much simpler things would be if he could just tell the woman that he had a girlfriend. Even better if Gia would show up and actually *be* that girlfriend.

Now he just sounded like a chicken. He didn't need to hide behind his girlfriend. He'd just have to man up and deal with it; her staring at him wasn't his problem unless he made it his. Hopefully, when he refused to respond, she'd get the hint and find somewhere else to look. He was here for the kids, not their parents.

Despite his lack of focus, Ricky's team plowed through every game like the powerhouse they were named for, and the night ended on a celebratory high. He knew the poor kids had to go home and do their best to get a good night's sleep, but he was too wound up to do the same, and he thought he might crawl out of his skin if he couldn't see Gia. Any other game night like the one they'd just had would have had him calling her up to share a large meat lover's pizza and a joyride with the windows rolled down, the rock and roll up too loudly to do anything but sing along. That's just the way it was between them.

That's the way it *had been* between them. Now, all he could do was hope and pray that it could be that way again. Except that maybe, just maybe, the next time they took that joy ride, Gia would be snuggled up against his side instead of leaning her head out the passenger window and singing "We Will Rock You" at the top of her lungs.

TWENTY-THREE

Wednesday crawled by at work, and Gia yearned to call Ricky, to see him. She didn't know if she could wait until Thursday night, now that they'd agreed to meet. She'd even considered bailing on her sisters, but she knew that tonight's meeting was an important one. They would finally be focusing on what had come of Phoebe and Trevor's dinner with Alice and Cal Masters over a month ago, a subject they'd all agreed to wait on until after the wedding. Because they all seemed to have conflicting emotions about the situation, they hadn't wanted a discussion of that caliber to take away from the joy of Jules' nuptials.

Two months ago, when they'd first discussed the dinner invitation, Gia had very few reservations about the connection, especially since it had been only Phoebe taking the plunge instead of all four of them. Sure, Jules was in contact with Angela by exchanged letters, but again, they'd been classmates years ago, and already had an established history, if not an actual friendship. Ren, a class behind, had known Angela, but hadn't run in the same crowd, and she'd opted to wait to interact with Angela until she came home, and they could talk face to face. Gia had been content to wait with Ren to meet Angela and her family.

But so much had changed since then, at least inside of Gia. It seemed that as Phoebe and Trevor made peace with their shared past and made plans for a future together, as Ren and Tim basked in the fragile place where grief and love still shared living quarters in the Dixon-Larsen home, as Jules and her Vic pledged their lives to each other with every look, every smile, every subtle touch, that Gia felt more and more acutely the chasm that separated her from everyone else in her circle. Even Ricky, with his full class schedule and part time job changing oil and rotating tires at Fleet Auto, seemed set on a course with a destination at the end of it. Maybe he still wasn't exactly sure what he'd do with his bachelor's degree, but he wasn't sitting around waiting for it to come to him; he was going after it.

And now, tonight, Gia felt what had become a constant unsettled tension brewing inside her as she thought about Angela Clinton, and about the efforts being made to bring closure or resolution or even restoration to the things that had happened between them all.

Sixteen years ago, Angela had plowed her el Camino into the side of Simone and Paul Gustafson's Buick, killing the couple and leaving the four sisters orphans, to be raised by their grandparents. Angela had been drinking all afternoon and was on her way to her high school graduation, to the same destination the Gustafsons had been headed; it was Juliette's high school graduation as well. Ren and Phoebe had gone early to save their parents a seat in the auditorium, and little Gia, sick with an ear infection and cold, had been dropped off at the home of her grandparents, so Simone and Paul had been alone in the car.

No, Gia realized as she made her way up the walk to Juliette's front door, she had no desire whatsoever to meet Angela Clinton. Or Angela's mother, Alice, and Alice's husband, Cal.

Especially Angela's mother.

Because Angela didn't deserve to have a mother, not when she'd robbed Gia and her sisters of their own mother.

Without bothering to knock, she pushed open the door of Juliette's condo and hollered, "Hallooooo!" Tonight, she hadn't brought anything with her. Usually Granny G packaged up some kind of dessert or leftovers for Gia to share with her sisters, but the grandparents had gone out to dinner with friends before their Wednesday night Bible study group at church, knowing Gia would be spending the evening with her sisters. So Gia had made herself a sandwich, showered and dressed in jeans and a sweatshirt, and then sat around waiting until the very last minute before heading off to join her sisters.

Bob, Juliette's best dog ever, came skittering across the floor tiles of the small foyer to greet her, barking up a loud and delighted welcome. Bob had stayed with Ren while Jules and Vic were gone, being loved on by the boys, as well as by Harry and Sally, Ren's two black labs, who welcomed the scruffy fur bag like family. Gia dropped to her knees and acknowledged the dog with petting and hugging and nonsense words.

As usual, the dog softened the sharp edges of her emotions with his silly, toothy grin, adoring brown eyes with the slash of black above them like painted-on eyebrows, and his unflagging exuberance every time anyone paid him even the least bit of attention. Bob had come a long way from the frightened skeletal mutt Juliette had rescued over a year ago now.

Gia took a deep breath and rose. Only then did she acknowledge Jules, who stood close by, waiting for a hug. "Hey there, married lady," Gia said, wrapping the glowing new bride in her embrace. "You look amazing."

"Why thank you." Juliette beamed, her cheeks coloring prettily. "I feel amazing."

"That's because she's finally getting some," Phoebe called out from the other room.

"Phebes!" Juliette exclaimed, her blush going from pink to crimson.

"Some?" Renata retorted, positioning the fussing Charise across her lap. "I would hope she's finally getting lots!"

"Renata Gustafson Dixon Larsen!" Phoebe hooted. "You're starting to sound like me."

"Gia, don't listen to them," Juliette instructed, putting her hands up to cover Gia's ears. "Nothing is sacred with them."

"It's all sacred with us," Renata contradicted as she unbuttoned the front of her shirt and pulled down the left side of her nursing bra. Baby Charise was nearly frantic with the object of her desire so close, but when Ren drew her daughter to her breast, the impatient cries instantly turned to appeased whimpers. "That's why we still do this whole G-FOURce thing, Jules."

Gia followed Juliette into the living room, and after quick hugs all around, she dropped to the floor on a pile of cushions next to the coffee table ladened with a tray of coffee fixings and a plate of chocolate chip oatmeal cookies. She glanced around at her sisters. "Should we do the pledge before I dig in?"

As the youngest sister, it was Gia's job to officially open the meeting. "Welcome Empress Juliette, Empress Renata, and Empress Phoebe." She pressed her hands together in a prayer-like manner and nodded her head to each sister accordingly.

"Welcome, Empress Georgia." The other three spoke just as somberly, nodding back at her.

They clasped hands, Gia sliding a finger into one of Charise's tiny fists since Renata's left hand was busy holding her baby, and they began the G-FOURce pledge, a time-honored tradition that had somehow survived adolescence into adulthood.

Let the words of our mouths
Be necessary, kind, and true.
Let the secrets we share
Be kept safe amongst us few.
Let the decisions that we make
Be brave, noble, and wise
Oogie-boogie-doggy-loogie
Wiggly-jiggly-fries!
G-FOURce unite!

The pledge was silly, none of them denied it, but it was like an unbroken cord weaving through their lives, binding them together, and none of them were willing to give it up.

Once they were settled back into their places, coffee and cookies in hand, Juliette started the evening out with some of the highlights of her honeymoon. She and Vic had taken a three-day road trip up the coast of California, ending up in Manzanita, Oregon, where they stayed in a beachfront cottage for another five days, before heading back the way they'd come.

"Everything about the trip was beautiful," Jules said, accompanying her words with dreamy sighs. "The weather couldn't have been better, the beaches were spectacular all the way up, and the sunsets along the coast were breathtaking. It was like the sky was celebrating with us. And the place where we stayed was perfect and tiny and quaint and romantic and...." She trailed off, her eyes beginning to glisten with what could only be tears of joy. "You guys, I love him so much. Sometimes I think it might actually be more than I can bear, and one day, he'll reach over to touch me, and I'll just burst into flames."

"Spontaneous human combustion is supposedly a thing, you know," Gia remarked, Juliette's happiness reigniting the conflicting emotions inside her. She felt petty, fickle, both glad for her sister and exceedingly envious of her certainty at the same time. "They haven't proved that it does happen, but nor have they proved that it doesn't. One of the theories is that a person can have a buildup of static electricity over time from some geomagnetic force. It sparks and then *poof!*"

Her sisters were looking at her like she was talking gibberish, even though it wasn't unusual for her to produce random tidbits of information during their conversations. She took a bite of a cookie, hoping the sweet chocolate would wash away the taste of shame in her mouth. Juliette's happiness had been hard won, and no one—*no one*—deserved to love and be loved more than she did. "I'm just saying it could happen. You sit in your office all day surrounded by geomagnetic force emitters like computers and printers and scanners, and then you rub up against Vic?"

"Poof!" Phoebe chimed in, lifting her hands to represent fireworks.

"You and your weird facts, Gia," Juliette said, rolling her eyes, but then she giggled. "Besides, I think if I was going to burst into flames from Vic rubbing up against me, um, after the last ten days, it would have happened already." As soon as the words were out, she blushed hotly.

"Juliette Gustafson!" Phoebe chortled. "Now you sound like me, too!"

"Great," Ren interjected. "A whole room full of Phoebes. Just what the world needs." A year ago, the comment would have triggered an argument, but tonight, it just made everyone laugh even more.

However, this was the kind of stuff that made Gia feel out of the loop. The decade-plus years that her sisters had on her held a lifetime of experiences that the three of them shared that she didn't. She'd only had her first real kiss a few days ago, and they were talking about sex and having lots of it. Trevor was a strong advocate for abstinence before marriage, so even if she wasn't yet engaging in it with him, it was no secret that Phoebe had taken her share of spins around the block. And although Juliette had really only had one boyfriend before Vic, they'd practically lived together for almost ten years. Ren? Well, she was on her second husband, but if the number of kids she'd birthed was any indication of how much she enjoyed the marriage bed, she wasn't hurting on that account, either.

So although Gia *knew* a lot—her sisters had always talked openly about the birds and the bees in front of her—she still felt the disconnect acutely.

"And on that note," Juliette said, waving a napkin in front of her face to cool her cheeks. "Let's get on with the business at hand. I have a super sexy husband—" She broke off, her eyes widening. "I think that's the first time I've said that to you guys."

"Woo-hoo!" Phoebe cheered and clapped. Charise, startled or curious, or both, popped off Renata's nipple to turn and stare at her boisterous aunt.

"Ow!" Ren flinched and pressed a hand to her breast.

"Sorry, baby," Phoebe said, her voice high and sweet as she apologized to Charise. "Did I interrupt your dinner?" Then she leaned forward and whispered, "Bite her again, girlie."

"It sounds good to hear you say it, Juliette," Ren said, ignoring Phoebe altogether. She cupped Charise's tiny head and turned her attention back to her meal.

"Thanks. As I was saying, my super sexy husband gets off tonight at nine, and I'd like to be home waiting for him when he does."

"Please tell me you'll be wearing something other than that ratty old pink thing you've had for a hundred years," Ren teased.

Juliette blushed again—more?—and wiggled her eyebrows suggestively. "Vic really likes that ratty old pink thing, I'll have you know. In fact, he likes it so much he got me a new one for our honeymoon, and let me assure you, it got a lot of use."

"La-la-la-la-la!" Gia burst out in song and covered her ears, feeling her own cheeks grow warm at the direction her mind was heading. "People!" she declared. "Naïve and innocent over here." Half the time she couldn't tell if her sisters simply forgot that fact, or if they didn't care how hard it was for her to be the oldest virgin in Midtown.

"Sorry, Gia." Juliette sounded truly apologetic, but her face still bore the glow of a woman well-loved when she turned to Phoebe. "So tell us about Alice. I know you've been holding out on us because of the wedding, and even though I've been dying of curiosity, I want you to know how much I appreciate it, Phebes."

"It wasn't just because of the wedding, you know," Phoebe said, growing serious. "I needed to process everything, so the timing couldn't have been better."

The room got quiet as Phoebe gathered her thoughts. "So, like I said, dinner was nice. Awkward, strange, emotional. But nice." From what she'd told them, the presence of the two men had been instrumental in breaking the ice. Trevor and Cal had hit it off right away, especially after learning they had a shared interest in target shooting. Granted, Trevor was a skilled archer and Cal preferred rifles, but the more they spoke about it, the more intrigued Cal had become, prompting an invitation from Trevor to join him and Vic the next time they went.

As much as she'd tried, Gia had a hard time imagining Phoebe in that setting. Her sister had the social skills to handle herself with great aplomb in pretty much any situation, but that was because Phoebe was a skilled masquerader. She'd spent so much of her life hiding behind her facade that she'd admitted it was a challenge to just be herself without fear. Trevor Zander, however, a man who had learned the hard way to be authentic, a man who loved Phoebe as fiercely as any man could love a woman, had become a sanctuary for her, a safe haven. Under his devotion, Phoebe was blossoming into a new version of herself that was truly magnificent to behold. Sure, she still looked like a pagan goddess in her tumbled hair, bold makeup, and her cleavage-baring, leg-flashing outfits, but that was just who Phoebe was. Ricky told Gia he'd once asked Trevor how he felt about the way Phoebe looked and dressed. Ricky wondered if it caused Trevor to be tempted, knowing that his older cousin had pretty strict rules about abstinence and being above reproach. His response to Ricky had made Gia love him for her sister's sake even more than she already did.

"If I'm going to blame Phoebe because she's too sexy for me to be around without stumbling or falling into temptation, then I'm pointing my finger in the wrong direction. I'm the one responsible for my own behavior, Rick, man. It's no one else's fault if I fall." It was under that kind of love and devotion that Phoebe was discovering God's love and devotion to her as well.

In the corner of the sofa, Phoebe tucked her legs up under her and crossed her arms tightly over her middle. Gia recognized the signs; Phoebe was feeling vulnerable.

"But then—we started talking—for real...." Phoebe stuttered to a halt. She paused, took a deep breath, and then as the other three girls watched, her eyes filled with tears and began to spill over.

TWENTY-FOUR

Six weeks earlier...

Phoebe waited while Trevor came around the car to open her door for her, delaying the moment of truth as long as she could. They were parked in front of the Masters' house, a lovely two-story home in a residential part of Midtown.

Trevor laced his fingers with hers as they made their way up the walk to the front door. "Are you ready?" he asked, squeezing her hand reassuringly. When she nodded, he reached out and pushed the doorbell.

A moment later, the door opened, and a young man in black pants and a white shirt greeted them with a warm smile.

"Oh, hello, Freddy," Phoebe said, her surprise evident in her voice. Freddy was one of Cal's employees at the grocery store, and he often delivered her orders to her, a service Phoebe was exceedingly grateful for. She hated grocery shopping.

"Hello to you, too, Phoebe. And you must be Trevor." Freddy introduced himself and stepped back as he held the door wide for them. "Come on in." Trevor and Phoebe exchanged curious looks as they stepped into the foyer behind Freddy.

Phoebe froze and let out a small, startled sound at the sight of the painting hanging on the wall in the front entry. Even though Cal had told her it was there, she'd all but put it out of her mind over the past few weeks, consumed with concerns of what they'd talk about over dinner, how she was supposed to behave, what it would be like to sit across the table with the mother of the girl who'd changed their lives so completely. So seeing it huge and real and so prominently displayed was an immense shock to her system. "Cerulean," she murmured when she could speak.

Freddy murmured something to Trevor before slipping away, talking so low Phoebe couldn't make out his words. He could have shouted, and she wouldn't have been able to hear him over the clamor of emotions inside her.

Trevor said nothing—she'd told him about the painting—but he slipped his arm around her, presumably just in case she needed his support.

Phoebe, however, needed to find her own footing in the presence of this painting that had been birthed from the womb of her pain. She squeezed his hand at her side, and then stepped forward, her arms crossed tightly, her eyes upraised as she took in the womanly form on the canvas. The figure, her features almost ageless, stood nearly naked with her arms wrapped around her distended abdomen, a length of gossamer fabric draped around her torso, barely covering her breasts and the shadowed apex of her thighs. The creature's face was lowered, her eyes closed in an expression of longing mixed with serenity. Dark hair flowed down her back, a blue-black slash against the cinnamon and caramel hued background that seemed to be lit from somewhere just beyond the edge of the painting. The woman's face, porcelain pale like Phoebe's, but with the distinct features of Theresa, the woman who had adopted Phoebe's daughter so many years ago, gradated into swirling hues of blues and greens from the column of her bent neck and down her chest, the colors separating into landforms over the orb of her belly so that it looked like she cradled the world in her arms. The colors on the canvas spoke of new life, birth, of regeneration, but something in the woman's posture resonated with such an ache of loss and longing that it nearly eclipsed the golden halo of joy and anticipation effected by the shimmering background.

Everything about the painting made Phoebe want to run for cover, to crawl beneath the comforter beside her mother the way she'd done when she was little. She wanted to weep and to laugh at the sight of it. She wanted to rip it off the wall and shred it before anyone else witnessed her private thoughts, or at the very least, cover it with a sheet to mask the woman's vulnerability, to hide the raw emotion exposed in every line of her face and body.

Her hand trembled as she reached out to touch the corner of the dark walnut frame, her eye drawn to the artist's signature in the corner, only the prominent P legible. But the name was hers, nonetheless.

"It's remarkable, isn't it?"

Phoebe turned slowly to face Cal, his voice kind and gentle as always. Beside him stood a woman who looked like an age-progression version of the eighteen-year-old Angela Clinton Phoebe remembered from high school. Petite and trim, her hair a pale blonde, but faded to ash tones that might have looked gray on someone else. There were fine lines around Forget Me Not blue eyes fringed with brown eyelashes. Alice's smile welcomed her, but Phoebe sensed a reservation, a holding back on the older woman's part, as though she worried what kind of reception she'd get.

Her voice barely above a whisper because of the emotions lodged in her throat, she simply said, "Hi, Cal." For a moment, she wasn't sure if she should hug him or shake his hand, but he took the decision out of her hands when he took her into his arms in a fatherly embrace.

"Welcome to our home, Phoebe." Then he released her and turned to Trevor.

"This is my fiancé, Trevor Zander," Phoebe offered. It still felt strange to introduce him that way, even after almost four months of being engaged. She'd said yes to him only six weeks after their encounter at the gas station, but she'd known that would be her answer much earlier than that. Trevor had waited until Thanksgiving Day to ask for her hand in marriage so their friends and families would all be together to witness their commitment to each other. Trevor had a summer tour booked, and since Phoebe had told him in no uncertain terms that she was going on the road with him, they'd made the decision to be legally married in a small family gathering the first week in May. They would have a full-blown celebration in the fall for friends and extended family after they returned from the tour, but a four-month road trip with her own favorite rock star sounded like a perfect honeymoon to the free-spirited Phoebe. Especially since the two of them would be traveling in Grandpa and Granny G's Airstream rather than riding along with everyone else on the tour bus.

Cal nodded. "Welcome, son. It's good to finally meet you." And then, with an arm around his wife, he drew her close to his side, and said, "This is my angel, Alice."

"I'm so glad you've come," Alice said, taking Phoebe's proffered hand in both of hers as though she held something precious. Phoebe could feel the slight tremor in the woman's fingertips—or was that her own hand shaking?—but she seemed to have lost her voice.

"Thank you for having us," Trevor stepped in, resting his strong hand on her back, lending his support once again. Phoebe arched slightly into it, and Trevor stepped closer so that she could feel the solid warmth of him just behind her. "The painting," he said, his eyes going back to the canvas on the wall. "Remarkable is right. I'm blown away."

"We wanted you to have a moment with it first, without us hovering over your shoulder," Alice said, her voice gentle, even though Phoebe heard a slight tremor there, too. The woman was at least as nervous as she was, and for some reason, that helped her calm down a little. "It's been a beacon of hope to me, Phoebe, and from the moment I saw it, I knew this was where it needed to be. A daily reminder of the beauty and sacredness and the gift of life."

Alice's eyes glistened as she spoke, and Phoebe didn't know what she'd do if the woman started crying. It was all she could do to hold back her own tears in the moment. "I'm so glad to see it again. Thank you." They weren't the words she meant to say—she'd wanted to compliment Alice on the lighting and decor, to downplay the impact the painting still had on her—but they were the words that found their way out of her heart, nonetheless. In the silence that followed, she wondered if she'd spoken out of turn.

But Alice, still holding Phoebe's hand, squeezed her fingers reassuringly. "We'll talk more about it over dinner. Come in, please." She led them into the living room.

Inexpensive art decorated the neutral-colored walls, and there was a large fireplace at one end of the room. Two enormous, overstuffed sofas in dark tones, along with two rocking chairs and a recliner like Gramps', were grouped together in a large seating arrangement, and a pile of toys in a plastic crate sat next to a pop-up playhouse against one wall. It was all very neat and tidy, but the scene looked straight out of a busy family home and wasn't at all what Phoebe had been expecting.

"Dinner will be ready shortly, but we can sit and visit for a few minutes first. Please make yourselves comfortable." Alice lifted a pretty glass decanter with lime slices floating in it. "Can I offer you a glass of sparkling water?"

Once again, Phoebe was so glad for Trevor beside her. He carried their end of the conversation, giving her the buffer she needed to get her emotions under control. After a few minutes of small talk, Freddy reappeared to let them know their meal was ready.

It was all rather formal—did Cal Masters, her grocer, have personal servants? It seemed so out of character to her, and Phoebe prided herself on being a good reader of people. Her bemusement must have shown on her face, because Alice smiled and patted her forearm reassuringly as they entered the large combination dining room and kitchen, the two spaces separated by an island countertop where a young woman was putting some garnish on a colorful pasta dish. She, too, wore black pants and a white shirt, along with a dark green apron over the top of the ensemble.

Freddy introduced her as his wife, Jill. "We're going to be your servers this evening," Freddy explained. "Go ahead and have a seat. We'll be right with you."

Cal directed Phoebe and Trevor to two of the places at the table. Phoebe ducked her head to hide the smile as the two men simultaneously held chairs out for their women, almost as though the move was choreographed.

As soon as they were settled, Freddy refilled their water glasses and offered them iced tea or raspberry lemonade, followed by Jill, who set bowls of deep red roasted tomato and corn soup in front of each of them.

What followed was a delicious meal of chicken in an olive sauce, a pan-seared artichoke and cauliflower vegetable dish, and the cold pasta with herbs Phoebe had seen Jill preparing earlier. In some unspoken agreement, they steered the dinner conversation toward everything but why they were there. They talked of Trevor's upcoming tour, galleries where Phoebe's art was displayed, how Cal's store had grown out of his parents' Mom and Pop shop to a gourmet grocery that catered to a younger, hipper generation than the original shop had.

Then they headed back into the living room where coffee was poured—Freddy left a full carafe on a serving tray near Cal's seat for them—and after Jill brought in small dessert plates of creamy vanilla ice cream spooned over chocolate cinnamon strudel slices, Phoebe saw Alice give Cal *the look,* and she knew the real reason for them being there was about to be disclosed.

TWENTY-FIVE

"Let me start by telling you about Jill." Cal began. "She's given us permission to share her story."

Phoebe glanced through the arched opening toward the room where they'd shared the wonderful meal. The young couple was just out of sight, but she could hear their quiet conversation over the sounds of clean up.

"We first met Jill seven years ago. Her name was given to us by a woman in our church—a good friend of Alice's—who knew about Jill's circumstances. Jill was fifteen at the time and had just learned that she was pregnant."

Phoebe, caught completely unprepared for Cal's statement, set her coffee down, afraid she might spill it, her hands suddenly shaking so badly that the cup rattled in the saucer. Trevor casually laid his arm along the back of the sofa behind her.

"When she went to her parents, their irrational response was that if she thought herself old enough to make adult decisions about sex, then she must be old enough to make adult decisions about the pregnancy. Since she hadn't come to them to ask for advice or help in deciding whether or not to have sex, well, then it wasn't fair of her to ask them for advice or help with the consequences of that decision."

Hearing the middle-aged Cal talk so openly about sex made Phoebe mildly uncomfortable, but not because the man was being inappropriate. She adjusted her thinking to accommodate this new side of the grocer.

"They didn't actually kick her out of the house, but they made it very clear they were not willing to have Jill's child in their home. Which meant if she wanted to stay, she would have to figure out what to do with her baby."

Phoebe had noticed Alice's face changing as her husband spoke, her shoulders lifting, her mouth setting in a grim line, and the thought, *Oh, Mama Bear!* popped into her mind.

When Alice took over the telling, her voice had changed, too. It was stronger, steadier; it seemed. "So Jill went to an abortion clinic, not knowing what else to do. After her initial consultation, however, she decided she could not go through with it. Unfortunately, at her age, her options were pretty limited without the assistance of her parents, all things considered. They ranged from living on the streets, to dropping off the baby with a Safe Haven, to getting on a waiting list for one of the teen pregnancy centers or maternity homes in the area. Our church actually has one, which is why she came to us, but it's more of a safe house for women who are escaping a bad situation. Jill didn't seem a good fit for the program, and the waiting list was long—there was no guarantee she'd have a place before her due date—so my friend contacted me about possibly taking her in. I spoke to Cal that night, and the next morning, we agreed to invite Jill into our home for the duration of her pregnancy." Alice's words grew gentle, poignant, and her features softened as she continued. "She chose to give her baby up for adoption, one of the most difficult decisions a mother can make, but one she believed was right for her. We were able to walk with her through that hard time and then help her get back on her feet as she learned to live with that decision."

Phoebe again eyed the doorway to the kitchen. She wanted to look into Jill's eyes now that she knew what the younger woman had gone through. She felt a deep connection with the pretty blond who had served her a delicious meal and then left to let the Masters tell their guests about her past pain.

"Jill was the first of many girls we've had in our home over the last seven years," Cal picked up again. "We recognized a great need while helping Jill, one we personally believe the church in general is mishandling, at least in cases like hers. We appreciate the good intentions of maternity homes and recognize the immeasurable value of places like that, but we struggle with the idea of sending a pregnant teenager into a dorm-like setting while she traverses such a difficult road, in essence, putting her aside until the pregnancy is resolved. We feel quite strongly that if a church says it is family-oriented, this is one way it can show evidence of that, and church families should be encouraged to open their homes to these young women. It's not a mission for everyone, we know that, but a pregnant woman, whether she plans to keep her baby or give the child up for adoption, is especially in need of a family setting where she can feel safe and defended and loved, regardless of how she got there." He patted a hand against his chest, and Phoebe realized he was dealing with his own strong emotions, almost as though his heart was pained by all that he shared.

Alice gently stroked his shoulder in a show of solidarity and support.

"To make a long story short," Cal picked up again after clearing his throat. "We turned that difficult experience into a ministry. It started out small and by word of mouth only, but after a few more difficult cases, we set up some parameters in which to work, and some strict guidelines the girls have to follow. We now open our home to up to two girls at a time who have chosen adoption as their course of action. Our ministry doesn't end after a baby is born, though."

Cal took Alice's hand in his, a gesture so tender, Phoebe had to look away. Alice cleared her throat. "A big part of what we do is help these young women find their way back into society while grieving the loss of their child; a loss that would be traumatic in the best of circumstances, but one made inconceivably more so for these mothers who are alone in the world and have made the most difficult decision they've ever had to make in giving up their child to be raised by someone else." Alice dropped her gaze to the napkin in her lap before continuing. "They usually start out working part time for Cal until they're ready to move into the next season of their lives. Then we make sure they have a stable living situation before we release them."

Phoebe sat still as a stone, her coffee growing cold in the mug between her cupped palms. Her heart wept inside her, grieved over the loss of her Lily all over again while her spirit marveled at the goodness of the people sitting on the sofa across from her. If only she'd had a Cal and Alice when she'd been fifteen and so desperate and alone. "What happens to them?" she finally managed to ask. "Do you hear from them? The mothers? Do they go on to do well?"

Cal chuckled softly, and Alice turned to smile up at her husband. "Sometimes I feel like Noah," he said. "The girls are our precious doves. Some of them get sent out too soon and they come back to us, their wings weary, in need of comfort and rest. But most of the time, they find their own way once they're out in the world."

"That said, we haven't lost touch with any of them. We keep in contact with all our girls via letters and phone calls, and visits whenever it's possible. They're part of our family now, you understand? We also have a private Facebook group where the girls can support each other and share their stories, and once a month, we have a dinner here for any of them who might want to come to reconnect, although Jill doesn't cater those meals. We all gather in the kitchen and cook together for old time's sake." Alice smiled up at the young couple who had just appeared in the doorway from the kitchen. "Jill is the only one who has stayed with us since the beginning. Thank you for the wonderful meal, honey."

"It really was delicious," Phoebe interjected. "Thank you."

Trevor made an agreeable sound beside her, and then added, "And thank you for allowing Cal and Alice to share your story with us."

Jill beamed, her cheeks pinking prettily. "My pleasure. I'm glad I finally got to meet the artist. I was about eight months pregnant when Alice brought your painting home, Phoebe. It took us pretty much the rest of my pregnancy to decide where to hang it." Jill glanced over at Alice as if to make sure it was okay to share. Alice nodded and took a sip of her coffee, so Jill continued. "We tried it in the room I was in—what would later become one of the two mama rooms—but it felt too overwhelming in there. Too intense. So we tried it over the mantle next." She waved a hand at the fireplace. "But Cal decided he wasn't comfortable with staring at a naked pregnant lady while dozing in his recliner."

"Hey, now," Cal chided. "I was fine with wherever you girls wanted to hang it." Alice patted his knee but didn't say anything.

"We tried it in the dining room, in the hallway, and then finally, when it seemed we were out of options, Cal suggested we hang it in the foyer." Jill grinned at Cal. "The moment it was on the wall, we knew it was the perfect spot for it."

"And it's been there ever since," Alice finished.

"Your painting, Phoebe, has spoken to each one of us who has come through that foyer," Jill said, her voice soft, vulnerable. "You are truly gifted."

Alice turned suddenly serious eyes on Phoebe, too. "I don't know exactly what inspired Cerulean or the other paintings in the Motherhood Collection, but the moment I first saw that one, it spoke to me. I know you and your sisters suffered a great loss when your mother was killed." Her voice trembled a little on the last word, and she took a deep, steadying breath. "In a very different way, I lost my daughter that terrible day so many years ago. I have the joy of seeing her home again soon, and if for no other reason, my loss can't begin to compare to yours. But I hope you believe me when I tell you that I have prayed for you and your sisters, and for my own precious Angela, every day since. Your painting became a connection between us, a daily reminder of hope in my life. Every time I walk by that image, I have asked God for restoration, for new beginnings for all who come through our home." She turned to smile up at Jill. "That prayer has been answered over and over in the women who have come to call this place their home, even for a short time."

"Remarkable," Trevor said, making eye contact with Cal. "You pegged it, sir."

"And now, having you here in our home..." Alice had to swallow hard before she could finish her thought. "It's really a miracle in the making."

Phoebe nodded, afraid to open her mouth to say anything for fear that her own story might come spilling out. It was still too raw, a bruise still too tender to touch.

"It's as though you painted it with us in mind," Jill spoke into the silence, as though she understood Phoebe's reticence. "It so perfectly represents the spirit of this home and the people in it." The young woman leaned into her husband's side. "The Masters are the best thing that ever happened to me."

"Excuse me?" Freddy said, wrapping an arm around Jill and squeezing her shoulders.

"The second-best thing," Jill amended, resting her head on her husband's shoulder. "They gave me a home and a place to recover, and a way to find myself again." She lifted her head to gaze up at Freddy. "And in the process, I found this guy, too."

"Jill runs a catering business out of our deli," Cal explained. "Almost all of our ready-made meals are her creations."

"Speaking of creations," Freddy interjected. "We're going to call it a night and head home to our little one now."

The young couple left shortly after, heading home to their own home where their one-year-old child was asleep under the care of a babysitter.

"It hasn't been easy," Alice said in answer to Phoebe's unspoken question, as the four of them stood on the front porch watching Jill and Freddy's van pull away from the house. "She'll always grieve for that baby."

She said nothing more, making no trivializing statements about God's comfort or the love of a good man, for which Phoebe was grateful.

As she herself knew quite well, God truly did comfort her heart, and the love of a good man was a rare gift, indeed, but not a day went by that Phoebe did not think of Lily, did not remember the weight of the baby inside her, or suffer the pain of releasing her child to another woman to raise.

TWENTY-SIX

"The coincidence is astonishing, Phoebe," Renata said, offering her the milk-drunk baby Charise. Dark wisps of hair capped the infant's round head, and she smiled blearily at her aunt as Phoebe propped her up on her lap and began gently patting her back until Charise released a rather unladylike belch. "And you're sure they don't know about Lily?"

"No one knew about Lily," Phoebe insisted. "There's no way they could have known about what I went through, especially not back then. It happened the year after Angela went to jail. Although the Clintons were still together then, from what Angela has told you, Jules, things were starting to unravel, so I doubt Alice would have been paying any attention to what was going on in my life during that time."

Gia glanced around the room at her sisters, their faces each bearing a different set of emotions. Ren analyzing the information Phoebe had just shared, Phoebe relieved at finally being able to share it, coupled with the warm glow of love in her eyes for the tiny niece she held cradled in her arms. Juliette worried her bottom lip between thumb and forefinger, her brow furrowed. She and Angela had been in contact by letter for the last year, and from the look on her face, she was scrolling through the pages shared between them, looking for clues or connections between Angela and Alice's stories.

Gia turned to Phoebe. "What happened to the Clintons?" she asked, trying to keep her voice level. Alice's ministry was pretty wonderful, truth be told, but how was it supposed to impact the four sisters beyond the relevance of a piece of Phoebe's artwork? "I mean, did Alice give you any information that would help prepare us for meeting with Angela? Isn't that the goal here; isn't that what we're gearing up for?" Alice had sent invitations home with Phoebe, asking that all four sisters come to dinner once Angela was home. A dinner planned for the coming Saturday night. Angela had requested a chance to talk to all of them together, face to face, so that questions could be asked and answered in person rather than via the written word, where emotions and sentiments could be misconstrued too easily.

Ren nodded and added her own question. "Yes. I'm curious about that, too. Was the divorce because of Angela? And does Alice's ministry have anything to do with what happened with Angela?" Then she turned to Juliette. "Has Angela ever said anything about her parents splitting up?"

Juliette shook her head. "She's only said that they divorced about a year after the accident. But I do get the feeling it's all tied together somehow. Something happened to trigger Angela's binge, we know that." Angela had confirmed as much in one of her letters to Juliette but had asked to be allowed to talk to them in person once she was back home. "Phoebe's right. Their home had to have been in chaos back then. There's just no way Alice could have known about Phoebe."

"I really believe that it's a God thing," Phoebe said, resting her chin on top of Charise's head. The baby had burrowed her face into the crook of Phoebe's neck, one chubby hand fisted in Phoebe's hair, the other pressed to her tiny wet mouth where she sucked on her knuckles as her eyelids grew heavy.

"I never thought I'd hear those words on your lips." What once might have been a not-so-subtle jab coming from Ren now held a tender note of teasing. "But that said, I think you might be right. We've seen a lot of 'God things' lately, and this is feeling that way, too."

"What do you mean, though? Isn't that a little trite?" Gia asked, wanting clarification, but also giving way to the contention in her spirit. As much as she appreciated hearing the Masters' story, and although she acknowledged the providential link between the heart of Alice's ministry and Phoebe's own experience, she wasn't sure how this was supposed to play out for the rest of them. "A God thing how?"

Phoebe spoke softly so as not to disturb the baby. "Well, don't you think it's quite the coincidence that her ministry speaks to my heart and my past on so many levels, and that Cerulean has played such a huge role in that home? And what about the fact that I buy my groceries from Cal because his store offers a delivery service? Cal, who coincidentally happens to be the husband of the mother of the girl who killed our mother."

Gia held up her hand to stop her sister. Something dark stirred up inside her, something twisting and ugly, and she felt it clawing at the back of her throat. "I. Me. My. Yeah, yeah, Phoebe. I clearly see how you might think there's a 'God thing' connection between you and Alice. But this isn't just about you, is it?"

The stunned silence that followed her words only served to heighten her disquiet. She turned to Juliette. "And I get your—" She struggle to find the right word. "Your *fixation* with this whole thing. Angela was your friend, and I assume you need closure or something."

"My fixation?" Juliette asked, her expression one of surprise, and slightly wounded.

"Georgia," Ren said, her voice quiet but firm, the way she spoke to her oldest son when he was getting a little too pushy with her or Tim.

Gia didn't look at her, but her words came out harsh and surly. "Don't 'Georgia' me, Ren. You're not my mother." She toyed with the handle of her coffee cup, her thoughts buzzing like angry bees in her head. "I—*we*—don't have a mother or father because of that—that—" She sputtered, trying to find a word that would encompass her chaotic thoughts, but came up empty. "Because of that Angela Clinton chick you all are trying to reconcile with. Why? Can someone tell me *why* we want to have a relationship with her?" She gripped the handle of her mug tightly, watching as her knuckles and nail beds whitened. Apparently, she *did* have some unresolved anger toward the girl, after all. "She got rip-roaring drunk and killed our parents, you guys."

Juliette made a noise that might have been her clearing her throat, but Gia pushed up off the floor before her sister could say anything. She stood, towering over them. She could feel the heat emanating off her, her scalp tingling, her shoulders tight with her bottled up fury. "What is wrong with you people? Why do you want to be all buddy-buddy with her and her family? She *murdered* our parents! And now she wants to reconcile with us, to smooth things over? She hasn't even had the decency to tell us what happened that day." Gia's voice was growing louder and more forceful the longer she spoke, and now her hands were gesturing madly, almost of their own accord.

Phoebe lifted a hand to cover Charise's ears, but Gia didn't care. It was as though the dam holding her emotions in check all these years was crumbling, collapsing in on itself, and once breached, there was no stopping the deluge that poured out of her.

"She claims to have had her 'come to Jesus' moment in prison and has spent the remainder of her sentence praising the Lord and sharing the gospel truth with her fellow inmates, right? Well, what about sharing a little of the gospel truth with us, the victims of her crime? She's left us all to live totally in the dark with our loss and grief—and not just us, but Granny G and Gramps, too!—because she doesn't *want* to tell us why she did what she did." Gia turned on Phoebe, pointing a long finger at her. "I bet a million bucks that the Clintons' divorce was a direct result of that day, or what led up to it. Which means Alice knows, too. Did she tell you? Did she give you even a morsel of an explanation to share with us? Anything that might shed some light on why we got to grow up without our parents?"

Phoebe's eyes were wide with concern, and she shook her head. "She said she felt that it was Angela's place to tell her own story." But Gia could tell her questions were sinking in, making Phoebe think.

"Who have they been protecting with their silence all this time? And why? Because it sure isn't us." And there it was. Suddenly, it all came clear to Gia. A reason. That was all she wanted. A reason for what happened so that she could accept things and move on. She didn't want to make friends with Angela or her mother; she didn't care what they did with the rest of their lives. She just wanted to know *why* things had happened the way they had happened. She needed to know why she'd been forced to grow up without a mother or father, why she felt adrift so much of the time. She wanted to know why Angela Clinton got to come home at the end of the day and reunite with her mother, but Gia and her sisters would never have that for themselves.

She had to get out of there. She needed to drive with the windows down and the music up too loud. She needed to think. She needed Ricky sitting beside her in his truck, holding onto the waist of her jeans as she hung halfway out the open window, singing at the top of her lungs so she could drown out all the confusion in her head.

Without another word, she snatched up her coffee cup and napkin and marched into Juliette's kitchen. She stood at the sink, shaking so badly her teeth rattled, holding the cup under the faucet. A noise behind her made her glance over her shoulder. Renata stood in the entry to the kitchen, her hands tucked into the front pockets of her jeans.

"Gia," she began, her voice sad, worried. "I'm sorry."

"For what?" Gia snapped, not ready to set aside her anger. "You didn't kill our parents."

"To be honest, I feel like we've been insensitive to you about all of this," Ren said. Gia kept her attention on the task at hand, not wanting to see the regret in Ren's eyes. "I hate to even admit this, because as a mother, I should know better. But I think we just assumed you were too young to be as deeply affected by all of this as we were."

"Well, I wasn't too young. And if you're really being honest about all of this," she said, using Renata's own words, "then you might consider that maybe I was even more affected by the accident than you three were. At least you have your memories of Mommy and Daddy. At least you can talk amongst yourselves about how great they were, how in love they were. You three can reminisce about the good times, about family vacations and holidays, about Mom's accent and her French curse words, about Dad's stupid jokes and how he loved Mom's hair and her smoky gray eyes. Which, by the way, you three have and I—I don't." Her voice caught, and she swallowed hard, trying to dislodge the lump in her throat. She set her clean cup in the drainer and dried her hands on a dishtowel that lay on the counter beside the sink. "You three at least have the years you got with Mom and Dad. Not me. I have nothing... because of Angela. Not even a reason why."

"This isn't like you," Ren murmured, stepping further into the kitchen. "What's going on? What's happened?"

"How do you know this isn't like me?" Gia asked, turning around to look at her sister. Behind her, Juliette had risen, too, and now leaned against the arm of the couch where Phoebe still sat with Charise clutched close to her heart. They were all watching her, misery etched into their faces.

"We know you, Gia pet," Ren said, using Gramps' nickname for her.

Gia shook her head slowly, firmly. "No, you don't. I don't even know me." Gia smacked a hand flat on the counter beside her hard enough to make her palm sting. The pain, however, seemed to sharpen her clarity, helping her to find words. "I have lived my whole life trying to be as good as everyone says I am. A good girl. A good friend. A good student. A good employee. A good Christian. A good leader. A good granddaughter. A good sister." She snorted; it was an ugly sound made uglier by the words that followed. "I don't ever recall being called a good daughter, though. Huh." She crossed her arms and leaned back against the counter, clenching her smarting palm into a tight fist. "I have been good all my life because I've been afraid to be anything else. And no, I'm not so self-absorbed that I think Mom and Dad left because I wasn't a good girl, so don't go assuming I need therapy or anything."

"Please, Gia—" But Gia cut Ren off.

"But I have been afraid to disappoint everyone. Do you remember how desperate I was to be included in this sister thing you three had?" She waved a hand around in a circle in front of her before tucking it back against her side again. "Do you remember what I had to do in order for you to let me in? If I recall, I was your slave—your *slave*—for months before I was allowed to join."

Juliette opened her mouth to say something, but Gia held up a hand, cutting her off, too. "I know, Jules. You were nice to me, but I was still afraid to do anything wrong, just in case I screwed up my chances. And do you all know that there is one—*one!*—person in my life I can truly call friend? Ricky. Just Ricky. He's the only person outside of family who still gives a rat's hindquarters about my life these days. All those girls I hung out with in high school? They weren't my friends. I was their good little leader, in charge of making sure they didn't get in trouble, or at least they didn't get caught. Do you remember my TDD badge? Do you know what that stood for? Team Designated Driver. Yep. That was Rickaroni and me. I got invited to parties so that everyone else could party. How sad is that?"

She paused to let that sink in, not just for her sisters, but for her, too. Talk about clarity.

"And before you bring up good old Granny G and Gramps," she said, knowing for sure that at least one of them was desperate to remind her of how much love they'd been given in the Gustafson home. "Please don't patronize me. I'm perfectly aware of how lucky we all are to have grandparents who took us in and raised us as their own. I have had many more years living with them than any of you, and I know how much of a sacrifice they made to make a home for us. But our grandparents are almost four times my age, you guys. They're in their late seventies. They're tired. They're old. I've never doubted their love, even for an instant. But I've always lived with the fear of losing them. Where would I go if they died, too? Even if one of you took me in, I'd be an obligation, a burden. It would be like having to join one of your clubs all over again. No thank you."

"No, Gia. That's not true," Juliette spoke up, her voice thick with tears. "You know that's not how any of us would feel."

"That's just it, though," Gia railed, pressing her clenched fist over her heart. "I'm telling you how I would feel. I'm telling you how I *have* felt my whole life. Like the afterthought, the odd man out." She felt the tears begin to well again, and she clenched her teeth together. She would not cry. "I'm truly the 'oops' baby in this family, and I have felt that as far back as I can remember."

No one dared contradict her out loud, not in the state she was in, but she saw on each of their faces the need to comfort her, to draw her to them. She wasn't having it, though. Not tonight.

"It's not your fault, you guys." Her words came out raspy, rough. "It's Angela's. And I, for one, have no interest in hearing what she or her mother has to say. Not now. Not after all this time." She shook her head, feeling stubborn and perhaps a little childish, too, but she didn't care. "She's had fifteen—no, more than sixteen years now—to tell us why she did what she did. It's too late, as far as I'm concerned."

"Gia," Ren began again, but Gia shook her head, not wanting to hear it.

"I think I need to go home. I don't want you guys to make your decision about Angela and Alice based on my feelings. If you want to continue with all of this, please do. I totally understand your reasons, but they're not my reasons." She skirted Renata, not wanting to be touched at that moment, and headed toward the door. She'd only brought her wallet and keys with her and she'd left them on the table by the front door. "Just please don't tell me about it, okay? If you need to have a G-FOURce or two without me, I totally understand that, too."

"Please, Gia," Phoebe said, her voice still soft because of the sleeping baby, but urgent nonetheless. "Don't go. I'm sorry I made this about me. You're right. Ren's right. We haven't asked you how you feel."

Gia stopped in the foyer and reached down to scratch Bob's head between his ears. "I'm sorry I said those terrible things to you, Phebes. You're not the bad guy here." She straightened and scooped up her belongings before turning back one last time. "I love you guys. This is your gig, though, not mine. I'll see you this weekend, okay?" And with that, she pulled open the front door and slipped out into the night, glancing briefly over at Mrs. Cork's door, grateful to find it closed. The last thing she needed right now was to have to play nice with the sweet old lady and her little dog.

TWENTY-SEVEN

"I'm worried about you, sweetie," Granny G said, sitting on the edge of Gia's bed. Her hands were folded in her lap, but Gia could almost feel her grandmother's desire to touch her, to stroke her hair, her back, the way she usually did when offering her comfort. She thought of Juliette's words from earlier, and Gia suddenly related. She, too, was a little afraid that she might burst into flames if someone touched her, but for completely different reasons.

"I'll be fine, Gran. I just need some time to think." Once again, she'd come home to find Granny G sitting alone in the living room, a cup of tea in hand, an Agatha Christie book open in her lap. But instead of joining her, Gia had made a few vague excuses and headed to her room. It was only just past eight o'clock, though, and Granny G had followed her after a few minutes.

"Renata called and told me a little about what happened," Granny G continued. "This isn't like you."

"Of course she did." Gia pulled a pillow over her head. "Actually, it is." Her words were muffled, but she didn't care. "This is exactly like me." How she wished people would stop telling her what she was and wasn't like. "Where's Gramps?"

"He was tired after our night out and went to bed."

Gia pulled her pillow down to her chest, but kept her face toward the wall so she wouldn't have to look at Granny G. "That's not like him. Why aren't you in there worrying about him?"

Granny G didn't respond, and the snippy words hung in the air between them.

"Sorry. That was uncalled for," Gia muttered. She still didn't turn around. "Is he okay?"

"He's fine," Granny G assured her. "Just tired. He's old. We're old. But then, you know that."

Gia sighed and finally rolled over. She took her grandmother's hand in hers and traced a purple vein on the back of it. "I'm not ready to talk right now, okay, Gran? I promise I'll come to you when I am."

"Okay, sweetie." Granny G patted her shoulder and rose to leave. "Let me know if you need anything. I'll be up for another hour or so; I still have some laundry to do." Granny G never went to bed with a load of clothes in the dryer.

When Gia came down the hall Thursday morning, she found her grandfather sitting in his usual chair, freshly showered and dressed for the day. Apparently, he was feeling up to snuff again; now that she thought about it, he hadn't dressed for breakfast in a while.

"You heading out somewhere, Gramps?"

"Nope," he said, smiling at her over his coffee cup. "I went to bed so early last night that my eyes popped open at five fifteen this morning. I moseyed around in my jammies and slippers as long as I could justify, but finally gave up and got ready for the day early." He held one hand out to the side. "So here I am, Dapper Dan."

Gia leaned over and kissed him on the forehead. He still looked a little wan to her, but his skin was cool to the touch, and his eyes were bright. "Well, good morning to you, Dapper Dan."

Gramps patted the table in front of the chair opposite him. "Grab a mug and take a load off."

Gia bit back a sigh. So Granny G had talked to him. "I have to get to work, Gramps."

"Give an old man a few minutes, girlie. I won't make you late."

Gia hesitated for another moment, squeezed her eyes tightly shut in an effort to reset herself, and poured herself a cup of coffee. She dropped into the chair Gramps had pointed to just as Granny G joined them.

"How'd you sleep, sweetie?"

Fine, fine. Get all the pleasantries out of the way. "It took me a while to get there, but once I passed out, I slept like a baby."

"Well, I won't beat around the bush." Without preamble, Gramps cut to the chase. "Your sisters are worried about you, and so are we. Is there anything we need to know? Anything you need to tell us?"

A sudden thought occurred to her. Ever since Phoebe had opened up about her struggles in high school, her grandparents had been far more attentive than usual. They'd admitted to being concerned about Phoebe back then, but they acknowledged that they'd been at a loss as to how to help her, and so they'd simply let things go, hoping everything would set itself to right in the end. They both shouldered a lot of guilt and blame for how things had turned out for Phoebe and Lily—were they worried that Gia might be in the same situation?

"I'm not pregnant, if that's what you're asking." Gramps snorted softly, and Gia cocked her head and shot him a curious look. "What? Is that so preposterous?"

"Well, no." He shook his head slowly, meeting her eyes, his own crinkling at the corners, as he smiled at her. "Not preposterous, but certainly not something I was concerned about."

"Why not? Because I'm the good Gustafson girl? Because I wouldn't do something like that?" Oh geez. What was wrong with her? Now she was lashing out at her beloved Gramps.

"Actually, that's about right." Her grandfather's expression grew serious. "I'm not saying it's impossible, Gia pet. I'm saying it's not something I'd expect to hear from you." He reached over and patted her forearm. "It was meant as a compliment."

"Sweetie, we're just worried about you," Granny said for what felt like the hundredth time to Gia.

"I know. I'm sorry." Gia took a sip of her coffee and tried not to grimace. Good old Gramps and his bitter brew. "Last night I told you I'd talk to you when I was ready, but I'm still trying to get my head on straight. I need a little more time, okay?"

Gramps sat back in his chair and studied his large hands he'd wrapped around his mug. A moment later, he nodded solemnly. "All right. I can accept that, but you know better than many that time is not really ours to order, Gia pet. So choose what you do with the moments you're given, okay? Don't be caught waiting for the right time to do the right thing."

Gia squeezed her eyes shut again, hearing echoes of her argument with Ricky from just a few days ago. A different version of her own words, but the message was the same, nonetheless. She took a deep breath and blew it out slowly, then opened her eyes. "Fine. I don't want to talk about this—I can't, or I'll be late to work—but I can at least tell you a little about what's going on." She took another sip of coffee, and this time, she didn't try to hide her reaction. "Gramps, your coffee is awful. How long has it been cooking?"

"Only about an hour," he said with a grin.

"Shall I make another pot?" Granny G asked.

"No. This will be quick. I'll get some fresh stuff at work." Gia stood and took her cup to the sink. "In a nutshell," she began again, turning back to face her grandparents where they still sat at the table. She held up her hands and started counting things off on her fingers. "One: I don't want to talk to Angela—or her mother—because although I can forgive her, I can't just pretend what she did didn't happen. It *did*, and we are all forever changed because of it, and I don't feel like pretending it's all okay now that a decade and a half has passed." She wiggled a second finger. "Two: I miss my mom and dad even though I never really knew them, and I'm jealous that Jules, Ren, and Phoebe *did* know them. Three: I love Ricky, but I don't know if I'm *in* love with him, and now he says he's in love with me, and I'm afraid his feelings will influence my feelings and I won't know if they're my real feelings or not. Four: I want to grow up, but I don't know what I want to do with my life. And last but not least, I don't want you two to get old. I'm afraid to grow up and move on with my life because what will happen to you two when I do?"

"Well, Gia pet," Gramps said after a stretch of heavy silence. "We *are* old. That happened long ago, I'm afraid, so you can check that off your list."

"Fine. I don't want you to get *older*, because after older comes death, and I really don't want anyone else I love to die for a while." Her words fell like lead weights around them, and Gia dropped her gaze to her feet.

Finally, Gramps spoke again. "Well, we did ask, didn't we?" In her peripheral vision, Gia saw his big hand cover her grandmother's.

"Sorry," she muttered. "That came out a little more... um, forceful than I intended."

"No, no," her grandfather said, waving his hand to dismiss her apology. "It may be that you haven't been forceful enough. You've given us several things to chew on today, Gia pet, things we should have realized long before now. Thank you for trusting us enough to tell us."

Gia looked up, surprised by his response. "You're welcome," she said, her voice tentative.

"And when you're ready, we'll talk." Gramps stood and crossed the space between them. "Give an old man a hug."

She did, resting her cheek on his shoulder, breathing in the smell of his old-fashioned shaving soap and the crisp scent of laundry detergent from his shirt. "Love you, Gramps," she said. "Sorry I've been such a poop lately."

Gramps chuckled and then Granny G was there, ready for her hug, too. Gia couldn't help but notice the frailty of the old woman's stature, the unmistakable curve of her spine, and how loosely the flesh covered her bones.

"We'll see you this evening, then," her grandmother said, patting her cheek.

"Oh! I almost forgot to tell you." She looped the strap of her purse over her shoulder and took her car keys from the key hook near the kitchen door. "I'm having dinner with Ricky tonight, so don't expect me until late." She smiled shyly at Granny G. "I'll start with saying sorry to him."

"Sorry is a good place to start."

"Yeah, well, it seems like I'm saying sorry an awful lot these days."

Gramps chuckled softly as she headed off to work.

TWENTY-EIGHT

Dumped a latte on my leg. *Going home to shower so I might be late.*

Gia sent the text and then waited to make sure it had been delivered. It had been that kind of a day, but Gia was determined to clear her head before going to Ricky's. She was ridiculously nervous, and she wasn't sure why. They'd apologized to each other over the years a thousand or more times, so it wasn't just the fact that she owed him an 'I'm sorry.' No, it probably had a lot more to do with the 'I want to be your girlfriend after all' bit that was making her clumsy and distracted.

Beside her on the seat was a to-go bag with a couple of sun-dried tomato and prosciutto sandwiches, Ricky's favorite from Ricardo's offerings. Thankfully, they were one of her favorites, too.

She didn't wait for Ricky's response, but took off for home, pulling into the driveway less than ten minutes later. Snatching the paper bag along with her purse, she launched herself out of the car and hurried inside.

Granny G was on the phone in the kitchen, but Gia could tell by her tone and posture that it was just a social call. Her grandparents had lived in Midtown all their married lives and had attended the same church for just as long. They had so many friends in their community, and the thought always made Gia glad. She and her grandmother exchanged a wordless greeting, Gia shoved her sandwiches into the refrigerator, and bustled off to her room.

After another record-breaking shower, Gia breezed into the kitchen wearing leggings under a short yellow sundress topped with a cropped denim jacket. On her feet were flip-flops that would be easy to kick off so she could climb the ladder steps nailed to the trunk of the cork oak tree in whose branches Ricky's tree house was built.

"Hey, sweetie. You look cute." Granny G was off the phone now and stood at the stove stirring a pot of something that smelled delicious. Gia came up behind her and peeked over her shoulder. Chicken and vegetable soup. A loaf of her grandmother's homemade bread sat on a cutting board on the counter. Simple fare for simple folks.

"Thanks, Gran. I spilled coffee all over myself at the end of my shift. Where's Gramps?"

"He's out working in his garden now that the day has cooled off. Would you mind hollering out the back door for him before you leave? Dinner is just about ready."

"Sure." Gia glanced at her phone to check the time. There was a message from Ricky.

Take your time. See you when you get here.

Her grandparents had the best back yard. It was large enough to have the whole troop over for barbecues, to host small gatherings for their church friends, and between the big trees, the detached covered patio with the two bench swings that made for quiet conversations, and the expansive kitchen garden, it was a wonderful place for kids—and grandkids—to grow up.

Gia spotted her grandfather on his knees, his back to her, his shoulders hunched as he rocked a little with the motion of his efforts. He wore a ratty old straw hat that always made Gia smile. On the ground beside him was a stack of empty plastic seedling pots, his long-handled spade, a three-pronged garden fork, and a versatile hoe—sharp edges all facing down—his three favorite gardening tools. "Hey Gramps," she called out as she approached the pretty picket fence that surrounded the garden plot. "Gran says dinner is ready. Time to come in and wash up."

Her grandfather turned to look at her over his shoulder and waved at her with the little trowel he'd been using. "Perfect timing. That's the last of the tomatoes in the ground, and I'm about done in." Leaning forward to brace his hands on the ground, he pushed to his feet and lifted his hat off his head.

As she watched from outside the fence, but not more than ten feet away, her grandfather's face went from exertion-tinted pink to ashen white, and then, as though in slow motion, he stumbled, took one listing step to the left, and then toppled to the ground like a felled tree.

TWENTY-NINE

RICKY LOVED THE FACT that Gia loved his tree house as much as he did. When his family had moved in here, there'd already been a platform with a railing up in the sprawling oak, left behind by the last family who'd lived in the home. Todd and Patricia Zander were a powerhouse husband and wife motivational speaker team, specializing in corporate business, and they were away more often than they were home, sometimes for weeks at a time.

The couple loved their work and had waited to have children until after their business was well-established. The moment they learned Patricia was pregnant, they began a hunt for the perfect nanny, whom they found in a woman named Nita Wiersma, a grandmotherly type who had recently retired from her position as a school librarian. But when Patricia's advanced maternal age brought on a slew of complications, and they determined there would be no more children after Ricky, he'd been delegated to the life of an only child being raised by a nanny.

Nita stayed with them for the first eleven years of Ricky's life, but then her own health problems began to interfere with her ability to drive, and eventually, she moved into a lovely, assisted living community, leaving the Zanders without anyone they trusted to care for a boy who was too old for a babysitter and too young to be left alone for extended periods of time. The Zanders had been at a loss. Business was good, but not good enough for either of them to slow down. So after almost a year of an unsuccessful hunt for a live-in housekeeper who would be willing to play nanny part time, they'd moved to Midtown to be close to Todd's side of the family, who were only too happy to help out with the well-behaved but lonely Ricky. So even though he had his parents, it was his extended family—he thought of Nita as family, too, even though he hadn't seen her in years—who had raised him, something else that linked Gia and him together.

When his parents were home, they had little time to spend with him, so he took on the project of the tree house. It had taken him less than a week after meeting Gia to know she'd be the first—and possibly the only—girl he'd invite up there to see it. At the time, it had been little more than the preexisting platform and the four walls he'd managed to erect on his own. She'd been completely awed by the project and had jumped in wholeheartedly, making him love her even more. Over time, with the help of Gia, and sometimes Trevor when his older cousin was available, they'd created a fortress in his backyard, and even though she still called it his, in Ricky's heart, it had become theirs.

He couldn't help but wonder what would become of it when he moved out. Every time he thought about it, his stomach knotted uncomfortably. He'd miss the tree house and all its memories far more than he would his parents.

By a quarter after five, Ricky had the thrift store coffee table they'd painted Bronco orange, covered in a tablecloth he'd snagged from his mom's meager linen closet. The Zanders never entertained at home, so what was there was rarely used and wouldn't be missed for the evening. Paper plates, tall plastic pirate booty goblets, and the two halves of a coconut bra Gia had turned into serving dishes, one filled with their favorite chip and pretzel mix, the other with Hot Tamales cinnamon candy, looked gloriously juvenile paired with the ornate candelabra Gia had found at an estate sale in the older part of Midtown. She'd draped it with strings of beads and random pieces of costume jewelry she'd collected over the years. In an ice bucket on the floor, a bottle of sparkling lemonade chilled, and there were several cans of soda and bottled water in the mini fridge nearby, another garage sale find. It had been a grand day, indeed, when they'd strung up a heavy-duty electrical cord from the garage to the tree house, and the little fridge had started to hum congenially.

He'd wait until Gia got there to plug in the twinkle lights. They'd strung them up to look like fallen stars in the branches around the structure, and there was nothing more magical than lighting up their tree after the sky had gone dark. Inside, where the table was laid, were a few more strings of lights, but tonight, he'd opted for candles. He busied himself lighting the seven tapers in the centerpiece: surely she'd be here soon.

Half an hour later, as the sun was bidding farewell in the west, Ricky blew out the candles and shoved the bottle of lemonade in the fridge. Sprawled in the hammock hung between two branches over the balcony, he fixed his gaze on the gate at the side of the house. In one hand he held a can of ginger ale, in the other, his phone, debating whether or not he should bother texting Gia. What had happened to change her mind this time? Did he really want to know? Did it have anything to do with Barista Boy?

And yet, she was the one who'd orchestrated this whole thing.

His chest hurt the way it did after too many sprints, like he couldn't quite catch his breath. He couldn't bear the back and forth, the not knowing. Where *was* she?

He set his soda on the rail nearby. "What have you got to lose, man?" he muttered to himself, keying in his phone's password. He pulled up her last text and started tapping in a brief message when he noticed the three dots indicating she was texting him at the same time.

His thumbs stilled, and he held his breath, waiting to have his heart broken again, but hoping she was on her way even more.

So sorry. At the hospital. Gramps passed out and hit his head.

Ricky sat up so suddenly, he almost toppled out of the hammock. With clumsy thumbs, he keyed a message back to her. *What hospital? Where are you? I'll come to you.*

It was several minutes before she texted again, telling him where they were, but it was more than enough time for him to batten down the hatches in the tree house and hurry inside to grab his jacket and keys. He hollered to his folks to let them know he was heading out for a bit but didn't bother waiting for a response. They probably wouldn't even notice he was gone.

Fifteen minutes later, he was at the hospital. He texted Gia from the parking lot as she'd asked him to, and then headed inside to wait in the main foyer where she would meet him. Gramps had been admitted and had been carted off for some tests while the girls—Juliette and Phoebe had already arrived, and Renata was on her way—were keeping vigil with Granny G in Gramps' assigned room. By the time Ricky passed through both sets of doors into the front lobby of the local community hospital, Gia was stepping out of the elevator. He heard her heartbreaking sob when she saw him, and without a word, he crossed the room and enfolded her in his arms.

"Thank you," she whispered against his chest. "I'm sorry I didn't text you earlier. You must've thought some awful things about me."

Ricky grinned to himself, his cheek pressed to her hair. She knew him too well. "How's Gramps?" he asked instead of admitting anything.

"Oh, Ricky," she murmured, pulling back a little to wipe at her face. From the puffiness around her eyes and her bright red nose, she'd obviously been crying for some time. "It was awful. I went outside to call him in for supper right as I was getting ready to head out the door. He stood up and—and you know how they say the color drained from someone's face? I always wondered if that was a literal statement or not. Now I know it is." She paused, and Ricky watched her eyes grow unfocused. He took her by the shoulders and gave her a little jostle to snap her out of it. She was beside herself. This wasn't his normal goofy-yet-solid Gia.

"Hey, Georgy Girl. Look at me."

"What?" She looked shell-shocked, her skin pale beneath the blotchy redness from her tears.

"Have you seen him? How is he?"

"Oh. Gran and I got to sit with him in the emergency room. She had me drive her to the hospital instead of riding in the ambulance with Gramps. I think she might have been more worried about me than him, though. I was kinda freaking out at first." She covered her eyes and let out a shuddering breath. "Anyway, when we got there, they were getting him all hooked up to stuff and getting him prepped to go back for some kind of a head scan and to clear his neck so they can take off the stabilizer brace. I think they just put it on as a precaution? I don't really know how all that stuff works; I'll have to look it up."

Knowing Gia, she'd be on Google before the night was over, collecting a slew of interesting facts about neck braces, spinal cord and head injuries, and a myriad of other emergency procedures. She was a sucker for 'Fun Facts' websites and a diehard Wikipedia junkie.

"Anyway, he was awake and responsive by the time the paramedics got to our place, but he was really confused, even when we all got to the hospital. He asked the same questions several times, wanting to know what happened, why we were all there, and stuff like that. He seemed to get better as time passed, so that's good, I guess. He remembered me coming out to call him to dinner, but he doesn't remember falling. They're doing a CT scan to check for bleeding or bruising or swelling on the brain, among other things."

"Did they say why he fainted?" Ricky smoothed her hair back from her face. It was all loose and wild, silken coils beneath his palms. He brushed away a stray tear with his thumb.

"The doctor said it could be any number of things, or even a combination of things, but she mentioned possibly a relapse of his pneumonia, dehydration, even a stroke, God forbid."

"Oh, wow."

"Yeah, I know. Scary. But he's old, you know? And I guess being sick for so long and after the stress of last year with John dying, followed by all the weddings—we still have Phebes and Trevor to marry off next month...." She shook her head. "Gramps has been tired a lot since he was sick, now that I think of it. He's been taking long naps every afternoon, and I've noticed that he goes to bed quite a bit earlier than he used to these days. I should have known something was wrong. His doctor said his lungs sounded clear, but she wants a chest X-ray anyway, just to be sure. So yeah, they're looking for evidence of a stroke, a brain bleed or bruising from the knock on the head, ruling out pneumonia, and clearing his spine so they can take off that neck brace. Poor guy. He kept pulling at it like he couldn't figure out what it was. I hated seeing him so confused." Gia made a sound like a whimper and gripped his biceps. "Oh, Ricky. It was awful. I was on the other side of the fence and couldn't get to him. I just stood there and watched him keel over. He went down so hard, too." Her voice rose in pitch, her hands tightened on his arms. "I keep seeing it over and over in my mind. And the sound of his head hitting the shovel—"

"Hey, stop," Ricky said, gently drawing her close again. "Enough. What can I do? Do you want me to take you back to his room? Or do you want to go outside for a walk?" He glanced around at the nearly empty lobby. "It's pretty quiet if you want to sit down here for a bit."

Gia took a deep breath and stepped back again. "I could use some air. Let me text Jules to let her know." She pulled her phone out of her pocket and started keying in her message.

While she waited for a response from her sister, Ricky asked, "Do you want something to drink? Or eat?" He pointed at the sign that directed visitors to the cafeteria. "The sign says they have a courtyard. We could hang out there."

"I don't know if I can eat anything right now, but you must be hungry. Our sandwiches are still in the fridge at home."

Ricky bought them both a green drink smoothie in lieu of food for the time being—the cafeteria had a surprising variety of vendors and options for such a small hospital—and they found a bench out under the shade of a purple plum tree in full bloom. Ricky let Gia tell him everything that had happened from the moment she'd walked out the back door until she'd met him in the lobby. He'd thought to grab a handful of napkins on their way out of the cafeteria, and Gia made good use of them to wipe her face and blow her nose throughout the telling.

"It was awful," she said for what must have been the dozenth time. "There was so much blood, Ricky. And it seemed like it took forever for him to come around. I knew not to try to move him just in case he'd hurt his neck, but it was all I could do not to shake him. It's just what you automatically do, you know?" She put a hand on his leg and jostled him on the bench in demonstration. "I kept yelling in his face like an idiot, shouting at him to wake up, wake up! And poor Gran. She had to do all the important stuff like calling 9-1-1 and holding a towel over the cut to slow the bleeding. I was a worthless basket case." She sighed deeply and then rested her head on his shoulder.

He wanted to put his arm around her, but instead, he took her hand and held it between both of his. Her fingers were chilled from her drink, and he thought they trembled a little, too. He didn't speak, but smiled contentedly when he felt her body begin to relax against his side.

The cool of the evening settled around them, and they sat that way for several minutes until Gia's phone chirped with a text message.

"Gramps is back," she said, pushing to her feet so suddenly, she stumbled a little. "Ooh! Head rush."

Ricky stood, too, and steadied her with his hands on her shoulders. Even in the glow of the lampposts in the courtyard, she still looked scary-pale to him. "You okay?" he asked, not wanting to let go lest she keel over.

"Sorry. Yeah." Gia took a shuffling step closer and wrapped her arms around his waist, pressing her cheek to his chest, ducking her head so it fit into the hollow under his chin. "I'm good now that you're here, Rickaroni. I love you."

It took everything in him not to respond to those sweet, sweet words that he wanted more than anything in the world to be true. Now was not the time to ask her to clarify *how* she loved him—as a friend who's a boy, or as a boyfriend—but he was certain she could hear the question in the way his heart rate jack-hammered in his chest.

A moment later, she pulled away from him and turned to head back inside. "Come on."

Although Ricky followed her closely, it took his breathing a little longer to catch up. In fact, it was still a little ragged when they arrived at the door to Gramps' room, and Ricky hoped the rest of the Gustafson gang would assume it was because of the haste they'd made getting there.

THIRTY

I LOVE YOU, SHE'D said, as though it was the most natural thing in the world.

It had just slipped out. Thank goodness she'd had her head tucked under his chin so he couldn't see her cheeks suffuse with color. Surely, even in the dark, they would have emitted a rosy glow. Man, did she know how to screw things up.

First of all, she was pretty sure she did love him, and in *that* way, too. She had to figure out how to get over the whole brother love stigma. Because what she was feeling didn't seem very brotherly after all. But she was also pretty sure she'd handled things all wrong over the last couple of weeks. It wasn't fair to Ricky for her to just blurt out her feelings after she'd raked him over the coals the way she had, and just expect him to be all okay with it. She owed him an apology, an explanation if she could come up with a reasonable one, and a huge barrel of sensitivity.

But the moment those words had escaped her lips, instead of wanting to take them back, she'd wanted to repeat them. She'd wanted to lean back in his arms, look him in the eyes, and say it again and again. They'd flowed across her tongue and poured out of her, each tiny syllable filling her mouth completely, the soft consonants forming between her parted lips. The phrase itself was a verbal caress that sent tiny vibrations through her from the top of her head where it made her scalp tingle, to the tips of her toes that curled in the soles of her sandals. Even her fingertips buzzed a little, and she didn't think it was from the cool night air.

She had to compose herself. Now was not the time to go all gooey brained. She needed to focus on Gramps. She needed to know he was going to be okay.

She walked ahead of Ricky into the hospital room, and even though he wasn't touching her, she was acutely aware of him right behind her. She reached back instinctively for his hand when she saw her grandfather, his poor battered face, a large gauze pad taped to his forehead where he'd split it open on the edge of the shovel when he'd fallen. His left eye was all shades of purple and red bruising, and dried blood still clung to his eyebrow below the bandage and in the creases and wrinkles around his eye. The hair at his left temple was also matted with dried blood, and Granny G reached up and pulled a piece of a leaf from the messy strands. His bottom lip was split, and there was an abrasion on his chin. In her mind's eye, Gia replayed his fall again. He'd gone down hard, without making any effort to catch himself, completely out even before he hit the ground.

Gramps looked so fragile laid out in the hospital bed, IVs and monitors hooked up to various parts of him, his skin, except for the bruising, sallow and almost blue-tinged. At least they'd replaced the oxygen mask with a nasal cannula, and the bulky neck brace was gone, too. Both good signs. Regardless, he seemed terribly old and sick, not at all like the patriarchal Rock of Gibraltar he'd always been in her mind. His eyelids fluttered open as she approached the side of the bed and touched his shoulder. He lifted a hand toward her, but he didn't really smile. Presumably because of his busted lip.

"Hey Gramps," she murmured, curling her fingers around his chilled ones while carefully avoiding bumping the IV taped in place over his wrist. She eyed the two pouches of liquid hanging on an IV pole near the head of his bed and followed the plastic tubing that fed the pharmaceutical cocktail directly into his bloodstream via the needle stuck in one of the many prominent veins on the back of his hand. "At least they didn't have any trouble getting a good line on you." Dehydrated or not, her grandfather had vampire fantasy veins.

"Gia pet." His voice was gruff, raspy, and he sounded exhausted, or in pain. Probably both. "I'm sorry I scared you," he began.

"Hush, Gramps," she interrupted. "I'm the one who should be sorry for hitting you in the face with that shovel while you lay on the ground all helpless and stuff." It was a terrible attempt at humor, but she didn't want to start crying again.

Gramps chuckled and then grimaced, and he lifted his other hand to his mouth. "Don't make me laugh."

"Sorry," she murmured. "Do you need some water?"

"Please," he said, blinking slowly. Granny G reached for a full plastic cup on a hospital tray nearby. She handed it to him without saying a word, and he drank deeply, slowly, and then rested his head back against the pillow. "I'm sorry, folks," he murmured. "I can barely keep my eyes open."

"You can sleep, honey," Granny G said, her tone gentle, soothing. His nurse had assured them that in spite of the concussion, it was no problem for him to sleep. "The doctor will be here shortly, and she can tell us all that we need to know for now. You just rest." She smoothed the hair back from his forehead, her brows furrowed with concern as she studied her husband's face. "I love you, Henry." And almost as an afterthought, she added, "You crazy old man." Gramps didn't open his eyes, but the corners of his mouth hitched up as he turned his face toward the woman he'd been married to for so many years.

Feeling gently dismissed, Gia stepped away from the bed and glanced around the room. Juliette and Renata sat in two chairs against one wall, their heads together, conversing in hushed tones. She could hear Phoebe just outside in the corridor talking to someone, maybe on the phone. For a moment, Gia didn't know what to do with herself, where she belonged, a feeling that was becoming all too familiar these days.

Ricky took her hand and drew her over to an empty chair in one corner near the door. "Sit," he said, moving to stand behind the chair.

Gia hesitated briefly, about to ask him where he was going to sit if she took the only chair, but the look in his eyes brooked no argument. And when she thought about it, she really didn't want to argue with him at that moment, anyway. She dropped into the seat and sighed deeply when his strong hands began to gently knead her shoulders.

"I'm next," Phoebe said as she reentered the room and eyed the two of them, albeit without rancor. They must have taken her spot. She reached up and patted Ricky on the cheek, but all she said was, "You're a good friend, Rick. Gia's lucky to have you."

"Almost as lucky as Trevor is to have you," Ricky returned, his smile as genuine as his words.

Gia lowered her gaze to the floor, not wanting Phoebe to guess what she was thinking, something her sister seemed to do easily enough. Was Ricky comparing their relationship to the white hot one Phoebe and Trevor shared? Whenever the two lovebirds were in the same room, the air itself seemed to smolder and shimmer around them. Gia knew Trevor had some pretty strict rules for himself when it came to dating and abstinence and sex being intended for marriage, but there were times when she wanted to holler at them to just get a room already and put everyone out of their misery. Fortunately for all, Phebes and Trevor were to be married in May, but Gia secretly wondered if things would get worse before they got better once the couple was allowed to have their way with each other.

Could things be like that between Gia and Ricky? All hot and bothered and intense? Did she want everyone to look at them the way they all looked at Phebes and Trevor, half pitying, half amused, and half in wonder?

"Wait. That's three halves." She didn't realize she'd spoken out loud until Ricky interrupted her train of thought, making her jump.

"What did you say?"

"Nothing." She shook her head and muttered, "Just thinking out loud, that's all. Stupid stuff." She should be thinking about Gramps, not about getting all hot and bothered with Ricky. Geez. Talk about self-centered.

Phoebe smoothed a hand over Gia's curls and then crouched down in front of her. "You holding up, Gia pet?" she asked, using her grandfather's endearment. "Gramps is as tough as a piece of old shoe leather. You know that, right?"

Gia met her gaze and nodded, feeling the tears well up again. "I'm just glad he's going to be okay," she whispered. She was also glad all three of her sisters had dropped what they were doing and come at a moment's notice. After her behavior at their G-FOURce the night before, there'd been a moment when she'd worried that they might think twice about coming to her aid. She knew that was silly. The four of them had endured much more difficult things than one sister throwing a temper tantrum, but this was the first time it had been Gia throwing the fit.

Phoebe straightened up and cupped Gia's face in her hands. "You *are* a good girl, Gia. You're a good granddaughter, a good sister, just like we've said to you your whole life." She was clearly referring to Gia's meltdown last night, but before Gia could speak, she continued, leaning closer. "And you're a good daughter, too. Maman would have been proud of you today."

The words, intended to comfort, made Gia lash out childishly. "No, I'm not. I'm mean and impatient and fickle and rude and scared out of my mind half the time. I'm angry and stubborn, and—and—I can't make up my mind about anything these days." She spoke softly, but with vehemence, and her words kept coming. "You can say it all you want, but that doesn't make it true."

Phoebe stood and took a deep breath. She glanced over her shoulder at their grandparents and Gia followed her gaze. Gramps seemed completely out, his lips slightly parted, his breathing steady, if a little shallow, and Granny G was bent over a folder of paperwork in her lap. She didn't fool anyone; the girls knew full well that their grandmother had the keenest hearing of them all. Phoebe offered Gia her hand. "Come out in the hall with me, okay?"

"I don't want to miss the doctor." Stubborn. Yep.

"Unless she uses a teleportation device to get in here, we won't miss her," Phoebe insisted, now waving her hand in Gia's face. "Come on. We'll stand right outside the door."

Gia finally took her sister's hand and stood to follow her. "If I'm not back in a few minutes, call security," she said to Ricky over her shoulder. He grinned and nodded and took the chair she'd vacated.

"I'll keep your seat nice and warm for you," he quipped, the concern on his face softening with his teasing. "Just the way you like it."

Both Gia and Phoebe wrinkled their noses and said, "Ew," sounding just like the sisters they were.

Out in the hall, Phoebe turned to face her. "Listen, I'm sorry about last night. I'm sorry I haven't been more sensitive to what you've been feeling about all of this. You're right about me, Gia. I'm really good at making things all about me, but I'm also really tired of it, and I have a feeling everyone else is, too. So forgive me, okay?"

Gia nodded, a little ashamed over the way she'd verbally jabbed at Phoebe. "I'm sorry, too. I wasn't very nice to you."

Phoebe waved her apology away. "I needed to hear it, and besides, I'm almost as tough as that old man in there."

Gia snorted. "You can say *that* all you want, too, but that doesn't make it true, either."

"Touché." Phoebe reached up to pat Gia's cheek the way she'd done to Ricky only moments earlier. "Regardless, you have a right to your feelings, which doesn't make you a bad person, Gia. You don't have to go to Alice's with us. We all understand, I promise. So will Alice. And when Angela gets home, she'll just have to deal with what she gets. It's your decision and no one else's." Phoebe took her by the shoulders, and even though she was several inches shorter than Gia, she wore platform heels today, so she was almost able to look her in the eye. "Okay? This is your decision, and no matter what you choose, we love you." She shook her a little. "And you're not allowed to feel guilty about saying no or guilted into saying yes, you hear?"

Gia nodded again, slowly. The stubborn creature inside still scrabbled to get out, but she only said, "I'll think about it, but I probably won't go this weekend. I want to be here for Gramps and Gran."

"You're absolutely right. Whether they keep him here for a while or he gets to go home, they'll need you." Phoebe hugged her quickly, then stepped back again. "Jules, Ren, and I will go this first time, okay? We'll scope it out, and if Angela is a freak of nature, it'll be the last time, too."

Gia nodded, hating the rush of relief that washed over her as Phoebe made the decision for her. Somewhere buried deep in the back of her mind lay the knowledge that she was just putting off the inevitable. Because if Angela Clinton wasn't a freak of nature—and all evidence pointed to her being anything but—there was no reason to believe this first dinner together would be the last.

THIRTY-ONE

When Dr. Rainey bustled into the room and approached Gramps' bed, Gia and Phoebe in tow, Ricky caught himself staring in appreciation. *Hello, Dr. Marilyn Monroe.* A remarkably well-endowed woman dressed all in black under her long lab coat, her lips a blood-red, and soft blonde curls framing her feminine features, the good doctor was not what he'd been expecting at all.

Unfortunately, Phoebe caught him staring. Arching an eyebrow at him, she chucked him under the chin, making his teeth clack together loudly enough for Gia to turn and cast him a curious look over her shoulder. Apparently, his mouth had been hanging open to boot. Phoebe just smiled and winked at him and then gave Gia a nudge in the shoulder.

"Keep a move on, Gia. I don't want to miss anything." They gathered close around the bed with the other Gustafson womenfolk to hear what the doctor had to say. It looked like it took some effort, but even Gia's grandfather kept his eyes open, his attention focused on the doctor. Ricky didn't blame him, not one bit.

He had no reason to believe that Gia was the jealous type, but he didn't want to give her any reason to be, especially after the way he'd acted about Barista Boy last week. In fact, knowing Gia, the minute Dr. Rainey left the room, she'd probably make some comment about how amazing the woman looked. But he wasn't stupid; he knew quite well that it had to be her pointing it out, not him.

He shifted forward in his chair and braced his elbows on his knees, watching the faces of the family he'd grown to love as much as—or even more than—his own over the years. He witnessed their relief as Dr. Rainey assured them that although Mr. Gustafson's lungs were not exactly clear, nor were they compromised enough to warrant putting him on intravenous antibiotics.

"If we start you on an IV course, you'll be stuck here for a minimum of 72 hours, possibly more," she explained. "But you, sir, need to rest, sleep, eat healthy food, drink lots of fluids, and get an inordinate amount of TLC from people who love you." She darted looks at the attentive faces gathered around the old man in the bed. "You'll only get a meager portion of that if I keep you here, you know. Ironically, hospitals are notorious for being the worst place to recuperate." She laughed softly, and Ricky found himself smiling along with the rest of the family. He liked her, and not just because she looked the way she did. Dr. Rainey really seemed to care what was best for Gramps.

She turned to Granny G and continued, and Ricky saw that Gramps was starting to drift off again. "Instead, I've ordered an antibiotic shot to get him started. The treatment might be considered unnecessarily aggressive if he only suffered from a mild case of pneumonia or only the laceration, but because he presents with both, because of his weakened immune system from having had pneumonia earlier this year, and the open wound having been caused by a dirty tool, I'm opting for aggression."

Slipping on a pair of gloves from a wall dispenser nearby, she gently peeled up one side of the gauze bandage they'd applied after suturing the wound in the ER. "They did a nice job," she said, before pressing the tape back in place. "I do, however, feel that it's necessary to keep you here overnight, just to make certain you're responding well to the antibiotics and to monitor you for any lingering symptoms of your concussion. Your CT scan came back looking good, but because of the way things happened, I think it's best to be extra cautious. Is that all right with you?"

"Works for me," his wife answered for him. The four sisters nodded in agreement.

"However," Dr. Rainey said, eyeing Granny G with a stern expression. "This good man must follow my instructions without exception, or we'll most assuredly see him back in here in no time." She placed a hand on Gramps' shoulder, and when he opened his eyes, she leveled her gaze at him. "Mr. Gustafson, I can tell you're the kind of man who doesn't go down easily. Which means that you probably did too much and then waited too long to ask for help. That can't happen again, okay?"

Dr. Rainey had him pegged to a T, Ricky thought.

Gramps reached up and patted the woman's hand. "Got it, doc."

"That means no strenuous activity, no gardening, no walking the dog, no climbing trees, no racing cars on the boulevard for at least a week, you understand?"

"No sexy time with Gran, Gramps," Phoebe interjected.

"Phoebe Gustafson!" her grandmother admonished, but Ricky thought he heard a hint of humor in the woman's voice.

"Ew, Phoebe. Why do you always have to go there?" Ren asked from where she stood at the foot of the bed beside Juliette.

"She's right, though," Dr. Rainey agreed, not missing a beat. "Nothing that might require heavy breathing until your lungs are no longer threatening mutiny."

Ricky grinned at the woman's forthright mannerisms, because if he knew Gia's grandfather at all, the old man would appreciate the doctor's dry wit and blunt talk.

"All in all, I'm pleased to say I see no reason you shouldn't have a full recovery, Mr. Gustafson," Dr. Rainey concluded as she waved a hand to indicate the bandage covering the forehead injury. "You'll have a dashing scar, but other than that, I think you'll be just fine."

After the doctor cleared out, Eunice, the nurse assigned to him, showed up to get Gramps settled in for the duration. Juliette and Renata said their goodbyes, and after turning down Ricky's offer to walk them to their cars, they left to return to their own homes.

Phoebe stayed behind to talk to the grandparents about what the next few days would look like for everyone, and Ricky leaned against the wall near the door, for some reason feeling a little like a third wheel.

"Will you need a ride home?" he asked Gia, who stood nearby looking like she, too, wasn't quite sure what her next move was. He wanted to help, but he really had no clue how. Sure, he'd felt the hero when he'd first arrived and Gia had cried on his shoulder, but now that Gramps was likely out of the woods and Gia's relief was evident, he couldn't avoid thinking about the talk they hadn't had. Other than her uncensored admission that she loved him—which, he acknowledged, she'd admitted under duress—their last real conversation had been brutal. He didn't want to just pick up where they'd left off. No, he wanted to take things in a new direction, which meant they really needed to have that talk. So now he found himself walking on eggshells again, and he hated it. This was Gia. George to his Fred. His Georgy Girl.

"No," she said, shaking her head contemplatively. "We drove in my car and I need it for tomorrow."

"Oh. Okay." He watched in silence as Eunice took Gramps's blood pressure and temperature. Then she handed him a menu and told him he could still order something for dinner if he was hungry.

"One of tonight's options was beef stew and biscuits," Eunice said. "And I can assure you that it's not your stereotypical hospital food. Everything is prepared from scratch in our own kitchen, and since you don't have any diet restrictions, I highly recommend it."

"You should eat, Henry," Granny G encouraged him.

The thought of food made Ricky's mouth water. He was starving.

"I'm starving," Gia whispered, as though reading his thoughts. "Do you want to go back down to the cafeteria and get something to eat?"

Ricky pushed off the wall, straightening with relief. "Absolutely." Turning to Granny G and Phoebe, he asked, "I'm taking Gia to get some food. Do you ladies want us to bring something back up for you?"

Phoebe declined, having just made plans to meet up with Trevor for a late dinner, but Granny G asked for a turkey sandwich.

As they made their way through the corridors, the awkwardness lingered. Ricky shoved his hands in his jeans' pockets, not sure if he should touch Gia now that the crisis with her grandfather had been averted. She seemed reserved, distant, and he couldn't quite figure out how to breach whatever had arisen between them.

"So are you going to work tomorrow, then?" he finally asked, and then wished he could suck the words back in. The last thing he wanted was for her to assume he'd been thinking about her work and the arguments they'd had.

"Yeah, I think I will, especially since Dr. Rainey said he's going to be okay, and he needs to rest. If I take the day off to hang out with him, I'll probably drive him crazy. You know me; I can't sit still and be quiet to save my life."

He chuckled softly. It was true; as much as she loved her movies, she could hardly manage to make it through one without talking. They'd been asked to leave more than one movie in their downtown theater. "You going to head out after we eat, then?" He just assumed they'd get their meals to go and head back up to eat in the room.

"I'll probably hang out with Gran for a bit. I doubt she'll sleep here tonight, but I don't think she'll be ready to leave any time soon." She turned to him as they approached the entrance to the cafeteria. "I hope you'll stay and eat with us, Ricky, but you don't have to hang out after that."

Ricky nodded, trying not to take her obvious dismissal personally. "Sure. I've got some homework I need to finish, so I'll head out in a little bit."

Then, as though she sensed that she'd hurt his feelings, she reached over and tugged his hand from his pocket, lacing her fingers with his. "Come on," she murmured. "We have a turkey sandwich to deliver."

On their way back to the elevator, both of them laden with trays of food, Gia said, "I might see if Ricardo will let me leave once Brad gets there." She frowned and pushed the UP button with her elbow, then stood back to wait. She sighed. "It's just that Friday afternoon is always really busy."

Jupiter. Merely the thought of Barista Boy made his stomach lurch, but he cleared his throat and asked, "What about Jupiter? Could he fill in for you?"

Gia lifted startled eyes to his. "Oh! I hadn't even thought of Jupiter."

"The sweetest words I've ever heard," Ricky muttered, not caring if Gia heard him or not.

For a moment, she just stared at him, and then, for the first time all evening, she laughed out loud. It might have been the sweetest sound he'd ever heard, too.

THIRTY-TWO

To Gia's dismay, Ricardo called her early the next morning to tell her he'd picked up some kind of flu bug that had him flat on his back. "I spoke to Jupiter and he'll cover me for the rest of the weekend, but he's not sure he can get out here until about seven this evening. Can you stay until then?" He sounded absolutely miserable, and because Ricardo was never sick, Gia didn't have the heart to tell him about her own woes.

When she informed her grandmother about Ricardo's predicament, Gran waved her off with a reassuring smile. "I already spoke to your grandfather this morning, and I believe he's doing just fine." She chuckled softly, and Gia was relieved to see that although Gran looked tired, she also seemed more at ease than she had last night. Gramps had spiked a low-grade fever a couple hours after Ricky left, and although the doctor attributed it to his body doing what it needed to do to fight off infection, she'd made the decision to keep him an additional twenty-four hours. "He asked me to bring him his own clothes, his own pillow, and his house shoes if he was going to endure another night in the clinker. His word, not mine," she added.

Jupiter called just after five to let her know he was on his way. Gia was taking a short break—her first all day—and they chatted a few minutes about how his week had gone. When he asked her about her own, she hesitated only briefly before telling him about her grandfather's injury.

"Does Ricardo know about your grandfather? He said nothing to me. I could have come earlier, Gia," he said adamantly.

"No, I didn't tell him," she admitted. "He sounded awful. Are you going to check on him before you come here?"

"No, no. I cannot get sick," Jupiter said. "My uncle promised me he is resting. His neighbor brought him soup, he said." He chuckled. "His neighbor likes to look after Ricardo."

Gia's eyebrows rose in question. "Really? Is this neighbor, by any chance, a woman?"

"A very persistent woman," he attested. "He is in good hands, I assure you."

Gia thought Jupiter might mean that literally.

"I will get there as quickly as I can, okay?"

Jupiter arrived about fifteen minutes before seven, sweeping into the cafe with his air of international appeal and ridiculous self-confidence. Gia couldn't help but smile at him from where she stood on the other side of the counter, and he, in turn, had eyes only for her.

"Gia. I am here now." He came around the end of the counter toward her and reached out to cup her face in his hands, his palms cool against her suddenly flushed cheeks. "Are you alright?" He dipped his head and gazed directly into her eyes.

"I'm fine," she assured him, wrapping her fingers around his wrists and pulling his hands away from her face. She wouldn't have minded his single-minded attention so much, except that the whole place had gone quiet as the customers watched the scene play out.

"How is your grandfather? Have you spoken to him? And your grandmother?"

"Everyone is doing well, all things considered," she said. Turning to Brad, who was stocking pastries nearby, she said, "Can you take over my register?" When he nodded, she headed back to the break room to gather her things. She knew Jupiter would follow her.

"Thank you so much for coming, Jupiter," Gia said as she pulled from her locker the denim jacket she'd stashed there when she'd arrived that morning. He stepped forward and took it, holding it for her while she slipped her arms into the sleeves. "I hope you didn't leave your aunt high and dry for tonight." She would feel terrible if she'd made things more difficult than they already were for him and his family.

"No, no. It worked out well. My aunt is taking the children to their grandparents' home in San Diego for the weekend, so I am free to help Ricardo until Monday."

Gia was greatly relieved. "Well, thank you all the same."

"It is no trouble. Now you must go to your grandparents and give them my best regards, okay?" He cupped her chin in one hand and lifted her face so their eyes met. "I forbid you to think of Ricardo's again for the rest of the weekend." Then he winked at her. "But you may think of me all you want."

Gia smirked and then nodded. "Of course," she said. For a moment, his gaze dropped to her mouth, and she wondered—surely he wouldn't—if he was going to kiss her. Then he surprised her by stepping back and gesturing toward the door. "I will walk you to your car, okay?"

Once she was settled in her front seat and Jupiter had closed the car door for her, a wave of fatigue washed over her. She leaned her head back against the headrest and took a deep breath, letting it out slowly before she stuck her keys in the ignition. She'd slept poorly the night before, partly because she'd been attentive of her grandmother's restlessness. Around two in the morning, Gia had gotten up to use the bathroom and had found Granny G in the dark kitchen, standing at the sink and peering out the window at the backyard. It occurred to Gia that her grandmother must have seen Gramps go down, too. By the time Gia had made it to his side, Granny G had already been hurrying out the back door.

Gia had made them both a cup of tea, and then crawled into the big bed beside her grandmother, her head resting on her grandfather's pillow. It smelled like him, so familiar and unchanging, like old man aftershave and decades of life experience. Gia breathed it in and reached over to take Granny G's hand beneath the covers, acutely aware of how fragile it seemed, how in the dark, she no longer recognized her grandmother's hand in hers. She lifted a silent prayer: healing for Gramps, peace for Gran, sleep for them all.

She'd eaten a sandwich at Ricardo's, so she headed straight to the hospital. She was half afraid the sight of her own bed would lure her in if she stopped by the house first.

Gramps' room was full, not just with family members—Tim and Ren were there with all five of their kids—but also visiting was the pastor and his wife from their church, as well as their neighbor from across the street, Mrs. Sherwood.

Renata took one look at Gia, and in a tone that brooked no argument, she said, "Half an hour for you, missy, then you're going straight home to bed."

Like a good girl, Gia didn't argue. She did stay a little longer than half an hour, but that was only because she fell asleep in her chair, and Ren had been out walking the corridors with a fussy baby and had lost track of time.

The house was quiet when she got home, and it occurred to her that she hadn't heard from Ricky all day. She dug her phone out of her bag and groaned when she saw the unresponsive screen. In all the hullabaloo the night before, she'd forgotten to charge it. She plugged it in and jumped in the shower; she'd call him as soon as she got out.

Sure enough, Ricky had tried to contact her several times throughout the day. She hurried into her comfortable old flannel pajamas and flopped back on her bed before dialing Ricky's number.

"Gia!" He answered after the first ring. "Is everything okay?"

She felt awful for making him worry. "I'm sorry I didn't call you earlier. My phone died, and I had to work late because Ricardo got really sick, and then I fell asleep at the hospital, so Ren sent me home. But everything is fine, though, I promise."

"Aw, man, Gia. Don't apologize. I was just worried, but I'm glad you're okay." He hesitated, and then in a voice that sounded a little unsure, he added, "I'm pulling up outside your house."

"Oh." Gia sat up and ran a hand through her hair. "Oh," she said again.

"When I hadn't heard from you, I finally just drove to the hospital. Your grandma sent me to check on you since you weren't answering her calls either."

Gia groaned. "That's all she needs, to worry about me, too. I'd better call her." She pushed off the bed and crossed to her dresser to look at herself in the mirror. "Want to come in?" she asked into the phone, frowning at her reflection. There were shadows under her eyes and her flannels were ancient—she and Juliette had bought matching puppy pajamas years ago for one of their movie marathon sleepovers—and her hair was still wet, but at least she smelled good.

"Sure."

While she dialed her grandmother's phone, she padded down the hall and through the living room, into the entryway and to the front door, feeling her weariness in her bones. She pulled it open just as Granny G picked up. Waving Ricky inside, she greeted her grandmother and apologized for her dead phone. "Ricky just got here," she said in response to Gran's question. "Yeah, maybe we'll watch a movie or something until you get home." She glanced over at Ricky; her eyebrows raised in question.

"That's fine." Ricky nodded. "I can hang out."

She hung up and turned toward the kitchen, expecting Ricky to join her. But instead, he grabbed her wrist, pulling her up short.

"Hey," he said, his voice gentle, husky. "Come here." He pulled her toward him, drawing her into his arms. Sliding her hands around his waist, she sagged against him, resting her head on his shoulder, her nose pressed into his neck, the curve of his collarbone against her cheek.

"I don't know how much longer my legs will hold me up," she murmured. "Will you catch me if they give out?"

"Yes," he said, his arms tightening around her. "I'll always catch you. It's what I do best."

She pondered that a moment, unsure whether she should be offended or not. She leaned her head back to look up at him. "Always? Do I ask too much of you, Ricky? I mean, do I—do I take you for granted?"

For a long moment, he just looked at her, but in his eyes, she saw his answer before he spoke. In a whisper, he said, "You don't ask enough of me, Gia."

And then he kissed her.

THIRTY-THREE

AND THEN *SHE* KISSED him.

He might have made the first move, sure, but there was no doubt in his mind that she was kissing him back. Her fingers clutched at the back of his shirt like she was holding on for dear life, and her knees did, in fact, buckle.

Somewhere through the fog in his mind, it occurred to him that his knees were a little shaky, too, and he tightened his hold around her, feeling every curve of her pressed into him, her firm breasts, the ridge of her hip bones against his own, her thighs mirroring the length of his. And when she sighed against his mouth, he echoed her, but in a deeper, more animal-like sound. *Hungry,* he thought, the word moving sluggishly through his senses. *Yeah, weak-kneed and ravenous.*

In a move so smooth one would think he'd rehearsed it, he slid an arm under Gia's knees and scooped her up against him. Then he staggered. Just a little, but enough to make his eyes snap open. "Geez, you're heavy," he muttered, and then kissed her again, realizing that might not have been the best choice of words, hoping she'd been so caught up in the moment she hadn't noticed what he'd said. Could he make it to the sofa without dropping her?

He felt her smile against his mouth, and then her lips traveled slowly away from his, moving in a path along his jaw to the column of his neck where he was sure she would feel the throb of his pulse as his blood raced through his veins.

Yes. Definitely, yes. He'd make it or die trying. A rush of adrenaline coursed through him. He could do this. He could.

"Ricky?" she whispered; her breath hot on his skin.

"Yeah?" He was having a hard time concentrating with her nuzzling the sensitive hollow just below his ear. He took another step.

"Put me down," she said into his neck.

"What?" Her words registered, but he couldn't seem to make sense of them. "Why?"

"Because you're going to hurt yourself," she murmured, pressing a kiss up under his chin.

"No, I won't," he said, now feeling rather indignant. He took another step, then another. Dang it, she was challenging his manhood. Right in the middle of the most romantic move he'd ever made, she was doubting his ability to carry this through. Quite literally, in fact. "I'm perfectly capable of carrying you across the room."

She started to wiggle.

"Stop squirming," he growled. "If I *do* drop you—which I won't—it'll be your fault."

She kept jostling around. And then he realized she was laughing.

Laughing!

"Are you laughing at me?" he asked, his voice tight with effort and chagrin. "Seriously?"

For whatever reason, that made her laugh even harder. "Put—put me down," she chortled, trying to swing one leg out of his grip. "Your face is turning red."

"No. Absolutely not." He was determined to prove her wrong. "You just need to hang onto me." And with that, he clutched her tighter, and practically lurched across the living room. He bumped the corner of the coffee table with his knee and grunted angrily, but he made it.

And she was still cackling like a crazy person, her whole body shaking convulsively, her arms wrapped around his neck.

"Geez, Gia. Let go now," he ordered, trying not to pant with exertion.

"No," she snorted, clinging more tightly to him. "You're going to drop me."

"I'll drop you either way, but at least if you let go, I won't fall on top of you," Ricky snapped, not quite sure if he was really angry at her or not. He was sure of something else, though. He couldn't hold her like this much longer.

"Say 'please,'" she teased, and began trailing kisses up his neck again toward his ear. When her teeth closed lightly on his lobe, he yelped... and the arm under her legs loosened its hold.

He didn't drop her after all, not exactly. As if someone had hit the slow-motion button, she lowered her feet to the floor, so that she stood on tiptoe, her arms still looped around his neck, her eyes only inches from his and crinkled with laughter. "That was very sweet, Rickaroni," she murmured, and then she kissed him again, this time more forcefully, her mouth exploring his, testing and tasting....

Wait.

Sweet? She thought his gallant effort was sweet?

But he found he didn't have the wherewithal to be offended—his hands settled into her low back, his fingertips splayed wide, brushing the top of her backside—not when she was kissing him like that. He clutched at her hips, pulling her roughly against him. She was leaning fully into him... *trusting* him to catch her.

Dang it. He groaned, and even to his own ears he sounded like a man in pain. He slid his hands back into a safe—*safer*—zone, bringing them to rest at her waist, his palms on her hipbones, putting the tiniest space between them.

Gia lifted her gaze to his. "Are you o—okay?" She stumbled over her words; she sounded winded, or startled, her voice came out breathy and uneven.

"I need—you need to—you're tired," he finished lamely, trying to garner the will to wrench himself away from her. "I need a drink," he declared, not sure his own voice sounded any more stable.

Gia leaned back, her eyes wide, and then she brought her hand up, clearly trying not to laugh again. "Am I really such a bad kisser?" she asked, her voice tight with humor. "I think Gran has some medicinal Jack Daniels in the cupboard above the fridge."

"Oh, Mary, Martha, and Lazarus Jones!" Ricky exclaimed, closing his eyes briefly and tipping his head back. "That's not what I meant."

"Maybe it was a Freudian slip," she said. "Or maybe it's a portent, a harbinger. Maybe one day I really will drive you to drink."

"Maybe you should stop talking and kiss me again," Ricky said. But the sight of her eyelids lowering and her mouth opening in acquiescence sent a combination of sheer lust and panic surging through him, and he gripped her waist hard and set her away from him, making her knees bump up against the edge of the sofa behind her.

She sat abruptly.

"Sorry," he murmured, stepping back in response to the overwhelming urge to push her down into the cushions beneath him. "I need to st—stop." It took all his willpower to get the word out. He brushed both hands over his hair, lacing his fingers behind his head, angling slightly away from her lest she see just how badly he wanted to finish what they'd started. "I need to stop," he repeated, a little stronger this time.

"I'm sorry," she whispered from where she sat behind him. But he heard her loud and clear, and those two words made his stomach roil.

"Please don't apologize," Ricky muttered, waffling between anger over his lack of self-control and the desperation wedged against his breastbone making it hard for him to breathe, making him long to throw caution to the wind with her and see just exactly how far this night could take them. "Don't apologize unless you really mean it." He snorted and pressed the heels of his hands to his eyes, then ground out, "Please don't mean it."

After a moment of silence, he lowered his hands and glanced at her over his shoulder. She was looking right at him, her eyes wide, her mouth—*that mouth!*—slightly open like she was trying to speak but the words hadn't quite formed on her tongue yet. Her expression, however, wasn't apologetic. She looked... *pleased* with herself.

"I'm not sorry you kissed me, that I kissed you, if that's what you're worried about," she finally said. "I'm not sorry we got each other all hot and bothered and—and *stuff*." She was blushing, but when she didn't look away, he moved toward one of the easy chairs close by and lowered himself into it. "In fact, I'm glad, because I've been worried about that for a while now."

Ricky raised his eyebrows in question. "Worried about what?"

"That all that stuff might not work right for us," she said, lifting one hand to wave it back and forth between them. "That I might not turn you on. Or vice versa. You know, since we're practically siblings and all."

Ricky took a slow, deep breath, and then leaned forward in the chair, resting his elbows on his knees, before letting it out. Bowing his head over his hands, and in a voice far calmer than he felt, he said, "I have never, not once, Georgia Amity Gustafson, thought of you as a sibling." Did she get it? Was she hearing him loud and clear? He lifted his gaze to meet hers. "I have always been—" he couldn't say hot and bothered, because that was only the tip of the iceberg where his feelings for her were concerned. "I have always been yours," he finally said. "And I have always wanted you to be mine." He studied her, willing her to understand, and then reiterated, "*Always.*"

"Oh Ricky," she finally said, his name coming out a sigh. "I think I need a drink, too." Gia stood and offered him her hand. "Come on. Let's go make some hot chocolate. I think it might be safer for us in the kitchen."

Ricky wanted to argue—kitchens had counter tops and tables and walls... and, well, Gia would be in there, too. But he swallowed hard, took her hand, and let her lead him into the kitchen, anyway. She only turned on the light over the sink, and for that, he was glad.

"Sit," she instructed, and then headed to the pantry to gather her ingredients. She preferred to make hot chocolate from scratch rather than a mix, and even though it always turned out delicious, she never stuck to a strict recipe, opting to add a dash of this, a smidge of that, according to her moods. The pantry door stood open, hiding her from his view, and Ricky couldn't help wondering what would happen if he followed her inside and pulled the door closed, shutting them together into the tight space.

"You know perfectly well what would happen, mate," he muttered to himself.

Gia stepped out of the tiny room and nudged the door shut with her heel. "What was that?" she asked, her arms full, her smile soft.

"Nothing. Just thinking out loud. Do you need help with all that?" he asked, starting to push to his feet.

"Nope. Sit." Setting her ingredients on the counter next to the stovetop, she began to concoct. Into a large saucepan she poured a couple of cups of milk, followed by a good helping of heavy cream, the stuff Gramps liked on his granola, and began stirring it with a whisk over medium heat. Once it began to steam, she turned the burner down, added part of a can of coconut milk to it, a healthy portion of cocoa powder, a spoonful of almond extract, two broken up cinnamon sticks, and some freshly ground nutmeg. From a drawer in the fridge, she pulled out a ginger root and cut off two slices, peeled them, and tossed them into the pot.

Ricky watched her in silence, growing comfortable with the familiarity of the task she was performing. He couldn't count the times she'd made them her special blend of hot chocolate, how many times he'd sat in this very seat and watched her flit around her grandmother's kitchen like she was doing now. Did she feel how right this was, too?

"Chili pepper?" she asked, turning to look at him over her shoulder. The dim lighting of the room highlighted the weary circles under her eyes, and a blind man would have noticed the slump of her shoulders, the shuffling of her footsteps.

"Just a tiny bit." If Gia had her way, she'd drop a whole dried hot chili in the mix. Ricky didn't mind a hint of spice, but coupled with the bite from the ginger, a little chili pepper could go a long way.

A few moments later, she poured the steaming liquid through a strainer into two tall mugs and brought them to the table. "No marshmallows, sorry."

When she was seated—at the other end of the table from him, far enough away that their knees wouldn't bump and their hands wouldn't accidentally brush, but close enough they could look each other in the eye—Gia took a careful sip of her hot drink and sighed with satisfaction. "Mmm."

"It *is* good," Ricky said, echoing her sentiment. "As usual." He made a show of taking a long sip, and then with a dramatic flair, set the cup on the table, smacking his lips together in satisfaction.

When she registered the wide chocolate mustache on Ricky's upper lip and the taunting challenge in his gaze, her eyes narrowed. She tipped up her mug, taking extra time to coat her own upper lip with the dark liquid, not breaking eye contact with him. He knew she could hardly stand it, the feel of the thick moisture clinging to her face, but he'd thrown down the gauntlet, and she had no choice but to accept the challenge. It was one of the sillier competitions they'd started back in junior high. Who could make the biggest milk-stache, and as they got older, who could leave it on the longest... oh, and if either of them laughed or looked away, it was an automatic win for the other one. Because Ricky's mouth was wider, he usually won by default.

But something in her eyes told him she might just give him a run for his money. Like a chess match, back and forth, first Ricky drank, then Gia, until finally, when he'd taken his last drink and set his cup away from him, she almost laughed. Almost. He'd had a lot of practice at this game over the years—he'd even worked on it in front of his mirror back in the day—so he knew his Fu Manchu with long streaks down either side of his mouth had to be impressive. There really was no way on earth could she top that. She didn't have that much chocolate left in her cup.

She blinked, and then a slow smile lifted the corners of her lips. It kinda scared him, and he found it hard to breathe. It didn't matter one iota that she wore flannel pajamas with floppy-eared puppies all over them, or that she had on no makeup, or that her wet hair and tired eyes made him think more of a damsel in distress than a seductress, because everything about the way she was looking at him made his radar go on high alert. In a voice he thought would make Phoebe proud, she said, "I'm thinking about crawling across this table and licking that stuff off your mouth."

Ricky straightened in his seat as though she'd struck him, and he couldn't help it; he looked away. He lowered his gaze to her mouth, then to the empty cup in his hands, and finally, he closed his eyes altogether, snatched up a paper napkin from the holder in the middle of the table, and dragged it across his face in an attempt to eliminate the temptation.

He could hear the grin in her voice. "So check out my epic stache. Cuz, you know, I win."

"You're a dirty, rotten cheater, Gia," he said, not looking at her.

"What? I broke no rules," she insisted.

When he finally looked at her again, something in his expression gave her pause. She picked up a napkin and made quick work of the mess on her own lip. "What?" she asked, the word laced with trepidation.

"We need to talk." Now. Tonight. He had to know where things stood. There'd be time for games later.

"I know." She practically sighed the words out.

For a moment, Ricky felt guilty. Gia was so tired she was giddy, clearly uninhibited, and he wondered if maybe they should have the conversation another time. But Gramps was getting out of the hospital in the morning, and then Gia would be caught up in caring for him all weekend. Work and school, soccer, and family would consume another week, and pretty soon, they'd just keep putting it off indefinitely. It would never be a good time to talk unless they made it so.

Gia seemed to be thinking the same thing. "I know," she said again.

THIRTY-FOUR

GIA PUSHED TO HER feet and reached across the table to snag Ricky's cup and then took his and hers to the sink to wash them. After she'd set them upside down in the dish drainer, she turned and pressed her back to the counter. Crossing her arms tightly, she said, "Look, I'm not sure I have it in me to have a deep, drawn out discussion tonight, but maybe we can start the conversation tonight—you know, exchange bullet points or something—and pick up when I've had more sleep?" Her hair fell forward as she studied the ground for a moment. "I can go first since you kinda already started things last week." She blushed when she recalled their confrontation in the parking lot of the taco stand, but it seemed so long ago now. Was that only due to her fatigue or because so much had happened since then?

"No," Ricky interjected, his words quiet but forceful. "I'll go first, but you have to look at me." He rose, too, and slowly approached her, stopping only a few feet away from her. He propped his hip on the corner of the table and gripped the edge on either side of him, hunching his shoulders ever so slightly. "Because the only real bullet points I have are that I love you, Gia, and I always have."

He held her gaze, not looking away, his expression so sincere, so intense. The bridge of her nose tingled, and she felt the prickle of tears; she swallowed hard, but she didn't speak.

"I want to go out with you. I want to marry you some day. Tomorrow, next year, next decade, if that's what you want. I want to have your children—" he twitched, and then grinned, and then she snickered. "I mean—"

"I know what you meant," Gia interrupted, overcome, and then she pushed away from the counter and closed the distance between them. She placed her hand over her heart. "I love you, too, Ricky. And if you want my heart, it's yours." She turned her hand up as though she held something fragile in it, and then pressed it against Ricky's chest, spreading her fingers wide, startled to feel his heart thudding almost violently beneath her palm. "There," she whispered. "Now it's right where it belongs, next to yours."

Ricky reached up and covered her hand with his own, his gaze darting to her mouth and then back to her eyes. She felt her lips twitch in a knowing smile. She was fairly sure she was thinking the same thing as he was; now would be a good time to kiss again.

Ricky stood and Gia closed the last of the distance between them, stepping into his embrace, sliding her arms around his waist. They didn't kiss, though. He just held her close, resting his cheek against the top of her head, rocking her slightly from side to side.

"How about a movie?" Gia finally murmured, keeping her voice low so she could listen to his heart beating, strong and sure, if a little fast, beneath her cheek.

"Sounds good to me." Without another word, they headed into the living room and settled into one end of the couch, Ricky's arm around her shoulders. She turned a little so that her back pressed against his chest and leaned her head on his shoulder.

"You choose something," she said, her words just a little bit slurred. "And here's fair warning; I'll probably be asleep in about thirty seconds."

He hugged her more tightly to him. "Sleep, then. I'll be here."

Later, Gia would remember only that he'd turned the television on and pulled up Netflix, but if someone asked, she couldn't say for sure what they'd watched.

Nor did she remember Granny G coming home.

But she *did* remember Ricky making her stand up and walk to her room. "There's no way I'm carrying you," he teased, his voice soft in her ear.

She was pretty sure he'd kissed her goodnight, too.

THIRTY-FIVE

Saturday dawned cheerful and expectant, but Gia awoke slowly, her whole body resistant to leaving sleep behind. Although she didn't feel so bone-weary and out of control as she had over the last week or two—she'd slept like a baby, it seemed—she turned on her side and curled around one of her pillows, burrowing her face beneath it to block the light. She relished the pleasure of not having to haul herself out of bed at the crack of dawn and put on her armor for work, her cheerful smile, and that she didn't have to immediately deal with her hair. She could feel the mess of it beneath her head and around her shoulders; she'd fallen asleep with it still damp and would need the patience of Job to restore order to it.

But there were other things she needed to remember, something they had to do today, something she'd done last night.

Yanking the pillow from her face—she'd been on the verge of suffocating anyway—her eyes flew open, and then she beamed as it all came back to her.

Ricky. Her Rickaroni.

Who would have known that the skinny little kid who'd fallen off his bicycle in front of her would grow up to be quite so scrumptious? And holy smokes! How he could kiss!

"I've been missing out," she murmured into the quiet room. Although he'd always been relatively closemouthed about any love life he had, she was pretty sure Ricky hadn't missed out on much. Maybe that was why he was so good at it. But then, she didn't want to think about any of that right now. All she wanted to think about was him. And her. Him kissing her. Them kissing. No more Fred and George, that was for sure. "We could have been doing that together for years."

The more she thought about it, however, the more determined she became that waiting until now, until after the madness of high school, might not have been such a bad thing after all. She'd seen some tragic demises of friends-to-lovers relationships, breakups that might have been avoided, friendships that might have been preserved, had they stayed out of each other's pants. But the expectation in high school to not just experiment sexually, but to be well-versed in it, coupled with the lack of understanding that intimacy was about far more than getting naked with someone else, put undue pressure on people to take steps they weren't ready to take.

The Christian beliefs Gia had embraced early on taught abstinence, which was all fine and good, but her reasons for doing so were not nearly so high minded. Sure, Gia knew her opinion was antiquated among her peers, but she hadn't wanted to have sex with just anyone. She'd wanted it to be special, with someone she really trusted. Having witnessed so many broken hearts over the years—those of her friends, yes, but also her sisters—she'd decided long ago that trust was even more important than love.

People could justify anything when they were in love. Love colored things, and not always in a good way.

Jules was a perfect example of that; she'd spent almost ten years of her adult life in love with a guy who treated her like crap. Oh sure, at first Mike had been awesome. But over the years, he changed. Juliette, however, hung on, loving him even when he didn't love her, unable to see the truth through her love-tainted lenses. Ren and Phebes? Their relationship had been poisoned by skewed ideals about love and sex and the criminal acts of a fellow student who thought sex was a right, not a precious privilege, and the loss of trust in each other, in the people who loved them, and in the world around them. Their experiences were as different as night and day, but both of them bore wounds that still needed tending, even after all these years.

So, between her misgivings about love and trust based on what she saw in relationships around her, and being terribly self-conscious over the lanky, awkward body she'd been saddled with for most of high school, Gia had been able to avoid the entanglements of angsty high school boyfriend/girlfriend relationships. It had certainly helped that she'd always had friends around to keep her from being too lonely, including Ricky, who was willing to be her partner in crime whenever one was called for.

But just because they were out of high school didn't mean the pressure was off. In some ways, now the pressure felt less like it came from outside influences, but instead, it was her own desires pushing her to experience everything all at once. Ricky's hands on her, so different than they'd always been in the past—sliding over her curves, clutching at her, pulling her to him in ways that shouted desperation—had stirred up a response in her that had been so unexpected and overwhelming and... well, *desperate* too. It had been quite eye opening. What would she have allowed had he not pushed her away first? And this was only their first round of kisses, no less!

Gia sighed blissfully. Oh, what kisses they'd been, too. The best part? Because they'd talked last night, because even though their words had been few, they'd been honest, because they had stopped when they did, she didn't feel guilty about any of it, nor was she afraid of seeing him today. She wasn't worried that he'd changed his mind, or that she'd messed things up, or any of those myriad of things she'd heard her friends bemoan time and time again.

In fact, Gia could hardly wait to see Ricky today. Maybe he'd called or texted; she turned toward her bedside table, but her phone wasn't there. She'd probably left it in the living room last night when she'd fallen asleep against Ricky's chest, a thought that made her sigh again.

Wide awake now, she pushed up out of bed. Gramps would be coming home today, too, and she'd promised Gran she'd be available to help out.

When she got to the kitchen, she was surprised to see Granny G's breakfast bowl and coffee cup already washed and draining in the sink. A note on the counter told Gia to sleep, that Juliette and Vic were going to help get Gramps home this morning, but that if Gia could be there to oversee lunch, that would be lovely. So she made herself a cup of coffee, stuck a couple pieces of bread in the toaster, and went searching for her phone.

She found it in the couch cushions, nearly out of juice from not charging it overnight, but she didn't even have to swipe it on to see several notifications of texts and messages, most of them from Ricky.

Jupiter had texted; she opened his message first and smiled when she read it. *I hope your grandfather is feeling better. Please tell me if you need more time to be home. My aunt has changed plans to have her children visit longer with their grandparents, so I will stay in Midtown with Uncle Ricardo next week.*

She shot him a grateful message back, promising to let him know once her grandfather came home. She had no clue how much help he'd need, but knowing Gramps, he'd not want her to miss work just to keep him company.

A voice message from Jules reiterated what Granny G had said, that she and Vic would help get Gramps home. "I brought a massive spaghetti casserole over this morning and left it in the fridge. It's for lunch, since it sounds like the whole gang is planning to join us there to welcome Gramps home." Gia grinned at the gentle sarcasm in Juliette's voice. "Apparently, we're going to try to wear him out completely his first day home. Make him wish he were back in the quiet of the hospital, you know?" She'd also left instructions to stick the casserole in the oven by eleven if they hadn't gotten home from the hospital yet, but that was it. Gia was footloose and fancy-free for the next hour.

She took a deep breath, surprised to find herself a little trembly, and opened the first text from Ricky.

Good morning, GG. I hope you slept well. Do you need any help today with Gramps?

Half an hour later, he'd sent another one. *Can't stop thinking about you. Don't ever get rid of those puppy PJs. Ever. Call me when you get home from the hospital. I want to help. And see you.*

What was it with guys and ugly pajamas? Vic still claimed his favorite outfit of Juliette's was her fluffy pink bathrobe. And now Ricky was mooning over her ancient flannels.

Two minutes later. *Actually, if I'm being honest, I want to see you. And help. In that order.*

She needed to put him out of his misery. But before she could do more than hit reply, another text came through.

You're awake! Or home from the hospital! Yes, I've been checking my phone every 30 seconds, I admit it, so I know you've read my messages.

Gia giggled and hit her call button. Texts were fine, but she suddenly wanted to hear his voice.

"Hey there, Georgy Girl." Ricky answered after the first ring.

"Hey there, Rickaroni-Baloney."

There was an awkward silence, and then they both began speaking at once.

"So how is Gramps—"

"Do you want to—"

After an even more awkward bout of chuckling, Ricky told her to go first.

"I'm actually here at the house. Granny G let me sleep in since Jules and Vic are going to help her get Gramps home. You want to come over and wait here with me?" The moment the words were out, she wondered how good an idea it was inviting him over when the house was empty. And suddenly, Trevor's rule about not being alone with a woman behind closed doors made a whole lot more sense than it ever had.

"I wish I could, but I'm working this morning," Ricky said. A wave of relief washed over Gia, followed quickly by disappointment.

"Oh." The word came out like a deflated balloon.

Ricky chuckled into the phone. "Don't worry. I'll come over as soon as I get off at noon, okay? Can I bring you lunch?"

"Jules made a massive casserole for everyone. You're invited." She smiled, fairly giddy with pleasure. "You're always invited."

"I'll run home first and shower, okay? Changing tires is dirty work." He said his goodbyes, and Gia released a happy sigh.

That gave her all the time she needed to do something with her hair, find the perfect outfit to wear.... She paused, considering her motives. Ricky had seen her in just about everything she owned, but still, she felt pretty today, and she wanted to look good, too. "I'm dressing up for me," she decided, and then said again, "For me."

THIRTY-SIX

The front door opened at 11:30 AM to let Ren and her troop pile inside the house. Renata carried a huge basket in her arms; Gia saw it contained a mountain of Ren's homemade 'healthy' cookies, as well as a box or two of Gramps' favorite Little Debbie treats, several books, and a few other things she'd have to check out when Ren put the basket down somewhere. There was also one of those fancy fruit-infusion water bottles tucked into one corner. Gia made a mental note to keep track of that in particular; she doubted Gramps would take much interest in using it except for when he knew Ren would make an appearance, but Gia would put it to good use when he wasn't.

She snatched Charise out of Tim's arms, sniffed her head with great gusto, and then nuzzled her in the neck, causing the baby to snort and giggle, and then greeted the boys in a much more subdued manor. She got grunts from the older two, both of whom had white cords hanging from the earbuds in their ears, and a quick hug and hello from the always warmhearted Levi. Judah, almost six, hugged her tightly around the waist, bumping Charise's diapered bottom with the top of his head. "Butthead, butthead, butthead," he chanted as he repeated the motion over and over again.

"Judah!" Renata chided, but Gia had to close her eyes so she wouldn't laugh out loud at the mixture of disapproval and humor on her sister's face. Judah shot his mother a halfhearted apology and loped off to follow Tim who was herding the boys into the living room. The poor kid was always in trouble for something, and Gia was pretty sure his "Sorry" was more rote than repentance.

A few minutes later, Trevor and Phoebe arrived. Phoebe brought a huge green salad in one of her fancy hand-thrown pottery bowls. She commandeered the baby, but Gia didn't mind. She loved watching Phoebe with Charise, knowing that her sister was regaining some of the experiences she'd missed out on after giving up her own daughter so many years ago.

"Hey, Taz—Trevor." She still called him by his old nickname every once in a while, but he insisted he didn't mind. She gave him a quick hug after handing over the baby to Phoebe.

"Hey, Gia. I hear Ricky's coming over."

Gia turned sharply at his tone. She felt her cheeks warm at the teasing glint in Trevor's eye, followed by the grin he exchanged with Phoebe. But she only nodded and said, "Yep. When he gets off work." Then she slipped away to the kitchen to check on the casserole.

Of course, Ricky had told Trevor; she knew how close the cousins were. In fact, Trevor quite likely had known about Ricky's feelings for Gia, long before Gia had. But still, it was all so new and unexplored inside of her, and she wasn't yet ready to bring anyone else into her bubble of happiness.

"My bubble of happiness," she said out loud to the casserole, as she stuck a knife into the middle of it to see if it was heated through yet. When she pulled the knife out, the layer of cheese that had puffed up in several places deflated, hissing and sputtering a little. "Nothing can pierce my bubble of happiness though," she insisted. "All is well in my little world today."

Right before noon, Gramps and his entourage made it home safely. Except for the horrible discoloring on his face and a brace strapped to his arm—apparently, he'd fallen on his left arm and strained his wrist—he walked steady and tall, not looking the least bit weak or out of breath.

"Thank the good Lord, I'm home!" he declared when he stood inside the foyer surveying all that he held dear before him. Then he was ushered into the living room and escorted to his recliner. He lowered himself gingerly and released an exaggerated sigh of contentment.

The women booted all the men and Charise—who sat on Gramps' lap and stared at his face with wide eyes—out of the kitchen so they could ready the feast. Without waiting for instructions, Ren and Phoebe set to work enlarging the table while Juliette brought the extra panel inserts out from the pantry. Gia slipped around behind her and grabbed the last panel, along with a stack of paper plates, bumping the door shut with her heel on her way out.

How many meals, how many memories had been made in that small kitchen, the five of them weaving in and out of each other's way, working together, creating together, doing life together.

Gia set the plates on the counter while her sisters maneuvered the table and then headed to the refrigerator to get the iced tea she'd made earlier and shoved into the freezer to chill faster. Tea in hand, she smiled and paused to look around at the warriors who made up her clan. It didn't matter that she was nothing like her older sisters on the outside, or even Granny G, for that matter. It didn't matter that she was more than a decade younger than them, or that Granny G was four times her age. What mattered was on the inside, in their hearts. She didn't just love these women; she trusted them with her life. This was family—*her* family—and she liked it just fine.

"So, guess what?" she said over the rise and fall of their conversations. The words were out before she could let herself think too much about it.

The kitchen fell silent, and Gia tightened her hold on the gallon jug of iced tea. She took a shaking breath in an attempt to bolster her courage.

"What is it, sweetie?" Granny G asked, stepping closer and putting a hand on her arm.

Phoebe, too, waltzed up to her, but she had a knowing grin on her face as she gestured for the pitcher of tea. "Would you like me to take that, so you don't drop it? Your hands are shaking."

Gia almost pulled it out of reach. That little girl she'd been, the kid sister always underfoot, wanted to stick her tongue out at Phoebe, too. But she let Phoebe take the tea, and then wiped her palms on her flowery skirt... beneath which she wore a purple ruffled underskirt, just for old time's sake.

"What is it?" Granny G asked again, but her tone was no longer worried, not after seeing Phoebe's face.

"I just want you all to hear it from me, okay? And please don't tease him."

"Tease him? Who are we talking about?" Ren asked from where she stood at the counter mashing a banana for Charise.

"Ricky. We're kinda—well, we're, um, you know." She pinched the bridge of her nose between thumb and forefinger and tried again. "We—I like him. We like each other. A lot."

Juliette, digging at the back of the silverware drawer for the extra utensils, grinned, but said nothing. Phoebe snorted.

"Well, I like him, too," Granny G said. "But you already knew that. He's a good friend."

Gia studied her grandmother. Was she really that clueless? No, she had to be teasing her. Or was she giving her blessing? "You know what I mean, Gran. We're, um—" What were they? He hadn't officially asked her out, had he? And just because they'd said they loved each other didn't make them boyfriend and girlfriend. Or exclusive, for that matter. Maybe she should have waited to get the details from him before she blurted this whole thing out to her family.

"You're *in* love?" Granny G asked. "I already knew that, sweetie."

"Me, too," Phoebe quipped, sidling up next to Ren, both of them now leaning against the counter with their arms crossed in a pose Gia could only describe as smug.

"Yep," Renata chimed in. "Nothin' new here, girlie."

"So did I." Juliette had started setting out the silverware around the big table, but she stopped and looked at Gia. The smile was still there, and Gia thought she saw a glisten of tears in her oldest sister's eyes. "Do you remember that Champion Qualities List we made up after the cockamamie Monday ManDates Intervention failed royally?"

"Still bitter, are we?" Phoebe quipped.

"No." Juliette stuck her tongue out at her sister. "It's the truth. That was the most ridiculous intervention plan ever in the history of the G-FOURce." She turned her attention back to Gia. "Anyway, do you remember what character trait you suggested for our list?"

Gia thought for a moment, but she didn't have to try very hard to remember. "Patience."

"Yes." Juliette nodded. "Patience. You said it was really important to you because you didn't want to be pushed into something you weren't ready for just because a guy might think he was ready."

"I remember that," Renata interjected, pointing a wooden spoon at her. "You compared it to Granny G's sunflowers but remind me what you said again."

A strange sense of peace settled around Gia's shoulders as she thought about the almost prophetic words she'd spoken back then; about the things she'd claimed were important to her in a man. "I said that love needs time to take root and grow strong before it blossoms. Like Gran's giant sunflowers. The roots and stalk need time to grow strong and sturdy before the plant can support the weight of the heavy blossom on top." She grinned to herself as she considered her relationship with Ricky and how much of themselves they'd invested in their friendship over the years. "That if the plant grows too quickly, it won't be able to support the huge flower head. That it will just fall over and die before any good can come of it."

"Yep," Juliette said, nodding again. "I still remember your words as clear as day, Gia. You said you didn't want to be in a relationship where all the glory was in the flower, only to have it fall on its face because you didn't put your energy into the roots and stalk first."

"Well, you and Ricky have certainly invested your energy into the roots and stalk of this relationship, Gia," Ren added. "You've been inseparable, the best of friends, since junior high."

"Seems to me you're good and ready to bloom," Phoebe agreed. "And I have a feeling it's going to be a pretty spectacular blossom."

"I just never put it together," Gia said, shaking her head in bemusement.

"Seems you're the only one who didn't," Granny G said, her voice gentle.

"So why didn't anybody bother catching me up to speed?" she asked, a scowl furrowing the line of her brow. "I mean, maybe one of you could have said 'Hey, that Ricky fella sure is a hottie, don't you think, Gia? Maybe you should start dating him now.' Or something along that line. Might have saved me a little teenage angst, you know?"

"Oh, please." Phoebe chuckled. "We've been saying it for years. Maybe not in those exact words, but still, we've been saying it."

"Seriously? You guys all knew?" Who was she kidding? Even Ricky had known for years.

"We've known since the day that boy followed you home," Granny G said, patting her hand. "And that's the God-honest truth. Is he joining us for lunch?"

Gia nodded slowly, still slightly confounded by the fact that she'd been the only one in the dark all this time. "He should be here any minute now."

As though waiting for her cue, the doorbell rang.

THIRTY-SEVEN

GIA JUMPED UP. "I'll get it!"

Judah and Levi charged into the foyer from the living room, arriving at the door just a moment before she did. A wrestling match started over who got to actually open the door, but Gia reached over their heads and managed to pull it open while simultaneously sweeping the wriggling mass of skinny arms and legs out of the way. "Sorry," she said around a laugh, grinning up at the guy standing on the front patio. "Hey, Rickaroni."

But he wasn't smiling. "Hey, Gia." *Not Georgy Girl.*

And then she saw the woman standing just behind him. Wait. She saw... *herself* standing there. Gia straightened, her shoulders lifting, her eyes widening. So did the woman's; it was like looking in a mirror. The long, red curls, the pale, freckled complexion, eyes the color of a sea swept day. And she was tall. Maybe even taller than Gia.

The boys on the floor stilled, quieted, and then Judah piped up. "You look like Aunt Gia!"

"Gia, this is Cheryl—" Ricky broke off and turned back to the woman. "I'm sorry. I don't remember your last name." His voice shook just the slightest bit.

Cheryl stepped forward tentatively, but in her eyes was a look of determination. "I'm Cheryl Wiley." She thrust her right hand out, and for a moment, Gia could only stare at the arm protruding from the flowered sleeve of the woman's dress. A dress that looked like it could have come off a hanger in Gia's closet. And Cheryl's hand—the shape of it, the length of the fingers, the pronounced knobby bones of her knuckles and wrists—it was like staring down at her own hand. When Gia didn't take it, Cheryl slowly, self-consciously, crossed her arms.

Gia blinked and then shook her head. What on earth was going on?

"Is that you, Ricky, dear?" Granny G called from the kitchen. A moment later, she bustled into the foyer, followed by Phoebe and Juliette. "Oh!"

When Granny G came to an abrupt halt, Phoebe ran into her, almost knocking her over. Juliette scrambled to keep the older woman upright, but no one could take their eyes off Cheryl in the doorway beside Ricky. Then Renata entered, already reprimanding the two boys for being in the way. She stopped mid-sentence and stared with her mouth open. The boys, not missing a beat, scrambled to their feet and dashed out of the tiny entryway that was suddenly way too crowded.

"Hi," Cheryl began. "Mrs. Gustafson—Sarah Gustafson, right? I'm Cheryl Wiley."

Instinctively, Phoebe and Jules closed ranks on either side of Granny G, Renata close behind them. Ricky stood like a deer in the headlights, apparently waiting for someone to tell him what to do, not exactly outside with the newcomer on the front porch, and not exactly inside with the rest of the family. Gia looked from him to the girl still hovering behind him, and then to her grandmother, who had gone white as a sheet.

"Y—yes. Yes, dear. I am." Granny G swallowed hard. "I think I need to sit down, girls."

Her words were like a starter pistol at a race. Suddenly everyone was moving at once, the three older girls practically sweeping their grandmother into the living room to the sofa, Tim corralling Levi and Judah out of the way—they'd gone straight in to tell him about the stranger at the door—and Vic and Trevor lurching forward to come to the aid of their womenfolk. Gia stumbled in behind them, not daring to look over her shoulder to see what Ricky was doing. Surely, he'd follow, too.

She didn't want to know what Cheryl was doing.

"Vic, honey," Granny G began, her voice tight, her face still blanched. She looked up at the man who stood at Juliette's side. "Can you please show Cheryl in?"

"Cheryl?" Gramps asked, having sat forward in his recliner, his footrest locked down. "Who is Cheryl?"

"I'm so sorry," the girl said from the living room doorway. "I didn't expect a crowd. I—I didn't mean to interrupt—" She broke off, clearly upset over the chaos she'd orchestrated. "Are you all right, Gra—Mrs. Gustafson?"

All eyes turned to the girl who'd stumbled over Granny G's name. Who *was* she?

"Whoa," Reuben said from where he was sprawled on the floor, reading one of the latest YA novels that had met his mother's approval. "Dude," he said under his breath to Simon, who leaned against the wall beside him with another book. "She could totally be Gia's twin."

The room fell silent…, and that's when Gia saw it. The look that passed between her grandparents was not one of surprise, no. It was a look that said they'd dreaded this moment, had possibly even known it would one day come. A look that told Gia the truth about one thing.

She'd been lied to by the people she loved—*trusted*—more than anyone else in the world. Her fingertips tingled, then her scalp, and she began to tremble just the slightest bit at first. When Ricky stepped up beside her and started to slip his arm around her waist, she jerked away. "Don't touch me," she tried to say, but all she got out was "Don't—" before her voice broke off into a sharp gasp for air. Oh God, she couldn't breathe, she couldn't breathe! She waved away Ricky's attempt to reach for her again, panting in short, shallow inhalations that left her lungs screaming for oxygen. Tiny lights flickered in her line of vision and she knew she was going to faint. She knew it as surely as she knew that this girl, this Cheryl Wiley held the keys to the missing places in Gia's life.

"Head down, Gia," Vic ordered, placing one hand on the back of her neck, the other around her waist, forcing her to bend forward. "Hands on your knees. Breathe in through your nose, out through your mouth. Slow down." Where he'd come from, she didn't know, but his authoritative tone steadied her and she obeyed, gripping her knees with clammy hands, letting her head fall forward.

Breathe-two-three-four, out-two-three-four. Again. And again, until the lights stopped snapping and popping behind her closed eyelids. Without straightening, in a voice she barely recognized as her own, she wailed, "What is going on?"

"Oh, Gia. My sweet girl." Her grandmother's voice was tight with grief and misery, and when she didn't continue, Gia lifted her head to look at her.

"What is going on? Who is she?" She stretched out a hand and pointed at Cheryl. Gia couldn't look at the girl, but in her peripheral vision, she could see her still standing in the doorway.

"Gia, let's sit down," Vic said, leaning forward a little to speak quietly to her, calming, soothing.

Gia lurched upright and shoved away from him, her hands fluttering in front of her as though to ward off anyone else who might try to approach. "Stop it! Stop telling me what to do." She turned to her grandfather, who had risen from his chair and was now crossing the room toward her. "Who is she, Gramps?" This time, her voice came out harsh and wretched. "Someone tell me!"

"I—I'm your sister," Cheryl said from the doorway. "You and I are sisters."

In her grandfather's anguished expression, Gia saw the truth of Cheryl's words. A glance at her grandmother confirmed it.

Gia fled, making it into her own room before her legs gave out beneath her. She closed the door and slid down it, wrapping her arms around her legs, pressing her forehead into her knees.

Breathe-two-three-four-out-two-three-four. Again. And again.

And then she began to weep.

THIRTY-EIGHT

RICKY STOOD ROOTED TO the floor as he watched the scene play out in front of him. If only he could have figured out a way to stop it, to hold back the tide that was washing over them all.

He'd pulled up out front and there she was, leaning into the driver's side of a little Nissan parked at the curb. He didn't recognize the car, but it had hardly registered through the thrill of anticipation he'd had at seeing her again, over the chance to greet her out here by herself rather than in front of her whole family inside. "Hey there, Georgy Girl," he'd called to her as he'd slid out of his truck, hoping she'd turn and make a mad dash into his arms.

She'd straightened, but kept her back to him, almost as though she hadn't heard him. She worked her fingers through her long hair, combing out the worst of the tangles as he'd seen her do so many times before.

"Gia!" he called again as he sauntered up the street toward her.

Then she stiffened, and ever so slowly, turned around.

The shock had just about knocked him off his feet. Not Gia, not in a million years, but in some strange, twisted way, it *was* her. Like another dimension Gia. A clone experiment that had veered off to the left a little. There was nothing innately *wrong* with this one—all the parts added up, the hair, the body, the skin, the eyes—it just wasn't her.

"Who—where's Gia?" he asked. As soon as the question was out, he realized how stupid it sounded. This wasn't a science fiction movie with body snatchers or aliens on the loose.

He approached her slowly, and she took a step backward into the protection of her open car door. "Sorry," he said. "I thought you were someone else."

"That's all right." She sounded exactly like Gia, too. Ricky squeezed his eyes shut for a moment, trying to make sense of what he was seeing.

"Um, can I... help you with something?" What could he ask her without sounding terribly rude? Surely, if Gia knew about this girl, she would have mentioned her to him, warned him.

"Oh. Well, maybe." The girl's nervousness was evident in the way she shifted her weight back and forth, the way she tugged a curl forward and toyed with the end of it. All things Gia did, too. "I'm here to see the Gustafsons." She darted a glance toward the front of the house. "This is where they live, right?"

Ricky nodded. "Are they expecting you?" His mind was still having trouble putting the whole thing together. Gramps just got home. Why would they have company today while he was still sick?

The girl frowned self-consciously. "Um, no. I should have called first, but I—" She broke off as though reconsidering what she'd been about to say. Then she sighed deeply, and her shoulders drooped like she was carrying the weight of a heavy burden. "I should have called."

Ricky stepped closer and stuck out his hand. "I'm Ricky. Gia's friend."

"Oh. Hi, Ricky. I'm, um, Cheryl Wiley." She shrugged, an apologetic grimace marring her features, but she shook his hand. Her eyes, he noticed, although eerily familiar to him, were terribly sad. "I don't know who Gia is. I'm sorry."

It was the strangest thing in the world to be standing here in front of Gia's house, talking to a woman who looked and sounded like Gia, whose hand even felt like Gia's hand in his, and yet she didn't know who Gia was. "Gia Gustafson. She's a Gustafson."

"Of course," Cheryl nodded, but Ricky was pretty sure she was just being polite, that she still had no clue who he was talking about.

He shoved his hands in his pocket, warring between offering to escort her to the front door to greet the family and drilling her to find out why she was here, what her intentions were. Some unspoken fear had risen up in him when she'd turned around, something that made him feel protective of this family he cared for so deeply. "So you're here to see...?" He turned the statement into a question, hoping he didn't sound rude, but opting for caution.

"Henry and Sarah Gustafson. And their granddaughters. Although they might not remember me." She smoothed her hair back over her shoulder and glanced away again, but he didn't miss the glimmer of moisture in her eyes. "It's been so long."

"But you don't know Gia?"

"I was pretty young the last time I was here. Just a little girl." She frowned, and then a strange look came over her face. "Wait. Is Gia... maybe Georgia?" Her eyes lit up momentarily. "Of course. Georgia. Gia." She swallowed hard and then lifted her gaze to his. He almost stepped back at the intensity in her eyes. "Is she here? Georgia?"

"She goes by Gia," he said, wondering too late if he should have mentioned her at all. But then, what was he supposed to do when this woman who could have been her twin sister stood not five feet away from him?

"Oh. Okay. I'll remember that." Cheryl took a step forward, making him move out of her way. She closed her car door and squared her shoulders. "I've come a long way to see her," she said, and started toward the sidewalk. "To see all of them."

Ricky lurched into motion, catching up with her in a few strides. "Um, Gramps just got home from the hospital maybe an hour ago. This might not be a good time if they're not expecting you."

Cheryl paused and then shook her head. "I should have called. You're right. But I can't leave now." Her voice grew tight, choked with tears that were beginning to pool in her eyes. "I can't leave without knowing—without seeing them." Then she swiped at her cheeks with her fingertips and started up the walk, determination in every step.

He didn't know what to say, what to do. In a quandary, he trailed after her, trying to imagine how this would all play out. By the time they'd reached the front porch, he was desperate to act, even though he remained at a complete loss. "Let me go first," he urged, stepping around her just as she pushed the doorbell.

He should have stopped her. He should have been more determined himself. He should have paid attention to his gut instinct that this was going to turn out badly for everyone.

No one had gone after Gia; they were all too busy trying to process the lookalike who still remained in the room. Although he desperately wanted to stay and learn who she was, he decided if no one went to see to Gia, he would.

"Please, Cheryl," Gramps said. "Come in, child." He stepped forward and offered her his hand. She shook it and smiled tentatively at the old man. Granny G rose and came forward, too, but instead of shaking Cheryl's hand, she opened her arms and gave the girl a gentle hug.

"I'm sorry for my initial reaction. You caught me by surprise, dear."

"No, no," Cheryl began, taking Granny G's hand in both of her own. "I'm the one who should be apologizing. I should have called, but I didn't have your number. The only one I had was Paul and Simone's."

Small noises of surprise—shock?—reverberated around the room at the mention of those names, but the grandparents seemed to take it all in stride. "We understand," Granny G said. But she withdrew her hand from the girl's grip, and for the first time, Ricky saw what looked like fear in the old woman's eyes. What was going on?

Gramps gestured toward the chair where Tim had been sitting. "Won't you have a seat, Cheryl?" He waited until she made her way into the room and lowered herself to the edge of the cushion, and then he returned to his recliner, although he stayed upright, his feet planted on the floor, his hands braced on the arms of the chair. "It's really quite remarkable to see you again."

That was one way to put it.

"I'm going to go check on Gia," Ricky interjected, but as he turned to leave, Trevor stopped him.

"Hold up, man." Trevor nodded toward the door. "Maybe you and I should head out and give the family some privacy."

"Whoa. Hold up, yourself, buddy." It was Phoebe. "You, my love, *are* family. And so is he." She waved her paint splattered hand at Ricky. "You're not going anywhere." She circled Trevor and put a hand on Ricky's arm. "I'll go get Gia. You two stay. And if I miss anything, I'll expect a full report." The last, she directed to Renata. "Take notes if you have to. This ought to be good."

Ricky's eyes widened when he heard the anger in her voice, and when he saw it reflected in her expression, he knew for certain that Phoebe was not going to let Gia face this alone.

It was also pretty evident that Gia was not alone in her ignorance, that none of the sisters knew about this Cheryl person. Juliette had moved to stand beside her new husband, and Tim, having sensed something from his wife, had handed her a sleeping Charise, and was just now returning from ushering the boys into the grandparents' room where they could watch television on the big bed. Reuben and Simon had complained quietly about missing out, but knowing Renata, she'd fill her boys in on things once she'd gotten the scoop. She wasn't one of those moms who hid stuff from her kids. At least not anymore.

Granny G made her way to the other armchair and eyed the group. "Please, kids. Someone take the couch. You don't all need to stand." After a long moment's hesitation, Vic led Juliette to the sofa and sat beside her, an arm around her shoulders.

Ricky stood with Trevor by the entrance to the hallway, but he wasn't so sure Gia would come out with Phoebe. He'd seen the look on her face, and truth be told, it scared him. When she'd pushed him away and wouldn't let him touch her, he'd wanted to argue with her, to remind her that this whole thing wasn't his doing, that he'd been caught in the blast, too.

"Did you drive here?" Gramps asked Cheryl, obviously struggling for a way to begin the conversation.

"I did. I drove down yesterday." Cheryl darted glances around the room as she spoke, but otherwise, her eyes stayed glued to the floor at her feet. "I'm so sorry," she said. "I didn't know how else to do this."

She sounded small, vulnerable, and it tore at Ricky's heart because she sounded so much like Gia.

"I know it must sound so selfish to you, but I had to see you. See her. I didn't know... before."

Ricky saw a tear land on the back of Cheryl's hands where they rested in her lap. "He didn't tell—"

Phoebe slipped into the room, interrupting Cheryl's quiet plea. "She won't come out," she said. "But she's agreed to leave the door open, so you all had better speak up." Phoebe aimed her gaze at her grandfather. "I know you're sick, Gramps, but that girl in there—" Her voice cracked, and she cleared her throat. "She might just be mortally wounded, so this better be good," she reiterated.

Ricky then remembered the part of Phoebe's story that had bothered Gia so much, how Gramps had automatically taken Renata's side against Phoebe, assuming the worst of her, just like everyone else did. It had been only the beginning of Phoebe's nightmare, because although the crime committed against her that night had been horrific, her grandfather's abandonment had been a near-mortal wound to her heart that had led to years of unnecessary suffering. How different things might have been had he looked past his anger and frustration to see the pain Phoebe was suffering. Last year, when Phoebe finally unraveled the dark shroud that had covered her secrets all these years, the old man had wept openly, and apologized for his part in her pain. But Ricky could understand why Phoebe, of all the girls, was not going to stand by and let Gia be abandoned in the same way.

Nor would he. "I'm going to sit with her," he said, his voice firm, solemn. Then to Phoebe, he added, "I'll let you know if we can't hear."

THIRTY-NINE

Gia lay on her side with her back to the door, her knees drawn up, her arms wrapped around a pillow. She didn't turn when he entered the room.

Without a word, Ricky slipped off his Vans and lowered himself to the mattress behind her. When she didn't make any objection, he curled his body against hers, sliding one arm under her shoulder and the other around her waist. Then he gently gathered her close. She let out a juddering sigh and tucked the back of her head up under his chin. A moment later, she laced the fingers of one of her hands with his.

From the other room, the conversation began again, and Ricky was surprised at how clearly the voices traveled down the short hallway to where they lay nestled together on Gia's bed.

"My dad died in January," Cheryl began, the abruptness of the words gentled by her soft voice. "Although he passed away in his sleep, it wasn't easy. He had a lot of unfinished business, and much of it he handed off to me to deal with." She stopped for a moment, and Granny G spoke up.

"I'm so sorry, Cheryl. Your father was a good man who was forced to make some difficult decisions."

"Yes, well, unfortunately, more often than not, my father chose wrong. When it came to difficult decisions, he typically chose the easiest option, even if it usually meant just prolonging the inevitable."

Ricky could almost taste the bitterness in the girl's voice.

"Don't get me wrong. He took care of me the best he knew how or was capable, and I loved him very much, but that doesn't make the things he did okay. He really was half a man after Mom died, and his inability to move on, whether by choice or not, marked every aspect of our lives." She sniffed, and someone—Ren, maybe?—offered her a tissue. "When Mom got sick, I was so young, not quite five years old. Most of what I know about her has been pieced together from Dad's stories, so that anymore, it's hard to tell which memories are mine and which are his."

Ricky felt Gia flinch. She'd also been four when her own mother—well, when Simone Gustafson—had died, and she, too, had told him the same thing about her own memories.

"I do remember her and Simone, though. Your mother."

Ricky could picture Cheryl lifting her gaze to each of the three Gustafson sisters still in the room.

"It's like I have these snapshots in my mind that I know for certain are my own experiences. Their heads bent together, laughing, talking quietly close by while I played."

She paused, and he thought he heard her sigh.

"I remember the *sound* of them together almost more than anything else. Their voices were the background music of my early years," Cheryl said, a wistful note in her tone. "Simone's accent was so strong, sometimes I couldn't understand what she was saying, but her smile and her eyes—oh, and the way she smelled, like a garden—said everything important, anyway. She was the best friend my mother could have ever had."

"They were lovely together," Granny G confirmed, her own voice tender with remembering. "Your mother with her hair like—like yours." Ricky was sure she'd been about to say Gia's. After a weighty pause, she continued. "And Simone's black curls. Whenever I see Gia and her sisters bent to a task, I remember what might have been."

"Do—do you know everything, then?" Cheryl asked after a few moments of silence. "Do you know about the cancer and the treatments and—and the pregnancy?" She sounded more adamant to Ricky's ears, but he sensed fear there, too.

"We do," Granny G said, but then she faltered a bit. "Henry and I know. About the...."

Ricky couldn't make out the last word.

"I'm sorry," Phoebe interrupted, and although he didn't think she was being intentionally rude, he heard the shock in her voice. "Can you repeat that, please?"

Gramps spoke up instead. "We know about the surrogate pregnancy, yes."

The silence that came from the front room was thick, heavy. Gia had turned to stone in his arms, and after several moments of utter stillness, he whispered against her temple, "Breathe, Georgy Girl." And she did.

"Wait." It was Ren's turn. "Are you saying—I think you'd better start from the beginning, okay? Because this is not making any sense."

Except that it was starting to, and that's what made it so difficult to hear.

"Would you like to tell the story, Cheryl, or would you like us to?" Granny G asked.

A moment later, as though she'd considered her options carefully, Cheryl said, "Why don't you start with what you know, and I'll finish with what I know. I have a feeling my knowledge of events begins about where yours leaves off."

"Sounds fair," Gramps agreed.

And so, while the spaghetti casserole grew cold in the kitchen, the tragic tale was laid out. No one seemed to mind.

Colleen and George Wiley had been Simone and Paul's closest friends. While the Gustafsons gave birth to one daughter after another, the Wileys struggled for years to conceive, but to no avail. Finally, with the help of *in vitro* fertilization, they gave birth to their precious miracle, Cheryl, and because they so badly wanted another child, they decided to go through the procedure a second time when Cheryl was just a few years old. It was during that time that Colleen's doctors discovered her uterine cancer and determined that a hysterectomy and aggressive chemotherapy would be the best treatment plan to keep Colleen alive. The couple had simultaneously been faced with another difficult decision: to terminate their IVF plans altogether or find someone who would be willing to surrogate for them. With her husband's blessing, Simone offered to step in and be that person for Colleen and George.

"We didn't know this," Renata interjected, clearly stunned by the revelation. Then she asked, "Did we know this?"

"Your parents opted not to discuss even the possibility of a pregnancy until they were certain the implantation was successful," Granny G said, although she didn't really answer Ren's question. "The IVF procedure had resulted in only one fertilized egg, so the chances of a successful pregnancy were slim. During that initial waiting period, however, Colleen took a dramatic turn for the worse. Her body reacted terribly to the chemo, and then she had a series of strokes that nearly killed her, putting a halt to further cancer treatments. A few days later, they found that the implant of the embryo had taken."

"Did Mom know?" Cheryl asked.

"We're not sure," Granny G admitted. "George was told, of course, and Simone said she talked to Colleen often while sitting at her bedside, but by then, your mom was no longer responsive."

In the beginning, it was George's despair that motivated Paul and Simone to not discuss the pregnancy with him unless he brought it up. He had been distraught, unable to believe that his beloved wife was dying, and one night, he'd shown up on Paul and Simone's doorstep, hysterical, wild, and drunk on a whole lot of grief and enough hard liquor to really scare them. George told them that he wouldn't go on without Colleen, that if anything happened to her, he would end his life, too. He made them promise they'd take Cheryl as their own after he was gone.

"They were already your godparents," Gramps said, presumably speaking to Cheryl. "So they agreed to his demands just to put his mind at ease, certain it was only his pain talking."

"Where was I during all of this?" Cheryl asked. "I don't remember my mother's illness at all. Just that she was sick, and that Dad was a mess. I remember being afraid of him."

"You stayed with Simone and Paul and the girls," Granny G said. "You were quite a bit younger than they were, so you spent most of your time with Simone while they were in school and busy with their lives. It wasn't for very long."

"I remember that now," Juliette spoke up. "I do remember you. A little red-headed thing always hiding behind Mom's skirt. My goodness."

The Gustafsons had waited, hoping and praying for miracles, either in healing for Colleen, or peace for George, and all the while, the baby inside Simone was beating the odds. But in less than a month after her original diagnosis, Colleen's body could no longer fight the good fight, and it was George's grief that made the ultimate decision for them.

He didn't kill himself. At some point, Colleen had extracted from him a promise of her own... that he would live, that he would care for their child—the only one she knew they had. But when Paul and Simone finally attempted to talk to him about the thriving child Simone carried, George hired a lawyer and had papers drawn up that terminated any and all of his parental rights to the unborn baby, signing her over to Paul and Simone. Then he'd packed up a truck and trailer with what few belongings he and Cheryl absolutely needed, and left town. It was months before they learned from the lawyer that he'd relocated to Northern California, away from everyone and everything he knew. He'd landed a grounds and maintenance job at the apartment complex where he lived, which meant he didn't have to worry about finding childcare for Cheryl while he worked.

Paul and Simone, brokenhearted themselves over the loss of their dear friends, considered the baby a cherished gift, a treasured remembrance of the little family they loved so much. Two months before she was born, the Gustafsons signed the court papers making Gia legally theirs.

Granny G's voice wavered a little as she continued. "George wrote one letter that we know of to Paul and Simone, asking them to let him go and respect his wishes, even if they didn't understand, because starting all over was the only way he could survive without Colleen. He promised them he would take good care of you, Cheryl, but he knew he could not raise a baby on his own. He knew the child would have a loving home and family with the Gustafsons, and it was the very best he could do for her, but he begged them not to tell anyone that he'd abandoned his baby; he would have to live with his failure his whole life, but he didn't want the child to grow up under the burden of it."

Right or wrong, Paul and Simone agreed. Other than Henry and Sarah, who'd known all along about their decision to surrogate, no one else needed to be told.

Once again, a silence settled over the room down the hall. Ricky thought it was possibly the saddest story he'd ever heard.

When Gia shifted, he lifted his arm to allow her to change positions. Without speaking, she pushed up to a sitting position and swung her legs off the side of the bed. Slowly, a little like he was dealing with a scared animal, he scooted over to sit beside her. She reached out and took his hand, once more lacing her fingers with his.

"I still think someone should have told us," Phoebe said in a troubled voice. "You should have at least told Gia. *She* needed to know."

"Believe me, Phoebe, sweetheart, we've thought about it many times," Granny G said. She sounded miserable. "Especially once she turned eighteen. As an adult, we reasoned she could choose what she wanted to do with the information, and of course, we'd have supported her in any way we could. But so much has happened in the last couple of years, and the time has never felt right."

Gia tensed beside him; Ricky knew those words struck a bruised spot in her.

Gramps picked up when Granny G stopped. "As you girls well know, we have made many mistakes along the way in parenting you. We have always done our best by you, but we know we have failed you in many ways, too. In trying to respect George's choice, in keeping your parents' desires in mind, we've felt—perhaps wrongly, I'll admit—that our hands were tied. It has taken us years, but we are slowly learning that withholding information is not always the best way to protect the ones we love. Sometimes for a season, it's okay to keep things close to the heart, but eventually, the truth does find a way to the surface, doesn't it?"

Ricky could imagine Gramps dipping his head in Cheryl's direction, or perhaps in Phoebe's.

"But don't you see, girls?" Granny G jumped back in, her voice urgent, begging them to understand. "Your parents did what they believed was right at the time, all of them. And had Paul and Simone still been alive today, they might have done things differently than we have. They might have changed their minds about not telling you girls about George and Colleen and sweet Cheryl, here, or they may have gone after the two of you, Cheryl, after some time had passed and hearts had mended a bit." She sighed so deeply, Ricky heard it, almost like a cry. "We don't know. We can't know. And right or wrong, we did what we thought was best, too. But the fact is, Phoebe, your parents claimed Gia as their own because that's what their friend asked them to do. From the moment the doctor confirmed that the implanted embryo was a success, they loved Gia without reservation, first as a gift for their friends, and then as a gift *from* their friends. She was always theirs. In every way that matters, she was theirs."

Gramps cleared his throat and added, "She's yours. She's ours."

Gia inhaled deeply, and then let her breath out in a slow exhale. Ricky found that he'd been holding his breath, too.

"And she's mine." Cheryl's words filled the air around them, taking up every ounce of space. Aching, bruised, hopeful, her voice trembled with longing. "She's all I have left. Until last Christmas, I thought I was going to be completely alone in this world." Her voice snagged, but she cleared her throat. "I didn't know I had a sister."

Ricky found it hard to separate the voice he heard in the other room from the girl he held in his arms. Cheryl sounded so much like Gia, and her sorrow, her loneliness, her need broke his heart. He wondered if it had penetrated the wall of pain around Gia's heart, too.

FORTY

Cheryl picked up the story from that point. "At first, we lived in a tiny apartment on the second floor. There was an elevator that never worked, so we always had to take the stairs."

George, who had worked as a mechanical engineer in the aerospace industry designing and testing high-performance engine components for Rolls-Royce, had walked away from the life he'd built to hide him and his little girl away from a world without Colleen. At some point—Cheryl couldn't recall exactly when—he started fixing things around the property, starting with that elevator, and eventually, he was hired on as the grounds and maintenance person for the forty-unit complex, and they'd moved into a larger apartment on the ground floor where Colleen had her own room and a tiny postage stamp of a backyard to play in. When it was time for her to start school, George opted to home school her to keep her close.

"My physical world was very small for a while, but over the years, people got used to me showing up with Dad on repair calls, tagging along beside him while he showed apartments and handed out notices, or sitting in front of him on his riding lawn mower. I'm sure there were all kinds of rules he broke having me as his sidekick, but he was fiercely protective of me, and for whatever reason, no one turned him in." Her voice softened, so that Gia had to strain to hear it. "I know now that he was afraid of losing me, too. In many ways, those were sweet times, mainly because I was too young to realize that our life wasn't exactly normal. I mean, it was *our* normal, right?"

"You were their miracle, Cheryl," Granny G said, her voice so kind. "They loved you so much."

I was their miracle, too. The thought careened around Gia's mind like a tantrum-throwing child, but as she listened to Cheryl talk, it was getting more and more difficult to ignore the waves of compassion surging up in her. While she'd been slow dancing at her own pity party for the past several months now, Cheryl had been figuring out how to survive on her own. Maybe even for the past several years. Her next words confirmed it.

"By the time I was twelve, I was pretty much homeschooling myself. I may have been sheltered, but I wasn't blind, and surrounded like we were by families of all different kinds, I knew how things were supposed to be. Which meant I knew things weren't right in our home. Oh, no, don't look at me like that." Who was she talking to? Ren, most likely? She had such a strong Mama Bear reaction to children who were hurting. "He never harmed me in any way, and I know he loved me the best he could. But he was simply ill-equipped to care for a teenage girl. He made sure I was safe, fed, and had a roof over my head, that all my needs were met. But I took care of my education and my plans for my future."

The room had grown terribly quiet, and Gia could hear Cheryl's words like she was in the same room with her.

"In many ways, I lost my father sometime during my high school years. He was there in body, watching out for me, but his heart, his spirit, had given up the battle, and by the time I finished my dental hygiene program, he was sick. I think once he knew I would be okay without him, he gave himself permission to let go. I used to hear him talking to my mother like she was sitting at the other end of the table, or beside him on the sofa." Her voice had thickened, like she might be trying to hold tears at bay, and she cleared her throat. "In the end, when he could no longer work, I took care of him. He was my father, and I loved him." She released a short, sharp sound that couldn't quite be called a laugh. "Even though part of me wanted to hate him, I just couldn't. I loved him."

"Oh, Cheryl, that's so hard for us to hear." Yep, Ren. A stranger might not recognize the censure behind the gentle words, but Gia knew her sister so well—

She knew *her sister* so well. She knew all three of her sisters so well.

"My sisters," Gia whispered, her voice rough with revelation. Not just one sister, but three amazing older sisters who loved her and watched out for her, who'd stepped in when they'd all lost their mother—because yes, Simone had been Gia's mother in every single way. She'd had Granny G, too, and Gramps, who'd become a father figure to them all. A loving man who'd made mistakes, yes, but who'd been more than just present in body like Cheryl's father. Gia had so much, a life bursting at the seams with people who loved her, while Cheryl had endured the loss of her own parents all alone.

"I know," Cheryl said in response to Renata. "It's hard to say it. I feel guilty even for thinking it, no less putting it all out there for everyone to judge. I know you must think my father some kind of monster, but he wasn't. He was just a man so much in love with a woman that he couldn't live without her. I truly believe that."

After a few more moments of silence, Ren spoke again. "I think that might just be the scariest thing about giving yourself over to loving someone completely. A parent, a child, a lover." Gia held her breath, realizing that her sister was sharing something she might never have said aloud to anyone before. "Sometimes you love someone so much you really don't believe life can go on without them."

"And when it does, you punish yourself by wallowing in guilt and shame and regret." It was Phoebe, and Gia knew she was thinking about Lily, about the years she'd spent under the burden of her secret.

"Fear," Juliette added. "You're just afraid to live, to be happy again."

Tugging gently on Ricky's hand—she wasn't going to let go of him now—Gia rose a little unsteadily and made her way from her bedroom and down the hall, knowing she needed to be with her sisters, her family. Ricky stayed right by her but said nothing, because he knew without her having to tell him that she needed him.

"Or self-pity," Gia said as she moved into the room to stand close to Phoebe, who leaned back against Trevor, his arms wrapped like armor around her. She kept her gaze lowered, not quite able to meet Cheryl's eyes. "Feeling so sorry for yourself that you think you're alone even when you're not, and you lose sight of all your blessings, of all the good things that make living an adventure." With her fingers still laced through Ricky's, she lifted his hand over her head and draped his arm around her shoulders. "I wish they'd told us." And then she lifted her head and looked right at the girl who might be her own reflection. "I wish I'd known about you a long time ago, Cheryl."

"I'm hungry, Mommy." Judah pushed between Gia and Phoebe and charged across the room to Renata. "I'm starving like a shark and my mouth wants to eat everything." He wrapped his skinny little arms around her waist and bent back to scowl up at his mother, but his little sister blocked his line of sight. "Better move that baby out of the way, or I might bite her butt, cuz I'm so hungry."

FORTY-ONE

THE MEAL WAS QUITE possibly the strangest one they'd ever had in the Gustafson home. As Gia looked around the table filled to capacity, she couldn't help but be overwhelmed by how much their family had grown in the last couple of years. Between the men in her sisters' lives, the growing number of children underfoot, and now, a new sister—another Gustafson girl, for surely, that's what she would become!

And of course, there was Ricky. There'd always been Ricky. In fact, when all the extra leaves were pulled from the table and it was put back to its normal set up, it seated four... and over the years, in her mind, that fourth seat had become Ricky's. He was as much a part of their family as any of them.

She felt the empty places, too. Maman and Papa, John, Phoebe's Lily, and now George and Colleen, too. But this was a table where life was happening, where hearts were healing. The past was never forgotten, but in this circle, new beginnings were born and nurtured.

Sitting across from Cheryl, Gia marveled at the similarities between them. The shape of their hands, the almost translucent webbing between fingers, the forked pattern of the creases at their elbows. The dip of their chin when listening, the smile that brought out dimples in their cheeks. The cadence of their voices, even the choppy laugh that Ricky liked to tease her about; now it came in stereo. At one point, they had reached for the salad bowl on the table between them at the exact same time, and it had been like watching a synchronized dance, the way their gestures mirrored each other.

She could tell she wasn't the only one disconcerted by it all. The boys, at least the younger two, stared openly back and forth at them, Levi's usual conviviality magnified by his delight in the situation. Gia couldn't remember the last time Judah had been so silent during a meal, transfixed as he was by the entertainment they provided. Her grandparents, too, kept eyeing the two of them, albeit much more surreptitiously, and she realized they must be wondering how this would all play out over time.

Because it would take time. No one was naïve enough to think otherwise, and although the conversations ebbed and flowed as dishes were passed and food served, although laughter and tears came easily around the table, it felt a little like trying to maneuver across one of the freshly planted vegetable plots in Gramps' garden right after the rows had been smoothed over. One false step could be disaster, but with the right amount of care, the seeds had the potential to take root and flourish.

Gramps, Gia hadn't failed to notice, looked exhausted, his shoulders drooping, his poor battered head seemed almost too heavy for his neck to hold up. Besides his physical condition, he had to be emotionally drained. Not only had he unloaded one of the biggest secrets he'd ever had, but he'd also talked more in one sitting than he had as far back as Gia could remember. However, he often said his favorite thing in all the world was sharing a meal with the people he loved, and so she knew he would remain at the helm until Gran forced him to go lie down.

When the late lunch began to wind down, Tim gave the boys permission to leave the table. "Stay in the backyard," he ordered, tipping back in his chair a little to make sure all four of them made it through the slider in one piece. Gia worried the poor old wooden chair would give under the man's bulk, but he lowered the front legs to the ground again without a mishap.

Thankfully, Ricky stayed close to her side, his hand steady at her back, or on her knee, or with an arm draped across the back of her chair as it was now. In all the upheaval of the week, his presence offered her the most stability, and she leaned into him, if not bodily, definitely in spirit.

Why had she, for even one moment, doubted that she needed him, wanted him? Loved him.

She *loved* him.

She traced a heart on the table between their plates. When his fingers curled around her opposite shoulder and gently squeezed, she glanced up to find him grinning knowingly. He mouthed the words, "Me, too."

Under the table, Gia's foot bumped Cheryl's. It wasn't intentional, but when their eyes met, Cheryl—her very own tall, redheaded, freckle-faced *sister*!—arched a brow at her in question. Gia started to apologize, but Cheryl chuckled—a sound that might have come out of Gia's mouth, so familiar it was to her—and said, "It's my fault. Me and my long noodle legs. You should see me when I have my combat boots on. Total klutz." She shrugged. "But I love them. What can I say?"

"Wow," Ricky moaned. "Two of you in combat boots? This might be more than I can handle. How long did you say you were in town for, Cheryl?" The question was asked in jest, but everyone turned to hear her answer.

"Oh. Um, I'm not exactly sure." Her smile faded slightly, and she began toying nervously with her silverware. "I kind of left it open-ended because I didn't know what to expect." She let out a self-conscious chuckle. "I never dreamed I'd be sitting here having lunch with all of you today." She raised her gaze to Gia first, and then toward Gramps and Gran. "I don't know how to thank you... for—for all of this." She swallowed hard and her eyes grew bright. "I didn't know what to expect—" Her voice cracked, and she looked down at the fork in her hand. "Thank you," she finished quietly.

"Where are you staying?" Juliette asked.

Cheryl smiled brightly then. "You know that Holiday Inn over by the mall? I have a room there. I have it reserved for a week, but I figured I'd stay as long as I needed to."

"Goodness, that's going to get expensive," Granny G began, then she glanced over at Gramps, almost as though for confirmation. Sure enough, he nodded and patted his wife's hand. Granny G said, "We have a spare room; you can stay with us. It will give us all a chance to get to know each other. It's certainly nothing fancy around here, not like a hotel at any rate, and you'll be stuck fending for yourself much of—"

"Oh no," Cheryl interrupted. "No, I'm fine where I am. You're just home from the hospital. You don't need a guest to worry about, too. Besides, it's not a bad price, and the room is really nice." She was blushing and Gia felt awkward right along with her. "To tell you the truth, I'm kind of enjoying my solitude." Her pretty pink coloring darkened considerably, and she hurried to explain. "Please don't misunderstand. I really appreciate the offer, and it's not because I don't want to get to know you." She leaned forward and slid her hand across the table toward Gia. "I do. I came here hoping against hope and praying for just that."

Gia studied her water glass, suddenly afraid to meet Cheryl's eyes lest the woman across from her be able to read her mind. Gia wasn't so sure she was quite ready to have this stranger—no, this *sister*—sleeping in the tiny guest room just down the hall from her, in the bed that had once been Gia's before she moved into the 'Big Girl Room' where her sisters had spent their teenage years. She needed a little time to process all that had happened today, this week, this last year and more, because it seemed like lately, every time she turned around, she was being hit with something new and monumental, something life changing.

Yet, wasn't Cheryl's presence in her life what she'd been waiting for, longing for as far back as she could remember? Hadn't she always known she was different? Not like the others? The ugly duckling, so to speak? And now, finally, she had answers. Finally, things were beginning to make sense. So why was she hesitant in this?

"Why don't you stay at my old place?" Juliette offered, slipping her hand into Vic's where it rested on the table. "It's sitting there, empty right now, until I can figure out what I'm going to do with it. It's almost fully furnished and everything."

"Oh goodness. Mrs. Cork and Mr. Bobo will just love you," Ren said in full agreement, and then explained, "Juliette's old neighbor and her little dog. She thinks Gia is the cat's pajamas, and she'll get a kick out of meeting you."

"It's closer to here than the Holiday Inn, too," Vic added. "And it would be free."

"Come on," Phoebe cajoled when Cheryl's mouth opened, then closed, clearly at a loss for words. "You know you want to say yes. There's no use denying it; it's written all over your face." Phoebe pointed a finger between Cheryl and Gia. "And we know that look perfectly well, girlie. We've been reading that face for almost twenty years."

Cheryl giggled self-consciously and lifted her hands to cover her warm cheeks. "That sounds... amazing. But of course I'd pay you."

Juliette shook her head, adamant. "No, you won't. It's yours for as long as you're here."

"I can't stay for free," Cheryl said firmly. "I won't."

"If you pay me, I'll just donate it to charity," Juliette replied, her quiet stubbornness rearing its Gustafson head. Suddenly, her eyes grew wide. "Wait. I know." She sat forward a little. "Instead of paying me to stay in my place, how about you donate to a charity of my choice? Because we know of a good one, don't we, girls?" Her eyes darted around the table, meeting Gia's, then Ren's, and finally Phoebe's.

"Absolutely," Phoebe concurred. "Good call, Jules. Good call."

Cheryl nodded agreeably. "Sure. That works for me." She glanced around the table just as Juliette had done a moment ago, also ending on Phoebe. "If you don't mind me asking... what's the charity?"

Phoebe's smile softened noticeably. "The Ark. It's a non-profit program run by a couple named Cal and Alice Masters," she said. Then she cocked her head and eyed Cheryl inquisitively. "Hey, you know about our parents, don't you? You know what happened to them?"

Cheryl nodded. "I do. My dad told me about them when he told me about all of you. I'm so sorry."

Gia was humbled that this girl who had lost everything in her life could be so sensitive and sincere.

"Well, Alice Masters is Angela Clinton's mother," Phoebe said. "Angela was the girl driving the car that day, the one that hit our parents."

"Oh. Oh!" Cheryl's eyes grew large as Phoebe's explanation sunk in. "You've stayed in touch with her?"

Gia didn't blame her for being surprised by the notion. "Jules started exchanging letters with Angela in prison almost two years ago," she began, not sure why she was taking it upon herself to explain. "And Phoebe connected with her mother over art. Alice has been following Phoebe's career all along."

"She's been keeping track of all of us all along," Ren amended, and for a moment, Gia couldn't tell if that bothered her or not. Then she added, "From afar. Making sure we did all right without our parents. And to let Angela know we were okay."

"Angela is being released from prison any day now," Granny G stated. "She wants to get together with the girls."

"Wow," came Cheryl's stunned reply. "That's pretty wild."

"Yeah, it is," Phoebe agreed, and then she chuckled softly. "We weren't all so thrilled about it at first, believe me. I wanted nothing to do with Angela when Jules first told us about her, but then I connected with Cal—long story, but he's my grocer, of all things—and he brought Alice and me together." She leaned over and kissed Trevor on the shoulder. "Trevor came along as my protector and defender and ended up having a bit of a bromance with Cal. It was a good night, wasn't it, my love?"

"A good night, indeed," Trevor agreed. He and Phoebe went on to describe to Cheryl the program that the Masters operated out of their home, the one they'd lovingly dubbed The Ark. "Because they offer women a temporary safe place to hide in the middle of the storm, and then release them when they're ready," Trevor finished.

"Speaking of..." Phoebe cast a tentative look at Gia, then turned to her grandparents. "Gramps, Gran, I need you to tell us if you need help the rest of the day. We have that dinner with them tonight, but I did tell Alice there was the slight possibility of needing to reschedule until we knew better how you'd be doing. I need to let her know one way or the other."

Gramps straightened in his chair at the head of the table, and then turned to Granny G with a raised brow. "I'm putting my feet up the rest of the day. Just as the doctor ordered. How about you, Sarah? Are you needing the girls for anything?"

"Absolutely not. I'm looking forward to the lot of you skedaddling out of here so Gramps and I can have some peace and quiet," she teased.

"Remember what Dr. Hottie said," Phoebe quipped, reaching over to pat Gramps on the cheek. "No heavy breathing allowed now, got it?"

"Phoebe Gustafson!" Granny G's reprimand was made less potent by the twinkle in her eye. "Your grandfather and I will find an old timers movie and fall asleep in our respective chairs before the end of the opening credits."

"I'll be here," Gia said quietly. "I can help if they need anything."

All eyes turned to her, some in question, some in understanding. But it was Ricky who asked, "Why aren't you going, Georgy Girl?"

Her cheeks warmed, and she ducked her head. Suddenly, her reasons for not attending the dinner with the Masters seemed childish and mean-spirited. In fact, she was having a hard time remembering exactly *why* she didn't want to go. Because they hadn't *asked* her if she wanted to? Because everyone had just assumed she would? Because everyone thought they knew her so well and knew what she'd say? Because they all thought she was such a good girl?

Well, maybe they hadn't exactly asked, but they'd been talking about getting together with Angela ever since she first wrote back to Juliette. It wasn't like Gia hadn't had any opportunity to voice her opinion on the matter. And they'd probably assumed she would be all right with going *because* they knew her so well. They were her family. Her family.

And a good girl? Well, when all was said and done, she was. "I *am* a virgin, after all," she muttered, and then slapped both hands over her mouth when she realized she'd said it out loud. She lifted wide eyes to peer around the table, hoping against hope that no one had heard her.

Not a chance. It was only telltale half smiles and quiet snickers at first as everyone tried to be gracious, but when Gramps quipped, "Thanks for sharing, Gia pet," the group burst into laughter.

Ricky drew her close and let her bury her face in his neck. She could feel his body shaking just the slightest bit as he, too, laughed at her expense, but it was contagious. Even though she kept her hands over her face, she gave in and snickered.

When things had settled, Ricky surprised her by saying, "If it makes you feel any better, I'm a virgin, too."

Gia straightened and stared at him. "You are?"

"Geez. Don't look so aghast," Ricky said, pretending to be offended. "John and Tim offered to take me hunting when I was sixteen. Back when John realized I was looking at you like you were a girl." He grinned down the table at Tim. "Do you remember what he said to me?"

Tim chuckled and cleared his throat. "If I recall, it was something about treating a woman right because it was really easy to get lost in big buck territory during hunting season, right? So it worked?"

Ren turned wide eyes on Tim. "John said that? And you stood by and let him threaten poor, sweet Ricky?" She shook her head in disbelief.

"Poor, sweet who?" Trevor cut in, patting his young cousin firmly on the shoulder Gia wasn't leaning against. "Are we talking about this guy right here? Have you seen the way he looks at your sister, Renata?"

"Okay, okay," Ricky laughed, ducking his head a little. Now he was blushing, Gia noticed with delight. Across the table, Cheryl looked like she couldn't decide whether to be appalled or amused by the personal nature of their teasing.

"It's not always like this," Juliette said to her. "Some of us in this household still have a shred of dignity."

"Oh, please," Phoebe quipped, rolling her eyes. "Says the sister who got pulled over for driving like a blind duck?"

Vic leaned over and kissed his new wife on the temple. "You had me at 'quack,'" he teased. Juliette blushed and laid her head on his shoulder. They were ridiculously cute together, Gia thought.

"You kids are going to scare poor Cheryl away," Granny G declared, laying her napkin on the table beside her plate. She took a deep breath as though she had something important to say, and then straightened her shoulders. "And Gia, sweetie, I've been thinking about tonight and this dinner with the Masters. I think you should go."

"At the risk of sounding pushy," Juliette said, reaching over to put a hand on Gia's arm. "I think so, too. Maybe hear Cal and Alice out tonight, and then decide whether or not you want to talk to Angela when she gets home. What do you think?"

When she didn't respond right away, Granny added, "God is a master orchestrator, sweetie, and when he all but rolls out the blueprint for us, it's usually in our best interests that we go by his plans and not our own."

"I know," Gia finally murmured. "I don't know why I'm so resistant to it. Maybe I'm just being a big chicken."

Ricky's arms tightened around her shoulders. "I think you should go, Georgy Girl. Your sisters will look out for you."

"You know it," Phoebe concurred. Ren and Jules nodded in a show of solidarity.

Granny turned her resolute gaze on Cheryl. "You know, we don't believe in coincidences in this house, my dear. You're here on this day, at this time, for a reason, quite likely for lots of reasons. When you consider how things lined up today, it's hard to deny, isn't it? You arriving when the whole extended family just happened to be here, Juliette's condo open and waiting to welcome you. We even had a meal prepared, as though we knew you were coming." She reached over and slipped her hand into her husband's large one, his nearly swallowing hers up. "I think you should go with your little sister to the Masters' dinner. I think she'll need you there."

FORTY-TWO

AND SO, IT WAS decided. Alice, of course, was thrilled to hear about Cheryl, and extended the invitation to her before Phoebe even had the chance to ask if she could tag along.

Vic promised to meet Cheryl at Juliette's condo to let her in and get her settled, promising his wife he'd introduce her to the elderly Mrs. Cork next door so the woman wouldn't call the police to report an intruder. When Mrs. Cork phoned the police station these days—which she still did on a regular basis—she usually asked for Vic by name. Sometimes he believed she might just be punishing him for stealing away her favorite neighbor.

Gia thought that sounded exactly like something the quirky Mrs. Cork would pull.

At 6:30, Juliette arrived to pick her up, then they went next to get Cheryl, who looked refreshed after a nap, albeit a little nervous, too. Since she was still the new kid on the block, Gia gave her the front seat so she wouldn't have to squeeze into the back with Phoebe, who was notorious for needing extra room to finish getting ready in the car, regardless of where they were going. It was a rare day, indeed, when she was completely ready for anything on time. Surprisingly, she climbed in beside Gia fully clothed and coiffed, shoes and makeup on.

When they got to Ren's, where they planned to switch vehicles so they could ride in the far more spacious family van, she informed them that there'd been a slight change in plans. "Call me chicken if you want, but Charise is coming with us." She kissed her fat baby on top of the beanie she wore. "My little security blanket."

Gia thought it only fair. Phoebe and Juliette had already formed bonds with Alice and Angela, and now she had Cheryl, even if they were still doing the getting-to-know-you dance with each other. That left Ren on her own. Besides, there was no better conversation starter than a beautiful cooing baby.

The drive from Ren's was a little more subdued than it usually was when the sisters got together in a vehicle, but Phoebe assured them they had nothing to worry about. "You'll love them, I promise," she said, leaning forward from the middle seat to include Ren and Cheryl, who once again sat up front. "And just so you know, Cheryl, this is the first time everyone else but me has met these people, so you're in good company, okay?"

At five minutes before seven, they pulled up outside the Masters' home, and in the continued uncharacteristic silence, they made their way up the walk huddled closely together.

"We probably look like a human amoeba," Juliette giggled from the center of the group, dispelling the awkwardness. "Spread out a little, you guys." She bumped Phoebe, who stumbled against Gia, and both of them veered off the sidewalk into the damp lawn.

"Agh!" Phoebe gasped. "I'm wearing sandals, Jules. Now my feet are wet!"

Ren lifted Charise to her shoulder and circled Cheryl to put a safe distance between her and the other three sisters who were now jockeying for position on the walkway. "Are you sure you want to claim this motley crew? We can get a whole lot worse, you know. Fair warning."

Gia glanced over her shoulder to see Cheryl smile and nod, her face alight from the soft glow cast by a few solar powered landscaping lights.

Like the single-celled organism Juliette claimed them to be, they converged as a single unit on the front porch, finding it difficult to stifle their nervous giggles. But before Phoebe could lift the brass knocker, the door was opened wide by Cal. "Come in, come in," he said warmly, standing aside to let them pass into the foyer.

Juliette gasped when she saw the painting on the wall over the entryway table. "Phebes, oh my goodness. I've never seen this one." She reached out and grabbed her sister's hand. "It's stunning."

Gia, too, stared at the painting of the dark-haired woman draped in nearly sheer fabric, her arms looped lovingly around her enlarged belly that had been painted to look like the landforms and bodies of water on a globe. "She kinda looks like you, Ren," Gia whispered, almost reverently.

"I think she looks a little like you, Phoebe," Ren said, resting her cheek on the top of her baby's soft head. "So beautiful."

Gia took a sideways step toward Cheryl in a show of solidarity. No one would ever look at the painting depicting a gorgeous raven-haired mother figure and claim it looked like either of the tall, lanky redheads. It was rather lovely having someone to stand together with. Hearing Granny G's words in her ears, Gia realized she'd been right. "I'm glad you're here with us—with me," she said, speaking softly close to Cheryl's ear.

They all gazed at the painting a few moments longer, then Cal ushered them through the family room into the kitchen where Alice stood at one counter stirring together the ingredients of what appeared to be a homemade salad dressing.

"Hi, ladies. I'm so glad you're here!" Alice exclaimed. She dropped the whisk she'd been using into the sink, wiped her hands on a dishtowel, and then turned to face them. Her cheeks were slightly flushed, either from exertion or excitement, Gia wasn't sure, and her smile, although wide and welcoming, seemed somehow forced.

And familiar. Where had Gia seen her before?

Introductions were made, and although Gia tried hard not to stare, she found it increasingly difficult to focus on anything except the notion that she should know the woman. The conversation stuttered and stalled a little at first, but Charise came to the rescue, charming them all with her gummy smiles, her marshmallow hands and feet, and the intoxicating smell of her head. By the time they sat down to eat, everyone seemed to be feeling a little more at ease with each other.

"In our home, we pray before our meals," Cal said. He sat at the head of the table, just like Gramps, and held his hands out to Phoebe and Alice on either side of him. When Alice placed her hand in his and bowed her head, her chin-length pale blonde hair swept forward... and Gia suddenly remembered where she'd seen her before.

FORTY-THREE

Alice was one of the two women who sat across the cafe table from each other, holding hands and praying over their food, and studying the Bible together. They'd been there the last three Tuesday mornings, and although they were very kind and polite to her, Alice had never made any indication that she'd known Gia.

Yet if what Phoebe said was true, that Alice had kept track of them all these years, then Alice had certainly known who Gia was as she bustled around the cafe. In fact, Alice's presence at Ricardo's might have been *because* Gia worked there.

What was going on? And who was the woman sitting with her? It couldn't be Angela, could it? Wouldn't she have told Juliette if she was back in town? Wouldn't Juliette have warned the rest of them?

No, there was no way it could be Alice's daughter. The other blonde had looked older than Alice, her hair more gray than blonde, the lines around her eyes and mouth delicate, but definitely there. So a sister? A friend from church? Gia couldn't help feeling as though she was missing something, like once again, she was standing on the outside listening in. It made her feel like a little girl again, and she was so tired of feeling like a child.

She sat rigid, her eyes fixed on the top of Alice's bowed head, while Cal said a short prayer of thanks for the food. "Father, we invite you to share our meal with us and be a part of our conversation here, guiding our words and our thoughts as we share our hearts tonight."

"Are you alright?" Cheryl asked, leaning close to Gia as soon as Cal had said his amen.

Gia, however, had just about had it up to her eyeballs with secrets. What was wrong with being truthful? Genuine? Real? She patted Cheryl's hand reassuringly without taking her eyes off Alice. "I know you," she said, skipping the niceties. "You've been coming to my work every week. Every Tuesday this month. Were you there to see me? Keep track of me?" She emphasized the words Phoebe and Ren had used earlier that day.

Suddenly, Gia wanted there to be any other reason for Alice to be sitting at the corner table at Ricardo's each Tuesday morning. If the woman told her that she went there because theirs was the best coffee in Midtown, or that the tables weren't sticky, or that they had the best gingerbread scones and chocolate croissants in town, Gia would have accepted it, at least for the duration of the meal they were about to share. She just wanted to be done with the relentless barrage of revelations that kept crashing into her these days.

But when she saw the way Cal looked at his wife, followed by the deep breath Alice took—the kind of breath that always preceded an unloading of some kind—Gia felt herself moving, scooting her chair back from the table, before she'd even made the decision to do so.

"Why? Did Angela put you up to it? Have you been keeping her apprised of how I'm doing?" *Stop, Gia. Please,* a tiny voice pleaded inside her head. But the words kept coming, an angry swarm of stinging insects. She turned to Cheryl and cupped her chin none too gently, turning her sister's face toward Alice. "Have you told her about my newest sister yet?" And then the final blow. "She's another victim of Angela's wild ride, did you know? Because my mother was Cheryl's godmother."

"Gia!" Ren began, her shock almost tangible. "Honey—"

"No," Gia interrupted with a snarl. "I am so tired of all the lies, of all the secrets, of all the ulterior motives. This whole family is built on half-truths and secret societies. We even have our own secret sister club. The Gustafson Four. G-FOURce," she said, her tone mocking. Her next breath caught in her chest, and for a moment, she thought she wouldn't be able to release it. "Oh. Wait." Her words came out almost strangled. "I guess I'm not really a Gustafson, am I?" Turning to Cheryl, she said, "But I'm not really a Wiley, either. At least, my father—my *namesake,* no less—didn't think so."

"Oh, Gia," Juliette's whisper drew her attention. There were tears slipping down her oldest sister's cheek.

You can't fix this, Jules. "Excuse me," she said, her throat tight. "I think I need some air."

Gia stumbled a little as she shifted her feet out from under the table, catching one on a chair leg. Cal, ever the gentleman Phoebe claimed he was, rose politely when she did, and started to circle the table to help her. She shook her head. "I'll show myself out." Then she hurried from the room, doing her best to ignore the shock and concern on every one of her sisters' faces. She didn't look at Phoebe's *Cerulean* as she passed through the foyer and closed the front door carefully behind her. If she hadn't just given them enough to go by, a slammed door would only prove that she was still the baby of the family.

Wasn't this exactly the same way she'd behaved at their last G-FOURce meeting? Toward Ricky last week? Jupiter? Even toward Cheryl and her grandparents not more than a few hours ago? Temper tantrums and ultimatums, lashing out with cruel, hurtful words. Storming out of the room.

Why? What had finally popped loose in her? Uncorked? It was like everything was coming to a head all at once.

Was this what growing up was like for everyone?

"Dang it, dang it, dang it!" she railed at herself as she stalked down the sidewalk, grateful for her heavily treaded combat boots. With all her might, she willed herself not to cry. She was almost as tired of crying as she was of secrets, so instead, she berated herself harshly in an attempt to keep her anger stoked. "You're such an entitled little baby. Who said life wasn't supposed to be hard, Georgia Amity Gustafson—or Wiley, or *whoever* you are? What makes you think you get to live in Candy Land, following a gumdrop trail lined with lollipop trees and rainbows and—and... custom coffee drinks?" She smacked her hand against the trunk of a jacaranda tree in full bloom planted in the parkway so close to the sidewalk, the roots were beginning to buckle the concrete. "Owww! That hurt!"

But to her surprise, as she stood there clutching her hand to her chest in misery, a shower of bright blue-purple trumpet flowers fluttered down around her, a nearby streetlamp illuminating the moment as though the scene had been staged.

Like Queen Frostine on her ice cream float while candy sprinkles rained down on her in the middle of the Ice Cream Sea... in Candy Land.

Gia snorted. Then she snickered. Okay, maybe it was more of a maniacal chortle, but at the moment, she'd take that over stupid tears any day.

With her uninjured hand, she reached up and shook a low branch that arched over the sidewalk, lifting her face to the flower shower, and breathing in deeply of the faint fragrance hovering in the air around the tree.

Finally, lest someone peer out the window and think she a candidate for the loony bin, she brushed several of the slightly sticky blossoms from her clothes and hair, and started off down the sidewalk again, this time at a much less aggressive pace. She wasn't ready to face the lot she'd left at the dinner table in the Masters' dining room; she really did need a few minutes to clear her head before going back. A walk to the end of the block and back might do her good, and even though it was full on dark now, the street was well lit and the neighborhood seemed friendly enough.

It was true, though. Life wasn't lollipops and rainbows and Venus Risings. It wasn't unicorns and fairy tales and happily ever afters. If there were happily ever afters, then Maman and Papa would still be here. John would still be alive, and Phoebe wouldn't have lost her Lily. Angela wouldn't be haunting them from prison and Alice wouldn't be stalking them for her, either. Colleen wouldn't have gotten cancer, George wouldn't have died from a broken heart, and Gia would have known her sister... her whole life....

But then, none of them would be who they are today, would they? Juliette might have gone off to college and the great beyond with her friend Sharon, never to return. She'd never have gotten pulled over by Vic for driving like a blind duck, that's for sure. What about Tim, who had loved John like a brother, whose love for Ren was all the more remarkable because of it? Phoebe might not have met Trevor so that he could face his demons, so that he could then pray for her for fifteen years before finding her again.

And Gia wouldn't be a Wiley *and* a Gustafson. In fact, being more than a decade younger than Jules, Ren, and Phebes, it was quite likely she wouldn't even be their friend, much less a part of the Gustafson Four. At best, they'd think of her as their mom's friend's snot-nosed brat... if they thought of her at all. She wouldn't have grown up in Gramps and Granny G's loving home, quite likely not in Midtown at all, since the Wileys had lived in another city because of George's job. She might never have met Ricky.

Ricky, who was maybe even more awesome than a unicorn, truth be told.

Maybe life was a little like Candy Land after all. Sure, there were sludgy molasses swamps and dive-bombing bats in black licorice castles. But there were also gumdrop trails to follow—accompanied by grandparents who'd rerouted their own path to give the Gustafson girls a home—and lollipop woods, where sisters danced arm in arm and chanted silly pledges and called each other empresses.

And rainbows? They appeared when the sun shone through falling rain, right? Evidence that even in the middle of the storm, the sun still shined. A symbol of God's faithfulness, of his promise never to abandon his people even when the waters rose, and hope seemed lost.

She turned and walked backwards a few steps, gazing down the block at the Masters' home, at Ren's SUV parked out front—which meant her sisters, all four of them, hadn't abandoned her either—and at the lights beckoning from several of the windows.

The Ark. She could almost imagine a rainbow arching over it.

She stopped in her tracks and whispered, "Help me, Jesus." In that one plea was all the things she wanted to say, but she couldn't manage to put into words lest she start bawling her eyes out. Help me forgive my parents—both sets of them—for abandoning me. Help me trust that you, God, won't abandon me, too. Help me love without fear—Ricky, Jules, Ren, Phoebe, and Cheryl. Help me trust you, God, that you do have a plan for me and my future, just as you promise. Help me to never set aside my rose-colored glasses—no, my rainbow-colored glasses—so that I won't ever stop seeing the gumdrops and lollipops and sprinkles along the way.

She knew her prayer would have sounded a little childish to anyone who could hear her thoughts. Candy Land references? What adult did that? And yet, Jesus did teach that his followers were to have the faith of a child, right? Not to be simple-minded or childish, but teachable, and humble.

Humble. Gia sighed as she started her trek back the way she'd come. Time to eat some humble pie.

The thought of Ricky out there somewhere, thinking about her and praying for her tonight, bolstered her. She pulled out her phone and thumbed out a quick text.

You are way more awesome than a unicorn.

FORTY-FOUR

GIA STEPPED BACK FROM the door, the sound of the brass knocker still echoing in her ears. A moment later, it opened wide to reveal all four of her sisters, Cal and Alice behind them.

"We were just coming to look for you," Phoebe said, her eyes bright, but her smile soft.

Cheryl stepped close and hugged her, then whispered in her ear. "I just found you, Gia. I'm not quite ready to lose you yet."

Gia swallowed hard, wanting to get her words out before she cried. "I'm sorry," was all she got out, and then Ren hugged her, too, so hard she grunted.

Juliette and Phoebe joined the huddle, and Phoebe hollered, "Group hug! Come on, Cal, Alice. Join us!"

"Don't squish the baby," Ren said from somewhere in the middle.

Cal chuckled and kept his distance. Charise nestled contentedly in the crook of his arm. "Steering clear," he said. "Although it really is a beautiful night for a walk, isn't it, princess?"

A few minutes later, they'd once again taken their places around the table, and as they passed around a basket of rolls that were somehow still warm, and a large green salad tossed with chunks of tomatoes and cucumbers, carrot slivers, and Greek olives, Alice spoke, her gentle voice a soothing balm over the group. She'd make a good mother, Gia thought to herself. And then remembered that Alice *was* a mother. A mother who'd been without her daughter for more than fifteen years.

So much loss around this table. So much grief and separation. And yet, here they were, brought together because of the sludgy swamps they'd traversed, and better people because they'd found each other.

Gia turned her attention to what Alice was saying.

"Angela is home. She got out a few weeks earlier than she'd expected, but she wanted to lie low for a bit, to get her land legs under her, so to speak. It's been a little harder to adjust than she'd expected, so she asked for some time."

"Wait, she's here?" Gia pointed at the table in front of her, and then at the ceiling, indicating what she assumed were the bedrooms. "In this house right now?"

"No, no. Tonight she's at church. She's in a support group that meets a few times a week," Cal was quick to explain.

"And she didn't want to mess up our plans, so it worked out fine. She'll stay and visit with some of her friends from her group until I let her know we're finished." Alice leaned forward at her place. "Gia? I'm sorry for not introducing myself to you at Ricardo's." She toyed with her water glass but continued without waiting for Gia's response. "It was one of those silly things that I just didn't think through very clearly. I had one of those crazy notions that I could come to your work, tell you who I was and how much I was looking forward to having you and your sisters come here tonight, and then we'd chat and be the best of friends." She shrugged and flashed her a rather endearing smile, recalling to Gia's mind Angela's picture from Juliette's high school yearbook. There was no denying the family ties. "But once I got there and saw how busy you were—and how well you took everything in stride, Gia! My goodness, I hope that Ricardo knows what he has in you. Anyway, once I realized how idealistic my little fantasy was, I decided to just sit and pray for you instead."

"I'm sorry for what I said," Gia began, but Alice waved her apology away.

"Don't be silly. You had every right to question my behavior." She smiled again, the expression making her look younger than her years. "Well, that first day, just when I was about to head out, Angela called to see where I was. When I told her why I was there, she teased me for being a goofy old lady, and told me to sit tight because she needed to get out of the house, that coffee and prayer sounded good to her. We've prayed for all of you girls quite a bit over the last few weeks."

"That was Angela?" Gia's shock must have been written all over her face, because Alice's smile saddened a little.

"Yes. Prison—" She broke off, and then cleared her throat to start again, but all she said was, "It was not an easy place for her."

After a tense silence, Cal reached over and patted her hand. Charise had fallen asleep on his shoulder, and he had yet to allow Ren to take her from him. "But she's home now, Ally."

"Yes. She's home."

"I think you should call her now," Gia said, not allowing herself time to change her mind. The thought had come to her the moment Alice had said her daughter would stay out until she got a call saying she could come home. How many times had Angela yearned, ached, longed to come home over the years she'd been behind bars? Who were they to keep her away from home—from her mother—a single moment longer?

"Me, too," Juliette chimed in. The other girls quickly agreed.

Alice's face lit up. "Are you sure?"

"Call your daughter, sweetheart," Cal said, squeezing her hand. "I'll add another plate to the table." He rose and gently laid Charise into the baby carrier Renata had brought in with her. The baby made sucking motions with her mouth, but her eyelids barely twitched.

"You have the magic touch," Ren teased. "Do you ever babysit?"

Alice was just setting out the main course—boneless pork chops slathered in a tangy mustard sauce—when the sound of the front door opening and closing brought the conversation around the table to an abrupt stop.

Cal stood and gestured for them to go ahead and get started. "I'll be right back." He shot Alice a reassuring smile, circled the table, and headed to the front entry.

Gia turned slightly to watch him until he disappeared around the bend, but she kept her ear tuned as he greeted Angela. A soft female voice responded, sounding tentative to Gia's ears, but she couldn't make out what they were saying. She took a bite of her pork chop and closed her eyes in sheer bliss.

"It's good, isn't it?" Cheryl asked from beside her. "Alice, this is amazing," she said to the woman who kept darting glances toward the archway.

Cal appeared a moment later, Angela's hand tucked into his arm. "Hi, everyone," Angela said timidly, and they all rose from their seats as one, reminding Gia of a dinner scene in a Jane Austen movie where everyone stood at the arrival of an unexpected guest.

She was just as Gia remembered her. Aged. There was no other way to say it. No longer the porcelain-faced pixie with flaxen hair, but a world-weary woman with premature lines tugging at her mouth, shoulders rounded beneath the weight of a heavy load, and eyes that had borne witness to the sins of the world. She was still tiny, and she definitely bore a resemblance to her mother, but Gia had been so sure this woman was the older of the two sitting at the table in Ricardo's. She darted a quick glance around the table, and she could see the same thoughts mirrored in her sisters' faces.

"Hi, honey. Come. Join us." Alice pointed to the empty seat across from her—Phoebe had moved down to make room for Angela to sit next to Cal. "The girls tell me your pork chops are delicious."

So, in a way, she'd been here all along, having prepared the food just for them.

And then Angela smiled. "Oh, I'm so glad," she said, and let Cal scoot her chair in for her. "I've done nothing but cook since coming home; it's been heaven working in Mom's kitchen."

Cal chuckled. "Talk about heaven. I've done little else but eat her delicious food since she came home." He patted her hand and smiled at her. "I think I've put on a good ten pounds or more."

"Well, Cal, thanks to you and your amazing store, I have access to whatever ingredients I could possibly dream up. So I'm thinking you might have to take some of the blame on this one."

It was then that Gia remembered Cal wasn't Angela's real father. What had happened to the man Juliette remembered from court, the one with the hard voice? How big of a part, if any, had he played in the whole ordeal, and where was he now?

Watching Cal, though, the way he attended to both Angela and her mother with such gentleness and sensitivity, no one would ever know he hadn't known and loved her all her life. Yet another example of God's faithfulness in the storm.

The conversation around the table once again picked up, but Gia sensed that they were all waiting for someone to address the great big elephant sitting in the middle of the room. Angela had asked the girls to meet with her at some point, but was she ready to talk to them about the past? Were they ready to hear it? They'd come prepared to get to know Alice a little, to maybe hear what she might share about Angela, but it had been pretty clear—at least in Phoebe's mind—that Alice was going to let Angela tell her own story.

When Cal put his napkin on the table and rose, everyone stilled, as though they'd been waiting for a sign and this might just be it. Sure enough, he began gathering plates, and Juliette started to rise to help. "No, no. Please sit," Cal told her. "Alice, why don't you and I do the dishes while the girls talk."

Alice stood, too. "Sounds good. Would you ladies like to head to the living room? I can bring coffee and dessert in there in a bit, and it might be more comfortable for you."

The girls all exchanged glances, but then Angela spoke. "Actually, Mom, if you don't mind, I'd like to just hang out in here with you and Cal while we talk. Is that okay with everyone?"

Moral support, Gia realized. She nodded, responding first. "I'm great with that. The Gustafsons are notorious for after dinner talks around the table." She winced and darted a glance at Cheryl. She'd have to remember to be more sensitive to her new—older—sister.

"And this way, we can help with clean up so it'll be done in no time," Ren added in agreement. She deftly gathered the silverware from the places closest to her, stacked the plates the way Gia had seen her do so many times over the years, and carried the load to the sink where Cal was already running hot water for rinsing. Sure enough, in short order, the table was cleared, dishes stashed in the dishwasher, coffee and tea brewed and served, and a platter of homemade sandwich cookies that looked like—

"Are these whoopie pies?" Cheryl asked, reaching for one and dabbing at the fluffy white filling with one finger. "Oh, my goodness." Her eyes widened as she licked her fingertip. "There was a lady in our apartment complex who made these for the kids every Halloween instead of caramel apples or popcorn balls. I love whoopie pies!"

"I do, too." Angela's eyes sparkled. "I requested them for every special occasion when I was growing up. This is actually Mom's recipe."

"And it was my mom's before me," Alice added.

"We've been missing out," Phoebe said, taking a bite of one of the cake-like cookie sandwiches, the filling squeezing out on either side. "I'm thinking Granny G is going to hear about this."

"Mona makes whoopie pies," Juliette quipped. "But these are even better than hers. Don't tell her I said so, though." The Gustafson girls all had a weak spot for pastries from Mona's Bakery. They were on first name basis with the whole kitchen crew, and Mona always threw in a few extra treats when the girls ordered a box of goodies from her for their G-FOURce meetings.

"So since we're talking about memories," Angela said, startling them all with her blunt segue. "I don't think there's any easy way to do this, do you? But I think if I put it off any longer, I'll go crazy." She took a long sip of her black coffee. "Please don't stop indulging while I talk. In fact, it might make it easier if you do."

FORTY-FIVE

Sixteen years ago...

It was over. It was time to move on, let go, be done. Her father could barely look at her anymore, even in public, and although she held her head high and kept her smile plastered on her face, she knew she couldn't keep it all together much longer.

But what choice did she have? The whole world, it seemed, depended on her, counted on her to be their princess. At least the world as she knew it. For most of her classmates, school was winding down to summer, and they had parties to attend, trips planned, new adventures to explore. Not Angela.

Tomorrow, she'd climb in the back of Daddy's car—she hadn't ridden in front with him since the night she'd told him on the way home from church—and he'd drive her out of town to the home of a woman named Beatrice, whom Angela had never met. There, she'd take care of the matter as promised, and then convalesce in Beatrice's care until she was ready to come home and pick up where she'd left off.

"A friend," Daddy had said about Beatrice when he'd first told Angela what was to be done. "One who knows how to keep quiet about things."

A friend, Angela discovered, who knew how to keep quiet about things because she had lots of practice as her father's devoted mistress.

He hadn't meant for Angela to find out. In his rage, it had slipped out before he could stop it. "You want to talk to your mother about this first? Are you mad? She couldn't handle it. She'd go on a drinking binge or curl up in a fetal position and take more pills. She's too medicated to care what this could do to your reputation, your future. To *my* reputation and *my*

"

future." His face had been purple with emotion. "You have no right to question my judgment on this. You came to me, not your lush of a mother, remember? You will take care of this, and then you'll stay with my—with Beatrice—"

He'd stopped talking abruptly and stormed from the room, but Angela had seen it in his eyes, in his expression, the knowledge that he'd just given away his own secret to the one person who could destroy him if she so desired.

What Daddy hadn't realized was that she'd have done anything to please him. She was his angel, his princess, his pride and joy, and she would sell her soul to the devil if it made him happy. He could hurt her, threaten her, scream at her, tear her guts out with his constant pushing and shoving, his unrelenting demands on her to be better, smarter, stronger, more, more, more than anyone else.

But even more than she cared what he thought, even more than she wanted to make Daddy proud, she loved her mother. If Daddy thought hurting Angela would make her a better person, that was one thing. But knowing he was hurting her mother was another thing altogether.

She would have the abortion, she would forget about Nate, the boy she wasn't sure she loved, but whom she'd slept with because he'd said he loved her in a way no one else had ever said it to her before. And she would continue to be her father's protégé, his sidekick. With her voice and her looks, her intelligence and charisma, and the fact that he didn't have to pay her more than room and board and a stipend, she *was* his publicity. She would help him win, and win again, first in Midtown, then in California, all the way to The Cabinet itself. Angela made him look good when his dear, beloved wife could not... because Alice's health didn't allow her to participate in so many, many things. At least, that's what he'd always led her to believe.

Up until that moment, that slip of the tongue about Beatrice, Angela had believed what he'd told the world, that her gentle, sweet mother was in poor health. She'd believed that he cared deeply for his wife and wanted to protect her and take care of her, just as much, if not more than Angela did.

It hadn't taken her long to figure it out. The sleeping pills and antidepressants in the medicine cabinet in her parents' bathroom, the cases of Gray Goose and Bombay in the back of her mother's walk-in closet, stacked next to the dorm fridge with an automatic ice machine and stocked with tonic water and ginger ale. If her father wasn't the one keeping his wife in a near-comatose state, he certainly knew she was doing it to herself. And for all intents and purposes, he seemed to be just fine with it.

An icon of the community. A pillar of the church. A family man. An advocate for the downtrodden. A spokesperson for those who had no voice. An activist for the worthy causes. A faithful husband. A loving father.

No wonder her mother self-medicated herself into a stupor every night. Her whole life was a lie.

And Angela's was quickly becoming one, too.

Well, if it worked for Alice....

FORTY-SIX

"And so, you see, I didn't know what to do. I thought my hands were tied. Even behind bars, I didn't think I could talk to anyone, because if they believed me and let me out, he'd hate me even more than he did already. I'd been so conditioned to take his word as gospel truth, to obey his every command—to the point that I was willing to have an abortion to protect his reputation and career—to believe that everything he did was for our good. I'd spent my whole life trying to make him love me, but it was never enough."

Alice sat beside her daughter, holding her hand, and Cal stayed close by, offering his support with a touch, a pat, or the offer of a tissue. "And I was so afraid for my mother. I didn't want to expose her addictions because I knew he would somehow turn it into a way to make himself into a hero for standing by her through it. And I was afraid for her, too, if I did. What would happen to her if he abandoned her, and I wasn't there to save her?"

"So you just kept quiet and took the blame for everything," Juliette said from her seat next to Phoebe. The two sisters sat so close that their shoulders pressed together, but Gia felt certain they'd intended it that way. Ren had moved her chair back from the table so she could nurse Charise. The baby girl had awakened in a temper so uncharacteristic of her it had made everyone laugh, a much-needed break from the heaviness of Angela's story.

"I was to blame, though," Angela corrected gently. "I could have told someone. I could have gotten Mom out of there. I could have packed us both up and gotten the heck out of Dodge. But I didn't, because all that seemed like it was too hard." She shook her head and made a small snorting sound. "Girl, I didn't know what hard was."

Gia's eyes widened at the way Angela's voice changed into something sharp, harsh, but laced more with regret than bitterness.

"No," she continued. "I took the easy way, the one that brought instant gratification." She lifted her gaze and looked directly at Juliette. "And you paid for it. Dearly. Every day of your lives." She looked at each sister, one at a time, as she spoke. "So did your grandparents. You, too, Mom." Even though she included Alice, it was pretty evident to Gia that the mother and daughter had already cleared the air between them, likely long, long ago.

"And so did you," Ren said, lifting Charise to her shoulder to burp her. Everyone nodded in agreement.

"But I'm the only one who really deserved to." She held up her hand when her mother started to protest. "Mom. It's over. It's done. You're well now, and that's what counts." So maybe it still wasn't completely resolved for Alice, but now that she had her daughter back, Gia felt certain it would happen.

"Can I ask you something?" Phoebe said, her eyes bright with moisture.

"Of course. Anything."

"What happened—what happened to your baby?"

Angela nodded and turned to her mother. "I miscarried because of the accident. I didn't know until after I'd been sentenced. And I was too afraid to ask anyone."

"They told me in the hospital, assuming I already knew," Alice explained, picking up the story now. "I had no idea her father already knew, so I kept it to myself until she was well enough for me to discuss it with her. When I told her about the miscarriage, she told me everything." Tears gathered in Alice's eyes as she recalled for them the agony of sitting across a table from each other, surrounded by strangers and guards, unable to hold her daughter while she wept for all that she'd done, for all those who'd suffered because of her decision. "But out of that horrible visit came my decision to walk away. From Dan—who is now a smarmy politician somewhere in Arizona near Tucson—from the alcohol, from the various medications I treated myself to. There was no way to undo what had happened, but I knew I had to take back my life so that I could give my daughter back hers when she came home to me."

"And The Ark?" Phoebe prodded. Gia knew where this was going. She knew what Phoebe wanted to hear. Just as she knew what Alice's answer would be already.

"The Ark. Yes. Because I want to provide a safe place for girls, for women, like Angela was, who need a place to go. Who will be loved unconditionally as they make some of the toughest decisions of their lives."

"Girls like me, too," Phoebe said, her voice just above a whisper. And then she shared her story with Angela and Alice and Cal. Cheryl, too.

It was at least another hour and perhaps a few too many cups of coffee before the sisters and baby Charise left the home of the people they'd bonded so intimately with, first in tragedy, and now in healing. Their hearts and minds were overflowing, and the ride back to Ren's was as subdued as the one that brought them to the Masters' home, but for a different reason altogether.

"I feel a little like Mary, the mother of Jesus, must have felt," Phoebe said. "When she treasured the things she'd been told and pondered them in her heart."

"Totally," Gia said, whispering so as not to disrupt the introspective mood of the women surrounding her. Even Charise sat quietly in her car seat, her eyes wide open as she stared out the window at the streetlights flashing by.

"I still have so many questions," Ren admitted from the driver's seat. "I feel a little like we've just opened a door to what we thought was a closet, but when we turned on the lights, we discovered a great hall full of treasures that might take us the rest of our lives to go through."

"And it feels okay, doesn't it?" Juliette asked. "I mean, I don't feel like I need all the answers today. I think it's okay, maybe even better, if they come a little at a time."

"I know I've kinda had my fill of revelations for now," Gia said, and then reached out to touch Cheryl's shoulder. "But I think more time might be the best thing for all of us. More time together, getting to know each other." She was speaking directly to Cheryl now, but she meant it for all of them.

"Me, too," Cheryl said. "Thank you for letting me come tonight. For including me in all of this. My heart is full to overflowing right now. I feel like I belong—" She broke off and glanced down at her hands in her lap.

"You do belong, Cheryl," Gia insisted, grabbing her sister's hand and squeezing it hard.

"You're one of us now, whether you like it or not," Phoebe teased. "A Gustafson Girl by proxy."

"Absolutely," Ren agreed as she pulled her SUV into her driveway. She shut off the engine and turned to Juliette. "You know, there was a time when I thought you'd lost your marbles. That day you brought out that letter from Angela Clinton?"

Juliette laughed. "I remember. I was there."

"Yeah. Well, I'm sorry, Jules. I'm sorry for doubting you, for being angry at you for following your heart on this, for listening to the Holy Spirit the way you did. I'm so glad we had this night, and I don't know if it would have happened had you not opened the door for us. So thank you, big sister. You're my hero."

A collective sigh peppered with words of agreement filled the interior of the car before they disembarked.

As Gia climbed out of her seat, her phone slid from the pocket of the black jeans she wore onto the seat cushion. She picked it up and saw a text notification.

And you are way more awesome than a pot of gold at the end of a rainbow. You're even more awesome than a rainbow itself.

EPILOGUE

ONE YEAR LATER...

Gia pulled up to the curb in front of Juliette's place. She still thought of it that way, even though it was now occupied by Cheryl, who had moved to town last summer to be close to her new family. It seemed dental hygienists were in high demand in Midtown, so finding a job had been easy enough, and she planned to rent the condominium until she was ready to buy a place of her own. Gia hoped to move in when Cheryl moved out; the grandparents were talking about finding a retirement community nearby where they would have twenty-four-hour assistance as needed, they wouldn't have to worry about transportation, and they'd be surrounded by others in their season of life.

"Besides, it'll free you up to live your life, sweetie," Granny G had said to her at least a half a dozen times. "You shouldn't be hanging around us old fogies all the time. You and your Ricky have some young folk living to do." And as much as everyone hated the thought of saying goodbye to their home, they all agreed that it was time for Gramps and Granny G to simply enjoy being old fogies for a change.

Gia and Ricky did have some living to do, in fact. Ricky was slowly whittling away at his degree so that he could teach—he had a special penchant for fifth and sixth graders—and the two of them were saving their money for their wedding. They hadn't yet settled on a date, but Gia wore an opal engagement ring that sparkled with rainbow colors every time she lifted her hand to look at it.

"Hello!" she called out as she pushed open the door. Juliette's car was already parked out front, too, so Gia wasn't surprised when Bob came careening into the foyer to greet her, his nails clicking and clacking on the tile, followed immediately by Mr. Bobo from next door. Mrs. Cork was probably ensconced in her armchair watching 'Murder, She Wrote' on Netflix—Gia got her hooked after once telling the old lady that she reminded her of Angela Lansbury in the show. She'd have to make sure she was the one to return Mr. Bobo to his mommy so that she could say hello to her.

"In the kitchen," Jules hollered from inside the house. Gia followed the voices, and after setting her box of cookies on the table, followed by a round of hugs, she poured herself a cup of coffee from the pot on the counter, still finishing its brew.

"It'll be strong," Cheryl pointed out.

"That's the only way I drink it," Gia responded.

They heard the door open, and the dogs made their wild circuit once more, eliciting squeals of delight from the foyer. Renata called out, "It's just Charise and me." She made her way through the roiling mass of dogs with her little girl in tow, and then stepped back as the rest of the sisters converged on the darling child, vying for first dibs on auntie hugs and kisses.

Juliette pulled out of the melee first. "Phoebe texted. She'll be a few minutes late."

"Surprise, surprise," Ren exclaimed drolly.

By the time they'd shifted the party to the living room and found their respective seats—Cheryl had kept Juliette's furniture right where she'd left it, and Jules hadn't hesitated to let her know that she still had dibs on the right end of the sofa—Phoebe was pushing her bulk through the front door.

"I hate being pregnant," she said by way of greeting. "Look at my ankles! How come you don't look like a puffer fish when you're preggers, Ren? I hate you."

"Tell me something I don't know," Ren quipped.

"Well, since we're all here, Gia?" Juliette stood and held her hands out to the women on either side of her. "Shall we begin?"

Once again, the girls began the G-FOURce pledge, a time-honored tradition that had somehow survived adolescence into adulthood.

Let the words of our mouths
Be necessary, kind, and true.
Let the secrets we share
Be kept safe amongst us few.
Let the decisions that we make
Be brave, noble, and wise
Oogie-boogie-doggy-loogie
Wiggly-jiggly-fries!
G-FOURce unite!

The G-FOURce. The Gustafson Four. A force of nature to be reckoned with; that's what they still were. But no longer were there only four empresses in their sister society, nor was Cheryl the only honorary member.

Angela Clinton was welcomed into the circle any time she was in town, and as soon as Charise was old enough to understand the responsibility that came with taking the pledge, she'd be ushered into the fold as well. Phoebe and Trevor, too, were bringing a baby girl into the world in about three months, and, of course, there was always Lily. Maybe one day she would know what it was to be a Gustafson Girl.

Angela had returned to the women's prison where she'd spent the majority of her adult life, but this time as a chaplain. She ministered to broken women on the inside, while Cal and Alice continued to offer sanctuary to pregnant teens who needed a safe place to make the tough decisions. Six months ago, Alice had recruited Gia as her assistant—a role Alice had hoped Angela would fill, but she was happy to have Gia in her stead. Gia loved everything about the work she did, but even more than the job, she was growing to love Alice, who was quickly becoming like a mother to her.

For whatever reason, Juliette was not yet pregnant, so although they weren't going to give up trying, she and Vic had made the decision to adopt. Alice connected them to one of the adoption agencies The Ark worked with, and the couple hoped to one day become the parents of a child who needed them as much as they needed him or her.

"You could always hire a surrogate," Gia told Juliette. "Look how awesome I turned out."

Cheryl sat in her brand-new armchair opposite Ren—the first piece of new furniture she'd ever bought—and beamed at the bevy of women in her living room. "Sometimes I still can hardly believe this is happening to me," she said, tucking her legs up under her and smoothing her skirt over her knees. "You Gustafson girls are the best sisters I could ever wish for. I love you. All of you." She turned to Gia and grinned. "You, especially, on account of the red hair and freckles."

• • • • • • • • • •

How cool was it that Gia and the Gustafson girls discovered yet another sister to join their G-FOURce club?

Their journey has come full circle with the healing that started back in **Juliette & the Monday ManDates** when Jules reached out to Angela Clinton. Wasn't it good to finally meet the woman at the center of their deepest wounds?

I hope the Gustafson girls have endeared themselves to you as much as they have to me.

• • • • • • • • • •

Are you ready for another series about sisters?
Check out the Seven Virtues Ranch Romance Series or keep reading for an excerpt from...

Gotta Have Faith: Seven Virtues Ranch Romance Book 1

Can a small-town cowgirl and a big-time city boy find their way back to a second chance at happily ever after?

Faith Goodacre has had to overcome major obstacles to save her family and bring Seven Virtues Ranch back from the brink of disaster.

So when her high school sweetheart shows up hoping to win back her heart - oh, and he's bought the ranch next door - her carefully ordered world she's worked so hard to build threatens to implode.

Cordell Overman is back, and he's ready to face his past and make things right. But he's got a whole town to convince that this time around, he's here to stay.

If you like sweet contemporary romance in a small town ranch and farm setting, life-altering surprises, and second chances, you'll love *Gotta Have Faith*, the first book in the Seven Virtues Ranch Romance Series. So come sit a spell in Plumwood Hollow where life happens a little slower and sweeter, but hearts might just be a little bigger.

It's another wholesome, swoon-worthy romance series about sisters.

From the Author

Dear Reader,

I have a special place in my heart for sisters. I grew up with a sister only eight months younger than I am. Yep, there are only eight months between us. But before you send those side-eyes at my poor parents, one of us is adopted. It was a case of...

"You can't get pregnant."

"Let's adopt."

"Yay! Your baby is ready to pick up at the adoption store!"

"Oh, and double yay... You're also pregnant! Surprise!"

"Wow! Let's keep them both."

"Sure. Why not?"

Or something like that.

In many ways, my sister and I are as close as twins, seeking security and support from each other in ways no one else can possibly provide. And in many ways, we are like oil and water... a beautiful mess. We now live in two different countries, and there is always far too much time that passes between phone calls and visits. But she is in my heart every single day, and I can't imagine my life without her in it.

I have another sister who arrived on the scene many years later, and with a beautiful adoption story of her own. She is the age of my children, so our sister relationship has a precious nature all its own. And again, I can't imagine my life without her in it.

You'll find "sisters" in most of my books: some by birth, some by adoption, and some in name only—friends who have become sisters.

If you're looking for fiction with realistic romance and redemptive story lines, I invite you to check out some of my other books and series.

You may meet your next BFF (Best Fiction Friend)! Or visit me online: **BeckyDoughty.com**.

I write heartfelt and wholesome Contemporary Romance and Women's Fiction. I write fiction because nonfiction is hard! Yes, I've tried. Let's just say I like to color outside the lines when it comes to facts. But emotions and feelings and the roller coaster ride that comes with all relationships? Oh yeah. That's where you'll find me.

Where hope lives and love prevails,
~ Becky Doughty

Let's stay in touch! **Sign up for my newsletter** for book and audiobook news (and deals!), and for fun subscriber-exclusive stuff.

An Excerpt: Gotta Have Faith

CHAPTER ONE
FAITH

"NOTHIN' FINER THAN A hardworking woman in a worn pair of jeans and a Stetson."

Faith Goodacre straightened and turned slowly. She'd know that voice anywhere. Even after all these years. She removed her safety glasses, wishing she'd worn her shades instead, and narrowed her eyes against the brilliant sunlight. It was uncommonly warm for early May, but the weather could still change on a dime this time of year. She settled her hat a little firmer on her head, then lifted her chin a notch so she could look down her nose at the man who'd just rounded the end of the barn to park across the gravel driveway behind her. Hooking her thumbs in the belt loops on her jeans, she watched as Cordell Overman took his sweet time getting out of his big Cajun Red Silverado, grinning at her all the while.

He stopped several feet away from her, thank the good Lord above, because even if she could get her feet to move, she wasn't about to retreat. He was on her turf, and she hadn't yet decided if that was a good thing or not.

She widened her stance and squared her shoulders. "Sure beats a city slicker with soft hands and a sunburnt scalp, kicking up dust in a shiny new truck, to boot," she said, letting her sweet tea drawl lace the words with just enough sugar to take the edge off.

"Ouch!" Cord clutched his chest and staggered backward a step or two. But he kept his eyes fixed on her face, and his smile didn't waver, making it somewhat difficult for her to maintain her disdainful expression.

Holy smokes, he looked good.

Not that she was looking.

Okay, yeah, she was.

"You're looking good, Cord." Dang it. She hadn't meant to say it out loud, but at least she sounded unaffected by his sudden appearance.

"Even with this sizable hole you just blasted through me?" He lifted his hand and peered down as though to gauge the extent of the damage, then looked back up at her again, his eyes sparkling with humor.

"Looks to me like you'll survive," Faith quipped.

He held his arms out at his sides, making his already snug gray t-shirt stretch even tighter across his chest. "Then how about a welcome back to the holler hug for an old friend?"

She forced her gaze to stay on his face but looking into his November sky eyes was proving to be just as troublesome as ogling his impressive physique.

Old friend. So that's what they were calling it these days? "Believe me; you don't want a hug from me."

"Sure, I do." He took a step toward her, but she held up a hand to stay him.

"As you so eloquently put it, I'm working. Hard." She tapped the shield of the chop saw she'd been using, then lowered the blade and knocked the safety into place. "I'm not exactly in the mood to cuddle right now." With the back of her wrist, she swiped at a drop of perspiration that trickled down the side of her face and clung to her jawline. She was sweating like a sinner in church, covered in sawdust, and her hair was plastered to her head under her hat.

Cord, on the other hand, could have stepped right off the cover of *American Cowboy.* Except he didn't have a two-day scruff, he wasn't wearing a hat, and she was pretty sure he didn't own a horse. Not anymore, anyway.

"Cuddle is your word, not mine," he said, flashing his pearly whites at her. "I wasn't asking you to snuggle up to—"

"Semantics, Cord." She rested her hand on a cocked hip and exchanged his grin with a grimace. *Speaking of pearly white...* Her imagination conjured up a holster slung low at her waist, complete with a pearl-handled Colt .45 poised for the draw. Heck, her little Glock would do the job just fine—.

Good grief, Faith. What job are you considering using any gun for? She cleared her throat, hoping he couldn't read her uncharacteristically violent thoughts.

"You're a long way from home. What brings you to our neck of the woods?" What she really wanted to ask him was what had brought him to Seven Virtues Ranch. And couldn't he have at least called first? Given her some kind of heads up? Wasn't that just common courtesy?

Cord turned his head briefly in the direction of Seven Virtues' closest neighbor, Whispering Hills Ranch. Although nothing was visible through the wooded tract that marked the property line between the ranches, Faith was pretty sure he was picturing the abandoned hay barn on the other side of the small creek that meandered through the trees. Same as she was. Not something she particularly wanted to dwell on, but his next words confirmed her suspicions. He spoke in a husky drawl. "How about a 'Welcome Back' kiss, then? Purely unselfish motives on my part, I assure you," he added, shooting her a sideways look that made something coil tightly low in her gut. Then he chuckled, making light of his request. "In honor of Uncle Judge, God rest his soul."

"I never once kissed Judge Flanner," Faith retorted, hating that he could still get to her so easily. She crossed her arms and dipped her head, hoping her hat would hide the flush coloring her cheeks. Just the thought of kissing Cordell Overman again made her blood run hot. "Besides, he was a married man, so there'd be nothing honorable about it," she added, narrowing her eyes at him. Judge had been, in fact, a widower, but he'd been married to Cord's aunt for more than fifty years before she passed away. "So, what did you say you needed? I really am busy, you know."

Cord let out a low whistle. "Why, Miss Goodacre, when did you get so prickly?"

Prickly? She tried not to be offended by his question, but coming from Cord, the barbed word smarted. It was self-preservation, as far as she was concerned. "Why, Mr. Overman, how do you know it's 'Miss'?"

"Because I made certain of it before I headed out this way to see you." The grin turned into a bold, piano key smile, one he'd used to charm her to his will a time or two—or two hundred—back in the day.

Even before he'd had his teeth straightened and bleached. Mercy, they were white. *City boy.*

"And I brought you something." He spun on his boot heel—at least those weren't new, she noted. He'd always preferred the Western work boots over more traditional cowboy boots. He reached into the open driver's side window of his truck to withdraw a pale blue mason jar spilling over with red and yellow columbines, the delicate star-like blossoms bobbing their heads in greeting as he approached with them. Holding them out to her, he said, "For you, Fair Maiden."

Faith couldn't help it. She smiled.

"There she is," he murmured appreciatively, dipping his head to look her in the eye. "There's that pretty smile I know."

She pressed her lips together, trying desperately not to be impressed that he'd remembered about the columbines, then she shook her head in surrender. Man, he was good.

She'd once pointed her favorite flower out to him where they grew in her mother's gardens. She'd told him the fiery wildflower with its flared petals, and backward facing spikes, made her think of fairy tale dragons. He'd plucked a small handful, dropped to one knee, and offered them to her, declaring he was her knight in shining armor, ready to slay dragons for her. Faith still carefully tended the bushes that grew in riotous disarray at the top of the long drive up from Carpenter Road. She had the sneaking suspicion that Cord had helped himself to them on his way in.

Except she remembered, too. She remembered just how not ready he'd been to fight for her when it came right down to it. Almost a decade ago, he'd kicked the dust off a pair of Ropers just like the ones he wore now, forcing her to armor up and fight the dragons herself. The fact that he stood in front of her today, that pie-eating grin on his face, told her he had no clue about the damage he'd left in his wake.

After a moment's hesitation, she took the jar from him, careful not to let her fingers do any more than graze his in the exchange. It didn't matter; the jolt was still there, sending a current of electricity coursing through her veins. She resisted the impulse to shiver and turned away to set the flowers on the stacked stone retaining wall nearby. "Thank you. They're lovely. But then, I do grow the finest columbines in town."

"You do, indeed," he agreed, not denying her assertion that he'd snagged them from her flower beds. "Only the finest for Faith Goodacre. That's what I always say."

She lifted her hat and fanned her face with it, turning away from him to gaze at the blossoms that now seemed to mock her. She had no clue what her hair looked like, and even though she shouldn't care what he thought, she did. "And I always say, 'If I want it done right, I'll do it myself.' As evidenced by those flowers."

"Only because you never did know how to ask for help." His words were gentle, but they practically knocked the breath out of her anyway.

She clapped the hat back on her head and spun around to glare at him, her eyebrows raised in indignation. "That's not how I remember it."

Cord shrugged. "Maybe you remember it wrong." His tone remained casual, but she saw the tension in the set of his shoulders, in the way he cocked his right hip just a little higher than the left. They were like a couple of gunslingers settling in for a standoff. She imagined his trigger finger twitching in anticipation, just as hers had a few minutes ago.

But Faith wasn't interested in going toe to toe with him. Not today. Not ever. It had taken some doing, but she'd let go of what might have been a long time ago, and up until this moment, she'd assumed Cordell Overman had moved on as well.

So, what in the Sam Hill was he doing showing up here at Seven Virtues Ranch, bringing her fairy tale dragon flowers, and smiling at her as though the last decade had never happened? It was bad enough that he was back in the hollow; did he have to try to breach the sanctuary of her heart as well?

"No, Cord, I remember it all perfectly well." She licked her dry lips and glanced down at the watch on her wrist. Her sisters teased her about it, but she refused to whip out her phone every time she needed to check the time.

Every minute of her day was allotted for something, and none of those minutes were set aside for the man in front of her. She'd erased his name from her calendar and had no plans to put him back on the schedule. She gave him a pointed look. "If you'll excuse me, I have to get back to it." She stepped up to the saw, removed the safety, and slipped her safety glasses back on. She bent to pick up a two-by-four.

He beat her to it. "Let me help."

"But I don't need your help." Faith didn't even bother trying to convince him to hand the board over. Instead, she grabbed another one. She swung one end away from her, nearly clipping him in the hip, and balanced it on the rock wall, then slid the other end into place under the saw blade. She made a quick cut, then stacked the two pieces on the other side of her workstation with others she'd already cut.

"I was only asking." He offered her the board he held, but she didn't take it. First of all, she wasn't going to risk touching him again. And second, now she was stuck standing on principle and couldn't accept his help, even if she wanted it. Even if he offered it with no strings attached.

Except she wasn't so sure there were no strings attached. "Actually, you didn't ask. You demanded that I let you help. Two very different things."

"Semantics, Faith," he said, tossing her word back at her. But he set the two-by-four back on the pile, then leaned his backside against the stone wall, bracing his hands on either side of his hips. The pose was casual enough, but she didn't miss the subtle shift in his demeanor, the slightly deflated posture, and furrowed brow.

The uncomfortable burn of shame made her skin crawl. She really was being prickly today.

And to give him credit, he did seem to be trying to make the best of a situation that was bound to be difficult, no matter how they approached it. A phone call to warn her of his visit may have proved just as volatile, truth be told.

"Where's Jack?" she asked, suddenly realizing that her dog hadn't alerted her to Cord's approach. Usually, the tri-colored Border Collie went out of his way to let everyone on the ranch know when visitors arrived. "Jack?" she called out before pursing her lips and letting out a piercing whistle. With a certain satisfaction, she saw Cord flinch.

The dog, however, remained AWOL.

Cord spoke casually. "I met up with Prudence and Jack at the front gate down the lane. She told me where I could find you."

Faith spun to look at him. "What was she doing down there? And why did she have my dog?" A momentary bout of irritation rose inside her. Prudence, the sixth of the seven Goodacre sisters, was constantly off indulging in some whimsy or another. Faith had corralled her at the chicken coop a little earlier where the girl was collecting eggs and padding the nesting boxes with fresh straw. She'd given Prudence strict instructions to check in as soon as she was finished, as Faith would need her help framing up the new chicken tractor she was making. Their chickens free ranged in the pastures behind the cattle, and the portable chicken housing kept the flock safe from predators.

"She was taking pictures," Cord said with a soft chuckle. "She'd put together a makeshift nest with weeds and flowers and chicken eggs and set it up on top of that old stump next to the Seven Virtues sign. She had your dog posing with it."

"Poor Jack," Faith said with a snort, as she settled the board onto the saw. "She's always making him model for her. Then again, he doesn't seem to mind." She made quick work of the last three two-by-fours waiting to be cut, then brushed the sawdust off her hands and removed her glasses again. She really should be wearing gloves, but her daddy never did, so neither did she. Oh, she paid for it with calluses, ugly nails, and rough skin, but Prudence had a knack for whipping up amazing herbal salves, and Faith was one of her best customers. "Did she say she was coming up soon? I asked her to help me with this thing." She waved at the cut lumber and rolls of chicken wire nearby.

Cord shot her a dubious look, his eyebrows raised.

"See? I do know how to ask for help." She grimaced; she sounded like a two-year-old, even to her own ears.

"Right. I see." Cord nodded slowly, that stupid grin back on his face. "So, speaking of Judge Flanner—"

"But we weren't." Faith cut him off, glad for the change in subject, but not liking his patronizing tone. "We were talking about you and why you're here."

Cord continued as though she hadn't spoken. "Frankie's selling the old place."

She frowned at him. He seriously didn't think she already knew about that?

Frank "Judge" Flanner—so named because he'd held the title of head judge at every Plumwood Hollow pie contest as long as anyone could remember—had died last fall, and although she didn't really miss the grouchy old rancher, Faith hated what had become of Whispering Hills over the last several years, and especially since his unexpected passing. Frank Junior—Frankie to his family and friends—was career military and had little inclination toward picking up cattle ranching where his daddy left off, and no one else in the nearby area was in any position to purchase the huge property and its dwindling herd of cattle. Which inevitably meant some stranger from out of town would be moving into the close-knit community, something that always took some adjusting to.

Once again, Faith locked the saw blade down, and this time, she unplugged it from the bright orange extension cord snaking around from the front of the barn. "So, you're here about your uncle's place? If you're hoping for an inside scoop, I don't really have much of one. I know Frankie wants to move it quickly and all in one piece, and he's priced it accordingly." She knew this because she'd contacted him about purchasing some of the acreage to expand Seven Virtues. "The big house is sitting empty right now, but Jordan Binks—you remember him? He lives on site in that cowboy cabin and keeps an eye on the place. He's a good guy, and he knows that place better than your uncle did, I'd wager, but he's old, and he's worried he'll get ousted when a new buyer comes in. He loves that place and is good with the herd. Granted, he lost a few calves and two first-calf heifers this spring, just because he was trying to manage what he could on his own. We helped out as much as we were able; Hope spent a fair amount of time over there early April." Faith frowned. "I hear he's considering keeping the bulls from breeding come fall if they haven't sold the place by then, but otherwise, he's been operating as though Judge was still calling the shots."

"Poor bulls." Cord winked at her.

Faith kept talking, choosing to ignore his juvenile comment. "Which means unless Frankie finds a buyer soon, the place is going to start losing some serious revenue." She worried about Binks. The old cowboy had made Whispering Hills his home for more than fifty years, and the thought of him having to make a new start this late in life just about broke her heart. "Anyway, it's a real steal for all that land, the house, and the outbuildings. What's left of the herd, too, I believe. I know Judge downsized pretty extensively in the last few years, but last I heard, he was still running a good two hundred head. Oh, and he's currently got eight or nine bulls, too. There are the two good-sized ponds, and a 5-acre lake—" She broke off, waving a hand as though batting away her words. "But then, you probably know that ranch better than I do. It's gotten a little run down, but otherwise, it hasn't changed much since you left." She swallowed hard, the words stinging the back of her throat on their way out.

For a few moments, he said nothing, just studied her. Faith held his gaze, even though it about killed her to do so. Her skin prickled with the urge to squirm, but she maintained her dignity and kept it together.

"You interested in the place?" he finally asked. "You looking to expand Seven Virtues?"

She shook her head. "I couldn't take all that, even if I wanted to or had the resources to do so. It's all I can do to keep up with what we've got going here. I know of several folks around here who'd love to have just a piece of it—Seven Virtues, included—but Frankie doesn't want to parcel it out if he doesn't have to. And at the price he's selling, he'll move the package deal without too much trouble." She shrugged again like it made no difference to her, but she'd been acutely disappointed when Frankie had explained that he already had a potential buyer.

Cord nodded slowly, but when he brought a hand up to rub the back of his neck, she stiffened. He was nervous about something. That neck grab thing he did, while awfully pretty the way it showed off his muscular arms, was as sure a tell if ever there was one, at least when it came to Cordell Overman. And one she recognized, even after all these years.

A rogue breeze whispered against the damp tendrils of hair clinging to her neck, and Faith lifted her face to it, releasing a long sigh of pleasure. She reached up to hold her hat on, closing her eyes against the brilliant sky, and shot him the same question he'd asked her. "Why? Are you interested in the place, city boy?"

The moment the words left her mouth, she wanted to suck them back in. She suddenly and acutely did not want to look at him for fear of what she might see on his face. She'd asked the question in jest, but now that it was out there, it struck her that Cord's arrival in Plumwood Hollow was quite a coincidence. What if he was back to take a look at his uncle's place?

Oh, mercy. What if Cordell Overman moved in next door? The thought made her knees go weak.

CHAPTER TWO
CORD

Cordell Overman had a really good idea of how a thirsty man felt staring at an oasis in the desert. The moment he laid eyes on her, his mouth went so dry, it almost hurt to swallow. When he tried to speak, he experienced a moment of sheer panic, because his tongue refused to cooperate. His pulse had been racing for two days at the mere thought of seeing Faith Goodacre again, but the real-life version of her literally took his breath away.

The beautiful girl he remembered—dreamed about, pined after, ached for—had become a beautiful woman. Her curves, already lush and feminine back in high school, had filled out in a way that made his palms sweat, and the upward thrust of her chin exposed the pale hollow under her jaw where he used to plant kisses just to hear the sweet noises she made. Those lips—

"I'm going to grab a glass of sweet tea," Faith said abruptly. "Can I—" She stumbled over the words, her cheeks growing pink when she caught him gawking at her. "Can I offer you a glass?"

Was he drooling? He wouldn't be surprised. He ran a hand over his mouth and along his jawline, just in case. He wasn't thinking about Whispering Hills, that was for sure, and from the look on her face, he could tell that *she* could tell exactly what he was thinking.

He glanced away, corralling his wayward thoughts. *I know, I know. But I am just a man, Lord, and you made Faith Goodacre a very fine woman.* He took a slow, steadying breath and counted backward from ten. At four, he braved looking at her again.

She kicked at a clump of tenacious fescue that had rooted itself in the gravel, her head down, her arms crossed tightly over her chest.

Don't shut me out, Faith. "Sure. I'd appreciate a cold drink." His voice held just the slightest rasp, but he cleared his throat, hoping she hadn't noticed. He took a step toward her, and she flinched, shifting backward and tripping over the leg of a sawhorse. When he reached out to steady her, she put an arm up as though to ward off an attack. Withdrawing his hand, he wasn't sure whether to be offended or not. "You all right?"

"Of course." She gestured down the driveway ahead of her. "Shall we?"

When Cord reached out again, she side-stepped a little and glared up at him. "What are you doing?" she asked.

"Just grabbing the flowers." He picked up the jar from where it sat on the rock wall, grinning in spite of her indignant tone. He kinda liked the fact that she didn't seem any more immune to him than he was to her. "I'll carry them for you."

"Oh. Right. Thanks." She turned on her heel and started toward the house, not waiting for him.

He didn't mind, no, indeed. Not when she filled out those jeans the way she did. He paused to take in the wonder of it all.

He was having a hard time remembering why he'd walked away from her in the first place.

"You going to join me, Cordell Overman, or are you just going to stand there ogling my backside all day?"

Cord laughed out loud and caught up to her quickly, his strides sure and long. "How did you know?" he said, intentionally crowding her just a little. He held the jar of flowers out in front of him, careful not to slosh the water on their toes. "You got eyes in the back of your head or something? And here I thought that was just a mom thing." He nudged her with an elbow.

A strange look crossed her face, quickly followed by a scowl. "You were practically burning a hole in my Levis. Cut it out."

"I apologize. You're right. Totally out of line." He meant it, too. Oh, he wanted to stare at her all day, and not just her backside. He wanted to pull her up against him and kiss her until her eyes rolled back in her head. He wanted to— "Stop!"

"What?" Faith jerked to a halt and planted her hands on her hips, glaring up at him once again.

Cord squeezed his eyes shut and shook his head before opening them again. "Never mind. Sorry."

"Wow. Really?" When he only shrugged, she said, "You know, maybe you should just tell me what you need, and we can forget about the tea." She narrowed her eyes at him and waited for his response. "I really do have work to do." The toe of her right foot tapped impatiently, making him smile again.

"And I really could use that sweet tea. Might cool us both down some," he replied, appreciating the high spots of color in her cheeks. "You taking back your offer of hospitality, Miss Goodacre?" He lifted the columbines pointedly and cocked his head to give her a cajoling look. "Even after I brought you your favorite fairy dragon flowers?"

The right side of her mouth twitched just the tiniest bit. She was fighting back a smile, he could tell. A rush of satisfaction coursed through him and he reached out to tweak the brim of her hat. She leaned backward, pulling out of his reach, but her glare had softened. He was getting through to her.

"Then let's go. I don't have all day." She took off again, not bothering to check if he was following or not.

He did not look at her backside. Not directly.

• • • • • • • • •

Keep reading – or listening to – Faith's story in **Gotta Have Faith: Seven Virtues Ranch Romance Book 1.** It's available in print, ebook, and audiobook, and you can find it at **Becky Doughty Books** or any of your favorite online bookstores.